The Last Days of the
National Costume

The Last Days of the National Costume

ANNE KENNEDY

ALLEN&UNWIN
SYDNEY · MELBOURNE · AUCKLAND · LONDON

Published by Allen & Unwin in 2013

Allen & Unwin
83 Alexander Street
Crows Nest NSW 2065
Australia
Phone: (61 2) 8425 0100
Fax: (61 2) 9906 2218
Email: info@allenandunwin.com
Web: www.allenandunwin.com

Cataloguing-in-Publication details are available
from the National Library of Australia
www.trove.nla.gov.au

ISBN 978 1 74331 386 2

Set in 11.3/16.4 pt Sabon LT Pro by Bookhouse, Sydney
Printed and bound in Australia by Griffin Press

10 9 8 7 6 5 4 3 2 1

The paper in this book is FSC® certified.
FSC® promotes environmentally responsible,
socially beneficial and economically viable
management of the world's forests.

For Kathy Phillips

CONTENTS

One is about to leave; the other is staying,
and suddenly it matters that there are trees
they know, fields they have farmed.
                                    They are only
poets dressed up as farmers, or you and I
got up as poets in farmer suits. But departures
are real enough and loss is nothing new.

from 'Tityrus,' *Eclogues and Georgics of Virgil*,

translated by David R. Slavitt

When you come to visit,
said a teacher
from the suburban school,
don't forget to wear
your native costume.

But I'm a lawyer,
I said.
My native costume
is a pinstriped suit.

from 'My Native Costume' by Martín Espada

Rip burn snag

1

When I'd been in this racket for a year, a year of clients coming and going with their garments bundled like babies in their arms, at which point the novelty had slightly worn off, I hid a man in my workroom. He wasn't there long, five minutes at the most. We barely talked, just to-the-point as you do with strangers sometimes. No traffic reports, no outlook for Saturday, no pleasantries. He told me about his lover. I suppose that's a pleasantry. Then he went home.

I had a husband, but that wasn't the reason I hid the man.

If I'd said no to the costume I would've saved myself a truckload of trouble. It was a difficult job, a right mess actually, and I nearly did my eyes in, if that's possible—I think they think eye strain's a myth now. But the fabric was so black it absorbed all the light. There wasn't a lot of light to go around (I'll get on to that soon). If I were ever in that situation again, not that it's likely, not now, but if I ever were, with a garment in such a shocking state on my worktable, the proverbial dog's breakfast, I'd say I couldn't mend it. If I ever again had a succession of clients, one after the other, snorting down my neck like that, I'd just say, Go away, go jump in the lake. No I wouldn't, I'm too polite. I'd say, Let things unravel—yes, *unravel*—without involving yours truly. I was involved from day one, just by saying yes to the dress.

The day it arrived was the very day the power went on the blink in Auckland: 20 February 1998. It was a Friday, late afternoon, and my workroom was getting dark anyway. It was the contrast—the blinding yellow sunlight, the deep secret fold of the hill. Our house was in a gully on the city fringe, in one of those messy post-hippy suburbs. I'd always liked the feeling of living close to a pulse—cafés, boutiques, used-vinyl shops. All the useful things. You couldn't buy a loaf of bread to save yourself. But now it had all gone dead. That Friday was just the beginning, only we didn't know it then.

Notice I've migrated to the royal We. I hope that this is going to be a story about We. Bigger than just me, GoGo Sligo. I hope it's going to be about history, large-scale cultural movements, diasporas, about humanity, because, really, that's what I'm interested in, despite everything that might come bumping along between now and the end of this book. I'm interested in the transforming power of literature. I am! But I suspect I might stray down a few self-centred alleyways occasionally. All roads lead to GoGo sort of thing. Stop me if I do. (You can't, of course, but I'll pretend you can, otherwise I may as well shut up shop. The literature shop, that is, not to sound too poncy; the mending shop is already shut, and that's what I'm going to tell you about.)

•

First, how the costume came to me: that Friday, high summer, the sun still only three-quarters of the way across the sky at half past five. Later, I thought about those long evenings, how it seemed as if the light had squeezed itself between the minutes on a clock, making them fat and pale. When I opened the door a rogue gust plonked me back in my Wellington childhood, when the wind always blew. The wind for me is like one of those famous cakes dipped in tea. Good old Proust. What would we think otherwise?

There was a girl on the doorstep—woman: punk-looking, kohl-eyed, hair dyed as black as shoe polish, almost blue. Funny how punk never dies. She was peaky and shaky, a slight lack of physical control as if surfing. Too many trips, I thought (sagely). But beautiful. She was beautiful. Under her arm she had a plastic bag. She asked me if I did invisible mending. They always ask that. She had an accent—Irish, I thought, or Canadian—and also a rasp like Marianne Faithfull. I gave her the speech I usually trot out: one, I could do almost-invisible mending; two, making it completely invisible would cost more than the garment was worth; and three, almost is usually enough. She said fine and clomped inside in her tartan Docs. A whomp of air blew a poster of a Colin McCahon painting off the wall (*The Blessed Virgin compared to a jug of pure water and the infant Jesus to a lamp*, in case you want to know).

She followed me down the passage, which was gloomy even though it was still sunny outside. It's these train-like villa conversions. The light that should have come from the other side of the house now belonged to the neighbours. I groped for the switch (troubling Pinnacle Power for a light), and the paper moon from Wah Lee's glowed. The punk woman was trembling like a goat. She asked me dully when it would be ready. I told her I'd have to—strange as it may seem—look at it first. Her pushiness was no surprise. The women were more trouble than the men, for two reasons: one, they were assertive; and two, they could actually see the garments (even this head case), whereas when it came to clothes most of the men were blind. I'm sorry to be genderist, but it's true. The punk woman went ahead of me into the workroom. She had that stalk of self-consciousness beautiful women often have. It's much easier to look ordinary, to have nothing to bother holding up. Take me, for instance. I'm medium all round, and I can just get on with it. Sorry to be lookist, but there you have it.

If the villa conversion was a train, my workroom was the middle carriage, plus it was cheek-by-jowl with the house next door and so—shadowy. I had the light on all day. The punk woman and I parted ways around the big table that filled up most of the room. We met up near the window. On closer inspection I saw she was thirtyish. She'd seemed younger because of her clothes. If she stuck to it (as people who dress in a certain style often do), she'd wake up one day and punk would have gone from making her look young to making her look old overnight, as if she'd had a terrible shock like the death of a loved one. I sort of admired it, sticking to your principles, not being swayed by fashion like a reed in the wind. I'd like to be like that, a style oak tree, but I've never known quite what to put on in the first place. Even though I like clothes—and I don't tell just anyone this—I never entirely trust how I look. There are too many possibilities. I quite liked this woman's black skirt and ripped tights, for instance, her military jacket. But I liked my Nom*D cardigan with its enormous safety pin. I like bohemian skirts and loose blouses, I like chic. I'd like to look like the women on Wall Street in their clipped suits, but you have to have the job to go with it. I never will. How simple it would be to have a tribe.

The punk woman smiled pertly, like an animé character. 'I'm in a bit of trouble, actually.' Mm. She didn't seem as worried by her trouble as some of my clients. (More on that later.) I waited for her to reveal the contents of her plastic bag. Over the years I've learned to be patient—although only on the outside; inside I'm fuming. They've done studies on this, how people build psychological walls against annoyances, but the wall is made of stress. I knew from experience that people are coy about revealing the tear in a garment. Once, when I first started mending, I unwrapped a red jersey-silk evening dress too quickly for its owner, a middle-aged woman with a puppet-like facelift. She snatched the dress out of my hands, and the red silk ran through my fingers like a bleeding cut. It still makes me flinch to think of it. In due course the punk woman tipped up her plastic bag and let a garment tumble unceremoniously onto the table, first its arms flapping, then its body. It reminded me of a film I saw at school of a baby being born, in which the baby's arm flung outwards from the mother as if taking a bow. Ms Punk gazed at the ceiling as if she found all this incredibly tedious.

My first reaction was, Christ, not knotwork. My next: Irish— the accent. This was a dancing dress, à la Riverdance. You'll be able to picture it. Short, flared from the waist, heavily embroidered with hose-like loops (the knotwork), and a cape swinging from the shoulders. I'd mended two of them previously, and they'd been hell. It was the strain the embroidery put on the fabric—the dresses could almost stand up on their own—that and the cut, the tightness under the arms. When a seam went, it shredded like spaghetti squash. In both cases, the girl had outgrown the dress. But they were expensive—you wouldn't get change from a thousand dollars—so the mothers wanted their daughters to *get the wear out of them*. A too-small dress, combined with prancing about, you were bound to end up at the mender. I read once that the Irish used to use their arms in dancing like the Scots, but one time an Irish dancer who was entertaining an English nobleman whipped a sword out from under his costume and lopped the Englishman's head off. He probably had good reason, but after that, the English banned the use of the arms in Irish dancing. I don't know why the Irish haven't reclaimed their arms. But I also wondered if the girls, the wearers of these dresses I'd mended, had flung their arms into the air with relief once Riverdance practice was over.

The girls' dresses had been brilliantly coloured—peacock blue, emerald green. The capes were fastened at the shoulder with shiny Tara brooches. The cartoonish knotwork was a riot. One of the mothers told me, starry-eyed (they were born-again Irish), that the loops were a symbol of the continuity of life, which probably didn't include emigrating to New Zealand after the famine. But this costume—the punk woman's—was different. It was black, or near black. Old, you could tell by the matted woollen weave, which had a grey bloom on it the way a black-haired person goes salt-and-peppery. The knotwork seemed at first glance to be silver, but when you looked closely you also saw gold and pale green. It wasn't shiny, it was dull, subdued, almost mournful. In the way of these dresses, the fabric was a vehicle for the embroidery, as if it only existed so there would be something to attach the thread to. It had been done by an amateur, you could tell, because the embroidery went right up to the seam.

I was accused of having a national costume once.

I don't, of course.

An odd story I won't trouble you with. Not yet anyway.

I fanned out the bell-shaped skirt. The design was concerned only with the arms and the torso. It had no interest in legs. Or the legs were everything, it depended which way you looked at it. A cape hung down the back like dark moth wings. But there was something odd about this dress. The knotwork covered the bodice *as per usual*, and ran around the edge of the cape, the hem and the cuffs. One sleeve was embroidered with a climbing thing like a creeper, which spread out with a flourish onto the shoulder, but the other sleeve was only three-quarters done, with the lower part and the cuff left blank. On the costumes I'd seen before, everything was symmetrical. Perhaps someone had run out of steam. Or thread. Perhaps they had died.

I'd seen straight away, of course, the great rent in the shoulder, where it parted company almost entirely with the sleeve, and I suppose I should have mentioned that first. Because the knotwork went all the way to the seam, I wouldn't be able to mend it without a heck of a lot of trouble.

'It's my grandmother's,' said the punk woman.

Pack of lies, of course. I shone the bright lamp on it. The punk woman peered over my shoulder, blocking the light. People like to feel involved. I undid the zip and peeled the dress outward. It was a system of tongues, a black orchid. From the inside you could definitely tell it was homemade—unfinished seams, uneven stitches. Where the sleeve had come away was the weakest part of the garment. The threads running sideways—the weft—were finer, and at this junction two areas of weft met as in plate tectonics. The rent had travelled like a shockwave into the sleeve, dislodging the old strands. The dancing girls' dresses had been torn only where they were plainest, but this rip had set the silver threads of the knotwork dangling like glow-worms.

'I wore it to dancing.' The punk woman was breathing close, and an odd, medicinal smell came off her. 'It caught on a nail as I was going through a doorway.' Her speech was unkempt, something about her tongue, but she was trying to keep it tidy. She gestured towards her shoulder, the site of the tear, and smiled. She had big yellowish teeth, like the inside of an orange, but strangely nice-looking. 'The whole thing just. Tore.'

There was no nail hole. I scrubbed the fabric between finger and thumb, like rubbing the fragrance from a leaf. I asked her how old it was.

'Old,' she said. 'Yeah, old.'

I thought it might be fifty years.

'At least.' She flicked her hair like paintbrushes. 'When can you fix it by?'

I held the dress aloft (yes, *aloft*), and it tumbled down like a theatre curtain. 'One of the problems,' I said, 'and this is just one of them, is matching the threads.' I explained how it would require a lot of thread, but that the dyes are different these days, and the textures.

'Oh,' she said, pouting a bit. 'So, no chance of it being invisible?'

I laughed lightly (yes, *lightly*). 'No chance.'

In a minute she'd beg me to do anything I could to save the garment. That's what they always did. Begged and pleaded. There was usually a lover involved, and a cheated-on spouse. I, as the mender, would be saving their life.

I said to her, 'It's so far gone even reattaching the sleeve would be a struggle.'

The punk woman considered. She tucked her lips into her teeth like tucking in a blanket. She reached for the garment. Her nails were black.

At that moment the lamp and the overhead light snapped out with no preamble. We were plunged into, well, the greyness of late afternoon. We both made involuntary *not again* noises. Because there'd already been a couple of power cuts. The transformers had been popping like party balloons. I tried the switch on the standard lamp in the corner. Zilch.

'Strange,' said the punk woman. She had this *awful gleam*. 'It's meant to be.'

'Meant to . . . ?' I might have started on a little rant about Pinnacle Power.

'No, I mean the dress,' she said. 'Dead, obviously. I tried to tell him.' She bundled it up, looking bemused. 'Well, I did my best.'

I must admit I was gobsmacked. She was taking it back! No one ever did that. People pleaded and whined, they begged me to save their garment. She didn't give a rat's arse. My heart was galloping in the Melbourne Cup—a ridiculous reaction, I know. I can't quite explain it. I needed the money, but there was something else. I put my hand on the poor, limp, knotworked sleeve just in time to stop her stuffing it back in the plastic bag. I said I would look at it again, that I may have been too hasty. She shrugged—which sort of annoyed me too—and I led her clomping to the front room where the sun was streaming in, and I had another squiz. The seams, the fuzz, the spaghetti—it certainly was a wreck.

I said I'd give it a shot. The sun warmed it a bit.

'It doesn't matter.' She had her hands out ready to take it.

I said, No, really, that I could do it. She went neutral and said fine then, and put her hands in her pockets. I said I'd do my best.

'You can't make a silk purse out of a sow's ear, can you?' Again, the unruly tongue.

Sometimes you can.

'It does look a bit like a sow's ear, doesn't it?' She giggled.

I wrote out a docket. Her name: Trisha, not that it matters. The job: Irish costume, black. When I asked for her phone number she said she'd just drop by one day and pick it up. Spare me. I hated this. *Don't leave a message*, they'd say, *under any circumstances*. The problem with dropping by was, sometimes they didn't. Sometimes they decided, apparently, that their lives could go on without the particular skirt or coat. Their life wasn't destroyed after all. The other possibility was that they'd been murdered by the cheated-on spouse. I never found out what happened to the people who abandoned their garments at the end of my rack (the sight of them growing poignant with familiarity). I did sometimes scan the crime pages with certain names in mind. Was Higgins, trousers, brown, the man bludgeoned to death by the jilted boyfriend at the barbeque? Was Ford, dress, blue, the woman poisoned slowly by her chemist husband? And of course when people didn't come to collect their garments I didn't get paid, which might sound petty, and of course I would draw the line at charging someone's estate.

A phone number was handy, then. But I didn't feel like arguing with Trisha. I told her the costume would be ready on Tuesday.

She was about to go, but I could tell she wasn't finished. She hesitated and reached for the costume. I let her take it and she put it quickly to her lips, as if to farewell it. I saw this as a bad sign, re being paid. I watched her while she closed her eyes and lingered over the fabric. It must have been rough and soft against her mouth, the harsh embroidery and the old fuzzy wool. Where a man's fingers had been, I knew that. I found myself saying, 'Your grandmother will never know the difference.' I didn't usually fish for information, but I knew there was no swollen-ankled octogenarian fretting over her Michael Flatley costume. I wasn't born yesterday. Or maybe I was, in some ways. No, I wasn't.

Sure enough, Trisha was momentarily puzzled. She put the costume down. 'Grandmother?' She'd forgotten her own story. Great crim she'd make. 'Oh!' she said finally. 'Well, not mine actually. A friend's.' She blushed, but happily. 'You know?'

I nodded. I knew.

'I should never've put it on in the first place. He did warn me, but I went ahead. Stupid me!'

I handed stupid Trisha the docket. After I'd watched her tartan Docs thump out to the gate, I went back to my moony workroom and reached for the light. I remembered the power was out. I hung the costume on the rack and watched for a minute as it swung, rippling out into the room, the beautiful ripped thing.

2

A bit about my little business (which was still moderately fun, and had just been for something to do, more on that later): Every day there was a procession of clients who, with their bundles, were like the survivors of a train wreck. They would drop off their torn clothes, tell me how it happened, then leave and I'd get on with it. While I worked, I'd mull over what they'd said. After a while, I began to suspect that at least some of them were spinning me a load of the proverbial codswallop. Was 'evening dress, red' really torn getting out of a .car? And seriously, were 'trousers, navy' chewed by a dog? The ragged tear did seem to be the work of *some* kind of teeth.

Perhaps there was a change in me, I don't know. Perhaps I started looking at the clients sideways. Because pretty soon, they started fessing up. The first time was when a schoolteacher cleared his throat and described how his girlfriend had, with her lips, glued him all over as if to wallpaper him. That's what he said. First she had ripped off his clothes, hence the torn dinner jacket. I had no idea why he told me this, as he stood in my workroom. Yes, I did know. It was because he knew I knew. I was becoming experienced. I was like a forensic scientist. I could tell, just from looking at a garment, how a pocket parted company with a panel, how a skirt split its pleat.

From then on I heard about the many uses of the hands, together with the tongue, stomach, neck, the arms, the area behind the knees, the crotch, breasts, and anywhere else clothing might be torn from. Not that I didn't know about them before, of course, just not like this. Or not anymore. I noticed that in their lugubrious descriptions, they all used the word 'passion'. So Baroque. They told me it was the kind of passion that was out of their hands, there was no deciding about it one way or the other, it just was. This was what they said. Not just one client, but many, over and over. They said these words—*passion, no choice, out of my hands*. I know. Tedious. What's more, they explained that the consequences of this passion were going to destroy their life, or would if it weren't for me, the mender. I must say I quite liked this bit. They were so grateful to me! They would tell me I was worth my weight in gold. I would shrug in a shucks kind of way. But underneath I was glowing. I imagined my bodyweight as a rough, glittering nugget. Of course I knew it wasn't my skill in mending they were grateful for. It wasn't the neatness of my weaving or the tininess of my stitches. Because really, there's no special trick to it. Well, perhaps a little natural dexterity helps. Perhaps having been a girl once, that helps. Having been a girl and because you were a girl having a bodkin put into your hands at school at the age of six, with a skein of bright wool and some hessian woven as loosely as fingers latticed together, and being shown how to make a running thread like the dotted line down the middle of the road. And over the years everything fined down gradually, from cross stitch in wool, to chain stitch in cotton, to satin stitch in silk, and it all got finer and finer until the fibres were like hair and the fabric was as tight as, say, the matt of the sky. It was as if you'd walked away from your big woollen running stitch and it receded into the distance, and at the same time your hands got bigger as if they came into the foreground. Nothing had changed. Everything was still there under my hands, but smaller.

But it wasn't my skill the clients were grateful for. No. It was my collusion. What lies are worth: their weight in gold. If it weren't for me, their lives would be over. This was such a lot of melodrama. Of course their lives wouldn't be over. Look at Clinton.

My neck would ache from being crouched over the sewing machine, thinking about all this. I really needed a visit from a health and safety officer to sort out my workstation. Not to mention the stories I was hearing. Also, my fingers would end up chafed from the needle, which poked me repeatedly as if to remind me I wasn't dreaming. The thing is, I didn't give a rat's arse what the clients did in their spare time. But why couldn't people be upfront about things? Why couldn't they be honest? What I really hate is deceit.

•

Some jobs I remember, others not.

Case 1: I remember a green shirt. I didn't do many shirts. This one was rayon, made from wood! The owner looked like he drank powdered protein drinks—somewhat pumped up. So the shirt might have burst anyway. Across the back was a long tear with bright threads like a fringe of grass. The man's skin would have shown through like a new road on his shirt. I wondered if a woman had traced it with her finger. Or another man.

Case 2: A winter coat belonging to a library assistant. The buttons were ripped off, all of them, each one taking a swatch of wool and leaving a little hole like a nibble. Impossible to nibble woollen suiting, of course. More like the frenzied chomp you'd need to tear into a Mars Bar.

Case 3: A black skirt with a pretty L-shaped tear. Piece of rubbish, one hundred percent polyester, badly cut—nothing wrong with that. The girl who brought it in was about sixteen, bit her nails, in a hurry, on her lunch hour. The tear caused by hurry in the first place, in a storeroom, with the manager, she said. She blushed, and was kind of proud he was so high up. The skirt belonged to her mother. Who must never know, of course. The girl couldn't find the exact same thing in the shops. I repaired the damage.

Case 4: Another black skirt, also inexpensive, ripped in gorse on Mount Eden. The owner in her thirties, married. She told me she'd scratched her thighs and her bum and had to soak her underwear in milk to get rid of the blood and keep covered up in front of her husband until the grazes healed. She was slightly shamefaced as she told the story, but also boasting. I suppose only a particularly desirable woman could have a man not her husband rip her skirt in the prickly undergrowth on Mount Eden. I told this woman she could buy a new skirt for less than it would cost to mend the old one, and her husband would never notice. Even if he saw it hanging in the bathroom with the tear visible. Even if he caught sight of it in the rubbish bin. I found myself getting quite worked up—*even if, even if.* The thing is, men don't notice that kind of detail. The woman wouldn't listen. She paid twice the value of the skirt to have it mended. She would never understand men, what they see, what they don't see. So I thought, in my great wisdom.

Case 5: A man who brought in a shirt his wife had made for him. Purple silk—no, indigo. She'd dyed the fabric from berries. Berries! A labour of love. The pocket was torn. The man told me the story standing in my workroom. His lover, not his wife (the categories so distinct), had ripped the pocket. He was ashamed and bursting with pride at the same time, literally, his jowly face swelling up. I looked at the flesh of the tear under the light—its fat, so to speak. It was bad. They'd been having a game, he said, in which he hid the condom about his person—that's what he said, *about his person*—and the object of the exercise was for her to find it, and for him to stop her. I felt my eyes roll involuntarily. This was a tame and childish game compared to some of the things I'd heard. We're talking objects and things that won't open in a hurry. (But why do people wear their best clothes? More on that later.) The man with the indigo shirt told me his lover had herpes, that was why they used a condom. So, no secret babies either. Strange how one thing leads to another, he said, and laughed. On eye contact he blushed deeper. Oh please! As they say in America. He was delighted to have a ripped shirt—but even more delighted, ecstatic, that *I* could see that another woman, not his wife, loved him, or something. Then he told me it was just a bit of fun. It wasn't as if he would play a game like that with his wife. His wife didn't need to rip his shirt. His wife *made* him the shirt.

I bundled up the indigo shirt as briskly as you can other people's clothing, and said I couldn't repair it. He *coloured visibly* and asked me why not. I said it was because his wife made it, and he asked me how that made a difference. I told him it made the job impossible. No matter what I did, the wife would notice. She would know it down to the last stitch. He said he didn't give a damn how much it cost. I told him money wasn't the point, it was whether it was possible. The man sniffed a bit, then sat back as if resigned. This could be the end, he said. I said, surely not. Then he told me something the others hadn't mentioned: he might leave his wife for the lover. There was always that possibility. I guess when you put it in that light, I said. And he said, I do.

I remembered this.

I mended it. Took a whole afternoon. It was labour-intensive, a word which used to be associated with carrying bricks, but has gone soft now that labour is carried out sitting down. I found the almost exact match of thread in the good afternoon light, the indigo of the berries. Thread by thread I wove the fabric back together. In the end I charged him peanuts compared to the hours it took. (I'm not good at taking money from people, which I guess means I'm not good at business.) I wondered if the wife would ever peer closely while she was embracing her husband, if her lips would press into her husband's chest and feel a line of roughness. Perhaps she would put her head back, retracting like a snake for a better look. I wondered if the wife was the kind of wife who ironed her husband's shirts. Perhaps she would reach suddenly for her reading glasses while she was at the ironing board late at night, thinking she'd seen something odd about the pocket. She'd peer inside and see the faint line of threads twisted and raised like a scar. Then turn her head to look curiously at her husband, who might be in the bedroom preparing for bed. Would she look at his naked figure with new eyes? I'd never know. I would never know unless, by some chance, I met the wife.

Enough case studies. The messes people got themselves into—up shit creek, basically. I was pleased never to have found myself in that kind of creek, which sounded very disgusting. All in the name of love.

But there is one more case study.

3

After the punk woman with the dog's brunch left, thank Christ, I pressed my ear against the flocked wallpaper in the passage and listened to the flat next door, but, as always, nobody home. Art had met them once when the rent was late. I looked out over Newton Gully. The high-rise construction sites on the ridge to my left were quiet, which was unusual. Ditto the dark, oily little mechanics' shops down the street that dinged till early evening. I walked along the brick path to our rickety picket gate. Yes, we had a house with a picket fence, but far from being a suburban idyll, it had gone to rack and ruin—like the set for a Tim Burton movie (sorry I can't come up with my own description). The front garden was a thatch of overgrownness you needed to fend off as you made your way down the path. This was the garden no doubt put in by some middle-class Victorian—no, Edwardian—woman, the wife of a banker perhaps. A pohutukawa tree presiding over exotics, pansies, geraniums and roses, which had gone to seed dozens of times over. She would turn in her flowery grave. Out the back was a little handkerchief lawn, all closed in and shady from the banana palms. From the front, though, you could look out over the strawberry patch of cottages than ran down to the North-Western Motorway. We were one of those strawberries, a red roof nestled in foliage. Among the houses, this Friday afternoon, there was no sign of life, but that wasn't unusual. After dark, it revved up a bit, when people got home, but often during the day it was so still you wondered if anyone lived there at all. Anyone home? Ah, me, actually, running my little business.

I went back inside and plonked myself in the late sunlight in the front window—we had a beautiful bay window—where the panes were so old they were bent like prescription glasses, making the red pohutukawa flowers fuzzy. I did a bit of hand-finishing—my machine out of commission, of course. Bell was coiled up asleep in her habitual chair in the corner. At this point I didn't know that the power was out all over downtown, and people were spilling over with the milk of human kindness.

Eventually the sun went all neony, how it does, and squashed down behind the Waitakere Ranges. I started to worry about Art. No, not Art as in Vermeer, as in Andy Warhol, but my husband Art-short-for-Arthur. He was late coming home. I folded up my work and wandered into the gloomy boomy passage. It was cavernous and the walls were timbered to halfway up, and I always felt like I was inside a mandolin.

•

So about half an hour after the power had snuffed it, I was peering *out* of the mandolin, imagining life as a widow at the age of twenty-eight. (Although can you be a widow when you only got married to go to America?) Bell slunk around my legs. She was mostly white and glowed like phosphorous. Just then I felt the bounce of the veranda as Art slapped up the steps. A squirt of relief fired somewhere in my torso when I saw his big rectangular outline. But Art was the one gasping—I'd given him a fright, looming there like a ghost, alone and palely loitering, apparently. He sighed when he saw it was only me. He said the power was out, and I said I could hardly miss it, could I.

'What are you doing standing in the dark, then?' he asked. Had I gone mad? I said very probably, bonkers. He said there were pills for that sort of thing that could keep people sitting at desks for long hours instead of lurking in dark passageways. Get me some, I said. Ah, he said, but you have to be sitting at a desk earning the money to buy the pills. I earn a bit, I said. Not enough, he said. More than you, I said, but that wouldn't be hard. (Not strictly true. Art had this lovely Grandma fund which flooded into his bank account every February.) We kept up this sort of banter. He came inside.

My McCahon poster was rolling on the floor as if in agony. The virgin and jug, rolled up inside, would be even more wonky than usual. 'It's a free country, isn't it?'

'Free for some.' Art liked to sound like a socialist, although the family on his mother's side, the Woolthamlys, was squattocracy. (You weren't allowed to use that word, I found out early on.) They owned 'the farm'—two thousand springy hectares in Taranaki—a fruit-drying business inventively called The Taranaki Fruit Drying Company, a few bungalows in Wellington, *plus*, four of the villas in our street, all in a row. They'd given us one. I should add that Art's father was a Frome, and not landed. Art was a Woolthamly-Frome. But anyway, that first evening of the power cut, Art clunked down his satchel, which was always impossibly heavy, as if it had brass candlesticks in it, as if he were a burglar, but it was just his dissertation on Settler Literary Ephemera. Not to diss it, of course. He kept printing it out, a wodge of a thing that he carted around with him while he worked on his series of off-and-on tutoring jobs. We pecked each other. He had nice

21

cheeks, Art, rough and smooth, and they smelled nice. He was gorgeous.

'We got stuck in the lift in Queen's Arcade,' he was saying. 'I was at the Denise Kum opening. Almost bought something—in fact, I still might. I thought you were coming. Why didn't you?'

I'd had a client.

I could just see, in the last of the western light, that Art was radiant. He had very white teeth, and a golden fringe of hair. 'Five of us, for two hours. This claustrophobic woman was going nuts, literally. I mean I've never seen anyone try to climb walls before, like Spiderman. So Roger read Joseph Campbell to us. We thought it was just the building, but the guy who winched us up told us the whole CBD's out, that's why it took so long. They're still going. They're winching every lift in town.'

Later, we heard on the news that seventy-four thousand workers had been plunged into darkness that afternoon. They waited to be released from lifts, like Art, or felt their way down hot, dark stairwells. Outside, the rush-hour traffic was chaos, Art said. Horns, road rage but not as much as you'd think. A few hours later, it all went very quiet. That was what we could hear now, as we stood in the doorway: the quiet. The thing is, I hadn't known there was noise before. Our house fell just on the edge of the Blackout zone. Yes I know, fell. It was a bit of a worry.

We felt our way along the passage. It was a beautiful passage, with a high wooden ceiling and a moulded arch, miraculously passed over by the seventies renovators. They must've had a crick in their neck that day. Lovely, that arch, when you could see it. Our fingers hissed along the old flocked wallpaper which lined the upper half of the walls. I knew these fuzzy shapes quite well anyway. They were like pet rabbits, and I liked to pat them. In the kitchen I scrabbled in my handbag for my pen torch and pointed it while Art climbed up to get the hurricane lamp from on top of a cupboard. He brought it down, dusted it off and held a match to it daintily, as if doing calligraphy. It gave a lovely warm light. His hair lit up like a sou'wester, and his face glowed underneath. He has a face of privilege—good food and happiness. I envied him that, still do. I fed batteries into the radio. It was like a snake eating eggs.

The news fizzed on, and we heard that the fourth cable had gone kaput at a quarter to six. Pinnacle Power said it was due to the heat and high demand for air-conditioning. Bollocks! said Art. The cables, which were forty years old, had been dying like flies over the last month. The third one had gone the day before. Pinnacle Power would get one going by Monday, they said. We yammered—the whole weekend ahead of us! Art said we could blow that for a fucking joke.

He'd found a bigger torch in a drawer and flickered out through the banana palms to the shed. I could hear him crashing around out there, cursing happily. I used my pen torch to investigate the contents of the fridge like a dentist looks into a mouth. Steak (we were meant to be vegetarians but both got cravings and attacked meat like lions at the zoo), broccoli, the good vanilla ice cream for afters. We were sticking to our gender roles, thank God. Art reappeared with a Primus stove, a disgusting rusty thing that would give you tetanus. He brushed off the cobwebs and fired it up—it was like a Boeing 747—and stood back with his arms folded, satisfied momentarily.

'Oh, and the wine,' he said. 'Chilled, but not for long.' He sloshed some into a couple of glasses. 'Cheers.' We clinked as the steak spat in the pan. 'This is fun, isn't it?' said Art. 'Like camping. We did this all the time on the farm.'

He'd grown up in town (his father did something in insurance, not very high up, strangely), but spent holidays on the Woolthamly sheep station. It wasn't what it had once been, apparently—carved up between the siblings, and there were a few of them. In fact, it wasn't much of a sheep station anymore. Art's mother, Prue-short-for-Prudence, ran the dried-fruit empire the grandfather had started—there were orchards and a drying plant on the property—and exported apples, prunes etc., mostly to Japan and Hong Kong. Made a pile. Good for piles, I'd say. We were hilarious. One day Art and his sister would inherit the whole shebang. A Prune of One's Own, I'd say. It sort of included me too, but we never discussed it. Money embarrassed him. Poor Art! I mean that.

He was on a roll, about the camps they went on. Days, weeks, near the creek, free as a fucking bird. Until a girl on a neighbouring farm was dragged from a tent in the middle of the night. They dug her up months later. No one went camping after that. As you wouldn't, I said. (Myself, I'm scared to do anything outside the city limits. Even within them.)

'But what are the odds?' said Art. 'Everyone stayed inside at night after that. Poor girl, though. Libby somebody. Raped. They—'

'Spare me,' I said. Seriously.

We ate at the kitchen table in the lamplight while the shadows danced on the raw, flaking walls. I'm not a materialist by the way. If I'm ever worried about having an old kitchen, take me out and shoot me. I asked Art how Work and Income was. We always said that, Work and Income, because we'd lined up at it in the university holidays to get the dole. I know, even with 'the farm'. These were the last days of the welfare state. Well, there was no casual work in the late eighties—none! But at the time of the power cut, Art's Work and Income was a temporary gig transcribing interviews for a film company called LambChop Productions. They mostly made docos. Art earned a pittance, but that was okay, he almost had his PhD. (Also, there was the spectre of serious money one day from the Woolthamlys. It was like a light in the passage, even when you closed your eyes at night: always on.)

He told me about his day. He'd been typing up conversations with a serial killer. There'd been an argument between a director and the producer like a bar-room brawl. Really, it was quite an eventful day. (He'd love a bar-room brawl. He would.) And how was my day?

Well: a commercial traveller—who I couldn't help thinking of as a cockroach waving its legs on a bedroom floor—brought in a waistcoat with a cigarette burn in it, pair of trousers with the fly gone (so many insects), both smelling of tobacco and the inside of a car. An elderly lawyer with a tweed skirt, zip gone. She was wearing another tweed skirt and a frilly white blouse and looked half-man half-woman, a kind of centaur. Oh, and a girl with yet another cocktail dress, which by then was making me think of Clinton and, well, cocks. I mended a lot of them. They should've worn saris—hard to unwind. After the cocktail girl, the mess of a dress arrived, and the power went off.

I thought of something and put my finger in the air. 'Um.'

Art looked over. (He had a very blue, lit-up gaze, by the way.) 'Idea, lightbulb?'

'If only,' I said. 'How will I work without electricity?'

'Oh,' said Art. 'It'll be back on by Monday.'

'What say it isn't?'

'You doubting Thomas,' said Art. 'You're a doubting Thomas, d'you know that?'

'I doubt that,' I said. 'I seriously doubt it.'

'A doubting Thomasina.'

We always went on like this.

It is true, though, that black absorbs all the possible light.

4

The truth is, at this point I was quite pleased about the distraction of the Blackout, for a specific reason. The night before had been a Ballet Night, always brittle affairs, but this had been a Ballet Night with bells on its toes. Art's parents, Prue-short-for-Prudence and Bert, were royal ballet supporters. The Royal New Zealand Ballet needed royal support. When Prue and Bert were up in Auckland they often took us to the productions they'd already seen in Wellington. The night before the power went kaput, we'd all had dinner in High Street (which was slumming it for Prue and Bert, they usually went to Antoine's, and I thought I detected a frisson of eye contact about the bill), then gone on to *Swan Lake* at The Edge. We'd walked up to the theatre together in our best get-ups, perfume trailing behind us, because it was such a beautiful evening, still light, still pink on Queen Street. There are worse things. Some weekends we went to 'the farm'. And anyway, the Woolthamly-Fromes were nice people, hospitable and full of bonhomie, as long as you bit your lip. And I did, for Art's sake, and because when I added up dinner (even that dinner) and the ballet tickets in my head, there wasn't change from a grand.

If there was any tension on Ballet Nights and Farm Weekends, it wasn't my doing. But I take full responsibility for what happened on this *particular* Ballet Night. I do. I feel terrible about it. As we were all processing down Queen Street, us women in our wafty finery in front, and the men in their, well, suits (Art changed out of his semiotician's zip-up polo-neck for his parents) bringing up the rear, we approached a group of street kids milling around outside a games shop, and I noticed Prue whip her head away as if disgusted, as if the very sight of them made her want to upchuck. I admired the Woolthamlys, even though they were such horsy-gentry types, but there was something comforting about their practicality. They were good at life, money, property. But I'm not a complete idiot. My parents, by the way, were Marxists, just thought I'd throw that in. Somehow Prue's head-tossing gesture stuck in my gullet. I did a sort of ostentatious thing; I rummaged in my purse and found a note, a five I thought, and as we passed I thrust it into the fist of one of the street kids, a boy of about fourteen with intense eyes and dressed in that baggy basketballish uniform they all wear. He was Maori, but the kids were mixed, Pakeha (i.e., white, like *moi*) and Maori. I was about to increase my pace to catch up with Prue when I noticed that the street kid was standing as if stunned. He was holding the note like he was a tree and it was a leaf. In a second I realised why: I'd given him a hundred-dollar note—egad, the red one, not the orange of the fives! (I didn't usually carry this much spondulix around, but a client had paid me in cash earlier in the day and I'd been happy to accept, re tax purposes.)

Everything around the street kid had gone like a tableau from 1910. He was rigid, ditto his friends, who were all staring at the note. Bert and Art had caught up with us. I saw Prue and Bert—once they'd twigged as to where the note had come from and what its denomination was—exchange Munch-like expressions in the evening light. I felt like a great philanthropist. I did. I felt like Warren Buffet. I smiled at Art. I remember his electrified face in a sort of torment, and I thought, Ah, he's torn, the poor bastard. But I didn't have time to get any further with my analysis because the tableau was over. A couple of the boy's mates were tackling him to the ground like it was a rugby game. All in fun. They were tussling and tumbling and play-fighting. But then, as I watched, as we all watched, one of the rugby players, the size of a fridge, grabbed the boy—who was quite slight—by the hair and punched him. I heard an awful moan, and the boy's neck jerked sideways. The fridge one punched the boy again, then let his hair go. His head slammed back onto the ground. The other kids leaned in around him like a scrum, poised. I was panicking and blabbering that we should do something, ring the police, find a phone booth. It was 1998. Not everyone had a mobile phone. Prue was already clipping away and saying over her shoulder, Come along, Megan, you only encourage them, the police will be in the vicinity. Megan's my real name. I saw Bert hesitate a second, then trot after his wife like a lamb. Art's warm hand was on my arm. GoGo, come away, he was saying, there's nothing you can do. I let myself be pulled away. Not pulled, walked. I went willingly, arm in arm like My Fair Lady to the ballet. As I looked back one of the girls, big, all boofy in her hoodie, gave the boy a kick in the head as he lay on the ground, and his head jostled and he whimpered like a puppy. In the distance, the shriek of a police car. There you see, said Prue. But the siren waggled off in the other direction, along the waterfront.

At The Edge we stood on the terrace sipping champagne, while Prue said *and this is our son Art and his wife* about thirty times to people in glittery dresses and suits. I had the impression of a lot of teeth, but couldn't get the street kid's head out of my head, and I thought about the possibility he might be dead. I pulled Art aside and said I thought I should go back to check, and he said, Are you crazy? It's dangerous. He said someone would have called someone by now.

When we went in, the auditorium was hushed, cushiony and perfumed. I sat clutching my program and listening to the orchestra tuning up, which was a *divine noise* but unsettling like a gale. I felt shit-scared, to coin a phrase. Not just, What am I doing here? but, What am I doing on the *planet*? The thing is, I'd felt this before, even when there hadn't been dramatic things happening like street kids being beaten up on my account. I know it's pathetic. I hadn't married Prue-short-for-Prudence and Bert, but sometimes I felt like I had, and that they were aliens. I wanted to go home to the pole house I grew up in and never leave it, even though when I'd turned eighteen you couldn't see me for dust. At one point, with the lake and the trembling feathers all bathed in blue, Art squeezed my hand. I hadn't ruined the evening. I was comforted, and concentrated on the swish and thump of ballet shoes as they landed on the stage. They were so human.

I haven't forgotten I didn't want to go down any self-centred alleyways.

On the way up Queen Street afterwards, just Art and me by this point (and I was on the lookout for street kids, I can tell you), I kept replaying the sick clunk of that vase-like teenage head. I said (ploughing uphill, under the verandas of the two-minute Chinatown) that we should've called an ambulance. Art said we probably should have. I said (out loud, which made it worse) that he might be dead. Art said nah, he'd be alright, he was a street kid, he was tough. As we passed the cemetery on Symonds Street I said we should've hung around though, and Art said we probably should've, but we didn't. He said it wasn't my fault, but I went on

29

and on. He was only trying to comfort me. The thing is, Art is a good person, but (and this might sound a bit nineteenth century, but it's the truth) when you have parents as rich as his, you can't cross them because it could cost you millions. I knew that.

5

Around ten, Art and I rolled together like marbles in the kitchen of the villa conversion.

Oh, villa conversion? That's what we lived in, and that's what we called it. 'See you back at the villa conversion,' we'd say. We were lucky to have it. They were rare as hen's teeth, a good villa ruined by being converted into flats in the seventies. Most of them were being knocked back into full houses. We didn't want the whole house, even though Art's parents owned it, along with its three neighbours. A whole house would be excessive. Instead, we lived with the doorways on one side of the passage blocked off and papered over as if they'd never existed. This night, in our seventies kitchen, we sat near the hurricane lamp. Art's laptop whined on and he thanked Christ it was charged. I reminded him he didn't believe in a Christian god. He said he might not, but the computer did. The laptop was full of bright gold leaking around the edges. Beautiful. Art furrowed his brow at the screen. He was telling me some new angle on Orientalism, to do with the settlers rather than the folk who stayed put in the motherland. Other was *in their face*, not at arm's length. I listened without looking at him, stitching

31

in my pond of light. (That's the thing about sewing, you can't look up.) His PhD was like a piece of knitting still on the needles; you could see quite clearly it was a jersey, but you wanted to go on looking at it as *knitting* for a while longer. I understood that completely. Because *I* was once about to write a thesis. (I never quite got to it.) When Art finished his dissertation, it would all be over. Settler Literary Ephemera (which was, you know, letters, advertisements, posters—all the stuff that wasn't writing) done, closed with a bang, yes, settled. Tick the box. Good. To tell the truth, I was a bit sick of it. *I* was sick of it!

Because Art was a nanosecond from getting his PhD in English from Columbia, he would have an academic job in a jiffy. There just wasn't much around at the moment. Not long after we got back to Wellington from New York—we'd barely *unpacked*—he got a tutoring gig up in Auckland, just temporary, but it seemed fun and he wanted to do it. He'd said to me, Do what makes you happy. More than once, countless times. The least I could do was return the favour. So we repacked our stuff and went to Auckland. Auckland would be kind of fun anyway. We knew people up there, as you do.

At the kitchen table that first dark night of the Blackout, I leaned close to the lamp with my reading glasses perched on my nose, and stitched the last of twenty-five white tutus back onto its mushroomy polyester bodice. (Yes, *reading* glasses.) It was an alterations job for a ballet school, and quite a good wicket, although the netting had continually pushed up under my fingernails. Swans were ruined forever for me. But in the end, they were still tutus. I sat there thinking (you can think a lot when you sew) about how when I was five I pestered Mary-France (my mother, who didn't like being called Mum) to enroll me in ballet class. I'd pictured myself in pink ballet slippers. Pink ballet slippers were the whole point. Mary-France was philosophically opposed to ballet—it would have been its cultural irrelevance to the Pacific, and the fact it promoted gender stereotypes. But in the end I went to a class in a brown church hall. The ballet teacher had a pair of black second-hand ballet slippers that were being given away. I tried them on. They fit. They fitted. I remember looking down at my feet. Free ballet slippers. Free, but black. I wasn't interested in ballet after that. If only I could have said, 'All I want is pink ballet slippers.' The agony of the five-year-old who can't say that, or even think it. But the worse agony, twenty-odd years later, of realising that that was what you'd wanted. Perhaps it was better never to have known.

But I know. I know now. Not to get too maudlin about it.

Sewing netting onto polyester in the half-light was driving me nuts, so I was glad when it was finished. It had really needed daylight. With my torch, I scalloped along the passage to my workroom. The tutus thrusting out behind me made my shadow look like an ostrich. I bounced my pen light around the room to see if there was anything low-key enough to do in the half-dark. There was the garment that the last client had brought in. Knotwork. Christ! Definitely a daylight job, and all in good time. Never put one job ahead of another. That was what I learned from Rip Burn Snag, Clothing Alterations and Repairs in New York (I'll tell you about that in due course). I ran my thumb over the tips of my fingers, which were tender from *Swan Lake*. The night air, usually thumping with next door's stereo, was silent.

Back in the kitchen, I read the paper until I thought I'd go blind, and then I just sat. Art's computer shut down suddenly. Those laptop batteries don't stand on ceremony. He rooted in his bag and brought out a settler studies person. No, it was Homi Bhabha—other side of the coin. All of which Art was still wading through up to his armpits. I was glad I didn't have to read Homi. I used to be into this stuff. But Art didn't open the book. He leaned back in his chair and said, GoGo, guess what? (He always used my nickname. I went to a poncy school, albeit Catholic, where the rich country girls came up with droll nicknames like Mimsy and Fifi. I was Megan Sligo, so GoGo was a giveaway.) (I have to add here, I was the poorest girl in school, although we weren't poor.) What? I said. Art talked out into the darkness. His upper lip caught the light. He told me about his walk home that evening through the choked streets. He was strangely serious, for him. He described how the light was peculiar and slanting as dusk came on, because there were no streetlights. An apocalyptic surge of pedestrians moved up Queen Street, and in every street to right and left there were crowds of people walking. They talked to each other, and had jokey conversations with people who'd been stuck in traffic so long they'd got out of their cars.

'It was eerie,' he said. 'This weird quiet, like the end of the world. People were talking, but all quiet and calm. They were streaming by, walking along together in the dusk, as if we were all walking towards something. I saw a man limping and someone was helping him. There was a woman with all these little kids and people were carrying them alongside her.'

Art's lit-up face: radiant is not too strong a word.

'GoGo,' he said, 'it was fantastic.'

He'd seen something, something I hadn't. I can't quite explain it, but it was this extra quality in him, this sense of wonder. Yes, I know, I'm sick to death of wonder, too—wonder in *the bone people*, wonder in *Alice in Wonderland*, wonder with chips—but it seemed to be true for Art. He'd felt real wonder, not just thought about it, and you could see the result coming off him. As I went back to my stitching, I wished I'd been out there on the street among people behaving differently from how they'd ever behaved before, people walking in the fading light, talking to strangers, and spilling over with the milk of human kindness. It seemed that something needed to happen for people to connect. It had happened, but I'd missed it. There might never be another time like this.

•

Later, I padded into the bedroom and cuddled up behind Art. We had sex, kind of quickly. Well, it was late. But good. Afterwards the sheets felt watery, steaming—I don't think I'm getting too fanciful—from the hot rock of Art's sleeping body. No dehumidifier, of course. I snuffed the torch, and blinked at the pitch-dark. It was almost painful. I could feel my eyelids yawning, gulping as much blackness as possible in case there might be a shred of light in it. There wasn't. After a bit of tossing and turning, I took the torch and went outside and looked at the blacked-out city. I felt like I was looking at Auckland for the first time. I know this is ridiculous. I couldn't see anything.

6

On Monday morning Art and I sat on the back doorstep drinking coffee, attacking our tough croissants, and reading about the outage in the *Herald*. Every time I encountered the word I read it as 'outrage'. We'd spent an inky weekend in the villa conversion, cooked twice on the 747. No, once. On Saturday night some friends in Arch Hill fed us lasagne at a dinner party, among interesting lamps. Art had regaled the table with the story of his walk home after the power went out—by this point it was an interstitial space, neither light nor dark, work nor leisure, but communal. It sounded lovely. Everyone was saying the Blackout would likely go on for a week. Pinnacle Power was fixing the ancient cable. This fixing theory didn't quite marry with the news I now read in the *Herald*—that every generator in the country was rumbling towards Auckland. There was also a map of the Blackout zone, and we were exactly on the edge. They were right about that. Walking home from dinner on Saturday we'd noticed that the other side of our street was carrying on as usual, lights blazing, TVs chortling at their own jokes sort of thing. We didn't know these neighbours, but suddenly they seemed shifty, privileged. I hated them. By contrast, our side of the street had been unnaturally quiet (although of course completely natural). As you passed the dark houses, you saw the odd single muted spark deep inside like an F-stop.

On the radio they were saying that little old New Zealand was big news around the world. The *New York Times* ran an article, the *Washington Post*, the *Guardian*. We were famous! (Picture a couple sipping coffee on their stoop in Manhattan. *Did you hear that, Martha, we got a mention in the* New Zealand Herald!) Art had a little rave. How the fuck, rampant capitalism etc. Not to mention the embarrassment. I wasn't embarrassed. Art said I should be. This great bloody feisty little fucking place.

Art had been doing his transcribing work at home, but needed to go into the LambChop studios in Mount Eden so he could plug in. When he'd trundled off, I went into my workroom and yanked back the curtains. A lemony sunlight fell obliquely onto the rack of clothes. By afternoon it would be angling onto my bank of spools. Usually I worked in the pond of electric light, but today the pond had dried up. You might imagine fish flapping tragically in it. My swanky new(ish) sewing machine was cold and grey. You'd think I'd have been disappointed, hot under the collar, outraged even. I wasn't. I felt a strange excitement. The thing is, nothing had ever happened before. I'd missed all the disasters—Second World War, Tangiwai train crash, Wahine storm, the Springbok tour (alive but too young). Now this, in the nick of time, before the end of the terrible century. We would live through the darkness in our half-villa in the middle of Auckland. I know it's pathetic. No one was going to die. But a charge ran up and down inside my body. You could have hooked me up to the national grid. Ah, but the transformers wouldn't have been able to transmit the power.

I took my workbook to the front room. There would be no new clients today, of course, with the city at a standstill. I thought I may as well see what I could get done by hand, taking advantage of the light from the big windows. I must say, it was nicer in there than in my workroom. The big blood-red velvet theatre curtains that someone had got from somewhere, the white-painted floorboards, and an enormous red brocade roll-armed couch that looked like an old Dodge. The only bum note was the abstract-patterned rug that Prue had hooked for us, but at least it was springy. In those years, things, possessions, just appeared. (Why don't they anymore?) I looked in my workbook. I only quote it here because you'll be able to see what kind of a business I was in.

Blouse, cream silk, torn front placket
Jacket, man's sports, navy, cigarette burn
Blazer, school, torn front panel
Blouse, woman's, sequined, torn buttonhole
Dress, evening, red, rip and oil stain
Dress, evening, pale blue, slit up back

And here's how these rips happened, according to my clients:

Desperate hurry, sex
Late night, yacht club, gazing at woman
Boy, innocent
Teeth, sex
Small car, gearstick, sex
Caught in car door, drunk, sex

And so on. Of course, I also had the standard letting-out and taking-in jobs, and the ubiquitous jean hems, and making a coat into a jacket. Why can't people ever be satisfied? I estimated that in three days I would get to the end of my list—even taking into account the item that had arrived last thing on Friday, which would of course be a nightmare, and which I should never have taken on, but I did.

I started on the cream silk blouse, which poured into my hands *like milk*. It did! I unpicked the remaining stitches on the placket so I could start again. The demure cut of the button-to-the-neck blouse, its neat collar, had been like a red rag to a bull, anyone could see that (even though it was pale). Shame, it was good-quality silk, and here's an interesting thing: people dress up to cheat. If I had some advice for someone contemplating having an affair, it would be *don't wear your best clobber to the rendezvous.* Wear cheap, easily replaceable stuff. No silk, no cashmere, no high-quality cotton. No designer labels, no retro. No custom-made, no homemade. Definitely no heirlooms. But would they take this advice? I doubt it. As for me, I don't know what I'd wear. Maybe that's why I would never have an affair—I wouldn't know what to put on. But no, it was because I was content. I suppose I could understand how my clients might think, in some weird way, that their best garments had no meaning without the lover. The other thing is (and I just thought of this), perhaps they wore these good clothes because they felt good—the cool of the silk, and the way cotton hugs you. The outer clothes would be of fabrics that might rub roughly against a lover's sleeve in public, in a lift, side by side on a bus, but innocently because it was, after all, just a sleeve. The lovers might have stared straight ahead going up to the tenth floor as this rubbing went on. There would have been no evidence of it to the naked eye. A forensic scientist, however, would find microscopic fibres hopelessly entwined. I only know this from what I saw. I would never have thought of rubbing woollen sleeves in a lift.

For the school blazer—something tender about the felty grey fabric a boy had torn on barbed wire—a patch would do, given the temporary nature of childhood. I took a snippet from inside the blazer's hem and transferred it to the elbow, robbing Peter to pay Paul. Dickybirds.

There was a wedding train with an almighty gash at floor level. I've mended a few of these. There are obviously a lot of nervous grooms out there in their big stiff new wedding shoes, and a lot of fragile trains teasing them playfully. Till death us do part. *Ri-ip.* I do. *Parp.* I began to reattach the filmy swathe as if it had sprockets. With such fine fabric, the trick is not to stitch too much or too tightly. As I sewed, I remembered my own wedding outfit: a black skirt, black mesh top, and a green Zambesi waistcoat—beautiful, but still a waistcoat. I hadn't set out to look like a man on my wedding day, but the photo (which someone took, I don't know who) is evidence that I could've been the groom. I think I had a fear of wedding dresses—not that I would've worn a fluffy white get-up, but there is a middle ground. When I was a kid, traditional wedding dresses were very last-year. I remember a photo sent in the post of a distant cousin all done up in her frothy gown. Mary-France opened the mail to this shock—*a ridiculous get-up, a collage of bourgeois ideologies.* This could also apply to the marriage. The case was also discussed in the conversation pit, on another occasion, with the English lecturers. *The poor, poor girl.* I sort of wanted to be a poor, poor girl, and I didn't. How to win?

I finished the train. I would have to tell the just-married woman to be careful with it, it was fragile. I was always telling clients that—just because it's mended, doesn't mean it's indestructible. It was a wound.

•

The next day, pretty much the same, except it was raining. Plus they were saying three weeks of Blackout, and an expert was coming from Australia to fix the cables. I woke up the bat.

Oh, the bat?

I trundled the antique Singer sewing machine from the corner of the bedroom where it'd been taking up space, but nicely, into the front room and parked it near the window. I swung the machine upright from where it hung underneath the little wooden platform like a flying rodent, shiny black, and eerily sculpted. It had been my bedside table when I was at university. There'd been a fashion for them, and I'd never been able to bring myself to get rid of it. I liked its long curly flourishes. I'd even used it once or twice, for a fiddly job. You could do a single stitch at a time. It didn't race ahead like a dog on a leash (yes, I know it's a bat).

I tidied the front room to make it fit for business—scooped up coffee cups, stacked books, plumped cushions on the red brocade couch. I shuffled Art's papers, which blossomed with staples in one corner as if it were spring. After my spring-clean, I started trollicking through my list of lettings-out, takings-in, takings-up, all on my trusty Singer. It was tedious work, but no more so than reading certain views of literature and culture.

By early afternoon I had almost nothing left on my list. I made tea and stuffed my face with bread, warmish cheese and banana, standing at the kitchen bench. Well, there was one item left. I went to my workroom, balanced a banana skin on the edge of the table like a soft clock, and lifted the costume down. It was as heavy as chain mail, from all the embroidery. I'd get it out of the way this afternoon. I carried it like a little body to the front room and spread it out on the table. I ran my hand over the wool, which was soft but with a slight prickle in it, a stubble and glint like grass. It was cold to the touch, as garments always are. They have their own microclimate. It was beautiful, but Christ, it was certainly a right bloody mess. There'd been violence done to it. That was nothing new; but the scale of it—appalling. What had this Trisha woman done! Or the man. I inspected the ripped seam closely. Someone, some amateur, had embroidered right up to the edge. The freed silver threads formed a mass. I was going to have to redo a strip of silver embroidery, there was nothing for it. The afternoon was wearing on, wearing out like a grey jacket getting more ragged every minute. Always match colours in good light. Matching fabric and thread is the first principle of mending.

I went back to my workroom, to my bank of spools. I loved those spools—a haze from the doorway, but the colours singled themselves out as you got closer. I chose a bunch of blacks, and the two or three skeins of silver embroidery silks that I had. Because there was no blinking electricity, I carted it all back to the front room. In the diffuse grey afternoon light, I matched the colours. There are gradations of black, of course, and finding the right one is like tuning a violin. You keep going, getting closer, going past it, coming back, until you're bang on. With this old costume, because it was so faded, it was always going to be a little off-key. Flat is better than sharp. Luckily I had a pretty darn good match in the silver silk.

With my incy snake-handled scissors I nosed a half-centimetre strip of knotwork undone so I could reattach the sleeve. I spent an hour leaning into the front room window with my glasses anchored on my nose, fusing the fine wool seam back together. The black fabric gulped the light like a sea anemone swallows water; a little factory. The seam was the easy bit. Next, the knotwork. There was a lint-like trace of what I'd pulled undone, and also I could copy the other sleeve. All the same, I squatted down at the Big Books shelf and looked in the index of a huge tome I have on costume. I read that these dancing costumes were descendants of Irish peasant dresses of the eighth century. From the twelfth century they were decorated with gold-thread patterns from the Book of Kells. Blah blah blah. I loved this stuff. The curly Kell designs looked like Maori carvings and I remembered reading some theory about how the Celts could've settled New Zealand before the Maori, and left stone circles scattered about the place before relocating to Ireland. Sounded like complete bollocks to me, but nice try. Hey, I'd be indigenous! Weren't the common curly motifs just the sea sloshing about in its communal basin? I couldn't find anything about the actual stitching, the loops and spirals. Didn't matter.

Soon I was pulling silver silk again and again through the old black fabric. Grandmother! I snorted to myself. Within a couple of hours, I'd put all the escaped threads to bed. It was an okay job, even if I did say so myself, considering the age of the thing, and the shambles it had been in the first place. A rider on a galloping horse wouldn't notice. I hung the costume back in my workroom and took afternoon tea to the front room. Eating a tepid Mallow Puff, I watched rain approaching over the western hills.

7

There was a man on the doorstep, wet—soaked. I showed him in and took his furled umbrella and propped it in the corner. He was jittery, but then the men always were. He didn't have a parcel or anything. There'd be a scrap of something in a pocket, no doubt, a silk shirt screwed into a ball.

But he didn't have a garment. He said he'd come to collect a dress. Nervous as hell, stuttering almost. It was kind of late for business hours. Half past six.

'A dress?' I said. I might've smiled to put him at ease, but I tried not to. Well, he'd cheated on his wife. I knew that for a start.

'A dress.' He squizzed into the tunnel of the flat. 'You in the Blackout?'

I said we were and led him down the passage. At the workroom door I asked him if he had a docket.

He puffed from behind his lips. 'It's a, you know, *dancing thing.*' He looked around as if he might find it hanging in the air. I'd noticed this before about the men. The women thought abstractly about a garment. It was folded neatly in their head.

44

When I looked puzzled, he said, 'A sort of dress. A woman brought it to you. Trisha.'

'Oh *that*,' I said. As if I could forget. 'You're collecting it for her?'

'She doesn't drive,' he said, and blushed. What agony to be a man. If a woman were picking up a man's suit, she wouldn't be all steamed up about being thought a cross-dresser. He stuttered on. 'She's my sister.' Yeah right. His face twitched, the palsy of a lie. My clients never lied. They always told the truth, because I knew it anyway. But what did it matter about this one? Let him fabulate through his teeth if it pleased him.

While I swept through the rack like The Woman of the Dunes, he made polite conversation from the doorway. Bit damp out there, he said. It was, I said. Actually it was a downpour. Unseasonable, he said. Mm, I said. It was bang-on for the season. His incessant decorum—I have to blame him—made me snag my finger on a garment. I flinched, and heard him wince in sympathy. I sucked on that metallic taste which never fails to surprise me—the table of elements are our relatives, Granny H, Grandpa He; we're the result of their unstable relationships. I wrapped a bit of interfacing around my finger; blood on a garment an absolute no-no of course. I was aware of the man watching me as I tied a knot in the bandage with one hand. 'Don't worry,' I said, to comfort him, because he seemed to have felt it more than I did, which is often the case. Thinking is terrible. 'Occupational hazard,' I said. 'And the dark.' When he didn't respond, I prompted him: 'The Blackout.'

'Of course,' he said. 'The outage.'

He read the *Herald*.

'Four days now,' I said, 'and they're saying weeks. Weeks.' It was a mantra.

He looked blank. A strange disconnect.

I spread the costume out on the table and invited him to inspect it. He stepped into the room.

'It's not perfect,' I said. I pointed out the slight roughness of the join, the differences in colour, and explained how when the tear was this bad, and the material this old, there was only a certain amount that could be done. He wouldn't look; he was petrified. While he *gazed into the middle distance*, I collected certain data. Thirty-odd, tall forehead, brown hair that was trying to be preppy but wasn't, was just badly cut, the solid upper body, and the way his hands hung beside him. The new jeans were a fraction too big. His face was pale, jutting, the eyes deep-set so their colour was impenetrable. He'd been unfaithful to his wife. That was the single fact I knew about him.

He cleared his throat. 'Rightio.' He did the puffing mannerism again. 'Is it, ah'—he hesitated—'invisible?'

Well, how could he know if he wouldn't look at it? I said it wasn't. I'd just *been* through all this.

He winced as if I'd pricked my finger again.

'To the naked eye,' I said, 'it's not too bad.'

He still wouldn't look. Anywhere but. 'The naked eye?'

'Yes, to the naked eye.'

'Not under a microscope, then?' he asked.

'No,' I said patiently, 'it wouldn't look good under a microscope.' He was a pedant. 'What I mean is,' I said as laboriously as I could, 'it's invisible enough.'

He wasn't convinced, but wanted this to be over. 'How much?'

I'm not good at fleecing people. It's my Marxist upbringing, which I think I've already mentioned. 'Um, a hundred and sixty dollars. It was quite a job.'

'It's a bargain,' he said quickly. He sorted eight shaky twenties from a very nice wallet.

'What do you do?' I asked. I never ask that question. It's rude.

'I'm in banking,' he said.

I must have looked unimpressed because he added, 'Donovan Brothers.'

Investment bankers down in the city. He wasn't a teller, obviously. I should have charged like a wounded bull. I said I'd wrap the costume, but he stopped me.

'It's alright like that. I've got the car outside.'

I insisted it must be wrapped. Anything could happen on the way home—car grease, spilled drinks, the risks are legion. Another assignation. He could have taken it right then—it's not as if I would've played tug-of-war with it—but he didn't. Things would have been different. He stepped into the tiny space between the door and the table while I fossicked on my haunches under the chair where there was a stack of paper, like a sponge cake. The doorbell rang and I jumped up, told him I'd be back in a sec.

He leaned away from me as I edged past him in the doorway and as he did knocked the dish of tiny amber beads off the table. They landed with a high-frequency crunch and washed over the floor.

'Ah, sorry.' He bent down to the beads as if to scoop them up, but they were escaping from each other as if changing from liquid to gas. An impossible task.

'Don't mind those,' I said. 'I'll get them later.'

He straightened, glancing at me on the way up. I felt sorry for him. 'Okay,' he said softly, just the consonant, the click of the K.

It was a client, a thirtyish businesswomen in a navy suit, high heels and very red lipstick—the powerful uniform I'd always had a secret desire to wear, but never would because of my *line of work*. Her dark blunt-cut hair was frosted with raindrops. The showers must have slackened to a drizzle. She greeted me with a firm hello, but no smile. I found myself matching both. We stood by the front door in silence, as if all our social calories had been expended on hello. Like the man in my workroom, she didn't have a parcel. No doubt there was a silky garment in her hardboiled briefcase.

'What can I do for you?' I asked, although I hate it when people say that. It's condescending. Her silence and her intense brown stare made me say it.

She said she hoped it wasn't too late in the day, but she'd come to pick up an *item*. She spoke with emphasis, as if talking to a class of five-year-olds. Positive, sure-footed, with important words in italics. It was a tone that left you in *no doubt*.

'A *costume*,' she said. Her face was shiny and oval like those shepherdesses you see in gift shops.

'A costume?' I didn't have it of course.

'The Irish one. The *dancing* outfit,' she said. Her italics.

I knew she wasn't a Riverdance mother—I'd have remembered them, happy and hyper—and the man in my workroom was collecting the only other Irish costume I had on my books recently. It wasn't as if it rained Irish costumes. I told her she must have confused me with another mender. That had happened before. I said I'd give her the number of Doris at Pins Alterations over in Kingsland, and I headed down the passage to get it. The woman clicked along behind me, saying, It's unmistakable, black, fitting, *heavily* embroidered . . . We stopped outside my workroom and she ran her hands around her upper body, leaving a wide margin the way a dead body on the street is outlined with chalk.

'It's *he-ah*,' said the woman. 'Don't you keep *records*?' She eyeballed me, and I was sick of her. This was what it was to be in the Yellow Pages.

'I have records,' I said (I've told you about my workbook), 'but I don't have your costume.'

She closed her eyes as if to contain something. It seemed she had a thin shell of composure, and that a scrawny chick of hysteria might peck through at any moment. 'Just *look*,' she said.

I wanted her gone—I had a client waiting, after all—but I felt sorry for her. 'Listen,' I said.

'No, you listen. You are Megan Sligo Mending and Alterations?' Unfortunately that was *moi*.

The woman put a hand on my arm, just lightly, but wow, the transgression. I wanted to wrest it away, but something kept me trained on her narrowed eyes. She lowered her voice. 'I saw a *docket* in my husband's *wallet*.'

I felt the sudden wallop of facts connecting. This was his wife. The man. His flipping wife! I looked at the door to my workroom. It was ajar. As if on cue, it creaked a little.

The woman went on: 'I thought it was *odd*, but didn't put two and two together. When I went to look for the costume, I really *thought* it would be hanging in the wardrobe.' Here she released my arm and leaned back to rest her case. 'It *wasn't*.'

She was anxious, and I felt oddly protective, but also drunk with a powerful, loose feeling. I could behave anyhow I liked with this woman. She was the poor jilted wife. I was the professional, in charge. Perhaps this is how psychotherapists feel when confronted with distressed clients. The woman drew herself up, as much as she could because she was petite, and said, almost viciously, 'It's an heirloom!'

I paused, thinking what to do. How odd it was that husband and wife should come to pick up the costume at the same time. It couldn't be all over between them, despite the obvious third party, if they were still running around synchronised. It was always the way, so I'd noticed, that the wife (or husband) still had enormous psychological, even spiritual (if you believe in any of that stuff) power.

'Please, just *get* the costume,' said the woman—the wife—and she folded her arms over her single-breasted suit jacket to wait.

The husband in the workroom would have been listening to his wife's voice, of course. He couldn't have missed it. At that moment, he could have stepped out into the passage and greeted her, marvelling at the coincidence of the two of them coming to get the costume at the same time, but he didn't.

I stood very still and changed my tack. I said to the wife, 'You didn't bring the costume to me, did you?'

'No. I didn't *b-ring* it to you,' she said. 'Obviously. My husband did. Either him or that little bitch.'

The word was like a knock on the funny bone—somehow still the most hateful word you could conjure, even taking into account the next generation of words, the reproductive parts. The woman looked, for a moment, forlorn. Her straight dark fringe fell forward. I would show her into the workroom and there she'd encounter her husband. There might be a scene, yelling and screaming. Or maybe they would keep it under wraps, escort each other tightly away. I buzzed with the awful anticipation. I'd give Art a blow-by-blow that evening as we ate fish by the light of the hurricane lamp. A man was caught out by his wife today, and the wife lunged at him on the path!

I hesitated and glanced at the workroom door, which was still ajar with the man behind it. 'Did your husband ask you to pick it up?'

The woman frowned. 'I don't think that's any of your business. *Actu-ally.*'

I thought about it for a moment. 'Well,' I said, 'I don't usually give out garments to, you know, people without a docket. Unless I've been told about it.'

The truth was the issue had never arisen before. Until the man turned up that afternoon. And I hadn't hesitated to hand the costume over to *him*. Things had got tricky with many of my other clients, but this particular bit of trickery, this Restoration comedy—it took the cake.

'I can *appreciate* that,' said the woman. 'And you probably don't usually have sullied garments brought to you either. Garments with the stain of adultery.'

Sullied. Adultery. Such old-fashioned words! It seemed that infidelity needed a few new words in the *Oxford Dictionary.* I replied grimly, 'You'd be surprised.'

The woman looked suddenly tired. 'Look, I just want to know what's going on.'

I nodded. I did feel sorry for her. It'd be best if she saw her husband, and they could sort it out between them. Let them yell, bicker, fume. This was nothing to do with me. I went to open the workroom door.

On the edge of the door I felt something foreign and warm at the tips of my fingers. I turned my head quickly and saw that I had encountered the husband's fingers. An electric current ran up my arm. I looked back at the wife. Had I gasped? It seemed not because the wife continued to stare at me without a blink. I let myself glance into the workroom. He was standing in the doorway looking at me. He moved a hairsbreadth, but I knew anyway, in that second, what I was going to do.

8

I saw the relief on the man's face when he understood I was going to hide him. The trace of a smile. I smiled myself and had to put my hand to my mouth and cough lightly. I remembered then to take my other hand from the edge of the door where it had been in contact with his fingers.

'Excuse me a moment,' I said to the wife.

She made to follow me, but I stopped her. 'I'll look,' I said. I needed to change my story. I didn't want this woman phoning Doris and hassling her. I stepped quickly into the workroom, skating on the beads, clinging to the jamb for balance. As I pushed the door closed I had a last glimpse of the wife's face, tilted with surprise as it slid out of sight.

In the workroom I faced the man in the metre-wide space between the door and the table. I was briefly aware again of the structure of his body, the long back and long arms, the square torso, the set of his neck, before I tipped my head back and investigated the Carrara ceiling, its beaten, cake-like pattern. Odd that there was copper beneath the whiteness. You'd never know unless someone told you. I wondered if he understood precisely what I was doing, that I was waiting, unaccountably, for an allotted time to flip by. The time that was to be filled with the retrieval of the costume. I was letting these moments go empty into the future. I could hear his breath, uneven, a swallow once or twice. The room was sealed by the intensity of the wind. The tree outside butted the glass, squeaking and making the light wobble. After a full minute I looked down from the ceiling. He must have moved forward slightly, or maybe I had. He was so close we could almost have kissed. But didn't, of course. We looked at each other. The expression on his face: disbelief? I stepped back out into the passage and pulled the door shut behind me.

I was aware that the wife was looking at posters on the opposite wall, the wall healed over like skin. At the sound of the door closing she spun around. Her arms were still tightly folded.

'Well?'

'I can't find it,' I said. I knew I sounded breathless.

The wife showed no visible reaction. If anything, she was more measured than before. 'I was given this costume for safekeeping for my daughter,' she said. 'It's an heirloom.'

Christ, there were children! It didn't bear thinking about. A girl, wide-eyed, hopeful. Perhaps she spread her grandmother's dancing costume out on the bed sometimes, ran her hands over it, felt connected to something, I don't know what.

'An heirloom?' I asked. Surely an exaggeration. It was half finished, poorly made.

I had a memory of a tablecloth blooming with wine stains. (More on that later.)

The wife sniffed and shook her head. 'It's not that, it's not even that.' She turned her brown eyes on me again. 'Can I tell you something?'

I made a yes/no sound. Did I have a choice?

'About two weeks ago,' said the wife, 'I saw a woman in the supermarket wearing a costume just like mine. I caught a glimpse of her at the end of an aisle—then, gone. I thought I must be mistaken because, you know, it's distinctive, this costume. Then I found one of your dockets in my husband's pocket.'

(That rhymed, but I didn't comment on it.)

'Megan Sligo Mending and Alterations,' she recited.

Yes, point taken.

'Even then I didn't think much of it. Maybe he'd picked up a stray bit of paper, written a phone number on it, I don't know. But something . . .'

She paused and I felt kind of pinned, yes, like a garment.

'. . . Something possessed me to check in the wardrobe to see if the costume was still there. And what do you think?'

Was I meant to answer this?

'*What do you think?* It was gone!' Her face crumpled. Something gave way. 'The little tart! You've never come across such a mess. Sometimes I think I'm going mad. I don't have much to go on. A glimpse, and—I don't know—a feeling. But then, the costume, gone! What's happened to it? You know, I wouldn't be surprised if this little trollop, whoever she is, wears the costume again. As if it's her own. The little Jezebel.'

How quaint these curly fin-de-siècle words (fin-de-the-previous-siècle)—tart, trollop, Jezebel. You half expected *harlot, fallen woman*. Where were the new words for people who screwed around? Women who screwed around. And what about the man in the workroom? Why were there no words to describe *him*, at nearly the end of the second millennium, and a blackout to prove it? An outage. I could almost see the wife's anger wafting off her body like dry ice. No slushy stage. No tears. Perhaps I should give her the costume after all, if it would soothe her. I had no loyalty to the man in the workroom. I didn't know him. From

Adam. I hadn't set out to hide him. There had simply been that galvanised feeling when I'd first seen him standing behind the workroom door. In all the transactions with my clients, I had never encountered the injured party. A garment was one thing, but a *spouse*. And a daughter waiting in the wings, to boot. I should hand over the costume. The problem was, I'd already told her I didn't have it. I didn't want to be caught lying. I didn't lie. I was honest. As the day is long.

At a tiny pinging sound from the workroom, the wife cocked her head and listened. She swivelled her gaze back to me, keeping her head at its birdlike angle.

'There's someone in there, isn't there?'

Later I wondered why I didn't answer that question. Some subliminal code stopped me. Later I would break out in a curious sweat thinking about it. Curious because—why? Why should I have cared, at that point? Why was I hiding the husband anyway? If my intention *was* to hide the husband, then not answering the question was the right thing to do. If he *hadn't* been in the workroom, if there had been nothing to hide, why would I defend myself against having a person in my own house? I somehow knew that to deny there was someone in the room was to give it away. And I didn't. I put on what I hoped was a puzzled but not too puzzled expression. I didn't move. I would not let the wife discover him. I'd save him from marital strife. After all, I had done this for so many of my clients. I would prop up some form of deception like a tent. That was what I always did.

The wife sighed. 'Ms . . . ?' Strangely formal.

'Sligo,' I supplied.

The wife looked down at my ring finger. 'You're obviously married. Or something. Tell me, has your husband ever cheated on you?'

Then I was moving away from the workroom door, ushering the wife down the passage. (Cheat? Never. We were open and honest.)

In the doorway the wife handed me her card. Milly Something. An accountant for a big firm. 'I think the costume is *he-ar*. When you find it, please *ring* me.'

I mumbled that I would.

'Do you know,' said Milly, 'when I opened the wardrobe I could *smell* her.' I recalled the acrid chemical whiff I'd caught off Trisha the previous Friday. Milly turned and walked out the open front door, which closed after her, an oofing slam as the wind sucked it shut.

•

The client was standing exactly where I'd left him in the doorway. For an instant he was like one of those human statues painted in bronze, the illusion shattered when his voice rippled through his body. 'That was my wife.'

'I think I worked that out,' I said.

A nervous laugh like a squeak. He sank back into the room so I could go past.

'And thank you,' he said. He looked waxy, almost luminous in the grey room.

'No trouble.' But it was trouble. A garment was one thing, a relic of infidelity—but a girlfriend, wife, whatever—I didn't want to see the *other party*. The client put his head in his hands briefly and I met his eye as he came up for air. I won't deny, I felt myself gloat over his misery as I got out my receipt book.

'Who shall I make it out to?'

'Pardon?'

'What name?'

'McGrath. Shane. There's no need.'

56

I scribbled the receipt and handed it to him. They're quite lovely these receipts, fluttery and bluish. 'You must have heard everything,' I said.

He nodded and looked unseeing at the receipt. 'Thanks.' He was trembling.

'Thank *you*.'

'Well, goodbye.' He took a breath as if to drag on a cigarette. A smoker. 'Oh'—he stopped—'the costume.' The word fumbled, as if he were holding it under his tongue like a thermometer. Then he lowered his voice, even though the idea of his wife hearing him from out on the street was ludicrous, and repeated, 'The costume,' quietly, as if that would cancel the loud version. 'May as well take it with me.'

I smiled. 'May as well.' On the table I folded the arms of the costume behind its back like a prisoner. He noticed it, a sudden but fleeting interest, and looked away. While I was wrapping it he said from the doorway, 'Do you mind if I stay a minute or two? So I won't, you know, catch her up.'

I hesitated. Harbour him, again, while the wife drove away? I gestured to a chair squashed up against the cutting table.

He shook his head and stepped further into the room. 'I'll stand. Only a minute.'

I put the parcel on the table and picked up a half-done hem. Peered at the stitches, put it down. I was used to filling in empty minutes, but it was too dark to sew. I glanced at the client. Shane.

'It's not as bad as it looks,' he said. 'Well, you know how it is.' A sheepish smile—but not really, I knew that; it was a proud smile in sheepish clothing. *Well, you know how it is* was an advertisement for himself. Like so many men who'd come before him to have their trousers and jackets mended, he was bragging. Two women found him attractive, at least.

I did stucco sweeps of the table, swatches and threads into the palm of my hand. A cursory act because the room was idle anyway in the Blackout. Lying fallow. I told myself not to ask him if he'd driven here, but went ahead anyway.

When he nodded I asked, 'Won't she have seen your car out there?'

A fresh look of comical anxiety. 'It's possible.'

'She might come back in.'

He let out a slow, tight stream of air. 'Here's hoping!'

Oh, a joker. I brushed the scraps into the bin and stood with my arms folded. A minute's silence. I looked at his face, which was, yes, still angsty. 'I had a friend,' I said, and he looked sharply at me. 'Who was seeing a man behind her boyfriend's back.' I stopped to see if he wanted to know the rest. He looked not so much inquiring as accepting of his fate—a touch of irony in his 'Yes?' I went on. 'One day her boyfriend drove past a house, completely random, you know, in a suburb, and saw my friend's car parked outside it.' I felt a wiry smile of triumph on my face, and a thrill ran through my body. Well what do you expect? He was a cheater.

'Jesus God!' he said. 'That makes me feel much better.'

I tried to stop my lips from pursing, but I suspect I looked like I sucked lemons.

He said, 'I've never been hidden before. Not even in a wardrobe. I didn't want to hurt her, you see. I had no idea she even knew. My name's Shane, by the way.'

'I know, you told me.' We shook hands as if we'd just met, which felt awkward because we'd already touched fingers. We waited for the wife—Milly—to get further and further away. At one point he patted his pocket in a gesture I recognised as checking for cigarettes. He cleared his throat carefully, trying not to make too much noise. He still looked white, but there was this humour behind it, a combination of self-consciousness and bursting confidence, like a comedian. It was ego, that was what I identified it as. Barefaced ego. They're all like that. I'd seen his dirty laundry, and he still managed to be wry.

Into the silence he said again, 'I really am sorry about this,' and I said, 'It's fine.'

'I didn't mean to drag you into anything.'

'I'm not dragged into anything,' I said. The self-centredness of the man.

'Good, well that's good. Sometimes things get . . . so there's no choice.'

'Yes, okay.'

'Especially when you throw in—'

'No need to explain,' I said. I'd heard the tangled stories of clients, the forbidden paths their garments took to reach me. I'd heard it all.

'—when you throw in a betrothal, almost.' He groaned softly but theatrically.

The wife had been gone four minutes. It was seven o'clock, ish. The evening was stretching out. There were still two hours of daylight to go, but in the workroom the walls were purpling as if bruised.

'I'll be off,' he said.

'She'll be well and truly gone by now,' I said.

'Yes, I've taken up enough of your time.'

These polite phrases, like retro clothing. Sometimes they were empty. It was all in the way you said them.

I reached for the parcel. 'Betrothed is an odd word. These days.' Well it is, isn't it?

A truncated laugh erupted under his T-shirt. 'Slight exaggeration. Family friend, more like.'

I saw him along the passage silently. He shambled down the weedy steps, a man with a wife who'd been picked out for him, and a mistress, which was a sexist word but it was hard to think of another that did the job as well. I suppose you couldn't blame him. *No choice. Out of my hands.* As he went down the path I remembered that I was still holding the costume and I started after him. 'Your costume!' He hadn't heard. I've never had a very carrying voice. I wouldn't be good in an emergency. He was in his car, pulling out and up the street.

I went back inside and, stepping over the beads on the floor this time, put the parcel in my workroom until someone should come and collect it.

9

I didn't set out to be a mender, in case you were wondering. No, no. I'd be an academic, and I still will, probably. I would be in an English department somewhere, perhaps in the Northern Hemisphere, which was, well, quite a big place—in a bright fat office, a professor, surrounded by narrow offices like strips of land occupied by lecturers. The seasons would be topsy-turvy of course, with the bulk of the work done in winter, the harvest of final assignments collected in bundles in the spring. The summer would be a time of deadness. But coming from the Southern Hemisphere, which was upside down anyway, this would seem normal. And the thing is, I'd always read a lot of literature, and if you like reading novels, and want to take them to bits and put them back together again like a clock and hope that they'll still work afterwards, and if your parents happen to be reading *If On a Winter's Night a Traveller* and leave it lying around the house, then you end up doing literary theory at varsity, and reading Saussure and Barthes and Foucault et al., who were all great guys, really they were. They were saying the blinking obvious, but someone had to say it. Also Kristeva, Cixous, bell hooks etc. All wonderful.

You read them nodding and saying to yourself, That's *so* true! It really was how things seemed, only you hadn't realised it before.

I once read that Jacqueline du Pré had never set out to play the cello. She was simply given a cello as a child, and so she played it. But sometimes she hated the cello. When she was grown up—and by this time a musical sensation around the world—she was given a very valuable cello and was told to be careful to keep it at the same temperature because of course changes of temperature aren't good for a wooden instrument. Between concerts she'd put her cello out in the snow, or stand it in sunlight in a glassed-in porch. The cello would shrink and swell.

I would've left Jameson out in the snow, but it never snowed in Wellington. It was Eurocentric to even think about snow, but you couldn't help missing it somehow in your bones and feeling a little cheated that you'd have to leave old Fred out in the horizontal July rain. The pages would swell.

It is true, though, while we're on the subject, that Derrida is a matchmaker. I met Art behind a pillar in the cheap seats at the back of the Michael Fowler Centre when the great man was visiting Wellington on his 'Derrida Downunder' tour. Within six months we were married—Art and me, that is. That evening in the Michael Fowler Centre, as I searched for Derrida, who was soon to appear about a kilometre away on the stage, I was aware of a black shape beside me. (Even then Art dressed in the semiotician's uniform. Boldface.) He was telling an anecdote to the person on the other side of him, a woman, also in black, who I felt annoyed with, even though I didn't know her, or Art. Later I understood what that feeling was. Yes, I got to know *sexual jealousy* very well. But at the time, I was a babe in the woods. All I knew was I wanted this man in black to be telling me, not the woman in black, the story about Derrida in Kansas. How when Derrida visited Kansas someone asked him, after his talk,

Don't you think all this is a bit like The Wizard of Oz? (because of course it was Dorothy country, flat and tornado-prone), and Derrida replied, *Yes, I suppose I am a bit like that little dog.* Art and the woman cracked up, and I laughed too. Art looked at me. As things turned out, it stayed that way. Talk and laugh, laugh and talk, a simple equation. When the tiny, distant figure of Derrida finally appeared on the stage, I stared straight ahead at him for a solid hour while he talked on 'Forgiving the Unforgivable'. He seemed to get smaller and smaller until he was at the end of the long tunnel of my vision. His head was too big for his dainty arms and legs.

At the end of the lecture, the woman who had laughed at the Derrida joke dematerialised miraculously (sucked up by a tornado, I said later), and Art turned to me and asked if I'd like to go out for a bite. I was already imagining a tooth bruise in my neck. We went to the Lido, Art doing his upright stride, and ordered pasta, which we couldn't swallow for wanting, and ended up soon after in his springy student bed. He was from Auckland but had come to Wellington to university because it was small and funky. It just went on from there. We talked about books and ideas and things, and laughed quite a bit. Art was great, he really was, and the more I got to know him, the nicer I saw he was. He was decent to everyone—old friends who he had nothing in common with anymore, shopkeepers, the girl he took to the Seventh Form dance, who wouldn't let him fuck her even though all the other girls seemed to be doing it: he was friendly to her when he bumped into her in the street. He brought me cups of tea, he pressed his palm onto my brow if I wasn't feeling well. I couldn't believe my luck. I hadn't even known people like Art existed. But also, I think what was so great about it was we weren't all tied up in knots with each other. We allowed each other freedom, we didn't stop each other seeing friends. I think the problem with some of my clients, for instance, is that they kept each other in a kind of prison. We were never like that.

•

Auckland had been trundling along in quite a fun way. It was bright and ferny, and the city sprawl all silvery. And I kind of liked going to gallery openings and parties—we knew a few people and met a few people, who were *new blood*.

Several nights into the Blackout, for instance, Art was telling me about Glenda, an old family friend who'd just got back from France and was working as an assistant at LambChop. She'd been taught by a woman who was taught by Julia fucking Kristeva. The Formica shone in the light of the hurricane lamp. The wine looked like plums. I took a whiff of the fish Art had gone all the way to Freeman's Bay for. It was acknowledged that I had the superior nose. I sniffed deeply and told him he shouldn't have. While he lit the 747 and zipped oil around in the bottom of a pan like kanji, I wrestled with kumara. Then there was Stewart, said Art, who along with six thousand other apartment-dwellers had to crawl up multiple flights of stairs in the dark to his flat, poor bastard. It stank to high heaven. The sprinklers had been set off by the power cut, and there was no air-conditioning. They might be forced out of their apartments anyway, by a state of civil emergency.

'We should have him to stay, shouldn't we?' said Art.

'Who's Stewart again?'

'I've told you. He's Shakespeare.' Art still referred to people by the topics of their degrees. 'Whoever Shakespeare was.' Because Shakespeare might actually have been the Earl of Something.

'I hate that,' I said. And I do. I hate it when every last thing is up for questioning, even poor old middle-class Shakespeare, who apparently wasn't educated enough to be himself.

'Why would he want to come here when there's no power? Aren't there other people he can stay with?'

'Stewart's a bit . . . he's a bit . . . how can I say?'

I generally say yes to everything. I'm famous for it. I'd said yes to the dress, after all. It would be kind to have Stewart stay. There was a lot of goodwill about re the Blackout. But I had a strong feeling that I didn't want any Stewart lurking around the villa conversion.

Art's blue eyes looked surprised, but he shrugged. 'Fine.'

We did a wobbly hug by the 747. 'We're doing alright, aren't we?' And we were. There are worse things. The fish, kumara and spinach were on the list of ten superfoods that Art had stuck on the fridge, of which it was good to eat at least three every day otherwise there might be a nasty shock waiting for you when you reached middle age. Free radicals running amok in your body. It was better to live in a constant state of virtual shock rather than wait for the real catastrophe.

Life went on across the street, hums, cackles, whines.

'Poor Stewart,' said Art again. 'But we've formed a sort of club. The five poor sods who actually *live* in the Blackout zone. Disparate people, all linked by darkness. I mean, Stewart and a feminist theorist from Paris. Darkness brought us together like a marketplace. I might write something about it.'

Art said at least he would invite the feminist theorist with the degree from Paris, who also sort of grew up with him, and who also wrote a bit of poetry. And her partner or whatever.

Choice between Stewart to stay and Glenda for dinner, Glenda hands down.

'Except we have no power,' I said, feeling practical.

'It's fine,' said Art. 'They're in the Blackout too.'

We were all equal.

Sometimes I think how different things would have been if I'd said yes to Shakespeare and spent the Blackout listening to someone wandering around the villa conversion reciting *What light from yonder window breaks?*

Art asked about my day. That afternoon, that evening, a man in love with a woman.

10

On Wednesday (Day 5 of the Blackout) I went out, to stop myself going crazy and to buy food. Up on the corner of our street, with the villa roofs falling away from me, I hit Newton Road and stood and looked out over the quiet parabola of the gully. At its nadir the North-Western Motorway took off into the green-grey distance where the Waitakere Ranges lay. The on-ramp was usually choked with traffic. Now its relative emptiness made the veering-off seem like someone's mad scheme. I turned and walked in the opposite direction, up the last of the rise to the Symonds Street–Khyber Pass intersection which normally was frantic, but today was like Good Friday—Good Friday when I was a kid. All the shops, the loan agencies, the boutiques were jailed with their squeaking security gates. As I walked, I peered into the long, dark shops. A few had lights shining deep inside, and a few shapes like bears shuffling about. People had been worried about looting, and they'd called out the civil defence the first week. But in fact there'd been less crime than usual, so I heard on the news. No one about. I was thinking about the apocalyptic novels I'd read in my teens—*Brave New World, 1984,*

Briefing for a Descent into Hell, The Day of the Triffids. They'd scared me stupid, that's why I liked them. On the footpath above Grafton Cemetery (where the Woolthamly who made all the dosh was buried, by the way), the street kids who normally hung out among the graves were sitting blinking like nocturnal creatures unaccustomed to daylight. I must say I did have a butcher's to see if the boy I'd given the hundred dollars to was there, but this was ridiculous—there were hundreds of street kids in Auckland. I stopped on the ridge to look back at the city. A strange pall of greyness hung over it. In the rain, the unlit buildings looked like a misty slagheap, dark, jagged and charcoaly. No traffic lights. The odd car, as if it were 1940. Way down Queen Street, where we often swanned around going to bistros, a lone bus. I could hear it lumbering from this distance—a kind of intimacy. But otherwise: quiet, quiet.

I turned back down Dominion Road, and tromped through that unpleasant bit of Spaghetti Junction where the familiar traffic fumes made me feel sick and comfortable at the same time, and continued on into Mount Eden. I picked up bread, salami, olives, fruit, and walked back home, glad I'd brought my umbrella because it started to rain.

The villa conversion, when I entered it, was full of natural light and darkness, somehow mixed, reminiscent of unbleached hessian and the slightly depressing atmosphere of health food shops. The rooms already smelled more humusy than usual, like a winter garden. Auckland was like that, even without the Blackout. In spring you wiped white film off your sandals and walked around smelling as if you were very old.

•

Mabel arrived with a job, calling from the front door, 'It's me!' No other 'me's in the world. She juggled an umbrella and a carton, which she peered over from behind her black-rimmed glasses. 'Tell me to piss off if you have to, but I thought you might be free, under the circumstances.' She waved her hand at the Blackout, which filled the air from here all the way to downtown. Mabel usually just turned up, or sent one of her fashionable young acolytes dressed in the clothes they bought for twenty percent discount from Mabel's boutique. This was to avoid the possibility I might say no to the job on the phone, which I did once when I was busy. Mabel had a label (I know), and was quite successful. Her designs were unmistakable, dark and voluminous. You could tell a Mabel walking down the street. But they also seemed to work within the bounds of some fashion dictum going on in Europe, season by season. Narrow trousers. Tulip-shaped coats. Ruffly blouses (roughly!). How these ideas spring up on different parts of the planet at the same time, like playground games, I have no clue. But Mabel also had perennials. She did a good flouncy skirt. And skirts with landscapes on them. That was where I came in. I'd been doing hand-finishing and embroidery for her for the last year. We'd become sort of friends—you couldn't avoid being friends with Mabel—although we lived in different worlds. My world had a hole in it—well, you know, the mending. Mabel's world was always on the boil—shapes, colours, textures, moving like a kaleidoscope.

She kicked off her shoes in the passage, and charged into the front room, which she filled: six feet, and her crinkly hair gave her another inch. Her perfume mated with every gassy particle. She scraggled the cat.

'We're *so* lucky to be just outside the Blackout, the girls and me, but I thought to myself, Well, GoGo will be able to do hand-sewing. Am I right?'

She plopped the carton on the floor. I think I nodded.

'I have these gorgeous, gorgeous things!' Mabel lifted shapes from the carton. They were organza, like filtered light. Drenched colours: green, salmon pink, butter yellow, a blue. 'Aprons! Welcome to the Fifties Housewife.'

With Mabel there was always a reference. I guess they're all like that, designers. I'd seen Mabel do the Seventies, War, Peace, War and Peace (big skirts, double-breasted coats). Never just clothes. Why not? (I really mean that.)

'Don't you love those colours?' said Mabel. 'You can almost taste them. In fact I can. I can taste them.'

The aprons were lovely. I fingered one, and saw the faint bluish markings where a few whorls of embroidery (executed by yours truly) would go.

'These are so post-war it's not funny,' Mabel was saying. 'It's tied-to-the-apron-strings colonial culture, of course, can't deny it, but also about reclaiming the fifties house*wife*. The lino-ed kitchen, kitchen *table*, lots of kids, veggie patch sort of thing. *Tu comprends*?' Mabel held an apron around her waist. It looked short on her statuesque figure. 'I can *just* remember all this,' she went on. 'The hand-knitted cardigan, the pleated kilt, the homemade biscuits. People think they were bad days, the fifties, and I do remember my mother taking things, pills, you know, but there were a lot of freedoms those women had that we haven't got. They didn't have to earn a goddamn living, for a start! I don't suppose your mother had an apron—you're too young.'

Actually—I told Mabel—there was an apron in the bundle of linen embroidered by my great-aunt (more on that later), but I don't think Mary-France would ever have worn it. It would've been a joke.

Mabel hurried on. 'There's another interesting angle to all this, a bit of social history. The rise of the washing machine—it was responsible for aprons dying out, did you know that? Before washing machines, if you spilled something on your dress you had to wash it by hand and it was such a bloody chore. By the fifties, aprons were getting decorative. You could just chuck your dress in the washing machine. It probably mashed it to pieces, of course. How's your husband anyway?'

Mabel could never remember Art's name.

I told her Art was fine and asked after Bill.

'Fantastic,' said Mabel. 'He's *fan*tastic.'

Mabel showed me where she wanted a few threads of colour, in a koru shape across the corners of the aprons. They were like spring. The spring that came after the winter of war and before the high summer of 1968. The blue embroidery lines were like veins. Mabel shook a semi-transparent plastic box full of stardust. 'I hope you won't mind,' she said coyly. 'Some beading.' I'd done beading for her quite recently (hence the beads that the client had knocked off the worktable), and I hadn't enjoyed it. It wasn't me. Seeing I didn't immediately object, Mabel charged on. 'A bead every so often, entirely up to you. Just to give them a bit of three-D. I'm thinking *dew in the garden*.' It wasn't really 'beading'. There was a man in Auckland did beading, ball gowns with thousands of sequins and seed pearls. That was beading. This was just the odd bead.

'Only fifty aprons,' said Mabel. 'To start with, anyway. It's not every girl in town will want one, only the adventurous spirits. The show's at the end of March, so no *desperate* hurry. Autumn's just gone. Gone to bed.' Mabel was always two seasons ahead. 'So, whaddaya reckon? The aprons.' The 'whaddaya' was an affectation, like '*tu comprends*'.

Of course I agreed to do them. It'd be almost pleasant. And I had my income to consider, though I never had before. Earning is strangely addictive.

'*Fan*tastic,' said Mabel. She tenderly wrestled open a plastic box and dipped her finger in. Pale amber beads stuck like pollen. 'Aren't they beautiful?'

'Good for intruders,' I said.

'The old beads-on-the-floor trick,' said Mabel. 'Oh, I almost forgot.' She dug into a plastic bag and pulled out a long gunmetal skirt, tight and wrinkly like a cocoon, and one of her long dark jerseys with fur polka dots. 'For you.' She tossed the clothes on the couch as if they were rubbish. They were samples. I had stacks of Mabel's samples. They were gorgeous. I never quite knew what to team them with, but I must've ended up looking as if I was at the cutting edge of fashion, because sometimes people stared at me in the street.

I fingered the fur polka dots and thanked Mabel.

'It's nothing,' she said on the way out the door, suddenly strangely shy. 'Last season's, but it'll look good on you.'

•

Change of subject but not entirely: do you know the story about the three sisters and the pair of trousers? Ah. A man bought a new pair of trousers because he had a job interview to go to, but the trousers were an inch too long. He lived with his three sisters. He asked his oldest sister if she'd take up the trousers by an inch. This was in the days before the sister would say, Go and do it yourself, you chauvinist bastard. Instead she said she was too busy making bread. He asked the second sister, and she too said she was busy, she was pruning the roses. The man asked his youngest sister if she'd take up his trousers by an inch, and she said she was too busy, she was starching the linen. So the man thought he'd have a go at taking up the trousers himself. He sat at the dining room table, threaded up a needle, and made an okay fist of it, for a man. He left the trousers hanging over a chair ready for the morning, and went to bed.

Late that night, the oldest sister decided she really should help her brother, and before she turned in for the night, she went to the dining room and took up the trousers by an inch. The second sister was just getting into bed when she remembered the trousers and thought she should do them after all. She took them up by an inch. The youngest sister woke in the middle of the night, troubled by something, and realised it was her brother's trousers, which he would need for his interview in the morning. She got out of bed, went down to the dining room, and took up the trousers by an inch. In the morning the brother put on his trousers and discovered they came down to just below his knees.

The moral of the story (which I was told by my aunt, Sister Jude (more on her later)), is blinking obvious of course: never put off till tomorrow what you can do today. But I always wondered about the man—and here's where we're privileged as readers and listeners, and the poor old character has to take what's coming to him. The poor sucker, if he never found out that his sisters also took up the trousers, would've spent the rest of his life thinking he was crap at hems, and probably never attempted another one.

•

When Mabel had gone I folded the aprons into a pile. Tomorrow. An apron wasn't for protecting a dress anymore, and sometimes a coat wasn't for keeping you warm. You could get sleeves that were just sleeves, no body. Sometimes I lay in bed and counted the garments that were becoming vestigial. Not really. I might do that now. I went to make a cup of tea. The kitchen was not quite the kitchen without the hum of the fridge. Afternoon didn't seem like afternoon when it grew its own long shadows. In the Blackout, everything seemed transient, and I liked it. I was in the interstitial space, I was in the Wahi, the Va—the Samoan space in between—not to put too fine a point on it.

I tried to remember how I had come to hide the man. I must have looked at him so that he stopped right there, motionless inside my workroom. Perhaps I pushed him back gently with my hand, but I don't think so. All I could remember exactly was standing close without breathing just inside the door, a hundred tiny beads under our feet.

Good afternoon light

11

That evening the client turned up to collect the costume he'd forgotten, or I had. I showed him in, he shook his umbrella, and when he was standing in the front room I told him the costume wasn't ready. He was, I have to say, speechless. Instead he turned one palm outward. I noticed it was pinkish, as if he stored a lot of blood there, more than usual. In the other hand he held a dripping briefcase. His dark, rectangular suit made him look a different person from the one in the new jeans, but still dishevelled. The suit behaved as if there was a wind in the front room. We stood in silence, flanking the table, me in my Mabel skirt, him in his means-business suit. The ball was in my court; I needed to tell him when to come back, that was the way the transaction should proceed.

I'm a terrible blusher. I don't need *blusher*, I can do it for myself, thanks very much. I could feel myself steaming and smiling stupidly, I didn't know why. Well, I did know. Rain was battering the iron roof, as it had the day before.

'I thought it was ready yesterday,' he said.

His high forehead had the look of a terrace house. People with foreheads are meant to be brainy, but that's a bit unfair on people with low foreheads.

'Yesterday?' My cheeks raving like a lava lamp.

'Or whenever it was.' Quickly, to get on with it.

'The day your'—I had to think—'wife was here?'

He half smiled, half pursed his lips. 'Yeah. That day.'

This is how he looked: like Mr Rochester. Read *Jane Eyre*. Like that. Craggy. What anyone would see in him, let alone two women.

'It wasn't ready,' I said.

His face went squarer. 'But it was. You wrapped it, remember?'

'I did,' I said. 'But when I looked at it again, I saw that in fact it wasn't ready. After all.'

I was being an idiot, a clown. I should give him his fucking costume and book in for therapy. I don't even swear. But there was something about the situation made me twitchy. I mean, I'd met the mistress *and* the wife. It was suddenly so transparent. I'd been doing this very thing, on and off, for three years, counting New York, but, well, maybe I shouldn't.

'Why?' he asked. 'I mean, why not?'

I blundered on. 'Because I didn't do a good-enough job on it. I can make it better.'

'Look, I've come from work,' he said. He looked tired, come to mention it; the eyes. 'It'll be fine as it is. Didn't you say it was invisible?'

I hesitated. I suppose we'd had the invisibility conversation—I did with most clients. It was all relative, it depended on circumstance. 'Almost invisible,' I said.

'Okay, almost.'

'But not to someone looking closely.'

He shook his head, which was a little shaggier than you'd expect with a suit. 'It looked fine to me. I'll just take it anyway.'

Something occurred to me. 'But you didn't look at it yesterday.'

He looked *slightly taken aback*. I smiled, but put it out like a small fire. He propped his briefcase against a chair. His hand looked stiff from it. 'I don't know anything about this sort of stuff.'

I said to myself, GoGo, just give him the costume. 'It's the Blackout,' I said. 'I don't have my electric light. I did this job under the kerosene lamp, but I should've done it in daylight.'

He followed my logic, looking from table to window.

'That's what I'll do next time,' I apologised, if not *profusely*.

'It's fine,' he said. 'I'll just come back.'

I hadn't planned this. I'd give him the thing the next day, untouched of course. But if I had planned it (and I don't know why the hell I would), I would've expected him to put up more of a fight.

'Tell me when,' he said.

He was a pushover. A tower of jelly, or jello as they say in America.

'I'll look in my book.'

Oh, I'd *look* in my *book*.

I ran my finger down the columns of the workbook, over the garments. The subtitles in my head, like the subtitles of the essays I used to write, the bits that told you what it was actually about. Coat, brown, woman's: *desperate hurry, sex*. Trousers, black, man's: *drunk, sex*. My finger came to the end of the list. Ah. I didn't tell him the jobs before the costume had all been done and that there were no new ones apart from the aprons. I could see him *out of the corner of my eye* squinting at the page. 'But it must've been,' he began, and stopped. I knew he wouldn't ask why the costume seemed to have slipped down the queue. He was like a man in a clothes shop, helpless—only worse, because this wasn't menswear, it was a fucking dress! Stop swearing, GoGo. I don't know where I got this habit. I'm really a polite person. Despite the pole house. I never wanted to be a raving lunatic. That's what I've always admired about Art. Nothing of the nutcase about him.

I told the client not to worry, that it wouldn't take long.

He nodded. 'When?'

'Couple of days. That wouldn't be too late to'—I took my finger off the page and looked up at him—'trick her, would it?' I was waiting for him to tell me to back off. He said nothing. I continued: 'What I mean is, are you still thinking you can . . . hide all this from her?' I could hear a lightness oozing out of my voice: contempt. The truth was, I was having a blast toying with the investment banker. I was a cat with a mouse.

'Hide the costume?' He was playing dead.

'Well, the *lack* of a costume was more what I was thinking.'

After a second he decided this was funny, and gave a short laugh. 'Yeah,' he said. 'I'm still thinking that.'

'That you can just put it back, and she'll never know the difference?'

'Yup, that's what I'm thinking.' He picked up his briefcase. His tight hand.

'Good,' I said. 'That's positive thinking. *I* was thinking it might be too late already.' GoGo, shut up, I was saying to myself, like a subtitle. Shut Up.

'No, it's not too late. She's in Wellington for a few days. Her firm relocated because of the Blackout. She's an accountant.'

Oh. This was a new development. Since yesterday. This was a bit unfair. 'I'm sure we can have it done by the time she gets back.'

'I'd appreciate it.' Polite. Formal. Slightly nervous.

I closed my book, formal too, prim. I was Jane blinking Eyre. He was moving across the room. I told him he'd have it back in time. 'That would please both of them, wouldn't it?' I could barely contain my distaste for him. 'Your wife, and Trisha?'

He shot a look from the doorway, the name of the other woman seemingly jarred from his mouth. 'Trisha?'

'Trisha. She'd be off the hook.'

'It won't "please her,"' he said tightly.

'Oh.' I was following him out into the mandolin, i.e. passage. The rain was fading away, some handfuls on the iron roof. 'She seemed to be, you know, keen to see it all fixed.' A lie, of course. She hadn't given a rat's arse about it. She was just going through the motions. If I remembered rightly.

He said over his shoulder, 'She's gone.'

I had a new, odd sensation in my cheeks: buzzing. 'Gone?'

He turned but I couldn't see his face in the dark passage, which was made so much darker by the low cloud. I'd never asked questions of my clients, not once. They offered me information, too much, about their complicated lives. Their eyes would start out of their head with the need to tell. It was gory. They told me so much I sometimes wanted to put my hands up to their mouths, crisscrossed like a bandage, and stop their *no choice, out of my hands*. But a man standing in the half-dark of the Blackout, he was hard to see, and it was just possible to ask a question of someone almost invisible.

'Gone where? Back to Ireland?'

I thought he cocked his head, its shape, in the dark. 'No idea. Why?'

'No reason. She seemed like a nice person.' Another lie. She was ghastly.

He ignored this, and peered back into the nothingness of the passage. 'Did you get all the beads up the other day, yesterday?'

I followed his gaze to the place where the beads had run under the door. Like honey. 'Yeah I did, most of them.'

In the grey light from the front door he looked blank. He didn't want to know about the beads, of course, it was just something to say.

'Tomorrow then,' I said.

'Tomorrow?' He seemed surprised, pleased. I suppose her nibs might be home for the weekend. 'Are you sure?'

'Yes.' I *might* be able to manage, seeing it was already finished. This was hilarious.

'Okay, tomorrow.'

He stomped down the overgrown steps, the slightly shambolic walk, and I watched him flicker away across the street. He had a car parked somewhere. The rain had gone off and the atmosphere was whitish, washed clean. The bougainvillea daubed its drenched magenta petals over the picket fence. Wildflowers and weeds poked at the dusk. That banker's wife—or whoever she was, in 1900—must have gone crazy with her forget-me-nots and daisies, her dandelions and lavender, in the unaccustomed heat while her husband was down in the city. Perhaps even during her lifetime she regretted planting so many English flowers in the semi-tropical hothouse of Auckland.

12

I learned 'almost invisible' in New York.

Oh, New York?

A bit of a long story. Art got a Fulbright to do his doctorate at Columbia. I know! Victoria University didn't stack up. You'd be able to think much more deeply at Columbia. I thought I may as well go too, for the ride. Joking. We were in love. Before I booked my ticket, I'd have to do two things: drop out, and get married, in that order.

The first one was temporary, of course. But strangely enough, I'd been having a bit of an existential crisis about university. I knew quite a few people who were having them and they seemed catchy. I'd written a whole essay without using the word *hegemony*, just a space where it should be. I imagined Professor Bleakley—Bob—having a chuckle in his jam-packed office, at the epistemological hole. Bob thought it was hilarious, but took marks off because this was university, he said, not drama school. My low mark was okay in the scheme of things, and I decided never to use that word again, which I'd always disliked because it reminded me of the gorse behind the house I grew up in. Next I wrote an essay without the word *hegemony* or the word *prolepsis*, which reminded me of medicine. *Discourse* reminded me of the opposite of soup or an appetiser, and the opposite of those must be regurgitation, so I started leaving that out too. Followed by *dialectic* and *normalcy*. So ugly. *Negotiate, unpack, problematise.* Gone. It was like that Haydn symphony where the musicians all gradually leave the stage until there are none. I thought old Wittgenstein would actually quite like that (I said 'old Wittgenstein' in my head, as if I were Holden Caulfield).

One evening after my second low grade, which was thrilling in a strange way, Art took my face in both hands like a goblet and looked right into my eyes. No one had ever looked at me quite like this. I remember looking away and back again. 'Do what makes you happy, GoGo.' I nodded as much as I could between his hands. Of course I would. Why wouldn't you? He put down my face. Where he came from, you could do what you damn well liked because you were so rich. Where I came from, you could do what you damn well liked because you were so highly educated. This was why we got on. This was what I thought later anyway.

•

You can spend a long time getting educated and drop out relatively quickly. On a Monday morning I took the cable car up to varsity. I usually rode the lift in one of those buildings that sits like a spirit level next to the hillside, and then I'd pound along The Terrace. I was broke, and the cable car cost money, and anyway you could think when you were walking. (Good with your feet.) But this day I needed the cable car. There was no point having a cable car if you didn't take it when you were about to drop out of university. When I got to campus, I remember being glad Dad (I actually thought that, in a Seussy kind of way—*glad Dad*) had lost his job at the university. There was no chance of bumping into him. I got forms from Registry (they should have Deregistry) and went around getting them signed by various professors, as if I was collecting for something. One said, Are you sure the situation can't be salvaged? I was a shipwreck. I said, This isn't spur of the moment, you know. And I realised with *sudden clarity* that this had been coming for a long time. Since the age of thirteen, to be exact. For ten years I'd been working towards dropping out, and now I felt drunk with the power of it. The drunken feeling came from the very fact I'd been a good student until recently. Otherwise this would have no meaning. I was a dropout! It was exhilarating.

From that moment I was officially unemployed, but something would turn up.

On the way down Church Steps (you didn't need the cable car when your business was done) it struck me that for the first time in my life I didn't have anything in particular to do. No books to ferry to the library before the fines kicked in, no chapters on post-structuralism to scatter with sticky neon petals as if there'd been a high wind at the end of spring. And nowhere in particular to go. Except the flat, our place in Mount Victoria where a pencil dropped on the floor rolled downhill. I'd go there, at eleven o'clock on a weekday. Art might be home, reading, writing, just as I'd done, until today.

But when I got home Art was out, and the flat had a desolate air. I saw, lying on the desk, the essay I'd been writing the night before. It stopped at the word *discourse*, which in any case wasn't there. I never touched it again, the essay. It lay there decaying as if someone on the *Mary Celeste* had been writing a paper on renegotiating the interstitial space at the time it was abandoned.

•

I felt my way along to the kitchen. I was getting used to negotiating the passage without the Wah Lee moon. Once the lamp was burning in the kitchen, it felt cosy, in all its yellow seventies glory. When Art's parents had first bought the villas I'd thought of painting the kitchen white, but the man in the paint shop told me that, considering the layers that would have been put on over a hundred years, the walls would need to be taken right back to the board. He said anything new would just fall off if applied to the present layer. I just left it, and we lived with the yellow. That was okay.

I turned on the radio news. The Auckland City Council was having a meeting right then about the outage, but Pinnacle Power hadn't turned up. There was a lot of yelling going on in the background, of *outraged* customers. I found a jar of pesto in the cupboard. Art would be home any minute. I cranked up the Primus stove and filled a pot with water for pasta. When I hoved near the sink, a smell, sweet and disgusting, rose up from the waste-disposal unit, the last few scraps left unground since last Friday. I plugged it up. What else to do? What did you do about these things while you waited for the power to come back on?

I looked out the back door to see if any lights had come on in the Blackout zone. Sometimes you could think this was just you, your own private blackout. But it was still completely black. It made me think of black gloves, I don't know why. I sort of liked it. I was getting to like it.

There was rustle of twigs. Did I mention we had a cat? Bell, short for Bella, short for Isabella, short for Isabella of Spain, because she had a black mantilla on her white head. Her eyes gleamed as she thundered through the garden. We laughed at her. There was a standing joke that she was so clumsy the native birds could party around her.

'Here, Isabella of Spain!' I said.

She wouldn't come. She'd heard something in the undergrowth and lumbered off. The banana palms were swishing now, as the wind got up. Couldn't see them, though, only hear them. I sat on the step and heard Art drop his dissertation and creak along the passage singing 'Between the Wars' under his breath.

•

From the start I loved rough wool in my hands. I remember the thrill of doing running stitch on hessian at school, aged six. It was the middle of the road. Crunchy asphalt. (Yes, thank you Gayatri Chakravorty Spivak.) Next I did wool tapestries like fields of Xs. The odd person, a visitor to the house, a colleague of Dad's (but only ever a woman), might lean over and look at a yellow rabbit as neat as a corn cob, and say, Good with your hands, aren't you? I would squirm with pride. 'She has advanced fine motor skills,' Mary-France would comment flatly, which made you think of cars suspended so their undersides were exposed. 'It runs in the family.' Unfortunately.

Sister Jude, of course. Not that I or anyone could be descended directly from Sister Jude, our great-aunt. Along with several nuns and priests who seemed to have ganged up in that generation of the family, she was a full stop when it came to potential cousins. The fun cousin-filled Christmases we might have had, but for the nuns and priests! Instead of having children, the nuns embroidered in their spare time. Every year Sister Jude would send by post several finely worked linen cloths and doilies. I would catch a glimpse of their starched bendiness, their multi-coloured arrangements, as Mary-France opened up a rough brown-paper parcel in the bottom of the hall cupboard and dropped them in. Poor Sister Jude, Mary-France would say. We always called her 'Sister Jude'. Like a married woman, no one could remember her name—and not just her surname, her first name. Annie? Patricia? It was lost to the Brown Josephs.

Once we visited Sister Jude in a convent in a strange town with milky light and a stillness that made it seem as if the world had stopped, after the wind of Wellington. Perhaps it was Auckland. The first thing you noticed was the smell—camphor, disinfectant, essence of old skin. And then the darkness of the polished wooden panels. Sister Jude was slipping away, breathing harshly, already halfway through a door. No one had thought to visit her while she had been fully in the room. She was lying in bed, a skeleton with wispy white hair like high cloud. While the adults huffed over her, I stood by the window, hoping to get some respite from the stench, but it was shut tight. I parted the dark curtain and looked down into a wet, sewer-like space which seemed at odds with the order and beauty of the Gothic convent. What was down there? Perhaps Sister Jude's real name, dropped like a coin a long time ago and still lying among the moss and mould. We didn't stay to see her die, but she died. And the stack of embroidered cloths—the dressing-table doilies, the tablecloths, the serviettes, the boiled-egg covers—were retrieved from the bottom of the cupboard and rehabilitated. Maybe old-fashioned was alright. Maybe it was daring. Mary-France decided that the embroidered cloths may as well be used, because what was the point of having them otherwise? What was the *point*?

And so one Saturday evening when she and Dad were having one of the parties they threw, mostly for Dad's English department buddies, but also for the odd publishing friend and an assortment of gas-meter readers who had brilliant minds, and smelly people who did nothing in particular but were also brilliant, Mary-France unfolded the first tablecloth and flared it out over the rough totara table. It was beautiful, with flowers and leaves done in thousands of the most careful stitches, so real that you thought you could pick them off the linen surface and it was a surprise to find the cool silk packed tightly under your fingertips. The crocheted lace edgings hung like icicles that would disintegrate and fill the palm of your hand with icy water. They didn't. I know because I sidled through the thicket of brown-and-green-clad English lecturers and tried it—they sat in your hand, cold but heavy. I remembered these moments, as if they were fined down to their individual stitches.

The English department and publishing friends would pour themselves a drink and settle down in the conversation pit to talk about books, books with titles like musical motifs. *The Leaves of the Banyan Tree, The Adaptable Man, Jerusalem Sonnets.* Then they'd get up to pour more drinks, a little less carefully, and settle back into the conversation pit, to talk about more books and the sexual habits of their workmates. More drinks poured, now with a kind of happy-go-lucky sloshing motion, and before long red wine stains began to appear beside the sprays of forget-me-nots and the big heads of the chrysanthemums which I'd tried to lift from the tablecloth. The blotches accumulated fast. How quickly that part of it was accomplished, the staining, compared to the hours that had gone into the stitches.

Over the years I became intimately acquainted with every embroidered cloth in the brown-paper package. I pored over them. I wanted to make these tactile pictures too, so I got a book out of the library and discovered that there were different stitches, and that you could follow a pattern or make things up. My first made-up things were wonky woolly cross-stitch affairs. A tennis player in whites on a green lawn. Another visitor to the house with an English accent thought it was the Long Man of Sussex. He wasn't. He was a she, for a start, and she was standing up. I kept going. I would go into what people call your 'own little world', which isn't that little because it has all the ideas and the people you've encountered in it. I once read in a novel by V.S. Naipaul (a raging misogynist but who cares?) about a character who could never be bored, even in jail, because he had a 'well-stocked mind'. I was patient. I discovered that each stitch was an act of patience. It all took a very long time. You had to not care too much about time passing. Maybe you had to be just filling in time until death with these little acts, these stitches. Maybe you had to not care about life too much, be clinging too tightly to it. Maybe you had to not fear death but even be, perhaps, looking forward to it and so filling up the minutes, the hours, the days until it should arrive. Not joking. That's how existential I discovered embroidery was.

It was alright, though, about my degree, in case you were wondering. I'd go back at some point and polish off my master's. Then I'd do one of those meandering degrees people do without tutoring jobs, without scholarships, without being able to bring leftovers for lunch and heat them up in the faculty microwave, but it would be fine. I'd do a PhD in the way of those older students you glimpsed around varsity when you started as an undergraduate, really nice people, and when you were halfway through your MA they were still there. You might have conversations with these students beside the lift occasionally. They'd tell you they'd decided to chuck it in, the PhD, it was like an albatross around their neck. Their relationship with their husband was suffering, their children were running wild, they were poor, and what's more they were fed up to the back teeth with the L=A=N=G=U=A=G=E poet they'd unfortunately chosen to spend ten years of their life analysing. They must have been crazy back in 1985. They never wanted to see another equals sign in their life. And you'd agree, yes, probably best to give it up if it was such a burden. But the next time you saw them, and expressed some surprise that they were still in the department, they were shocked, offended even that you'd thought they might drop out. Drop out! Of course they weren't going to drop out, in fact they had never for a second considered it. Well, perhaps for that moment once while waiting for the lift, otherwise, all that research, all that thinking, all those conferences, all the readings of the poems would be wasted, *wasted*.

That's what I'd do. It would be okay.

The thing is, I'd known since I went off to kindergarten with my plastic lunchbox that I'd go to university. That was what we did: improved our minds. Why emigrate if it wasn't for Uncle Vince to get a BCom, and Uncle Pat a flipping Doctorate in Divinity? From Rome. And lately the women. But you know what? (This is what I realised after I met Art.) They collected degrees because they didn't own anything, didn't produce anything. If they'd had a few thousand hectares dotted with fat cows, a few flocks of blinking sheep (yes, blinking), it would've been alright. As it was, no choice but to slog it out at school so they could work with invisible things like philosophy, literature, business *theory*.

If you didn't do this with your mind, if you didn't—what? I don't know. Body and soul could go to hell.

•

In the night I lay awake beside Art staring uselessly into the dark. I started panicking about the costume. Well, about the strange game I'd fallen into with the man—the unbearable formality, the awful closeness, and the fact I was an accomplice. I had threads on my hands. When he came the next day, I'd have the costume ready to give to him.

13

Thursday was nothing to write home about. Art went off to LambChop, the centaur came to collect her tweed skirt, a society matron picked up the blue gown with the slit up the back. I went out and snipped a few tendrils in the garden. The rain had cleared and it was a fresh, clean day. If the Blackout went on for weeks, as people were saying it would, I'd be reading a lot of books, I'd be drinking cups of tea and reading the paper—which was what I did next, in the front room. Megan Sligo Mending and Alterations would close. The hairs stood up on the back of my neck. But as one door closes another opens. I was brought up on that expression. The world was full of doors. I felt jumpy.

The flat was dead quiet, as if it had gone back in time—hey, to the Edwardian banker's wife. But hang on, the suburb would have been inventing itself around her, houses being built all over the valley, footpaths tarred as she walked along them, children everywhere. There were no kids in this part of town anymore. I fossicked for Mabel's aprons. May as well get on with them, although the show wasn't for a few weeks. I rattled the beads. They really would be lovely, these aprons, when they were finished.

Mabel was right—the juxtaposition of function and beauty. Not that I gave a rat's arse. Soon I was making the olivey stems of koru in stem stitch (although 'olivey' is an example of Western centricity if ever there was one), and every so often sliding a bright bead down the thread. Usually I would've spaced this kind of work out over days, weeks even. But I spent most of the day at the window embroidering. It drove me nuts.

Around seven I showed the client into the front room. On his tense face, more a grimace than a smile. I can't blame him—the oddness of it, an eccentric little ritual already solidified. Sunlight poured in the bay window. You brushed it out of your eyes like a fringe. He was in his suit again, but carried the jacket over his arm, prim as anything despite the wrinkly shirt. I offered him tea. He shook his head as if the idea was ridiculous. I half smiled. I hadn't really meant it. Tea!

'It's not finished,' I said.

'What?'

'The costume. Isn't finished.'

He dropped his jacket over the back of a chair. 'Again?'

Again! He'd guessed. That it was already mended, and I was keeping it from him.

'Still. It's still not mended.' I'd broken out in a sweat. 'Sorry. I have these aprons.' I indicated the pretty tufts of organza.

He didn't give them a second glance. One hand was clenched under his chin like *The Thinker*. 'Are you going to do this or not?'

'I'll do it, don't worry, it's just that I have . . . all this.'

'Because if you're too busy, say so and I'll take it somewhere else. Maybe you can recommend someone. Doris of Kingsland.' I laughed. He laughed through his nostrils. He remembered that I'd mentioned Doris to his wife, outside the workroom door.

I went serious. 'The thing is, there isn't really anyone else. Not who'd redo the embroidery. The way I would.' He frowned and I felt myself flooded with an awful power. I was holding his future like a hand of cards. I'd often been in this situation but had never withheld anything. 'We don't grow on trees, you know,' I said.

'I didn't mean that.' A tightening of the mouth.

To show how busy I was, I fished around twitching fluff out of a dish of beads on the table. I shook out an apron. From under my eyelashes I could see him watching. It occurred to me he might ask to see the costume, to check its progress, and in my head I hurriedly prepared a convincing performance of *not being able to put my hand on it*. But of course he wouldn't ask. A man wouldn't ask to see a garment, at least most men. I was trading on stereotypes. What a relief it was. My little one-act play was unnecessary.

'The thing is,' he said, 'I'm kind of busy myself.' Of course he was. I mean, Donovan Brothers. He narrowed his eyes at the bright window. 'And there is sunlight today.'

'True,' I said. 'Good old sunlight.'

'There's a wee bit of urgency about it.'

'Oh, I know,' I said. 'I know that.'

'I don't mean to drag you into all this.'

I shook my head. 'You're not. Not at all.' I was loving this. I gestured at a chair but there was no reason for him to be here. He reached for his briefcase. It's strange how the words 'sit down', 'have another cup of tea', make people leave in a hurry. I picked up an apron and, standing there at the table, busied myself with a bead. 'Tell me,' I said, '*why* exactly are you so concerned?' I was being dense. 'I mean, now you have Trisha.'

'I don't,' he said quickly, getting a little het up. 'She's gone. Remember? You asked me that and I told you.'

'Ah, no. I don't remember everything. I have a lot of clients.'

He looked sideways as if checking for evidence. 'Well,' he said, more to himself, 'I was an idiot. But you don't want to throw everything away just for being an idiot, do you?'

I held up my hand with the needle in it. 'No need to explain.'

'It's just simpler,' he said. He put his briefcase down again.

I was genuinely curious. I was. I asked, 'Is it possible to hide this from someone?' I reached for a fresh amber bead from the dish. 'The costume?'

'Well, yes, but not just the costume. I mean, can you really keep someone in the dark? You must think she's pretty naive.'

'No, not at all!' He was bursting. 'She's . . . funny and wise. You didn't see her at her best the other day. I just don't want to hurt her. When the thing's mended I'll put it back where it was.'

It occurred to me that she'd already seen it wasn't there.

He'd thought of that, he said, he had a plan. He was watching my hands jabbing away at the organza. I'm pretty fast, though I say it myself. I told him he was thorough. The eyes: they were grey, no, green, marbly, and intent. His plan: he was going to put the costume on the wardrobe floor.

'There's a pile of junk there, shoes and things. It'll look as if it fell off the hanger.' He looked at me pleadingly for verification, the thumbs-up. I made my lips into a sceptical twist. The man thought his wife was a moron.

Another bead, like sticky pollen. 'That day here, she said she saw a woman wearing the costume in the supermarket.'

'Did she?'

'Didn't you hear her say that?'

'No.'

Lying through his teeth, of course. He'd heard all about Doris of Kingsland. I continued. 'It is a beautiful thing, I mean, I can imagine any woman wanting to try it on.' For some reason I blushed. I'm a terrible blusher, as I said. I moved things along. 'It was your mother's, right?'

'I suppose so.' He looked out the window at the dark wild garden and the bright western sky.

'You suppose so?'

'It's not like she wore it or anything.'

I nodded.

'Will it be done tomorrow? She might just turn up, if the power comes back on.'

'Don't be anxious,' I said.

Because he was anxious. I didn't mean to be comforting—he was a cheating bastard—but it just came out.

He took a step over to the window and looked back at me. 'I have this feeling.'

'Yes?'

'That you're on her side. And that's why you won't get on with this. I don't blame you.' He held up his hand as if to stop traffic.

'I'm neutral,' I said. I squashed down my smile. 'But I never put one job in front of another.' I pointed to my workbook on the table. 'It wouldn't be fair otherwise, would it?'

'Neutral?' He gave an ironic guffaw.

When I was a kid I used to read guffaw as gawuff.

'But I'm paying you,' he said.

I couldn't argue with that.

'I'll tell you how you can be even more "neutral".' His fingers doing quote marks. He was suddenly animated, the grey-green eyes leaping. 'I'll pay double.'

I did a bead. 'I knew you'd get to that.' And I did.

'For God's sake, triple. Whatever happened to supply and demand?'

I must say I was tempted. I had no work to speak of, apart from Mabel. I sat down. At that point he noticed the organza apron for the first time and frowned. 'What about this? Is this urgent?'

'Of course *this* is urgent,' I said. 'It's fashion.'

He hesitated, and seemed to decide I was joking. 'I'll go now.' He took his jacket from the chair.

'Does your wife sew?' I asked.

'I don't know. Perhaps.'

'Ah,' I said. 'I just wondered if she might recognise a mend.'

He stopped in the middle of the room. 'Hopefully she won't go looking at it with a magnifying glass.'

Our voices had gone quiet, like the day we waited for his wife to be out of earshot.

'Well, not a real one,' I said. His silence indicated he wasn't going to be drawn into what sort of magnifying glass I meant. But he didn't turn away. 'I mean,' I said, 'she might look at it with the eyes of someone who—'

'Who can sew, yeah, okay.'

'The eyes of someone close.' I held my hand a centimetre from my eyes to demonstrate. 'Close to you, I mean. So close she can see everything.' My metaphor astounded even me.

When I looked up I saw he was blushing, an odd sight on his white face. 'If you're so concerned about Milly, why don't you . . . do whatever you do to these things and mend it?'

It seemed something had given way in him, a cell wall. I burred at seeing a bit of him, however tiny, undone. 'I will,' I said. 'I just need good light.'

The smallest pursing of the lips. 'About tomorrow . . .'

There was a sudden greyness, the exciting loss of the sun leaving the room.

'About Milly,' I said. 'I only meant if she looked right inside. She'll be happy it's there'—and I looked directly into his eyes because I'd just remembered something about him—'waiting for your daughter to grow up.'

He peered at me as if I'd suddenly gone small. 'Daughter?'

'It's for your daughter. That's what your wife said.'

'We don't have a daughter.'

I looked at the apron. I'd worked the whole thing, the koru, the white flowers the shape of stars.

'Not that I know of.' He smiled. 'She meant *if and when.*'

'So you did hear her through the door that day.' I neatened the thread and picked up my little snake scissors to snip it off. 'Maybe in the future,' I said lightly.

'Anyway, tomorrow?'

'If you like.'

'I *like.* But will it be ready is the point?'

'Yes.'

'What time?'

'What time can you come?'

'Sevenish. After work. I work.'

Oh, he worked.

I smiled. 'I'm surprised you've got time then.'

'I've got time to come and pick up a dress that should've been ready days ago.'

'I meant time for all this,' I said.

He winced. I'd overstepped the mark. Somehow our roles had gone topsy-turvy. He was supposed to brag about his conquest while I fixed things. 'Early evening then?' I said in a conciliatory manner.

'Okay. I hope it'll be ready. My wife's in Wellington, but she'll be back any day.'

'Yes, you told me. Because of the Blackout. See you tomorrow then.'

I watched him tramp down the path between the wiry garden beds. I noticed that he wore no clothes, like a lot of men. His clothes were almost invisible, his suit like nothing. His car was parked right outside. It was almost invisible too, a grey sedan.

14

The ring was so shiny it was meat-like on my finger. Getting married at the registry office with two friends as witnesses was so po-mo I couldn't stand it. Enshrined in culture but, in 1995, also spectacularly *other*. We surged up Willis Street afterwards and went to the pub. I loved it. I didn't mention it to anyone in the family. Mary-France wasn't a fan of the institution of marriage, Dad was long gone of course, and Lisa would be too stoned to take it in. Anyway, it wasn't like we getting *married* married.

I did find though—and it had all happened so fast that I hadn't anticipated it—that I became a *spouse*. And because the spouses of students weren't allowed to work under the terms of their F2 visas, and because it was impossible for two people to survive on a scholarship in New York City, the spouses got jobs under the table. The spice. It was expected. What were these regulations for if not to provide cheap labour for the hardworking taxpayers? From another spouse I inherited a series of gigs cleaning apartments in brownstones on the Upper East Side. I tooled over from Hoboken, and all day I swept parquet floors and dusted surfaces while someone sat in another room listening to the cabaret songs they all seemed to like so much in this part of town. 'It's De-Lovely'. I did the toilets and the sinks. Wiped up piss and slime and mould. 'You Go To My Head'. Crumbs and dust and ash. I had no doubt that Something Would Turn Up.

Sure enough, I got a lead from another spouse that you could get piecework from alterations businesses in the Garment District. I could *have* the old sewing machine the spouse was giving away because she was going home anyway, as they all did, in the end, urgently, like peristalsis. There wouldn't be any more money in it than cleaning, but it was cleaner.

•

I took the PATH across to Times Square and walked into the Garment District, found a narrow building on 37th Street squeezed between two bigger blocks. Up three flights, and in the sepia-coloured corridor was a metal door with a framed sign done in ornate red cursive: *Rip Burn Snag Clothing Alterations and Repairs*. Underneath, in smaller letters, the way a subtitle defines an essay: *Specialists in French Re-Weaving and Invisible Mending*. There was a piece of paper taped to the door. *Help Wanted*. I knocked and the door was unlocked noisily from within. As I stepped inside, a woman with a streak of nicotine going up through her greying hair was already walking away from the door, calling over her shoulder, 'Close the door!' I closed it.

The tiny workroom was a riot of clothes, spools, bolts of material, and a table so littered with offcuts it was like Jackson Pollock had run his lawnmower over it. Another woman, older, plump, with jowls and short legs tipping her off the edge of her chair, whirred away at a machine by the window. She looked as if she never left her station. The first woman, with the nicotine-stained hair (and you could see how she got it, because she had a fag stuck to her lip), had one of those two-tone New York accents—abrupt and friendly. She was small and wiry. She asked me my name, what experience I had. When I told her I could do embroidery she laughed.

'Em*broid*ery! Are you kidding? Who sent you?'

I reeled off the name of the spouse.

'Jesus Christ! Well, whadda we gonna do here? We're snowed under—yeah, just like the outside. It's snowing out there, it's snowing in here.' She called to the woman by the window. 'Whadda we gonna do, Nance?'

Nance called back without looking up from her machine. 'What choice is there? We got no choice. We're snowed under.'

Snow seemed to be the way they gauged business.

'You're right,' said the nicotine woman. 'No choice.' She looked about the room once more, and gave a sigh that at one or two points seemed endless. 'Okay, I'll tell you what we'll do, we'll try you out. We'll try you out on this, this, this'—and she yanked a few bits of clothing from a pile like a magician doing the tablecloth trick. The pile stayed put. 'Simple stuff. Hems, mostly hems. They're all marked, see?' She showed me the grainy chalk lines.

Nance called over from the window, 'Don't give her that jacket, Rose. Snag on the pocket.'

'Oh yeah,' said nicotine woman, and snatched the jacket from the bundle. 'I'm Rose.'

'Hello,' I said.

'Under the table?' asked Rose. I nodded. She held a few spools up to the light to match with the fabrics. 'Next Thursday. See you next Thursday. Okay?'

I tried to give her my phone number. Rose waved her hand. 'Yeah, okay, gimme your number. You can gimme a fake one. If you're gonna steal them you're gonna steal them, nothing I can do about it.' She scribbled down the number madly, saying at the same time, 'You look trustworthy to me. Been in this business long enough to know an honest face. Been looking at honest faces and dishonest faces since I was knee-high.' Rose gathered in my mending from the table like a harvest and bundled it into a plastic bag. 'My mother was a mender, my grandmother was a mender. I know honest, I know dishonest. Dishonest is the ones getting their clothes mended—sometimes, often enough. Got things to hide.' Rose slid the carry bag across to me. 'Haven't got things to hide, have you?'

Nance gave an admonishing click of the tongue—'Rose!'

I shrugged helplessly.

'No, you see,' said Rose to Nance. 'I know an honest face. You hang around here long enough you'll see some faces, you'll see some real doozies, won't you, Nance?'

'Say that again,' said Nance.

'Okay,' said Rose, opening the door, 'see you Wednesday.'

Hadn't she said Thursday?

'Did I? Whenever—Tuesday, Wednesday, Thursday, Doomsday. These are the Whenevers. They know I do them for cheaper, whenever I got a minute.' She poked a finger at my bundle. 'The Next-Weeks. Now those'—she crooked her thumb back into the room, to a long rack of clothes—'those are the Two-Days and those'—pointing to a smaller rack against the opposite wall—'are the Same-Days. Never get 'em mixed up, and never—*never*—put one in front of another within their own category. Wouldn't believe the trouble you can get into, doing someone a favour.' Rose laughed her tinselly cigarette laugh and unlocked the door. On the landing, I heard the door lock from the inside.

I carried the bundle of clothes home to mend them under the table, like the girl in 'Life of Ma Parker', the girl crouched under the table in her grandfather's hairdressing salon, the girl who goes on to have the *life*. I found that the jacket Nance had spied from across the room had been scooped into the pile after all. I wasn't sure what to do with it. I thought of taking it back to the workshop, making a special trip on the PATH so the jacket wouldn't become overdue, which would mean other garments would be put in front of it. Rose had been so emphatic that should never happen. But when I looked at it, I saw that I could mend it easily. So while the snow fell outside, I pulled a few threads from the inside hem and used them to reattach the ripped pocket.

On the Thursday before Christmas I carried my bundle through the snow to Rip Burn Snag. Rose let me in—'How ya doing?' She tipped the garments onto the cutting table and ferreted through them, going, 'Mm, mm,' to each one. When she came to the jacket she stopped and screwed up her face. 'You did *this*?'

I was going to be fired. I should have just left it. Back to cleaning the stinking bathrooms of the stinking rich.

But Rose was looking at me. 'Why didn't you *tell* me?'

'What?'

Rose snapped her fingers, which were tea-coloured from all the ciggies. 'Nance, we have someone who can actually sew!'

I did that palms-upward thing that I must have learned in America.

Rose put out her hand and we shook. Something swelled up inside me, not connected with my hands. Then Rose brought out a pair of beautifully made suit pants with a puncture in the back of the leg that a nail might have made, and a drag in the material streaming away from the hole like a comet's tail. 'Sit down, honey'—now it was honey—'I'm gonna show you something. I'm gonna show you how to mend this, 'cause I know you can pick it up fast. See this hole here? We're gonna mend this.' Rose was investigating the insides of the trousers. 'God knows how it got here. I mean *here*. I don't mind betting this swanky financier or whoever from over on Wall Street who came in this morning, don't mind betting he's in trouble. Don't know how he made this hole in this fine suit of clothes, but it sure looks fishy to me.' Nance laughed from the window. 'I mean,' continued Rose, 'what's he doing in the boxroom in his good pants, huh?' She looked up over her glasses. 'Ripping and burning and snagging 'em.' I laughed too. Rose smiled—'Uh? Uh?'—and tossed the pants onto the table. She angled a strong lamp onto them. 'You need good light for this. Now this, this is not worth re-weaving. Re-weaving'll take all afternoon, cost an arm and a leg. Not worth it, not where that hole is, not half hidden down near the ass. And not worth you learning how to do it either, unless you wanna spend a lifetime learnin'. Do ya? I didn't think so. We'll do Plan B.'

'Plan B?'

'Plan B is piece-weaving. Take an incy little bit of material from the hem and sew it in the hole. Quicker than re-weaving, but still takes a long time. You got anywhere you need to go to?' Rose perched magnifying-glass plates across her nose, big rectangles like blowtorch glasses. 'Now watch carefully. I'm gonna show you how to make time go backwards. But be warned'—she looked up between the magnifying plates and her two-tone, Bakelite-looking hair—'you're gonna help that man on Wall Street cheat on his wife.' Rose waited for my surprised expression, then dissolved into laughter and coughing. 'His wife is never gonna know he's been in that boxroom once we finished with this. So you're gonna be *complicit*. You gotta know that.'

I raised my shoulders. 'Okay.'

'Okay,' said Rose. 'As long as we're straight on that one. Now.'

That afternoon I had my first lesson in piece-weaving. We took a swatch from a hidden part of a garment (I was in the Garment District, and I was saying 'garment' now. There needed to be a word for clothes without people in them) and wove it into the hole. It was like a skin graft, it was the way a bird makes a nest, the way rescuers hold a net to catch a person jumping from a building. I could go on till the cows come home with the metaphors. As the afternoon closed in, and even the glare of the snow subsided, Nance worked away in her pool of light, and I watched Rose fill in the hole where the nail had been. And then another and another.

Over the next two years in New York, I learned about fabric, how a tear will follow the warp or weft of the fabric, or both. Up and down, sideways. It'll run along the weave like a mouse along a rafter. I learned how to fill in a bigger hole—more of a rip—with new threads carefully matched. I learned not to call it invisible mending, although it was almost invisible and the clients who came and went from the door, which had to be locked and unlocked each time, always wanted *invisible*. Rose said, 'I'll show you invisible'—her fine sift of rewoven threads. 'But you know what? Almost invisible is usually enough.'

If you went out with Rose at lunchtime, it was like walking along with Mayor Giuliani. Hi Rose, Hiya Rose, all along the street. Everyone knew her. Back in the workshop, Rose had a churning voice and liked to exchange flirtatious jokes with the men. I listened to the talk, to the clients, most of them men, some of them nervous.

One day, after a jumpy man from uptown had left with his almost-invisibly mended jacket, I asked Rose, 'Is almost invisible really enough?'

'Why do you ask that, honey?'

'Well, what say the wife—or the husband, for that matter—looks at the mend carefully? What say they put on their reading glasses and hold it up under a light?'

'If that's the case, the marriage is already doomed.'

I nodded sagely, thinking about my own shiny new marriage, my thoroughly nice husband finishing his dissertation on Settler Literary Ephemera.

As the first winter got colder, I snipped and wove. Over the quiet Chinese New Year (the New Year Giuliani banned fireworks), I threaded and trimmed. On into spring. I mended as the year turned into summer. I wove threads through dog days, my fingers sweating next to wool. Through opera in the park. I mended on into autumn. The frayed rents in jackets and skirts disappeared in my hands. And all the way around again, retniW, nmutuA, remmuS, gnirpS—that's how I thought of it, the seasons topsy-turvy.

That's how I got into this business; I fell into it by accident, if you can fall up the stairs of Rip Burn Snag. Well, when your world's been turned upside down you can. That was how invisible mending—which wasn't really invisible, was Plan B—began.

But as time went on, Art's dissertation, always a volatile thing, morphed into something that couldn't be finished in New York, could only be finished, in fact, at the Turnbull Library, Wellington, New Zealand, The World, The Universe. And so we came home.

One last observation. Well, not really *last*, but on the subject of dropping out and getting married, I promise it will be. Looking back, it seemed slightly unfair that there had been only two ways left to go ape-shit. Dropping out *for good*, and getting married *for good*.

How good meant forever.

•

The first thing I noticed, back in New Zealand, was that I earned a living, albeit a modest one. I hadn't set out to do this. I was going to go back to varsity as soon as I'd sorted it out. But I knew a woman who knew a woman who asked if I'd do some alterations for her. She'd been on a dramatic diet and needed everything *taken in*. Then someone else asked me to do some mending, then more alterations, jeans to take up, hems to let down, and next thing I was buying myself a proper sewing machine and a good light. Well, I needed them anyway, because I liked doing the odd bit of sewing. I've never bought a ready-made curtain, for instance. But I think if Mabel (who I'd recently met because Mabel knew everybody) hadn't rung me to say, *You do know it's the last day to put an ad in the 1997 Yellow Pages, don't you?* it would have all petered out. None of this would've happened. None of *this*. But I did, I phoned in an ad—Megan Sligo Mending and Alterations. I know! The odd client came. I did the work and they paid me. It was a blast, it really was. Such a straightforward transaction, simple but profound. I was in business! In the English department *business* had been a dirty word. Thinking was enough. The thing about thinking was, you couldn't really argue with it. Well, you could, but nothing changed. You couldn't squeeze it, or weigh it, or buy it or sell it. Well, maybe you could, but not easily. It was slippery. A garment (I continued to use that ugly word), on the other hand, came through the door and was an exquisite centrepiece of doing. I took the garment, the client, the light, my hands, I argued with it, and I won.

Within a few months I was earning more than Art—but I have to say, that wasn't hard—and I never had to leave the house. I didn't have to slave over a hot computer, listen to a bar-room brawl, or read *Writing the New Land: Pakeha and Their Letters 1835–1885*. I worked. And thought. I thought. But it was different. I liked my quiet snow of thinking, and underneath it, the grassy kerfuffle of thread, fabric, needles, scissors. After mending a garment I often couldn't remember my fingers ever coming in contact with it. The dress or jacket would hang on the long clothes rack, mended as if by a miraculous cure. Of trousers I would think, Take up your bed and walk, a line that popped up from a brief childhood phase of Mass-going. These tasks seemed to be done by another self comprised only of bones and nerves and muscles, and muscle memory.

15

It was a week into the Blackout. Friday. Don't you love the way we divide up our time into weeks? I can say *last Friday* and you know what I mean. I don't take this for granted. Imagine if I had to say *an interminable length of time ago,* which was what it felt like. At about four in the afternoon, I went over to Grey Lynn. The feminist theorist and her other half were coming for dinner—takeaways, but we needed bits and pieces. Down I went, into Newton Gully and up the other side, past low-rise sixties office buildings, service stations, a few tumbledown cottages. Deserted as Christmas Day. Merry Christmas! Normally you couldn't hear anything for the traffic and the graunch of machinery, but now, the flap of iron roofs, roller doors shuddering in their sockets.

From the top of the gully the city was spread out before me. It had the air of an archaeological dig, as if another way of life, another people and their clumsy habits, had grown up over the old, fast city. The entombed objects—traffic lights, shops, neon signs—were sunken away into the claggy air from which they might one day be gouged. The sensation vanished when I stepped over the line of the Blackout zone, and began to pass brilliantly lit showrooms with Porsches and Lamborghinis parked at rakish angles. There was traffic, people. I walked to Foodtown and bought bread, fruit, nuts, olives, canned fish, which I know has too much mercury but you have to eat something. Over the course of the Blackout, Art and I ate so much canned fish we could've taken someone's temperature.

Back home the villa conversion gave out a gust of mildew as I opened the door. The wood seemed to be doing the kind of disgusting things humans do, sweating and shedding and farting as it turned over in bed. I creaked along the passage and deposited my parcels on the kitchen bench. There was another smell, worse. Like a sniffer dog I tracked it down. The fridge. The smell was leaking in a refined kind of way from around its seal. I suppose we should have propped it open at the beginning of the Blackout. I now tugged it open a crack. A tidal stink of rotten cake just about knocked me backwards. When I crept back closer I could see the insides were covered in pretty antibiotic pink. I spent half an hour, gagging occasionally, sponging away the glutinous coconut-icy mould. I made it like an altar.

In the front room, my hands all mermaidy, I took the costume out of its wrapping. It wasn't half bad, as well mended as you could hope for under the circumstances. If you peered closely at the inside you'd see a tight thatch of new threads, ever so slightly darker than the original, but it blended in well enough. And on the front, the hoses of silver, the twisted knotwork, as confident as ever.

•

The client didn't come in but asked, slightly breathless on the doorstep, 'Is it ready?'

'No.'

He laughed, and I could see the silhouette of his square-jawed rictus against the blinding yellow sunlight. He looked out over West

Auckland—the motorway, the Waitakere Ranges (like dresses), the sun—then back at me. 'Look . . . when? Just tell me when.'

Such power I had. I smiled a gory smile. 'I'll check in my book.'

'Your book?' He followed me inside. 'Your *book*?'

In the front room I offered him tea because there was a freshly made pot. He shook his head but I took a cup from the china cabinet, an eggshell cup with a dragon on it, and poured one anyway. He picked up the cup without thinking and blew steam across the surface so it was like a thermal pool. I didn't ask him to sit down. When I couldn't stand the silence any longer I said, 'The thing is.'

'Yes?' He was cold.

'It's turning out to be a much harder job than I thought. I can do it. I just need good light.'

He looked into the *middle distance*. 'Is it good light this afternoon?'

I squinted out the window. It was sunny as hell. I'd even had to move, earlier, away from the heat.

'Because my wife,' he said. 'Milly.'

Oh, I was getting used to *Milly*.

'Believe me,' I said, 'I'm actually looking forward to mending this costume.' God knows where I dredged that up from. 'I don't often get to work with such lovely garments.'

He was glazed, yes, glazed like a wheelbarrow.

'It's beautiful,' I went on. It was. I wish I could tell you how beautiful. Glittery and hard and tight. Sumptuous. 'There should be a law against it,' I said.

He shrugged. 'I've never really looked at it.'

I knew that for a start.

He roved over to the bookcase, restless. I picked up a needle and lime organza.

'Oh,' I said, almost gaily (shut up, GoGo!), 'I thought you would have looked at it quite closely.'

'The dress?' He had his head on one side at the bookcase.

'Yes, the costume.' Jesus! He gawuffed. I went on, encouraged. 'I suppose these costumes were two a penny for you in Ireland. I suppose every time you turned around there was another one.' I pointed at the air. 'Look, there's a costume, there's another. With someone in it,' I added.

GoGo, stop.

He straightened up from the books and was preposterously serious. No sense of humour. Oh dear. 'I don't think so,' he said. 'There was only ever the one. I wouldn't even remember it, but—'

'You never look at it.'

'It was the only thing we brought with us from Belfast.'

'Really?' Everything had gone pink from the slant of the afternoon sun and the glow of the red curtains, as if seen through rosy cellophane.

'Well, that and the clothes we stood up in.' After delivering his snippet of hyperbole, he patted a pocket with cigarettes in it. I'd guessed right—he smoked. Black mark. On top of everything. Like a train, it turned out.

I went on with my stitches, white on lime. I asked him why he was leaving in the first place.

'Because the dress isn't finished,' he said, as if *obviously*.

'No, I mean Ireland.'

'Oh. Oh. God knows.'

'The Troubles?' I ventured.

A little laugh like a bubble. 'Troubles. I suppose it was that. A spot of bother.'

'What do you call it then?'

'Anything you like.'

'Sorry,' I said.

'It's fine. I was ecstatic as a child, by the way. Were you?'

It was my turn to guffaw. To gawuff.

'If it's a good light,' he said, 'couldn't you do the costume?'

'I work in order,' I said. 'Remember? I told you. I've got to get this done.' I held the organza aloft. 'I have a deadline.'

Now we both looked out the window. It was half past seven and the sun was squashing down into a lozenge over the Waitakere Ranges. The garden through the window seemed like a lit room.

He turned to me. 'Where's the thing now, on your list. Is it next?'

'The costume?'

He said with exaggerated patience, 'Yes, the costume.' Might have rolled his eyes. 'Is it next?'

Later I remembered that as the first exciting breakdown of politeness, the first brick from the wall. I reached over the apron and opened up my workbook, ran my finger down the page, not reading but thinking, thinking of a tablecloth, my husband, a drumming inside me. 'It's very soon,' I said casually.

He cleared his throat. 'I'm thinking, if it's not done by tomorrow, there won't be much point. May as well flag it.' He was scanning the evening through the window, restless.

I felt a fine net of something string me up inside—of hurt! Ridiculous, I know, because I didn't even know this man. 'But what about Milly?'

He met my eyes from the window.

'Her finding it on the wardrobe floor,' I said, 'and thinking it'd never been missing. What about that?'

'Oh, I still hope to do that. I'll just take it to another mender. Surely there must be someone.'

I could hand it over to him now. I mean it *was* hanging mended in the other room. I'd make up some story about why I hadn't given it to him before. I forgot, I was mistaken—something far-fetched which he wouldn't believe for an instant, and I'd see the look of contempt on his face and he would see me see it, and there would be another unbearable moment of intimacy, such as when I touched his fingers on the edge of the workroom door. It wouldn't matter, because I'd never lay eyes on him again. Or I could simply tell him that I'd lied. He'd be surprised and might ask why, and I'd say, I don't know, some madness. And he'd shrug and say at least he had it now, the costume, before it was too late. He'd take it home and drop it carefully on the wardrobe floor under a hanger, perhaps putting something on top, a raincoat, shoes, so that the sudden appearance of the lost costume wouldn't seem too outlandish. He'd go to Milly and kiss her, but not too hungrily in case she suspected remorse. He'd kiss her tenderly, lovingly, in the hand-in-glove manner of long-term lovers. And then perhaps they'd move like a two-headed monster, joined all the way down, to their own bedroom, and make love there in that same manner.

'It's a beautiful thing, you know,' I said. My voice came out rough, and I blushed and cleared my throat. 'The costume. I don't think you realise.'

'I probably don't.'

'You're lucky, with your traditions, you know,' I said. Well he was.

He shook his head. 'It's not like that.'

'No, no, believe me, the sentimental value, etcetera. Like your wife said. You can't buy it for love nor money . . .' I petered out. Then started up again. 'Especially when you throw in a betrothal.'

He looked at me oddly.

'That's what you said, the first day you came to get the costume, the day—'

'Yes, I know, the day Milly was here,' he said, singsongish. 'Well, I exaggerated.'

I knew that for a start.

He shrugged. 'Family friend. I suppose they thought we'd . . . get on. You know how it is?'

Rhetorical question, but I pictured the pole house, the A-frame ceiling and the conversation pit. 'My parents were too busy picking out partners for themselves,' I said.

He laughed and I followed suit. I was hilarious.

'I take it your parents are still an item,' I said.

He did a Jim Carrey look, eyebrows dovetailed. Not worth answering.

'Maybe splitting up is for when everything else is going swimmingly,' I said.

Complete garbage, of course. There's nothing like poverty to send people to the divorce courts in a handcart.

'Anyway, it must mean that you love your wife, if you go to all this trouble—I don't mean trouble.' I blushed.

He smiled and picked up his briefcase. 'So anyway, if you can't do it by Monday . . .'

I put down my beading. I'd give him the costume tomorrow. Then he'd be happy. Happy his marriage would be saved, happy his affair with Trisha would stay secret. Who could care less? Certainly not me. I'd seen it all, the lies, the excuses. I just did my job. I used my hands, I earned money, I thought thoughts. It was a nice equation. You couldn't fault it.

'It'll be ready,' I said. 'Come back tomorrow.'

'Monday, you mean.'

'Yes, Monday.'

'Really?' An ironic half-laugh. 'When on Monday?'

'Late afternoon. It'll be done by late afternoon.'

'Okay!' An elation in him. He took his jacket from the back of a chair. As if to smooth things he said, 'You have a lot of books,' without looking at the shelves—perhaps he'd noticed them earlier and stored the information in his cheek like a hamster.

'Yes, and Art.'

'You studied art?'

'Oh, no, my husband. That's his name.'

'Ah.' He ran his hand over the cobbled spines of literary theory. 'You're a pointy head.'

'No, not at all. Only my needles.'

He laughed. 'Did you go to Auckland Uni?'

'Vic,' I said. 'You?'

'Auckland. MBA.' He was moving towards the door.

'Oh,' I said. 'You'll be raking it in, then.' (GoGo, stop!)

'I wish.'

He was rolling in it.

Then I thought to ask him what he'd been doing when the power went off. As time went on this became a question people asked.

'At work,' he said, as if this was blinking obvious.

'Were you stuck in the building?'

'No.'

'How was it getting home? Was it wonderful?'

He looked at me as if I were crazy. 'No.' In the doorway he turned. 'Monday, seven o'clock.'

'Yes,' I said. 'But aren't your offices blacked out?' Donovan Brothers were in High Street, right in the CBD.

'We've moved to Mount Albert,' he said, 'temporarily. Monday it is.'

He stuck to the point, you had to give him that.

There was something I wanted to ask him, and I thought I would, standing there in the doorway. 'Tell me, is part of the thrill of all this that you might, you know, end up with the person? With the lover?'

He seemed about to speak but didn't.

I went on: 'That there might be no going back, even if you hadn't set out that way, you'd—'

'No, I know what you mean.'

'Even if it hadn't been that way in the beginning.'

'Yes.'

'Yes? You mean, it is part of it?'

'Yes. I said yes.'

For the first time I looked at him fully. It was an unfamiliar feeling, as if I'd shone a light on him. I didn't even know I had a light.

16

He must have passed my husband in the street because moments later Art slalomed in the door with a polystyrene tower of takeaways. Like the Cat in the Hat he swooped them to the table in the front room. The feminist theorist and her boyfriend were close on his heels. Art made intros in the darkness of the passage. Glenda, Grant. We all laughed because no one could see anything—just a flutter of Art pumping Grant's arm up and down as if milking a cow, which was a habit of his. And a voice from the direction of Glenda. 'Wife? That's right, Aunty Prue told me. How wonderfully committed of you.'

'GoGo performs miracles on clothes,' said Art. 'She learned this amazing technique when we were in New York, didn't you, darling?' I could see his lovely teeth, and I smiled too.

'What a day at LambChop, eh?' said Glenda. 'That place! But listen, I've got news. For later.'

There was a Shakespearean sigh I didn't recognise. Grant. (More Shakespeare.)

'Mysterious!' said Art. 'What?'

'Just wait!' said Glenda, like a slap on the wrist. 'Wait till we're sitting down.'

'Why? Will we fall down if you tell us now?'

'You just might.' Glenda giggled.

'Anyway,' said Art, 'let's not talk all night in the passage. Follow me! Mind your step.' He was like a scout leader, minus the sexual abuse, tromping us into the front room and lighting the hurricane lamp. Everyone appeared. Grant's long black coat, which in the dark of the passage had seemed New Romance, was revealed to be a boxy Wall Street affair, although it was February. He had a staid, clean-cut face to match, with a five o'clock shadow at this hour of the evening. He held up the booty that had been tucked under his arm. 'Cham*pagne*,' he said with overblown reverence, and handed the bottle to Art. Glenda was dark-haired and petite, gamine. She dangled a plastic bag of something like a stork bringing a baby. 'This is quite fun, isn't it, roughing it?' she said. 'Honestly, I've come to the conclusion we'd all be better off without electricity.'

'Great,' said Grant. 'The takeaway bar might need a spot of power, though, to make the, you know, fast food.'

'Sit, sit,' said Art.

'We're not dogs, Art,' said Glenda. 'Next you'll be telling us to roll over. For God's sake.' She slid onto one of the splintery bentwood chairs which wobbled bandily. 'Oh my Gahd!'

It was apparent that Glenda would like to wrestle Art to the ground and fuck him. I didn't mind, because I knew he wouldn't. If you stop people having friends, that's when they'll go off and have an affair.

I sleepwalked to the kitchen and returned with champagne flutes on a tray, the torch tucked under my arm. I edged into the room, smiling at the complexity of my manoeuvre. 'Help, I'm going to drop it!' The cork popped in Art's hands. He handed the bottle to Glenda and jumped up to take the tray. We were all laughing. Perhaps Glenda was right, it was fun having no electricity. It brought people together. Glenda poured the bath-like froth into glasses and said, 'Well, my news.'

Art's face floated near the lamp. 'You're not . . . ?' He gestured in Grant's direction, a nod oversized enough to be visible in the gloom.

'No!' said Grant. 'Good God, no! Never.'

'Okay,' said Glenda. 'We've got the message. My news is, I've had another manuscript accepted.'

'Oh, well done, Glenda!' said Art. 'Congratulations!'

I joined in, finding the strange seam of elation I had for someone I'd met ten minutes before. 'Congratulations! That *is* good news.'

Grant receded into the darkness. No doubt he'd already congratulated Glenda.

But Glenda hadn't finished. She squeaked the next instalment. 'In *England*. It's being published in England! Not just New Zealand.'

'In England!' said Art. 'That's fantastic. That is such amazing news! Isn't it, GoGo?'

'England! Yes it is.'

'Home,' said Grant, re-emerging from the shadows.

Glenda stopped with her champagne halfway to her lips. 'Grant, for fuck's sake, stop saying that.'

'It is global, though,' said Art doubtfully. 'England still means global.'

'The planet Earth,' said Grant. 'No matter how big our publishing aspirations, we're still limited to the planet Earth.'

No one listened to Grant. There was a feeling he was banned.

I asked Glenda, 'Is it fiction? Poetry?'

Glenda turned her face towards me, but her eyes were on Art, with a puzzled expression in them. 'Hasn't she heard of me?'

'Ah, Glenda, Glenda, Glenda,' sighed Grant.

'Grant, shut the fuck up.' This Scorsese-esque phrase sounded odd coming from her mouth. Glenda now looked at me. 'What exactly is it that you do?'

I told her about my alterations and mending business.

Glenda put her head back and said, 'Aah,' as if everything had fallen into place. 'From what Art said—I obviously got the wrong end of the stick. Poetry. I write poetry.'

'Well, that's just wonderful news,' said Art. 'Let's drink to it.'

'Yes, to conquering England,' said Grant. 'The Romans couldn't do it. The Germans *almost* did, and would've if it hadn't been for the Americans. This is the first *direct* occupation since 1066.'

Glenda clobbered Grant on the arm, hard. He said, 'Ow,' and looked at her deeply.

'To Glenda,' said Art loudly.

I think he liked her too, which was fine, because she was clearly out of the question. We all drank. The Chinese takeaways were opened up. While we ate Glenda told the story of the coincidences that had led to her sending her manuscript to the publisher and after that, well, the rest was history. She talked exclusively to Art, which some wives-or-girlfriends might not like, but I knew there was nothing in it, and I hate petty jealousies. I'm not that kind of person. I struck up a conversation with Grant like polyphony. He was a lawyer. We established that Grant's firm was working out of a makeshift office in Manukau, and that I was one of the eight thousand five hundred businesses affected by the Blackout. (I wasn't sure if I counted. Maybe it was eight thousand four hundred and ninety-nine.) Grant had a pinballish delivery to his speech, jumpy and circuitous, that made you not quite sure if he was joking or not. You could imagine this unsettling quality having sway in court. He and I did our best to talk while listening with half an ear to the low, slightly intimate-sounding conversation (when I thought about it) that was going on at the opposite corner of the table. I heard the phrase Settler Literary Ephemera. Grant was listing recent changes to the Education Act, 'Tomorrow's Schools', which had been a *complete disaster*. He had more than one client suing the Education Department for damages—trauma. He was a whiz, Grant, you could tell. Tomorrow's Schools was all part of the gigantic divesting of responsibility which had begun with selling off the state assets. I heard myself murmuring, I know, I know, and had the sensation of going in and out of consciousness. There was something about a teacher throwing herself off the Auckland Harbour Bridge. Grant poured himself another glass of wine from the gathering thicket of bottles on the table and said, deadpan, that he and Glenda had met a long, long time ago, when they were kids, virtually. Before she had—he groped for the word—crystallised.

Across the table, Glenda was on a roll, excited, incandescent, a good thing in a Blackout. But Grant was swallowing his wine and telling me how he had done better than Glenda at university, getting A-pluses for tort law (quoting grades was the teensiest bit pathetic, I thought), while she did a mediocre job at subjects you couldn't really put your finger on, that is, other people's texts—yet now that was all they talked about. It made him sick. While he, of the A-pluses for tort law, wore a suit Monday to Thursday to his stuffy law firm downtown at which he sometimes represented stepfathers in abuse cases, although not so stuffy as they wouldn't have casual Fridays, when you saw Aloha shirts perched around the office like exotic birds. Eradicated by Monday.

Grant fell silent and we both listened to Glenda telling Art about the English publisher, an astonishing man who circumvented the gatekeeping that kept cutting-edge writing out of bookshops—he printed copies on demand.

'It works the way tits do,' said Grant, and knocked back a slosh of wine.

This time, everyone looked at him from the dark periphery.

'I mean, you know, breasts, to be more biological, and politically correct. The baby sucks and it excites the glands into producing more for next time. That's the general idea.'

'Grant,' said Glenda, 'are you hoping for sucky-dicky tonight? Because if so, you're heading in the wrong direction.'

There was a silence. Then Glenda told Art she might have a spare copy for him and Grant said he was sure she would. I looked at Art and thought I could detect a blush in the candlelight. I had thought being squattocracy absolved you from blushing.

Grant was leaning right back in his chair, which groaned. His voice was disembodied. 'Tell them what it's about, Glenda.'

Glenda looked at Art and gave a light laugh. 'It's not *about* anything. It's poetry.'

We all ate some more chow mein. Art said it was jolly good, and I agreed. Thank god, said Art, for ta-kay ah-ways in an outage. I thought I saw his eyes roll in the lamplight.

Everyone had a general rave about the Blackout. Only a matter of time before *something* happened. The inevitable culmination of years of privatising. A late-twentieth-century long jump at complete capitalism. Grant asked what we should expect, when we ritually divested ourselves of the postal service, the medical system, the railways. Everyone joined in like a chorus in a Gilbert and Sullivan operetta. *The roading, the airline, public housing, public television, the provision of electricity.*

'And the administration of schools,' said Grant sagely.

'Grant, don't rabbit on,' said Glenda. 'He rabbits on,' she told Art, and me sort of. 'I live with this all the time. It drives me absolutely nuts. Will he stop? No.'

Grant rabbited on. These services, which the country had built up over a hundred and twenty years, were now owned by profit-driven consortiums like Pinnacle Power. Who, did we know, had quadrupled their profit and halved their staff over four years, and raised managers' salaries by thirty percent.

Art moved to the narratological present. 'And while the consortium grows fat, the cables, two of them over forty years old, grow thin. They become so waif-like they let their waif hands come unclasped.' One of Art's hands let go of the other, like the Sistine Chapel in reverse.

'That's very poetic, Art,' said Glenda, and Art leaned back.

There was a pause. We'd exhausted the subject.

'Well,' said Glenda, 'in some ways it *is* about something.'

'Pardon?' asked Art politely.

'My book,' said Glenda.

'Your book!' said Art.

'Although I'm still not sure if you could always apply *about* to this kind of textualising, but okay, it might be an interesting framework to look at it in. Within which to look at it. It's *about* embrained notions of transference, you know, in which language is a character, fleshed, that walks about freely in the text.'

Grant said, 'Freely?' He put down his chopsticks to think.

'It sounds great,' said Art.

'Who walks about in the text,' said Grant. He had his eyes screwed up in exaggerated thought. '*Who walks about in the text.*'

'I just told you,' said Glenda. 'Language. The character.'

'No, the character *who* walks about freely in the text, not *that* walks about freely in the text.'

Glenda looked at Grant with her head on one side, pouting. 'Is language a person?'

'Well, you just told us it was. Didn't she?' He appealed to me, for some reason. His sparring buddy.

I raised my shoulders. 'Um.'

'Honey,' said Glenda—she called her boyfriend honey like a rerun of *The Dick Van Dyke Show*, and smiled an American smile revealing all her teeth, the lower as well as the upper set—'honey, save your pedantry for the Family Court. Okay?'

'O-*kay*. I certainly will. I certainly will do that. And. You can spend the result flying to writing conferences that won't pay your fare to get there.'

Glenda hit Grant again on the arm and he smiled.

Art splashed more wine. 'Glenda? Grant? Here, man.' He and I exchanged a smile as I got up from the table with plates and a torch. We'd cackle in bed about it afterwards. It might turn into a discussion about whether they were happy or not. Art was interested in people's happiness. I thought it was hard to tell.

'You know what this reminds me of, Art?' said Glenda. 'Camping at the Woolthamly farm. They were wonderful days, weren't they?'

'Free as a fucking bird,' said Art.

•

With the torch tucked under my arm I ferried the plates to the kitchen. I planned to make coffee, but stood looking at the 747, suddenly exhausted. The *outage* had made everything trouble. The days had once run like clockwork, but now, the planning involved in lighting small fires, using ballpoint pens, peering and groping—at that moment it was more than I could stand.

I wavered with the torch back along the passage. A bubble of laughter swelled in the front room. I hesitated a moment, then turned. I was on the periphery of darkness. I put out my hand and brailled over the flocked wallpaper. I was retracing my steps, a moving cave. I came to my workroom and became one with my shadow. On the other side of the big table, light from the street shone obliquely in through the windows. I lay the torch on the table, a clunk. It rolled back and forth once either way like a beached fish with a waggling fin of light. I stood there for a moment, in need of something—air, darkness, the duration of a cigarette. I don't even smoke.

Change of subject but not entirely: the issue of tearing. I'd had the odd client who'd brought me a garment deliberately cut. Chopped. Usually I couldn't mend them, they were irreparable. It seems that people do a lot worse damage when they set their minds to it than they do by accident. There was a *callow youth* once, twentyish, still pimply, with a jersey, knitted by his mother, unravelling like Harry the Dirty Dog's coat. (I suppose this is Case 6.) Of course I told him straight away I couldn't repair knitting, but I gave it the once-over anyway, to soothe him. He was so anxious he had a smile plastered over three-quarters of his face. At first he told me he'd snagged the sleeve on a fishing knife. The wool was a nice shade of brown like tea with a drop of milk in it. While I was looking at it he told me how his girlfriend had cut the sleeve in a fit of rage. She'd just missed his wrist, which she was aiming for. I stayed blank. They wanted me to be blank. He worked it out for himself, then and there. He said he'd let the sleeve unravel.

I'd seen two shirts mutilated by wives (Cases 7 and 8). How you could bring yourself to cut up a perfectly good shirt, I don't know. The wives brought them in. The husbands probably didn't give a damn. The whole scenario—the effort that went into the shirt, then its quick demise—might make you think about the nature of construction in the first place, that the stitches were somehow invested with the very ingredient that would bring them down. Take a tablecloth, for instance. Made to catch the drops. Embroidered over hours, days, weeks. Stained in an instant.

Murmuring and a high giggle came from the front room. I felt my way along the edge of my worktable, familiar like a body. The rack of clothes caught the beam of the torch. So many shoulders illuminated. I saw a flash of my dim self in the mirror in my World

126

satin trousers. An old Mary Hopkin song Mary-France used to play came into my head—'Those Were the Days'. I came to a chair against the wall and bent down to it. My fingertips arrived on the paper parcel at infinitesimally different times, picked a tune out of its crispness. I snatched it up, quickly. Then tore it open in the prism of light on the table. The costume lay in the wrapping, soft and floppy, dark, bloodlike or black, like innards. I touched it. It was cooler than you'd expect, so cool it seemed damp. But no, just cool. I lifted the costume and held it to my mouth. Put it down again, picked it up. I held it away from me, by both its shoulders, as if I were giving it a talking-to, and I pulled. Nothing. It was tough, tough for an old garment. And my mending job was tight, the threads woven in securely, the ends tied. I should've been pleased with myself. I was. I tried again, grasping it and dragging at the seams. Not a sausage. It was certainly more solid than you'd think, this costume. I bunched a shoulder in each fist, and wrestled with it like a demon for a solid minute. Nothing. I gave up. I looked at my hands in the torchlight. They were reddened. Suddenly I picked up the costume again and gave it an almighty wrench. It gave way with a farting sound. As it did, I wasn't sure, but I thought I heard another sound, a strangled cry like a seagull, ring out into the room. When I looked at the costume, at what I'd done, it was a bit more than I'd intended. The tear, once it had started, had run along the seam it had traversed once before, and the silver threads splayed out like a sea anemone. I looked down at it, my handiwork. How violently the warp and weft had parted company.

●

In the front room they all went silent and spun their heads around when I came in. Grant looked amused, Glenda pitying. Art half got up from his chair.

'Alright, darling?' He'd had a few, and was all soppy. He toppled back down again.

'Fine.' I slid into my seat.

'Where were we?' asked Glenda.

'Bets,' said Art. He turned to me. 'We're going to bet on how long we can stick it out in our houses. And when the fuck, when the *fuck* they're going to fix the cables.'

'A hundred dollars it's out till the end of March,' said Grant.

'Two hundred on April,' thundered Art. 'They've given up on fixing the forty-year-old cables. They're getting a stopgap cable, which will take two months.'

I sat back. 'Do you have two hundred dollars?'

Art looked hurt. 'I might have.'

'I prefer this,' said Glenda softly, but blinking vividly. 'I like the dark.'

'Do you?' asked Art, suddenly quiet too.

'Yes.'

I looked at my hands, which were trembling slightly. I remembered what I'd come back to ask. 'Coffee anyone?'

'Thanks,' said Glenda.

Art noticed my hands and put his on top.

I smiled, aware of my teeth.

Grant said, 'Don't have coffee, Glenda.' He turned to Art and me. 'It keeps her awake till four in the morning.'

'It does,' said Glenda. 'But I write, so all is well. I mean, it's not as if it's wasted.'

'No coffee for me, thanks, either,' said Grant. 'We'd better be going.'

'You don't need to go,' said Art.

'No, we should,' said Grant, getting up.

The rest of us followed. Glenda said she'd put a copy of her first book in the mail for Art. She wouldn't be seeing him during the shoot.

'Is there mail?' someone said. During the Blackout. No one knew.

'That'd be great,' said Art.

'Lucky for you.' Grant was shuffling into his coat. 'She's only got three hundred and ninety-five copies left.' On the way out the door he turned and said, 'We're hoping the books will outlast the Blackout because, you know, poetry makes good fuel. Embrained poetry that is. The other sort's probably not so efficient. Embrained is definitely best. It's all the methane.'

When they got to the bottom of the steps, Art called out, 'Goodnight! Take care!'

But Glenda had already wrenched Grant towards her, and they were kissing violently. I looked at Art. He was transfixed. The kiss went on and on, their bodies writhing, until Grant yelped in pain and pushed Glenda away roughly. She staggered slightly and said something, a curse, and he laughed. He took out a torch, shone it down into the gully, and they linked arms and walked off.

We tidied up in the kitchen in the leaping shadows. I said the evening had been a rousing success, and waited for Art's funny rejoinder—Glenda and Grant, their bickering, Jesus. There wasn't one. Art was slightly glum, for him, as he put out the rubbish. I suppose they didn't need electricity to collect the rubbish. I looked out the back door after him at the snippet of city. Tonight there was the first moonlight since the electricity went off. It picked out just enough jaggedness to make the city look like a beautiful ruin.

17

On Monday the client was in the doorway to the workroom like the first day, the day Milly came. He stood watching me. Art and I had spent the weekend making trips to Mount Eden to eat takeaways (none of which conformed to the ten superfoods), washing clothes by hand and lugging them out to hang in the back garden (me) (thankfully it was windy and fine), squeezing the last drop of power out of a laptop in order to tweak Settler Literary Ephemera, which was apparently *coming apart at the seams* (Art), and reading about Ponsonby artists in the Saturday paper by candlelight and joking about setting the villa conversion on fire. On Sunday afternoon I'd noticed that the neighbours in the other half of the villa conversion were moving out. I called Art and we peered at them through the front window—a couple in black with stylish chairs. We'd never laid eyes on them before. On Monday morning there'd been a sense that everything would return to normal, but it didn't.

With the client watching me, I lifted the costume down from the rack like a puppet, and brought it out of the cave of the room.

'It has pins.'

He backed out into the passage to let me through. I signalled he should go ahead of me, but in the end I went first, my head high and self-conscious. He followed at a short distance but somehow I could feel him against me like an overcoat. In the front room I spread the costume out on the table. It fell into a rugged landscape—black crags and the shadowy folds of hills. In places the light caught the bloom on the wool as if it were obsidian. I saw him looking fiercely at it, as if seeing it for the first time. I shook it out again quickly and it was strangely soft, mashable. As if my hands did the work of millions of years of erosion, but quickly.

He stared up at me. 'You haven't even started it!'

He really was like Mr Rochester, and what I'd discovered was, I quite liked Mr Rochester, even though not many women would. Only Jane Eyre, and, well, Charlotte Brontë I suppose, but she had led a very sheltered life. Oh, and Blanche Ingram, aka Trisha the Punk. I decided I'd quite like to go for a walk on the moors in a hooded cape, thinking about this revelation, but hopefully not catching a chill. I'd pulled *Jane Eyre* to bits in the Sixth Form, you see. And other works of literature.

'Sorry,' I managed to say. 'I was snowed under.' I found myself remembering Rose and Nance and the gauge by which busyness was measured. 'Must be the darkness,' I said. 'People've been ripping and burning and snagging . . .' Nonsense, of course. I hadn't had a client since the previous Friday.

'I don't care,' he said. 'I don't care how busy you are, you said it'd be ready.'

'I know. I'm sorry.'

He took a breath and smoke-ringed it out. No cigarette, just pa-pa-pa-pa-paa. Dying for one, no doubt. 'Okay,' he said. 'I'll take it now.'

'Pardon?'

'I'll take the costume now, as is.' He sniggered bleakly. 'As-is-where-is. It is a wreck, after all.'

He wouldn't take it. I knew that. I said to him, 'I'll do it. Really I will.'

He smiled and looked up at the ceiling. I noticed his Adam's apple, which was slightly prominent. 'You must think I'm an idiot. You've held me up for, what, a whole week? I have my wife arriving home any minute. It's a miracle she hasn't turned up already. She could be there now, looking in the wardrobe.' Here he looked right at me. 'I've waited a week, and now I'm taking it somewhere else.'

We were flanking the table. 'The problem with taking it to someone else,' I said, 'is that you'll go to the bottom of their list.'

'List! I'll take my chances.' He did the pat-for-cigarettes reflex. God, he was desperate. 'Couldn't be slower than this.'

I watched his face stretching and rippling like a canvas. He was going to take the costume. With my rip in it. My very own tear. So what? Let him take it. I didn't give a rat's arse. He'd half turned to the window, gagging for a cigarette, you could see that—the fluttering hands. What a jerk. He was killing himself. I said to his back, 'Whereas I suppose I could do it after hours—i.e. now.'

'Now?' He didn't turn.

'Yeah,' I said to his back. 'It's next on my list. I could sit down and do it right now.'

Why not?

He spun around. 'While I wait?' The idea did seem ludicrous, coming from his lips, which were angular. Twin peaks in the upper lip.

'While you wait.'

He thought for a moment, then: 'Nah. Sick of mucking around. I'll just take it.' He stepped towards the table. Perhaps sensing some movement in me, he said, 'Don't bother wrapping it.'

I snatched the costume from under his hand. In mid-air, like a trapeze artist, I quickly repinned the torn seam. I stepped back and held it against myself, looking down. It wasn't bad, pinned like this. Even I didn't know I was so good. When I looked up I saw him frowning at the costume in a narrow-eyed way, as if he had astigmatism. 'How long would it take?'

I shrugged. 'An hour. No more than that.'

'An hour?'

I didn't answer.

'Okay.' He squinted out the window at the late afternoon sun, and laughed. 'Will there be enough *light?*'

I ignored the sarcasm. 'Yeah, course. It's beautiful out there.' I indicated the sky, the drenched-pink bougainvillea, the daisy bushes planted a hundred years ago, the forget-me-nots that had gone nuts in the Auckland sun.

He sat down at the table on a bentwood chair which wobbled ominously—well, they're eighty, ninety years old, and made for small English people. I noticed the way his thighs occupied his trousers. 'Alright,' he said.

I slid onto my chair but kept the costume bundled against me (avoiding pins, of course; I'm usually a dab hand at that). 'Before I start,' I said, 'tea?'

'No! No thanks. Just . . .' He waved his hand at the costume and looked away, as if he couldn't bear the sight of it. The *site*: the table Art had brought home from an auction on the back of a truck, my sewing things, my hands.

'Actually, you know what? I'll just pop out for a fag.' Yes, pop. 'Okay.'

I felt the veranda throb like a piano as he bounced down the steps to the garden. A moment later a tendril of cigarette smoke floated past the window. It smelled exciting. Death. I spread the costume out on the table and flattened the seams that needed to be reattached. There was a nest of broken black fibres, shot through with trails of coloured silk from the knotwork. Boy, if last time was a mess, this took the biscuit. I didn't want him to see it quite like this, so I worked quickly. I pulled each coloured thread away from the torn seam. I threaded a needle with the black thread I'd chosen the first time, and I began the job all over again.

By the time he came back I was weaving like a maniac. He reeked of smoke and brought the coolness of the late-summer afternoon inside with him. I saw him glance at the costume as he approached the table. Was it shock on his face at the state of it? No. He didn't know anything. He didn't know one end of the costume from the other. I have to admit, though, the tear wasn't pretty. The threads pulled away from the rip like veins pegged back for open-heart surgery. He pulled out a chair and sat at the table, looking at me. It was a gaze. I blushed.

'Right,' I said. It needed something, a word.

I was working on one side of the rent, weaving the needle in and out, in and out, as if making a kete of black and silver, the black of the thread, the silver of the needle. Checks. I was rebuilding the fabric. Then I'd do what I could going the other way, using the threads I was putting in place now to fill in the missing weft ones. It was a confidence trick, a high-wire act. You had to believe in it. Once you doubted, it all disintegrated, the threads, every which way. We sat in silence while I worked. At one point he looked at my hands, and up at my face through my reading glasses. Then looked away again. Or I looked away. Everything seemed fat: my fingers, his face, the air. There was an unbearable silence. But it had to be silent, didn't it? If we talked—I mean, we were mender and client, we might shrink back down to our neat and tidy proportions. If we talked, the odd thing that had happened between us the day I hid him might flare up again. What then? The threads of the costume would get tangled, he would scrape back his chair and go home, I would tidy my sewing things, perhaps sweep up the last few beads from the workroom floor. But because I'd hidden him, there was silence. I bent my head over the black hole I was filling in. The day outside was quiet—the Blackout. Cicadas. I was looking at swing bridges disappearing into black, wet bush either side of a ravine. I was thinking of bush walks. I noticed, from the corner of my eye, his hand come out and touch the costume. It was a long hand, slightly knobbly, with tiny gingerish hairs on the tops of the fingers. Strange, because the hair on his head was brown. His middle finger passed back and forth over the black wool. He looked up at me and seemed to hold his breath. I kept the costume still until his hand had gone.

He was fidgeting a bit, his hands on the table like birds.

I kept weaving. In out, in out. It's pretty relentless, but you get results. That's what I like. As long as you keep at it. Progress.

He cleared his throat. 'What do you do while you're sitting here sewing?'

I didn't look up. You can't. This isn't so easy, you know. It's intricate. 'I sew,' I said.

'I mean, do you, you know, listen to music or something?'

'Sometimes. But the Blackout.'

'You could sing.'

Sing! I kept sewing. 'Actually,' I said, 'I just think.'

He was quiet for a while, then asked (of course) what I thought about.

I was finishing a row. 'I don't know. What do you think about?'

He said nothing.

'Well?' I looked up and saw that he was a bit dazed. The afternoon, the heat in the room?

'Oh,' he said. 'I thought that was a rhetorical question.'

'What does *one* think about? No. No, it wasn't.'

He shook his head. 'I asked it first. Because you're doing something . . .' He trailed off (as they say).

It was a bit vague—you couldn't squeeze it—but I liked this question: what I thought about while I was sewing. See, I've thought about this myself. Thought about thinking. I said to him, 'And you—I suppose when you're at work, you think about the economy, etcetera.'

'Yeah. But the economy isn't a set piece, it's volatile, so you know, you think about risk, you think about what could happen. Wonder, if you like.'

If you like.

'I think about what I'm doing,' I said. 'It takes a certain kind of concentration.' I was leaning close over the costume, working carefully as if to illustrate my point. 'I think about the threads, I think about how they're all working together; really, they're almost like people—well, ants anyway. They're not quite inanimate. They're altered. Actually, I've never thought that until now.'

'Really?'

'Yes. Yes!'

'Altered?' He looked anxious. 'But it'll look the same as it did before, won't it, when it's fixed? How will I know? I mean . . .' He faltered and smiled sheepishly. 'It's not my strong point.'

I'd filled in the rip one-way, with lines, telephone wires, a stave, refill paper.

'I know that.' I smiled. 'I could do anything, couldn't I? I could make a total mess of it and you'd never know the difference. Because you don't actually *look* at it.'

'I look at it.'

'No you don't. You'll just have to trust me.' He looked so forlorn that I said quickly, 'Don't worry, I'll do a good job. It'll look the way it did when your mother, or whoever it was, wore it dancing at the Irish club.'

'Irish club! It *was* Ireland.'

'Okay, normal club. Dancing at the Normal Club and winning medals.'

'It wasn't like that. They didn't do that sort of dancing.'

'Didn't they? What did they do?'

'I don't know, the twist or something, or whatever came after that.'

'Nothing came after that,' I said.

'Shuffling,' he said.

'That's so true!' I said. 'I've always felt kind of hard done by that proper dancing had gone out by the time I was born. There are no rules. If there were special moves, I could be quite a good dancer, I know I could.'

He smiled at my outburst, and I blushed.

While we'd been talking my sewing had come to a standstill. My hands were rested on my wrists like a Frenchwoman having lunch.

'You've stopped,' he said. 'Look, I'm only interested in getting this done. Milly . . .'

'Yes, yes, I know, *Milly*.'

I started weaving in the weft, weaving thread after thread in among the old threads.

'Well, you're married. You understand.'

Burrowing like a termite, in and out, in and out. My needle. 'I am,' I said.

With my head still bent I saw, in my peripheral vision, the client getting up from the chair. He paced about but paused every so often, no doubt to look back to make sure I was still sewing. It made me self-conscious. I'd noticed that when we talked he didn't watch my hands; when we talked he forgot about the tear.

'I suppose you think about stocks and shares, do you?' I asked. When he looked blank I added, 'Our conversation . . .'

'The financial markets. Yeah. Of course.'

'Futures?' I attempted. My superior knowledge of finance. Well, I had to say something.

He laughed. 'Yeah. And the past and the present.'

'That just about wraps it up.'

'It does,' he said.

We went silent again.

'My sister,' I said.

He frowned at me from the window.

'Had a kimono from Japan. She was an exchange student.' (Well, I was desperate.)

He did his Jim Carrey rendition, as if I were mad. Or he was.

'A national costume,' I said. 'One of these! This!' I held up the costume. Exhibit A.

He shook his head. 'That's not a national costume. It's a dress.'

'Alright, if you want to deconstruct it.'

He stepped over to the table. 'Look, it's in bits! I took it to bits myself. I'm Jacques fucking Derrida.'

'Derrida?' I smiled. I mean, he was a banker.

He rolled his eyes. Fair enough. I've heard of Alexander Hamilton.

The thing is, *I* had taken the costume to bits this time. It made a change to have a female post-structuralist. I had performed this exercise in deconstruction in my workroom while a dinner party hummed away along the passage.

'You're making me jittery,' I said.

'*You're* jittery? I basically have one more day to save my marriage. I think Milly's coming home tomorrow. It keeps changing. I suppose that's a good thing.' He patted his pocket and turned to the window again.

I made a noise.

He looked back at me. 'What do you mean, Mm?'

I didn't know what I meant, but I said anyway: 'Maybe she'll forget about it.'

'No. She'll ask me, as soon as she gets home. She won't forget. I'm not a good liar.'

I did a few more in-outs with the long needle. 'I thought you were quite good at it actually.'

'No,' he said, dead serious. (Seriously.) 'I'm crap at it.' He was pacing again. He stopped and looked at a work of art on the wall—*Construction Site No. 14*, by Art's sister Issy. She was doing sculpture at art school even though she was thirty-five.

'Well, that's why I'm doing the lying for you,' I said.

He laughed and turned from the artwork, whose mish-mash of twisted metal had not had much effect on him. 'Good point.'

We were silent for a bit. The light falling in the windows was ageing, getting golden. He came close to the table and was gazing at my fingers, their busyness. From the corner of my eye I could tell he was mesmerised. I wished he would look away. 'I have a story about a national costume,' I said.

This did snap him out of his mini-trance. 'It's not a national costume,' he said. He sounded tired.

'Yeah, alright, this'—gesturing with the costume—'has nothing to do with costumes, national, native, whatever. But I really do have a story about a national costume. I just remembered it.'

I had. I'd just remembered it.

Silence. God, this was like wading in mud up to your armpits sometimes.

'Do you want to hear it?'

'Is this costing me?' he asked.

'No!'

He laughed.

'What?' I asked.

139

He shook his head. 'Just, never mind. The story.' He gave a little gawuff. 'Will you keep . . .' He fluttered his hand at the costume. I was snipping the tiny threads left after a section of weaving.

'Of course.'

'Alright. Fire away.' He sat down, grating the chair and angling himself towards the window. The low sun showed up the odd red hair on his head like an electrical wire among the brown.

I poured two cups of tea from the thermos I'd made earlier and pushed one across to him. It rippled.

•

I told the client a story which I was kind of proud of. A real story, but with meaning, vis-à-vis migration, culture. You couldn't make this stuff up.

'I went to a birthday party for a one-year-old,' I said. 'Daughter of a sort-of friend, Evangeline, who was our next-door neighbour when I was a kid. She was brought up Fundy, but married a Hindu. Indian. Long story, but anyway, the baby—gorgeous baby—they had a big party for her with all the relatives. The relatives on the father's side. Evangeline's parents disowned her. Anyway, the women, the aunts, were wearing saris, and the girls were wearing beautiful coloured dresses, blue and pink and yellow, with their hair tied up in matching ribbons. The boys wore white shirts and trousers. There were a few Pakeha kids and I noticed they were wearing jeans and T-shirts, and not even their best jeans and T-shirts. They looked as if the invitation had said, Come in your scungiest clothes. There was this Pakeha woman there, and I could see she was making a beeline for me, probably because I was the only other white person in the room. Apart from Evangeline.'

He creaked in his chair and looked at my hands. Not just looked, glowered, like a cartoon. The eyebrows. 'Are you sewing?'

I quickly did a stitch.

When he was satisfied, he said, 'That doesn't surprise me. I had a Maori girlfriend.' I looked at him and he stopped, then hurried on. 'If there were just a few Pakeha in the room, they'd be all over me like a rash.'

I nodded, and continued. 'This Pakeha woman at the birthday came up to me and you know what she was wearing? A Scottish costume.' Here I put down the costume so I could describe with my hands the long white dress with a tartan sash thrown over the shoulder. 'Like this, with this big medallion thing, the size of a fist, pinned *there*,' (holding the sash in place). 'She told me she was their neighbour or something. She said, I don't discriminate, I don't care what colour people are, as long as they're decent. She said she'd worn her national costume because she knew the Indians would be wearing theirs. They wore their saris every day.'

He glared at my empty hands, at the costume, and I picked it up again.

'That's what I was talking about,' he said. 'Before. It's not a national costume.'

'It might be a wee bit different for a dancing outfit,' I said, stitching now. 'But generally, generally speaking, I *know*. That's why I'm *telling* you this.'

'Okay.'

'Anyway, the women were wearing their saris. Did you know they're the oldest fashion item? Five thousand years.'

'No.'

'The women had spencers on underneath, by the way, and cardigans. It was freezing, even inside, because, you know, Wellington in July in a rickety wooden house, it was eleven degrees outside and twelve inside.'

I paused for effect. He nodded, unimpressed, and I continued.

'The woman in the Scottish costume—who was called Fiona Campbell, which is about as Scottish as you can get (except it would've been Anglicised)—told me again why she'd worn her national costume, and asked me if *I* had one, and I said I didn't. Of course. She asked me where I was from, and I said Wellington. She looked disappointed, so I said, Well, if I had a national costume I suppose it'd be Irish, but it was all a long time ago. She must've been a bit deaf, because she lit up and said to me, Ah, you should've worn your national costume, everyone else is! One of the cousins, who I knew a bit actually, was coming around with nibbles and stuff, and as she offered them to us, Fiona Campbell said, Megan has an Irish costume and she would've worn it if she'd known we were all going to be wearing ours.'

He smiled and leaned back in his chair. It creaked again ominously—they always creak.

Oh, he liked it. I felt the thrill of the storyteller. I continued.

'I said to the cousin, I don't have a national costume, but she looked me up and down with a funny expression on her face, as if she was imagining me in a strange get-up. I struck up a conversation with a couple of the aunts, and the grandmother who I'd never met. Fiona Campbell was still hanging about—because, remember, I'm her desert-island Pakeha—and she leaned over to the aunts and the grandmother and said, You know, Megan would've worn her national costume if she'd known we'd all be wearing ours. Jesus. I said to the aunts and the grandmother, I don't have a national costume, really I don't. Then I moved away and talked to a couple of uncles about how some of their children's friends, their New Zealand friends, were dropping out of high school, and how astonishing this was, blah blah blah. One uncle was saying, Why? Why do these young people who are offered an education say, No thanks! Well, I didn't know.'

Actually I did. But it would take a very long time. I went on with the story.

'Then Fiona Campbell hoved in sight and told the uncles about my national costume. The men looked me up and down and I blushed and said, I don't have a national costume, I don't. There was a bit of a lull, then later on Fiona Campbell came and talked to me again. I felt sorry for her, the poor old bat, and I asked her what part of Scotland she was from, just for something to say. I couldn't give a rat's arse, not knowing one end of Scotland from the other. She reared back, literally, like this'—I arched back in my bentwood chair, which creaked—'on her hind legs and looked at me the way old people read price tags and said, Goodness me, I don't have a clue, I'm a fourth-generation New Zealander. I'd hate to live in Scotland. New Zealand's a great little place, apart from the Maoris. If only they'd just get on with it. They were given good money for their land.'

I waited for his reaction. 'She really said that,' I said.

He nodded. I continued.

'I was trying to move away from Fiona Campbell, I couldn't stand it anymore, but old Fiona was telling some Indian friends of the family about my national costume. I kept saying, again and again, No, really, I don't have one, I don't *have* a national costume. I looked them straight in the eye so they could see that I was, you know, normal and that this Fiona Campbell woman was crazy. But nobody would meet my eye. They all looked me up and down, they looked at where my national costume might have been, if I'd had one. I was *entirely* sick of it, and the last couple of aunts who were being told by Fiona Campbell about my national costume, how I would've worn it if I'd known, I just nodded at them and smiled and I was imagining I had this old tartany green thing, or embroidered thing, hanging in the wardrobe at home.'

He laughed, out loud, no secret squeaking like the afternoon Milly was there. It was the first time I'd heard him laugh like that. I quickly took up the costume, which I'd been holding in my lap all this time. I hoped Art wouldn't come home and find me having a cup of tea with a stranger at an odd hour and, for no reason whatsoever, a man who was laughing at something I'd said. I didn't usually offer tea to clients. I didn't tell funny stories to clients, or joke with them. It was nothing really, but I didn't want to hurt Art's feelings, which I knew could be hurt despite his lucky life, his landowner mother, his father in insurance, his tertiary education—perhaps because of it. It might seem as if there was a hint of collusion between myself and the client, even though there was nothing, nothing. Except a way of talking that was all confidences, a turning inside out of all the words inside you.

Because I knew about his wife. I knew about his wife and his mistress and how there was no choice.

18

The sun had sunk further but there was still enough light that I might make serious headway with the reweaving. I was still going in out, in out. The client rearranged himself noisily at the table.

I asked him if he thought his parents had done a good job choosing a wife for him. I'd wondered about this, you see. He professed to love her, but he was, well, cheating on her.

The tea, going cold, was fluttering as I wobbled the table—my stitches.

He crunched back in his chair. 'Mm, gosh, that's a bit personal.'

I paused. 'I suppose it is. And so is this.' I held up the costume briefly, and laughed. 'Personal! My *Gahd,* as they say in America.'

It seemed he wasn't going to answer, then he said, 'Long story.'

'That's alright,' I said. 'Mending is slow.'

He blinked. 'I thought you said it wouldn't take long.'

'So I did,' I said, perhaps a little too hastily. 'And it won't take long. Tell me the quick version.'

'Even the quick version . . .' He considered his watch. 'I suppose there's nothing else to do, is there? But you must be almost finished. What was the question?'

I spoke with exaggerated enunciation: 'Do you think your parents did a good job picking out a wife for you?'

'Trisha?'

'No, Milly. Your wife.'

Did I have to spell it out?

Suddenly he snorted. 'Milly! You thought Milly—good God, no! Milly is the *last* girl they would've picked for me. Jesus. *The last girl.*'

'Oh,' I said. 'Okay.'

'Milly! The irony of it is, if Milly was Irish she wouldn't give a toss about the costume. I wouldn't be standing here.' He quietened down and went all sombre. 'I wish to God I wasn't.'

Charming, when we'd just been having an interesting discussion about a national costume.

'So let me get this straight,' I said. 'Milly wasn't the betrothed?'

'Stop saying that.'

'You said it. That day.'

'But stop saying it.'

'Okay. Friend. Family fwiend.'

He checked his watch and squinted out at the sinking sun. 'No, it was Trisha, of course.'

I think I stopped in my tracks. Whatever my tracks were, I don't even know. 'Trisha?'

'The buck-toothed girl from Clonard. I hadn't seen her since I was twelve.'

Trisha. Christ. *She* was the betrothed, and he'd—what a mess.

Well, I knew that for a start. But this was interesting. Trisha was the betrothed.

Stop saying that, GoGo.

Okay.

I asked him if his parents thought he'd go back to Ireland with *Trisha,* and he said, Good God, no. No. No.

Clearly they didn't.

He shrugged. 'Maybe the other way around. For my parents she was sort of a link to something. You wouldn't get it.'

No doubt. But, then, perhaps I was meant to find a boy at university. It was just that no one said it out loud. And I did! I did find a boy. Who was a bit like my parents, only richer. Engaged with the culture, had a degree in something useless, and liked to drink. Joking.

'You're right,' I said. 'I don't get it.'

'I know, it's pathetic,' he said. 'You need to know the background.'

I re-engaged with the black thread. In out, in out. 'Fire away.' My turn to say that.

'First of all—this'll be quick—we left Belfast in a hurry. In ten minutes. When you leave that quickly, there's something, well, unfinished.'

I snipped a thread and clattered the little silver scissors onto the table, scissors with a snake twisting up the handles. 'Why such short notice?'

'Um.' He cast a glance at the ceiling as if there was a cue card up there. 'Well, it was to do with council housing, in retrospect.' He swung his gaze back down to the costume, then back up to me because I had paused.

'Go on then,' I said.

He was restless and scraped back his chair and went and stood looking out the window, patting the pocket where his cigarettes were and looking back at the costume and my hands. 'Is this light good?'

'Yeah, it's fine.'

'Okay, good.' He came back to the table. 'It's funny how things turn out. If we hadn't had to move out of council housing—this is years ago now—maybe none of this would have happened and I wouldn't be here, but'—here he smiled and gestured to the room—'we did, and here we are.' He turned away in his chair, as if I couldn't possibly want to know about council housing.

'Oh, and why-did-you-have-to-move-out-of-council-housing?' Facetious as hell.

We smiled, then he went serious.

'Rats.'

I looked up. 'What's the matter?'

'No, rats,' he said.

'Oh. Rats. I thought you meant "oh, rats".'

'No, I meant rats. Specifically.'

'Is there a "generally"?'

'Well, yeah, actually, there is. Was. There'd been a general hoohah going on about housing for years. Our row in Clonard, and lots of the rows, were condemned in, like, 1890 or something. Roofs were falling in, one by one. When it rained the families at the end had to move in with the next-door neighbours. That sort of thing.'

'Jesus.'

'Yeah, shoe-box-int-middle-of-road. And we weren't even English.' He laughed.

'But the rats.'

'The rats were the last straw. Hundreds of them. They'd pulled down an estate nearby and the rats had, you know, packed their bags and moved in with us. You could hear them scratching at night. I didn't mind, actually, but I remember Ma shrieking in the kitchen in the morning when she saw what they'd done.'

'My Gahd,' I said. 'Terrifying.'

He frowned and shook his head. 'It wasn't fear. You're not scared of rats when you've seen a lot of them. It was rage. Blind rage. I was more scared of my mother than I was of the rats. Then she'd take a Valium and calm down a bit.'

'Ah,' I said. 'My mother took Valium.' Something in common.

'It was cheaper than a fag because it came on the National Health.'

I laughed. 'Is this true?'

'Of course it's true. Why would I tell you otherwise?' He went faintly puffy, put-out.

Why would he tell me? Because I'd trapped him here and there was nothing else to do, that's why.

As if to back up his story, he said, 'All the mothers in the lane took them. They'd say, Can I bum a Valium off you?'

I nodded seriously. No laughing. Then I laughed. This was hilarious. I had a vague memory of sitting on the stairs while Mary-France told someone on the phone about her new generation of antidepressants. *They're the grandchildren*—hooting with laughter, and performing the fridge-suck, slosh and clink that indicated another glass of wine. Valium was passé by that time. (Wine was still first generation, I suppose.)

'Anyway,' he said, 'we moved. We were going to get a new unit, everyone in the row was. In a new housing estate, with two bedrooms, wardrobes, hot water and a bath. We were all excited, my sisters and I. We were going to go swimming in the bath and play hide and seek in the wardrobes. There was just one problem.' He held up his finger. Hamming it up.

'Ah. What was it?'

'First of all, you are sewing, aren't you?'

'Of course! Look.' I was motoring. He'd be out of here soon. 'What was the problem?'

'We had to find somewhere else to live for two years while the estate was being built.'

'Oh. It was being built on the same site.'

'No. It was being built across the road.'

'Then?'

'Exactly. Why couldn't we just stay put until the new estate was ready? Most people had been in them all their lives, and their parents before them, grandparents sometimes, so what's the fuss all of a sudden? But the FHE, which stood for—I remember this, all the talk, I was about eight or something—Fucking Housing Executive, the Fucking Housing Executive said the rows weren't fit for human habitation. All of a sudden. It was the rats.'

'Ah, the rats.'

'The rats. The FHE—'

'The Fucking Housing Executive.'

'Them. Said anyone who wanted a new unit had to move out of the row houses *im*-mediately. So we moved in with Granny and Grandpa, who had a squat in Clonard since they'd had to move from *their* row at Cupar Street, which had been condemned. Just for a while, it was meant to be.'

I remembered the thermos. 'More tea?'

He shook his head and gulped down the stone-cold stuff in his cup, glanced at the costume. 'Keep going.'

'I am.' I was. Poke poke poke into the fabric. I was going great guns. 'Did you get your unit?'

'Well.' He wiped his mouth.

'Oh dear.' I looked up. 'Another problem?'

He shook his head, as if to say never mind. 'On moving day—I remember moving day. Everyone in the row was moving. There were pushcarts being lent round from neighbour to neighbour, and it was cheerful even, although everyone was going somewhere worse. I was out in the lane getting in the way of everything when I heard a smashing sound coming from next door and I thought it was the RUC doing a raid and I ran inside to tell Ma and Dad. In the house you could hear the smashing going on next door. Dad said, It's only Pat next door smashing his basin and his toilet. And all through the morning, there was the sound of glass breaking, and wrenching. What transpired was: we were all meant to smash the windows and the pipes, and tear out the wiring, and pull up the floorboards so there wouldn't be any squatters coming in after us.'

He was joking, of course.

'Not joking,' he said. 'It was a farce. Dad said—I remember this—he said we weren't going to do it because the squatters would need it. And Ma said we were doing it alright, or we wouldn't get a unit. You had to smash the place to go on the list for a unit. If you didn't smash it, you didn't go on the list. Ma and Dad argued about it all morning—as if it could get any crazier—while we were loading stuff onto the cart. In the end we left the house without smashing anything, even though the rest of the row looked like a bomb site. Ma was saying to Dad as we trundled away, You're a fool, you're an idiot. And we trundled over to Granny and Grandpa's, which was only a few streets away. But in the night—apparently—he must've agreed with her, because he went back and smashed it up. So I heard. The next morning when I woke up, he was in hospital. While he'd been doing the smashing, someone saw him, some jumped-up little IRA gunman, and thought he was robbing the place. They didn't like petty crims among their ranks, the IRA. And they kneecapped him.'

He patted for his fags.

'Shot him?' I'd pricked my finger. Occupational hazard. But not badly. Spot of blood. Which I sucked.

'Yup,' he said, almost comical. 'But it was poetic justice, he even said that himself. He'd kneecapped a few Catholic hoods himself, for joyriding. They were tough on their own. They didn't want trouble, except for the cause. He got new knees. Reconstructive surgery, and compo for them, in the end. That's how we got the money to come here.'

He craned his neck to peer at the costume. Looked away.

The afternoon was wrinkling around us like a poppy, rotten in its seams. He asked me if I'd be able to keep working in the light, or lack of it, the sun just about to go, and I said I could, just, and tried to thread a needle again and again.

He watched me. 'If it hadn't been for the Fucking Housing Executive, we'd never have had the money to leave Ireland. I'll just step outside.' He got up from the table, but halfway to the door he discovered through some sleight of hand that his cigarette packet was empty. 'Actually, I won't.' He went and leaned against the windowsill, his back to the light. His silhouette was like a cast in my eye. He drummed his fingers on the sill.

'You must've got your unit,' I said, 'after all that smashing. After the trouble your father went to.'

'Trouble. No.'

I snorted. 'No!' Unbecoming. Then tried to unsnort. You can't.

'It was too late. We weren't on the list.'

'The two bedrooms, the wardrobes, the hot water, the bath . . . ?'

He shook his head.

'Rats!'

In out, in out. But the light was crap now.

'Couldn't put it better myself.' Mocking (I think). 'But it was alright. We stayed on in the squat with Granny and Grandpa, and it was fine. There were always people coming and going, my uncles, never a dull moment. And Dreadful and Frightful.' He smiled and rearranged his legs. A rustle. 'How long now?'

'Not long. Dreadful and Frightful?'

'My second cousins, Ma's cousins, Deirdre and Finoula. They'd totter up the lane in their high heels and their furry jackets. *Hey-ho.*' Here the client did a little cross-dressing manoeuvre. 'They were scary but they'd give all the kids money for sweets. Piss off, they'd say, piss off to the shops. They were ship girls. I didn't know it at the time, but they were. Granny would go all lemon-lipped and retire to bed when they came round. My dad would go out. He had his mates anyway. (They'd lean against the houses. There was a greasy mark right down the row from it.) Dreadful and Frightful would sit at the table sipping tea. Give Aunty our love. They'd been to Liverpool and they'd tell Ma she should get out of this dump and come to Liverpool. Us kids would stand around listening, our mouths gummed up with toffee. Dreadful and Frightful would say, Little pigs have big ears. Go and play in the middle of the road. But in fact,' (as if he'd just thought of this) 'it worked out well us being there, because Granny and Grandpa got sick and Ma looked after them. They had these terrible coughs.'

He looked out over Newton Gully. 'It's rush hour but there are hardly any cars.' He came over from the window and stood close to me.

I'd stopped sewing. There was a bit to go, not much. The light had gone yellower, like magnesium, and would burn out soon. 'It's the Blackout.'

'Will it be finished today?'

'The Blackout? Hope so.'

'Not the Blackout! The costume.'

'I know.'

He stood watching. I snipped a bit. Thin air, actually. I asked him what happened and he said nothing happened. They stayed on in the squat for a couple of years. I asked him if it was terrible. He said, Nah, it was alright, it was fine. I thought Art might be home soon, but so? Could I not have a client telling me a story in the dusk?

'But it's already been an hour, surely. Yes it has, look.' He checked his watch. 'It's after half past eight.'

'Oh.' I held out the costume but he didn't look at it. 'It's almost finished. But the light's going. Unfortunately.'

He clicked his tongue and looked worried. 'Tomorrow then,' he said. 'It can't be too much longer, can it?'

'No.' I shook my head.

He rustled himself together, briefcase, jacket. I stood up. It was very dim in the room as he made his way out.

At the front door he said, 'You're sure it'll be done?'

'Oh yes.'

He smiled as if relieved, as if it was already done. He stood back and looked at the villa. 'This house'd be worth a bit.'

'We're lucky,' I apologised. 'Art's parents. They bought four of them.'

He did a single, big-gauge nod, as if everything had fallen into place. 'They must be worth a bit.'

I told him about 'the farm' and the Taranaki Dried Fruit Company.

'Oh, they own that?' He was a bit surprised. 'They're in trouble, aren't they?'

I said I didn't think so.

'No, they are. So I've heard,' he said.

I was kind of taken aback.

'I'm sure they're getting advice,' he said.

I thought about it for a moment and said, 'What do you think they should do?'

He shrugged. 'Pull in their horns. Be prepared to lay off a few staff, as a last resort.'

'Should they warn them?'

'The staff? Of course not! Unless they want to be left in the lurch. You don't want people walking out. If they have to sell in the end, they'll want the business fully functioning.'

I was almost taking notes.

'The vultures will be circling,' he said.

I shuddered, there on the cooling veranda. 'Thanks,' I said.

'No problem.' The client thumped down the steps and batted away fronds on the front path. On the street I could just see him looking at the row of houses as if he was checking out a woman's arse.

•

When the client had driven off I noticed that a box had been delivered to the veranda. I lugged it over to the doorstep and ripped it open. Prue-short-for-Prudence had sent a relief package from 'the farm' to tide us over during the Blackout. Stone fruit in trays, each piece wrapped in purple tissue; tinned oysters, candles, woollen socks, even though it was February. And also, cellophane bag after cellophane bag of dried fruit from, yes, the Taranaki Dried Fruit Company. Oh well, it was better than a slap across the face with a piece of dead fish. Art groaned when he came up the steps a few minutes later and saw the trays. Poor Art. I would've loved to have been sent supplies by my family, but that's because they wouldn't cross the road to piss on you. It wasn't Art's fault that his folks were industrious and clannish. The same traits that prompted the box of goodies had made them expand all over Taranaki, and then Wellington, with their big leadlighted bungalows, and in Auckland—the very row of villas we lived in. It also made them smug, self-serving bigots, but you can't have everything. I took this in in a heartbeat when I first met them.

Change of subject but not entirely: when I encountered Prue and Bert's politeness for the first time up on 'the farm' one weekend, I knew they'd be every ist under the sun. Sure enough, on hearing my name, Prue paused for a minute, a fixed smile on her face, and said, 'Sligo. What kind of a name is that?' I knew what she meant, even though I'd been brought up as atheist as hell. I felt a rush of solidarity with my poor Catholic forebears. I wanted to say, Actually, we're Hibernians, the Pope is too radical for us, the Pope is a hippy. But I didn't, because, well, because I loved this boy, Art. I loved him. And because I'm polite. (Remember, that's how I got into the mess with the dress. I should've told Trisha to run a mile, I should've told the client to scram, when Milly arrived I should've thrown open my workroom door and said, See for yourself.) So when Prue asked about my name, I told her I didn't know anything about it, which was true, and we moved on, and Bert, spilling over with hospitality, pointed through the big picture window at the hills—There was a Maori pa up there, there was a battle, see where the sheep are running. It wasn't so bad. It took a weight off your shoulders.

Art hefted the box along the passage (I did love our gender roles). I followed, saying long day at LambChop kind of thing. Oh, he said, a bit breathless, he hadn't been at LambChop all this time, he'd been at Glenda and Grant's charging his laptop. That's strange, I said, I thought they had no power. They'd found a temporary flat, said Art, in Sandringham. Couldn't stand the fun of roughing it anymore. We sniggered. Art said he'd meant to tell me, he'd dropped around there the last few evenings after work—his diss. No need to explain, I said. Seriously, we weren't the kind of couple that keeps tabs on each other all the time.

In the kitchen we twitched our noses—the pong of the waste disposal was getting industrial strength.

'We can't eat in here,' I said. I got up and opened the cupboard under the waste-disposal unit. The innards looked complicated. 'What do we do?'

Art said I could search him, and oh, apropos his dissertation, he'd seen some anti-Pinnacle Power graffiti around town that was *quite subversive*. Not that it was exactly *settler*, but it might be useful as some kind of epilogue. Perhaps the Blackout was a corporate plot to kill small businesses? To be honest, though, he said, he was getting tired of ephemera. So was I, *frankly*, I said.

We sat on the back doorstep (away from the smell) with a candle and gorged on the oysters, ate some dried apples and prunes (even though I'd said I'd never look at another piece of dried fruit in my life) and put on the socks, even though it was February. Kill me, I said, I'm a small business. We laughed. Art went thoughtful and said he thought his mother wasn't doing as well as she used to, apropos the dried fruit. I said, Oh? For some reason a buzz of *transgression* ran through me, and I remembered the advice of the client. Just an impression, said Art, about the business; he didn't know anything.

Normally I told Art about my clients, I told him anecdotes. *We laughed.* But I hadn't mentioned this one. 'I have this client,' I said. I was a little breathless.

Art said he thought I didn't have any clients at the moment, thank you kindly to the Blackout. I told him I had one—oh, and Mabel—and he thought that was good. It was, it was good. I ploughed on.

'This client said he'd heard the company wasn't doing well.'

'What does he know?' asked Art, a trifle defensive.

'He's an investment banker.'

Art said, Oh. He was sure his mother would be getting her own advice, but anyway, what did the investment banker say?

'The investment banker said they should be pulling in their horns,' I said. 'And they should prepare to lay off staff.'

Art shook his spiky head. 'Mother would never lay off the Murus, unless she had to.'

'He said the vultures will be circling.'

Art looked at me, a little frown stamped between his eyes like the edge of a pie crust. 'Vultures?'

I nodded. 'Circling. Should you mention this to them?'

'Perhaps I will,' he said.

Then *I* said they must have lots to go on with, his parents. The villas, for a start, and I bet they had investments stashed away all over the place.

They did, he said. They would have.

That night, once again, lying in bed blinking, I tried to pan for light in the darkness.

19

It was seven-thirtyish when the client arrived on Tuesday. That's *pm*, of course. Sunny as hell. He stood in the front room, his shoes very black against the white-painted floorboards. The floorboards were best in summer. In winter they were cold, but in summer.

'Is this after hours?'

'Well, yeah.'

It was, it was after hours.

'So you can work on it now and finish it today, tonight?'

I said I could. I sat at the table and gestured for him to do the same. He did, and held his wrist up in the air to look at his watch ostentatiously. He was hilarious. He glared at my hands.

I'd be finishing it today anyway. I'd finished the reweaving, and now I busily threaded up an embroidery needle with the silver silk, hamming it up for his benefit. Ostentatious? Two can play at that game. The needle. The silk. The scissors.

'Tea?'

'No thanks.' He glanced about the room. 'You're still getting work, despite the Blackout?'

I said yes/no.

'That's good,' he said. 'A lot of small businesses are going under. People aren't coming into the city. Retailers and restaurants have a ninety percent downturn. If there was ever a good time to buy a business, it'd be now.'

I shook my head in sympathy as I stitched. I might have even clicked my tongue like people from two generations ago. 'I had a backlog,' I added, in case he thought I was putting other jobs in front of his. This was partly true: I had had a backlog. Last week.

'You're lucky,' he said. Out of the corner of my eye I could see he was still gawping about. 'But I guess you're on the very edge of the Blackout zone. And your overheads would be minimal, wouldn't they?'

I nodded. I'd started in on the edge of the knotwork. *Not* that there was a lot to do.

He leaned back in the chair to wait. Carefully, so it didn't creak. He folded his arms.

I did my neat silver stitches. I was going like nobody's business. I'd be done soon.

He watched me with his arms set in stone.

'What were we talking about?' I asked.

'Your business.'

'No, no. Well, yeah, but why your parents picked out Trisha for you.'

'Oh, yesterday. Was it?' He looked genuinely mystified. 'I finished with that.'

'And the rats,' I said.

'The rats weren't that bad. I was embroidering.'

We laughed.

'Wine?'

He shook his head in a slight trance. *Wine?*

'No thanks. I have to go soon. I have to drive.'

'Okay. And there was Dreadful and Frightful. Yesterday.'

'God, yeah, Dreadful and Frightful!'

'In order to get to Trisha.'

'Well, only because you wouldn't understand the Trisha thing.'

But I did. I did understand. I just wanted to hear it.

I'd *met* Trisha. I'd met all the members of the poxy little love triangle.

'Okay,' I said. 'Tell me about the-thing-to-get-to-Trisha.'

He smiled behind his hand. Maybe not.

I stopped. I stopped sewing. 'This isn't a joke, is it?' Because it occurred to me all of a sudden that he was having me on. There were no rats, no betrothed, no family fwiend, no Dweadful and Fwightful, no mail-order bride. He was just spinning me a yarn so I'd keep sewing.

He was offended, or mock-offended. 'No, it isn't a joke. It's *no joke.*'

'Okay.'

'What's the time?' he said. His watch was the size of Big Ben and he was looking at it.

'Um, quarter to eight, give or take.'

Actually, Big Ben isn't that big, to use a grindingly obviously post-colonial metaphor.

'Because I have to go soon . . .' Twisting in his chair. 'Because Milly.'

'Yes Milly, I know. But Trisha, Dreadful and Frightful etcetera.'

'Dreadful and Frightful went back to Liverpool. We waved them off from the wharf. Not Granny, of course (good riddance to bad rubbish). You'll keep on with that—with the . . . embroidering?' It was like a dirty word, the way he said it. They'd pix it out on TV.

'Of course!'

He looked and I busied myself with the silver silk.

'One day,' (talking fast) 'after we'd moved to Granny and Grandpa's, I heard piano music coming from a house and I moseyed along the row to have a look. It was the marching season—you could smell stuff burning after the parade. I hung about listening to the music, which was sort of thwanging off the row like a tennis ball.'

Tennis ball was a nice touch. Especially seeing he was in a hurry.

'Eventually it stopped and a kid came barrelling out of the house and up the street. By this time I was sitting on the footpath mucking around and humming, and this man came out and said in a pompous sort of way, I see they've been celebrating the fall of Ireland—because the sky was all red over the roofs. Then he said, Keep singing, I was enjoying it. But I didn't, of course. He asked me if I wanted to have a go on the old ivories. I said, What's ivories? And he said, That's French for piano. I remember he was laughing all the time. He was grey like all the other adults, but there was something different about him. But I just thought he was a weirdo, so I ran home. He called out after me to tell Ma that Mr O'Connell said I had a good ear. So I told Ma and she said, Oh, Mr O'Connell, does he? She'd known him since she was a girl.

'I started learning the piano from Mr O'Connell like a lot of the other kids in the row. It's strange, circumstance, isn't it?' He smiled a bit, looking at the costume but not looking. 'I mean, how you come to do what you do.'

'What, you mean this?' I said, indicating the sewing in my lap.

He shook his head vigorously.

Remember I wasn't going to get self-centred? Someone would tell me if I did? Well tell me.

'I mean, everything.' He cast around the room, the red couch glowing in the sun, the white floorboards gleaming, the theatre curtains looking black against the glare, and ended up back at me, his expression hard to read. 'Where we fetch up. There's no choice.'

Please don't let him be a New Age philosopher type, I prayed. To some New Age god or other. I mean *fetch up*, for Christ's sake.

'If there'd been a tree,' he said, 'we would've climbed it, but there was a piano teacher so we played the piano.'

Alright. Yeah. It'd been the same for me. It was education or education. But it did occur to me that Trisha was like a tree or a piano. No choice.

I said this to him and he shook his head and laughed. 'No, not that. Bigger than that.' He ruminated. Yes, ruminated. 'No one had a piano, of course.'

My turn to gawuff.

'Mr O'Connell let us all practise on his piano. He had a timetable on his door which got so faded you couldn't read it, but we knew our practice times by heart, like the notes of a piece.'

Oh, the notes of a piece.

'There were always kids coming and going.'

I did some more silver stitches. The mend was beginning to look very nice, though I say it myself. Very neat. 'Including Trisha?'

'Yeah, Trisha.'

'*The* Trisha?'

'Well, she lived in the row. She was the gawky gap-toothed girl.'

'Poor kid.'

'She was fine. But I'm sick of Trisha.'

'*You're* sick of Trisha?' I said. '*I'm* sick of Trisha.' I was. I hated Trisha.

'Sick of talking about her.'

'Well, why are you here?' I asked, widening my eyes and offering the costume, which he looked at but not really.

Where we fetch up.

'Good question. That's the best question.'

'Because you had no choice. Ah, you see!'

He was talking over me, shaking his head, 'Nah. Nah,' and the chair creaking.

'But you said you had no choice. That first day.'

'Nah.'

'Okay, but you did say.' Something occurred to me. 'One thing. How did you afford the piano fees?'

'Oh.' He sat back, relieved to change the subject. Creak.

But he'd *said* he had no choice. That was what had got me in the first place. No choice.

'Mr O'Connell didn't charge.'

'That was nice of him. How did he live?'

At school they told us we could be anything we wanted to be. And I believed them.

'On the dole, like everyone else. There was no work. There were factories around Belfast, but they didn't employ Catholics. Well, there was a shirt factory my grandmother worked at once. But generally speaking.'

'She's pretty, isn't she?' I said.

'Who?'

'Trisha, of course, who else?'

'Argh!' He put out his hands as if to strangle me. 'I suppose she is.'

Come to think of it, she wasn't pretty (so I remembered). There's a funny thing about attractiveness. If you think you're attractive, you are. It's quite common to see a woman who's done up to within an inch of her life in a way that says, I'm gorgeous, and she's actually quite plain.

I wish I was like that.

'Did you fall in love with her?'

He shook his head. 'No!'

'Is this true?'

'Of course it's true! Why would I be in such a freaking mess otherwise? If it wasn't to do with some truth or other?'

I went to the sideboard and asked him again if he wanted wine, and he said yes, ta. Polite. I poured red left over from the dinner with Glenda and Grant. Offcuts. Okay, going too far. But when I brought the glasses over, their shadows did lie on the table, pressed flat by the angle of the sun.

'Cheers.'

'But remember I have to go soon.'

'I haven't forgotten. Where is she now then?'

'Don't know. Didn't I tell you this?' He stopped. 'What were we talking about?'

'Trisha.'

'Mr O'Connell. He'd moved from Dublin to marry his wife, for love people said.'

'For love?' I had moved for love.

'Yeah. There'd have to be some good reason to move to Clonard, wouldn't there?' He laughed. 'Except it was a good place. It was.'

I nodded. The room seemed suddenly like a room I remembered from a long time ago, but it was just the late rays of the sun giving it a filmy air.

Just!

•

They were in the squat in Clonard for three years, he told me, and after a couple of years his father had his knee surgery on the National Health. The last winter, his grandparents died.

'First Granny, then Grandpa. Everyone said Grandpa died of a broken heart after Granny died. They'd been childhood sweethearts, growing up in Cupar Street when it was alright to live there. Ma said it wasn't a broken heart, it was too many years in the damp, and she'd never forgive the FHE, the Brits, the Catholic Church, and the whole fuckin' lot of them.'

'This is before she'd taken her Valium of course,' I said.

'Yeah, exactly,' he said. 'Before she'd had her yellow pill. But seriously, Ma seemed to lose her marbles after Granny and Grandpa died.'

'You hear of that,' I said. Because you do, you read in the paper about people going nuts after their parents die. Me, I wasn't going to be losing any marbles over anyone in my family.

He seemed to brighten a bit. 'Or maybe she gained her marbles. Anyway, Dad had his compo money coming for his kneecaps, and I remember Ma saying we were moving as far away as possible, when the compo came through.'

'Ah, finally New Zealand comes into it,' I said.

'No, Liverpool. We were moving to Liverpool.'

What I realised was, I sort of liked this man. I mean, even though he was a prick.

'Dreadful and Frightful had sent Ma a postcard of The Cavern, saying Liverpool was great. Dad didn't want a bar of it, of course. He'd rather die than live among the swine over the sea. Ma said we lived among swine anyway.'

He stopped and his face was glowing in the strange slanting light, the last rays of the sun. I asked him if he got the money in the end, his father. Well, I couldn't leave the client in the squat in Belfast, could I?

'Yeah, in the end Dad got his bloody compo.'

'How much?'

'Six thousand pounds.'

'Wow.' I hate 'wow'. 'A tidy sum in those days,' I said. I hate that expression, too. For some reason I blushed and inspected the costume, its neatness. When I looked up I saw a puzzled expression cross his face.

'What?' he said.

'Nothing.' I shook my head.

'You just looked . . .'

I smiled. An idiot. Wow. A tidy sum.

'It was a tidy sum,' he said, and cleared his throat. 'Yup. Three grand for each knee.' He checked his watch. 'You are . . . sewing, aren't you?'

I brandished my needle. He couldn't tell. He didn't know anything.

He went and stood in the window, broodily. Mr blinking Rochester.

'We had roast pork and got new jerseys.'

And Milly was Bertha Mason, the madwoman in the attic.

'You'd get a fair bit of pork and jersey for six thousand quid,' I said.

It wasn't often you could use the word 'quid', but you could when it was a quid. I liked it.

'Some of it would've gone in the pub,' he said. 'Sometimes Dad came home smelling like the Guinness plant—he'd had a drop courtesy of So-and-so's right arm. It was good for the Catholic pubs, the compo. Apparently. I was only twelve.'

'Catholic pubs? A font to bless yourself?'

He shook his head, laughed a bit. 'It wasn't about religion. In case you were thinking that.'

'Oh, I wasn't.'

I was of course.

'It was about the haves and the have-nots. But anyway, the Liverpool fund, that was Ma's idea, and in fact Dad might've come around to it. I picked this up, I was twelve.'

'I know you were twelve.'

'She might have persuaded him. But then Bobby Sands died.'

'Bobby Sands?'

'Bobby Sands.'

'You're going to tell me about Bobby Sands, aren't you?'

He looked across at me from where he stood by the curtain in the wincing sun. 'You're not slowing down, are you?'

'Not at all. I'm going as fast as I can—and do a good job.'

'Alright. It just looked like you'd stopped for a minute there.'

'Stopped? No. You do want it to be a good job, don't you?'

He said he did.

He'd tell me about Bobby Sands, he said, *quickly*, because the light was going. The line of sun that ran along the tops of the hills like highlighter disappeared. The yellow room changed into another room, its grey twin sister. As if in keeping, our voices got quieter. I was almost finished, wasn't I?

I was.

'One morning I woke up to all this wailing going on out in the lane, and my sisters and I went outside and the men were standing around bawling their eyes out. Our dad was there, blubbing his heart out with the rest of them. They looked ridiculous, standing upright like guards, with the tears streaming down their faces. They weren't even trying to hide them, like men were meant to. Ma came out, and the other mothers. They were all crying, and Ma told me Bobby Sands had died in Long Kesh. I knew a bit about him. I was only—'

'Twelve. I know.'

'He was a member of parliament, elected in the prison. Young— in his twenties, I think. He'd been on a hunger strike for weeks. Sixty-six days. It took him sixty-six days to die. I remember it was a beautiful day, May, and all the men were crying. And the women, but it was the men that got you. I'd never seen my dad cry before. I went and stood beside him, as if that would stop him, but Dad said, We're crying for joy. For Bobby Sands, and for joy. So that was alright, then. It was for joy.'

The client reached out to touch the costume, hesitated, looked at me. After a second I took his hand—gently, it was heavy—and put it on the costume. I know—talk about unprofessional! His fingers curled around mine for a nanosecond. Then gone.

'I remembered Dad sitting at the table that night and saying the newspapers from all over the world were there, parked outside Long Kesh. Eight hundred years, and Bobby Sands had finally got the attention of the whole fucking world.'

It had felt leathery, his hand, like an Italian purse, but warm. Animal. That was what shocked me.

'Ma was tight-lipped. I suppose she knew where this was going. Sure enough, now Dad wouldn't leave. Not now we were actually getting somewhere. Dad was saying, You can take the fucking compo. Ma said she would, that's just what she'd do. She'd take us kids to Liverpool on her own, and leave Dad to the height that he grew. But Dad wasn't going anywhere while there were prisoners of war dying in jail. Because a few weeks later, another man died, and another. Ten altogether. And the Brits would pull out of Northern Ireland any day, and Kevin McGrath would be there to see it. That's what he said.'

'But he wasn't there.'

'He wasn't.'

'And they didn't.'

'They didn't. They haven't.'

And in the end, as he told me, they left in a terrible hurry.

'It was something that happened the next year, on the twelfth,' he said. 'To this day, I'm not sure what it was.'

The client stopped. He said he'd just step outside and have a fag, if I didn't mind, and I watched him through the wonky glass of the bay window, shifting on the veranda, the smoke flying like a scarf out into the garden. I thought of the Petit Prince.

•

Back inside, he scowled out the window. A pale glow from the garden silhouetted him as if he were a plant.

'The twelfth?' I said.

The glow of dusk was draining away.

'On the twelfth of July every year the Orangemen paraded through the Catholic areas. Celebrating the downfall of Ireland— where you could walk you could dominate sort of thing. It wasn't always violent. Ma said when she was a kid the Ulster parade was a bit of fun and they used to run along beside it. Until the Derry parade, 1969. The Bogside fought back against the RUC. They brought in the English army. So what I remember is the Apprentice Boys marching through the streets, the Catholics trying to stop them with barriers, the RUC knocking down the barriers.'

'Gosh,' I said.

'It was fine,' he said. 'You can be run over crossing the road. But this particular day, something happened. Dad had been at the parade and was laughing because he'd heard Ian Paisley talking to the crowd and he said—and everyone said this—Ian Paisley was God's gift to Ireland because after hearing him raving on, half England wanted to join the IRA. And we were all laughing, but there was more to it than that. Dad was in this heightened state. I could tell something was different.'

He came and sat down at the table, sat back squarely in the bentwood chair.

I was snipping busily, unnecessarily. Fluff. 'What?'

'A few days later I came home from school and saw Ma leaning against the kitchen drawer like she'd just shoved it shut that instant. She had this possum-in-the-headlights look, and I knew there was something in the drawer I wasn't meant to see. So later on, when she'd gone next door (she was always going next door to Aunty Theresa's), I went and opened the drawer.'

I smiled and mimed gliding open a drawer with thumb and forefinger. This was great.

He shook his head. 'Nah. Like this.' He mimed wrenching the drawer open. 'It always stuck. You had to wrestle with it like your enemy.'

'What was in the drawer?'

The chair creaked. These chairs, antiques, sought after, and flimsy as hell.

'At first nothing out of the ordinary. I knew all the stuff by heart—holy pictures, rosary beads (mine blue, my sisters' pink), baptism certificates. I'd seen it all hundreds of times, so it was sort of sacred, and sort of nothing. I was just about to give up when I saw, underneath all the other crap, a new thing. It was a card with a photograph stuck on it. I scraped it up off the bottom of the drawer. It was Dad, all blurry, but you could still see it was him coming out of the corner shop, his head sideways, but his eyes swivelled around to the front, starting out of his head. There was a red smudge on the edge of the print. Letters, but I couldn't make them out. A photograph of Dad! No one had a camera. I stuffed it back in the drawer. By the time Ma got back I was away out the door into the lane.'

He looked at me and laughed, and I laughed back. We laughed inanely for no reason.

The thing was finished. I was sick of sewing anyway. Sick to death of it. I decided then that I was absolutely sick of mending and alterations. You could feel this about anything. I'd thought this about reading and writing.

'Anyway,' I said.

'Anyway, later on I was out throwing stones at a Prod and—'

'What's a Prod when he's at home?'

171

'Protestant.'

'No kidding? Did you hit this Prod with a stone?' (I mean, he might have hurt someone.)

'No,' he said. 'Couldn't even see him.'

'It was dark?'

'It was summer. July, remember. The marching season.'

'Why couldn't you see the Prod? And was it a boy?'

'Yeah, a boy.' He sat up. He'd been slouching before. I noticed his hands again. They were square. 'There was a barricade. We'd toss stones over it. There was a barricade down the middle of the road.'

I pointed out the window. 'You mean, like if there was a barricade down the middle of this street?'

He looked out. 'Yup.'

I looked at the villas opposite. Across the road was Electricity. We didn't know anyone there.

'Made of what, this barricade?'

'Iron, wood, barbed wire. Anything.'

'Anything?'

'Old car doors.'

'What was the name of the street?'

'Does it matter? I don't know. Cupar Street. It was Cupar Street.'

'Made of iron and wood and barbed wire?'

He sighed theatrically. 'And car doors.'

'I just want to see it.' And I did.

'No one lived in Cupar Street anyway. The windows were concreted over and the roofs were fallen in. Although Granny and Grandpa lived there when they were young.'

I put the costume down. I mean, this was fascinating.

He paused. He'd lost his thread (yes, thread!). 'Where was I?'

'The Prod.'

'Oh yeah, I'd arranged to meet him there.'

'You mean you'd actually jacked it up with the boy, this Prod? To throw stones at each other?'

'It was a bit of a game,' he said impatiently. 'Anyway, that wasn't the point. The point was, I was tossing stones at the Orangie kid, and we started talking and I told him how I had a picture of my dad. I was bragging, because no one had pictures. I told him all about the photo, my dad coming out of the shop and it was stuck on a card. The Prod called out from over the barricade, that he knew what it was, it was a Wanted card. I said, What's a Wanted card? and the Prod said, It means your dad's wanted. I remember thinking, My dad's wanted! My dad was so great people wanted him! The Prod asked me if I knew what it meant, and I said of course I knew. And he said, Why'd you ask then? He said, So you know it means he's a dead man, sooner or later? I said yes I did know. But I didn't.

'I ran all the way home along the row, breathing like crazy, in and out, drying everything out inside my throat, which was good because I didn't want to cry in the street. When I got home, there was Dad sitting at the table plain as day. Alive. He said, You look like you've seen a ghost, son. Well, I had, and I said, You got the Wanted card. Dad laughed. He laughed! It wasn't funny. I said, *Did you get the Wanted card?* and he said, I did. This was terrible. We were all dead. But Dad said not to worry. He said, We're all wanted. Ma had her back to him and she was muttering that he was an idiot. I was beside myself and I was saying, Am I wanted? Are Dana and Sharon wanted? (They're my sisters.) Is Ma wanted? And Dad said, No, not you. The men. The men.

'Which was true, of course. It was only the men. All the kids gave cheek to the English soldiers. Ma could stand in the doorway giving them a piece of her mind as they passed, all the women did—*Anglo bastards! Go back to your mammy.* The soldiers would tramp by, all stony-faced.

'It was just the men, the Provs.'

I asked him what was a Prov *when it was at home*. Provisional IRA, he said, formed when the regular IRA had gone soft. I remembered this from the news anyway, once upon a time, in the pole house. The news of the world, and the evening cocktails.

'But the women and the kids—you could be in the wrong place at the wrong time.'

'Could you?' I said. I wanted to know, I really did.

'You could.'

I looked outside. The daisies were just visible, little smudges. Quarter to nine.

'Was your dad a Prov, then?' I asked.

He shrugged. 'Yup. He was waiting for the day I'd join. I never did of course. Anyway, Dad said it was nothing, the Wanted card. And that was the end of it. I remember that, in the candlelight. But it wasn't the end of it.'

'Candlelight?'

'It was a squat.'

'Oh yeah.'

Squattocracy.

'No electricity, like this,' I said, indicating the room. The dusk had settled over it like felt. There were only minutes of light left. I knew the light quite well, its relationship with this room. Soon I wouldn't be able to see his face. In an hour Art would be home and I'd continue with my Blackout life, my pools of light, my carefully heated water.

'Not like this. You're almost finished, aren't you?'

'Almost,' I said, bundling the costume in my hands as if it were a cat, so he wouldn't see.

'Because I have to go,' he said.

'Why?'

'Why!'

I mean he'd just told me about the Wanted card.

He pulled something from his pocket, a mobile phone, clunky as hell.

'A phone call,' he murmured. 'I'm expecting a phone call.'

'Milly?'

He nodded. 'But also.' He looked around the room. The red couch and curtains were wine-coloured. The white floorboards had a moony glow.

Art would be home any moment. So what? I was seeing a client. I was earning a living. And anyway, we weren't like that, controlling with each other.

'But what were you going to say? Tell me quickly: what next? Please.'

Please? GoGo, stop.

'You're sewing?'

Of course I wasn't blinking sewing. I held the costume in my hands. Like a cat.

'I'm sewing.'

He was talking. He was getting up from the table and reaching for his jacket, and going on.

'Another photo came in the mail.'

I stood up too. 'Another one? Was it in the drawer?'

'It came in the mail. Dad was out.'

'Work?'

'There was no work. Slight exaggeration—a day here, a day there, from the Brew, the Labour Exchange. He wasn't idle though. Always on the move, wound up like a spring.'

The client was putting on his jacket.

'Are you going?' I asked. Slight panic.

'No, it's cold,' he said.

Ah, late summer, and a chill outside now. You needed a jacket.

'The mail came and it was another photo of Dad, a worse one.'

175

'Worse! Oh no!'

He laughed. 'Oh no!'

I repeated seriously, 'Oh no.'

He took his briefcase.

'Ma opened the letter in the passage, dropping the envelope as she walked into the kitchen. I remember that, like a husk.'

A husk, he said. A husk.

'She flew into a panic. She'd never panicked before. In fact, her motto was, No need to panic. It was probably the Valium, but ah well. Now there was a definite need to panic.'

'And she'd lost her marbles, remember,' I said.

'Yeah. Or gained them.'

'What was it? The card?'

He transferred the briefcase to the other hand. 'It was a Mass card, for a requiem. As if he was already dead. Ma went into a whirl. We're going to Liverpool, we're going, we're going! She had a cardboard box and was tossing things into it. I went and got my Superman and put it in the box. I'd outgrown it but it was the only thing I had that was from a toy shop. In fact it was from the tip, but it had once been in a toy shop. Ma flung it out of the box. Necessities. We needed necessities.'

I nodded. Necessities. The sky to the west had a violent streak of pink. The client didn't see it. He had his back to the window.

'Later that night, Dad came in and he'd had a few drinks. *I couldn't refuse a drink when it was Jacky Quinn's leg, now could I?* Ma threw the Mass card at him, and it fluttered away. He looked at it on the floor, but wouldn't pick it up. I was watching all this through the crack in the bedroom door. Ma screamed at him, Pick it up! He said, I know what it is. He said he'd faced execution every day for a long time. But Ma was yelling, You've done something, Kevin, what've you done! Over and over. And he was raving on about Bobby Sands and the other martyrs and how we were getting somewhere after eight hundred years. They were going at it, yelling into each other's faces, and they stood really close and I thought they might grab each other. But they didn't. When they'd stopped, Ma said, We don't need the Housing Executive to stove our roof in, we'll do it for ourselves thank you very much, with our yelling and screaming.

'She wrenched out the kitchen drawer and tipped it into the box we were packing for Liverpool—the pink and blue rosary beads, the birth certificates, what-have-you came tumbling out. She went into the bedroom and came back with her old dancing costume.'

My neck twitched in surprise. I could feel my cartoonishness. 'What—*this*?'

He looked at the costume bundled in my arms, which was done, done like a dinner. It was finished. Finis. Finito. The End. He didn't look. It was too dark to see anyway, the blackness. You could just make out the shine of the knotwork. He looked at me. 'Yeah. That.' He smiled. I hadn't seen his teeth before this close, and now I could just see them like the white floorboards. They were pleasantly crowded, they got along well together.

'Ma tossed it into the box and Dad said, What the fuck d'you want that for? You only had it on five minutes. She said she loved dancing, or had before she'd ever laid eyes on Dad. Dad was saying, No you didn't, you did not love the dancing. And Ma was saying, Yes I did, I loved dancing and you're not to tell the story of what you know nothing about. They went back and forth like this. I hated this, my parents fighting. They didn't usually fight. Ma was saying she belonged to some club and people thought it was a good sign that there was dancing again and things were getting back to normal, after 1969. And Dad was roaring, A good sign! A good fucking sign! Your ma couldn't even rustle up a few pennies to finish the thing. And Dad tugged at the sleeve of the dress, and Ma tugged it back, and I thought it might tear. Dad was saying, Oh yeah, great times. Back to normal! Then he said, Your own da used to say, what's normal after eight hundred years? Ma said, My da was a bitter old soul, that's why I ended up with you: I was used to bitterness and griping and bile, it seemed normal. I was listening to all this. Dad was saying—a bit slurred—But he was right, wasn't he, your da? Because then there was 1972.'

The client moved to the front room doorway. He stood against the jamb. '*Now* I'd better go.'

'1972?' I said.

He shook his head. 'Bloody Sunday. I suppose no one was thinking about dancing then.'

He was fishing for his car keys and moving into the dim passage. Everything was fuzzy, half formed in the dusk. I followed him and we picked our way to the front door.

'Did you go then, that night?' I asked.

'No.'

'No?'

'No. We probably never would've gone, even if Dad had, you know, if they'd got him. We never would've left Belfast.'

'But what about Liverpool? And Dreadful and Frightful?'

'Talk is cheap,' he said. 'We never would've gone. But do you want to hear this?'

'Yes.'

He turned his head. No. I couldn't see. I couldn't see a thing. Only his teeth. We were standing in the doorway by the front door but I didn't open it. There was a shred of pink light through the stained-glass window above the door. These villas, they're beautiful. I could see him looking at the costume which was wrapped around my hands. I'd give him the costume. When he'd finished, I'd give him the costume. But what I thought was: he wants to tell.

'A few days later I was going for my lesson. I'd forgotten it, what with everything going on, and then I remembered it, and I got my music and went along the row and I remember thinking how you can forget things, like birds, pianos, even people, and then they're there again. And there was Mr O'Connell, standing on the doorstep looking out, as he often did, having a fag. He was looking over the roofs at the sky, which was still smoking a few days after the parade. When he saw me he waved and I broke into a run. As I ran I noticed that a car was cruising behind me, going along at the same speed as me. I thought someone was trying to park and I looked back and I saw a big dark car. As I reached Mr O'Connell's house he said, How's 'The Happy Farmer' and I said he was grand, and then I saw this look on his face and there was a huge, thunderous bang. It was like the whole world had blown up, it was the end of the world. Mr O'Connell crashed from his doorway out onto the lane like a tree being felled. Blood was pouring from the side of his head. I felt like I was in space, or I was like some sort of ghost hovering over Mr O'Connell. I might've been yelling but I couldn't tell. I remember I didn't know what to do, I was paralysed, and I was petrified the sniper might get me as well. But the car had gone. I stood in the middle of the lane, the blood pounding in my ears, and music, 'The Happy Farmer', plastering itself against the houses. Then neighbours came rushing. I remember Mr McKinley dropping to his knees next to Mr O'Connell, and you know what I thought? I thought his knees must hurt, the way he dropped like that. And Mrs Touhy taking his pulse, and Mrs O'Connell running out of the house and sinking next to Mr O'Connell and wailing. Then I looked at Mr O'Connell, who was undressed in the worst possible way. Exposed. From then on I knew the meaning of undressed, the side of a head taken clean off, showing these glistening ropes and wads that make us go, up to a certain point.'

20

The costume was like a thing alive, the way it jumped in my hands. Half alive, then dead again, in and out of consciousness. The client swivelled his head quickly to look at it.

'Don't worry,' I said. I meant the costume. I was shaking my head. I didn't know what to do, whether to fawn over him or to be cool. I was never good at this sort of thing. But I found, while I was looking at him, that I had tears in my eyes.

Because he had told me. He had told *me*. He said, Thank you. I said, You're welcome. As they say in America. I opened the front door and we stepped out onto the veranda. I went very sensible.

'Go on,' I said.

'Me go on?' He looked pointedly at the costume but I didn't say anything. I could see his face now. The sky had a last bit of pink.

'The whole street was at the O'Connells', adults and kids packing in, and Old Mrs O'Connell (that was his mother) was being held up under the arms by two women because she'd collapsed like a puppet. She was whimpering and Aunty Theresa and a couple of other women were trying to get her to drink tea out of a saucer but it kept spilling down her front and Young Mrs

O'Connell (his wife), who was shaking like a leaf, was saying, Leave off with the tea, will you, can't you see she doesn't want it? But the other women kept trying to give her the tea and saying, It'll do her good. Ma was saying, Leave her in peace, won't you. But still the other women kept trying to give her tea, until after a while everyone seemed to have forgotten about Mr O'Connell being dead. We were there to debate the issue of whether Old Mrs O'Connell should have tea or not.

'I remember at home we had soup.'

Soup. A gas ring because it was a squat.

He shook his head. 'I couldn't swallow, even the soup. I had some kind of trapdoor in my throat. Ma was smoking in the candlelight and swinging her foot and saying, It's alright, son, he had a good innings, he was getting on. It's a tragedy when someone young dies, but he had a good life. She went on thinking up more good ways of looking at Mr O'Connell's death. At peace now, gone to a better place.'

He was motoring. I wouldn't interrupt him again.

'Dad wasn't there,' he said. 'Probably down the Working Men's Club.'

'Working Men's Club? But I thought they didn't—'

'They didn't. There was no work. But there was a Working Men's Club.'

'Fair enough,' I said. Shut up, GoGo! 'And?'

'And, nothing. Except I could sense something coming to a head during the evening. When Dad came in, us kids were in bed. I heard Ma say, It's in the pot. Then, They mistook him for you, you know that, don't you? And Dad saying, That's rubbish. They were silent for a while. Dad was eating. I could hear his spoon. Then Ma said, You're a stupid fool for hanging round here, and Dad was saying, Stop it, will you, you know nothing about it. Ma said she knew something happened on the twelfth, and she asked him what it was. Dad told her to keep out of what she knew nothing about. Ma said, I know this—you have Jack O'Connell's blood on your hands.

'I got out of bed and looked through the crack in the door and saw in the light of the candle that they were leaning forward in their chairs, clinging to each other. I wondered how they could be slagging each other off, and the next thing be hugging. Ma said we'd all go to Liverpool now. We'd stay with Deirdre and Finoula. Dad stiffened and leaned back. Ma was staring at him, her eyes looking crazy in the candlelight. She said, Well you don't think we're going stay now, do you? Dad got up and slammed out the door. Ma called after him, Hope you die out there, you bastard! Ma sat there and you could tell she was thinking away like anything. You could see the thinking coming off her.

'I must've been a bit slow, because it was only after lying there for a while that I put two and two together. If the sniper was meant for Dad, then I had led him to Mr O'Connell.

'In the morning Dad wasn't there, but that was nothing unusual. Ma was like the head of Sinn Féin, she was like a little general. She marched next door to Aunty Theresa's.'

'This was your aunt?'

'No, everyone called her aunty because her two sons had been shot joy-riding through a checkpoint and now she had no children. She had the only phone in the street. Her husband had got compo for his arm, but he'd been on the blanket in the Maze and the only way he was coming home was in a box. She was in the money.'

'The blanket?'

He shrugged. 'They didn't wear clothes or wash. Well, they were political prisoners, treated like criminals. Thatcher said, "Crime is crime is crime." Apparently. I was only—'

'Twelve, yes. Very poetic. Very Gertrude Stein.'

'You've finished it, haven't you?'

'Just get on with it, get on with the story.'

'It's not a story.'

'Okay. Get on with it anyway.'

He nodded as if he could read the fabric, which was just a blob in the dark, and which I knew he wouldn't be able to see anyway, even if they got the stop-gap cable going. But he was scrutinising it, his face twisted as if he were illiterate and trying to figure out his letters. 'So the phone, anyway, Ma came back after using the phone and said matter-of-factly, We're booked on the ferry on Friday.'

'What day was it?'

'Tuesday maybe. A few days to go, anyway.'

'Shouldn't you have gone right then?'

'We should've.'

'Why didn't you?'

'Just listen.'

'I am listening.'

'Because I don't have long. I really don't.'

'Ooh, Milly's waiting!' I tooted.

'Wasn't it you who wanted me to tell this?' he asked. He sounded indignant. I couldn't see.

'I thought it was you wanted to tell the story.' I did.

'It isn't a story.'

'Okay. Whatever it is. I thought you wanted to tell it.'

'No. I don't.'

'Okay.'

'I had no intrinsic interest in telling it,' he said. 'It was just to pass the time.'

Oh, intrinsic.

He went down the bouncy steps to the garden. I felt each step.

'Tell the story,' I said from the veranda. 'Or whatever it is.'

'Alright.' He turned around and addressed me from the garden. 'At teatime that night . . .'

'What night?'

'The night after Mr O'Connell—wasn't that what we were talking about?'

'We were.'

He stood in the wild garden. Tonight I would heat water.

'We were having our tea. Just us kids. Ma never ate. She'd hang around in the scullery doorway, smoking. There was this bashing on the door, bang bang bang, and it was Aunty Theresa. She was yelling, Concepta, Concepta. I remember there was fried bread on my plate, the colour of copper. It was about Dad. There'd been a man killed at the parade. Aunty Theresa told us kids to get our things. Dana and Sharon—my sisters—ran into the bedroom, but I stayed in the kitchen. Aunty Theresa was saying, Concepta, you've got to go. They know they got the wrong man. But Ma was dazed. She said, How do you know? It was a leak in the prison. There'd been a leak. Aunty Theresa was saying, Just go for Christ's sake! But Ma was asking where Dad was. Aunty Theresa said she didn't have a clue, and not to worry about Kevin, he knew what was going on. This was us, Ma and us kids, we had to go from the house, now.

'Then I knew he'd killed a man at the parade. A Prod.'

Well, I knew that for a start. I boinged down the steps myself, to the garden. We stood on the path among the tendrils, the clag of datura in my nostrils. He spoke close to my face.

'Suddenly Ma seemed to come to, like a switch flicking. She said, We'll go! Aunty Theresa was all excited, as if Ma had won a raffle. Then there was general chaos. Dana—ten years old—going crazy. The UDA, the UDA! And then Sharon started up. The UDA! Ma said, Keep quiet about the UDA, will you? It's a lot of nonsense. So I knew it was true. Aunty Theresa ran back next door to book us on the ferry. I'd never seen her run before. I said to Ma, who was whirling about plucking at random coats and things, They're after Dad, aren't they? She didn't answer. Her eyes were bright, as if it was Midnight Mass. She said, We're going to Liverpool, we're finally going. Dreadful and Frightful would meet us there.

'Aunty Theresa came back to tell us we were on the night sailing, and a taxi was on its way. Ma wanted to know how she'd got a black taxi to come over here at this time of night. Aunty Theresa said she just did, and they laughed. They actually laughed. It really was like Christmas. Ma had the box she'd packed under her arm. There was no time to take the sheets from the beds, or anything. We had our jackets, our schoolbags. As we were going out the door, there was a woman waiting in the lane with five or so kids and a whole lot of supermarket bags. She said, Can we have the house? News travelled fast. You had to be bold to get a squat. Ma said, sort of quiet, that it was a marked house and she wouldn't be wanting it. That was the first time I knew this. It was a marked house. I saw the woman's face, like a mushroom under her scarf, all blank. Ma told her to come back in a few weeks, but the woman said it would be too late by then, and she went away.

'As it turned out, the black taxi didn't come. We had to walk to the Falls Road! As we ran I looked back and caught a glimpse of the tea table, everything on it, the dishes and the half-eaten food like the *Mary Celeste*.'

Yes, the *Mary Celeste*. I was looking into his face with the garden framing it, but couldn't see it.

'We were kissed by neighbours all along the lane. They'd never kissed us before. All the way along the lane, people were calling in whispers from the doorways. We walked through the streets of Clonard till we got to the Falls Road. There was a checkpoint on the way, and we were trembling. We got a taxi which smelled like an old leather trunk I hid in once at a friend's house, and then couldn't open again.

'Dad was waiting on the wharf, smoking, looking nervy. Ma said, So you're coming then, are you? He ground his fag under his shoe and took the cardboard box from Ma, and we all walked onto the ferry.

'We watched Belfast getting smaller and smaller.' He held up his hand to the westward sky, comparing it with the Waitakeres. 'When we were turning out of the Channel—I remember this because suddenly the sea was boiling, it was the Irish Sea, and that was what everyone said about it, it boiled. I thought about my Superman being left behind, and I started to go on about it. A couple of kids stared at me, and I did the classic what-the-fuck-d'you-think-you're-looking-at, and Ma shooshed me and said we didn't want to be drawing attention to ourselves. I asked why not, loudly, and Dad gripped my shoulder and hissed through his teeth, It's just the way it is, which were the first words he'd spoken on the journey. I can still feel his thumb poking into that soft bit under your shoulder blade. He held it there, saying, There goes Ireland, there's your last glimpse of Ireland. The lights of Belfast were disappearing into the mist, and then it was just black water slopping about. We went and sat in the cabin and I started up again about my Superman. Ma said, For goodness' sake, you're too old for a toy like that anyway. But it wasn't for playing with, it was for keeping. For *keeping*. I knew who would get my Superman—the boy who would move into the house after us, from the family with the plastic bags. I couldn't stand it. I was wailing. The girls were saying, Tell him to be quiet, Ma! Ma said, We'll buy another Superman if it means that much to you. Well, we had six thousand pounds, give or take, burning a hole in our pocket. But I knew we wouldn't. All the way across the Irish Sea I said under my breath, *I'm going back, I'm going back to get my Superman*. At one point Dad said grimly, None of us are ever going back, and Ma said, Well you've changed your tune all of a sudden. That was us leaving Ireland. When you tried to look out the window all you could see was us. From now on it was just us.'

Insects brushed against me on the path. I thought I felt warmth coming off him. I heard Bell crackling in the undergrowth, and his breath. There was more. 'What?' I said.

'The boy with the plastic bags didn't get my Superman. They did move into the house, a few days later, and it was firebombed and he lost an arm and bled to death before they could get him to the hospital. That's what I heard. The boy who'd taken my place. But I didn't know that then. I heard it later.'

I caught my breath. No words. None. I supposed this was some kind of end, the end of the story, the most tragic bit. You couldn't get more hyperbolic, could you? He should've died but he didn't, he came to paradise and lived happily ever after. End of story. There are more pages to go in this book, and so we know there is more. We're privileged as readers and writers. And as immigrants.

I recovered. 'But what about Dreadful and Frightful? Weren't you meeting them in Liverpool?'

'They weren't there. When we got to the address they'd given us, we were told they'd got on a ship.'

'Well, they were ship girls.' He laughed. I laughed. It was almost completely dark.

'Are you still there?' he said.

'Of course I'm here.'

'But none of this is what I meant. What I meant to say.'

'What did you mean to say?'

He shook his head. I felt the skim of his hair.

I cuddled the costume, my muff. It was finished.

'Seeing it's not finished, am I coming back tomorrow?'

'Do you want to take it to another mender?'

I heard his sigh. 'She's probably not coming home tonight or I would've heard.'

I couldn't make out his face anymore in the dark, and among the trees and vines.

'Milly?'

'Of course Milly.'

'Come tomorrow then. It's almost finished.'

It was done. It was done, despite everything.

'This can't go on,' he said. I felt his lip brush my upper lip. Hesitate. And again. The smell of cigarettes. A warmth coming from him. I stepped back.

'What?' he said.

'Nothing.'

'The power will come on.'

'I know.'

'What should I call you? All this time and—'

I told him.

'GoGo?'

I explained about my posh school.

I knew *his* name, of course, but I liked to think of him as the client. Perhaps I was always the mender to him. I don't know.

He made his way along the overgrown path. I heard the gate click and him curse gently as he dashed his keys against the car door. He was meant to be dead, and this was his new life. I felt a rush of excitement that I was in it.

21

Then Art was coming in and there was a party we were meant to go to a few streets away, Helen Someone we knew vaguely from Wellington. People were starting to have Blackout parties. I wasn't sure if I wanted to go, I wasn't in the mood for inane conversation, and Art said, Same. We hoed into cold meat and potato salad, deciding, and sculled a bit of the white wine Art had couriered in from outside the Blackout zone. Art said they never knew when to stop with the d-d-d. I looked at him. He sneezed. Dressing. We both said, Oh no, and soon he was sneezing like a starter motor.

'It's the d-d-d—achoo!—dust.'

'Only a matter of time,' I said, and I laughed for some reason.

It was true. The carpets were like someone's felting hobby. No hope of vacuuming them, of course. (Or of hanging them on the line and attacking them with a carpet beater, I thought, like the Edwardian housewife's maid would have done. Nailing them down had no doubt seemed like a good idea at the time.) Art was a card-carrying hayfever-sufferer with a bona fide diagnosis, like a visa to the mythical world of mites—you couldn't see them, you just thought you had when the sun shone.

'It was a r-r-race,' said Art, and sneezed, 'between Pinnacle Power and m-me.'

'You did come second,' I said. 'Silver.'

We were good.

He asked me between sneezes whether I minded him going around to Glenda's and I said why would I mind? I mean, he was honest.

We moseyed over to the party with a torch. It was in a villa like ours, but a whole one. There were candles all through the house so it looked like Diwali, and people crowded into room after room, leaning against walls or dancing. The house shook a bit. Nirvana was straining out of a ghetto blaster. I moved through, talked to someone I went to university with but I couldn't remember her name through the whole conversation. I went to get a glass of red wine from the kitchen, passed Art having an animated conversation with a group of people, including Glenda. *Three fucking weeks.*

After a couple more conversations, one about property values, another about late capitalism, I drifted out onto a huge deck where there were more candles and people smoking. It was a beautiful evening. It was quite noisy, just talking, but a neighbour yelled from next door to shut up, it was midnight. There was general laughter. Then I saw, at the corner of the deck where it looked like a boat, the client. He was smoking and nodding with a group of three or four other people. He caught my eye, and put his cigarette in the other hand. I felt a bit nervy, like if I'd had a cigarette, I would have juggled with it.

I went back inside, but when I looked over my shoulder, he had followed me. The room was crowded and there were people trying to dance to some New Romance, good luck to them. He was in front of me. I noticed the way his white shirt was tucked into his jeans, a preppy look I wasn't into. He said, Do you want to dance, and I said okay. You can't really say, No, no I don't. We jived around looking a bit stupid. I didn't look at his face, only his body. Everything from the neck down. We didn't touch. As you don't. He was a terrible dancer, robotic. It was kind of funny, really it was. Then the song finished and people melted away from the middle of the room. We stood about not saying anything, but then Art appeared from another room.

'Shall we go?' He looked at the client.

I said, 'This is.'

'Shane.'

'Shane, sorry. I knew that. A client.'

They shook hands. I said yeah, I was ready to go. As I turned to the passage I saw a woman flit across it, from a room on one side to a room on the other, which was the side we didn't have in our villa conversion. And I thought, from the split-second flash I took in of black hair, clompy shoes, surfing gait, that it was Trisha.

We were going. Art was saying goodbye to some people, Glenda, Grant et al. I turned to the client.

'I thought I just saw Trisha. Did you?'

'No,' he said. He smiled.

Art and I sailed home along the empty streets, arm in arm, in the dark, and talked about whether we should stay in the house, because of Art's hayfever. He said he couldn't be bothered moving, but did *I* need to because of my, you know, business (because it wasn't quite a business), which was thoughtful, but I said no, *I* couldn't be bothered. Our voices were bouncing off the houses across the road. It would be fine as long as it didn't go on *too* much longer. Another three weeks might just be bearable. I was about to be paid for quite an involved job, I said. Art said, Oh good.

I was feeling blasé, buoyant, I don't know. I said it wasn't *too* bad, was it? It wasn't, he said, not bad at all. You couldn't really ask for more. Perhaps some electricity occasionally. A light once in a while wouldn't go amiss. He could live without almost everything else. Well, that and the computer. And the vacuum cleaner.

We were coming up the steps and he said, 'That wasn't the investment banker, was it?'

'Oh, actually, it was,' I said.

'I meant to tell you, I told Mother what he said about the business. Remember? About pulling in their horns, laying off staff?'

'I remember,' I said. I was in a trance.

'They think they can ride it out. They've been through bad times before.'

'Okay, good.'

When the client came the next day, the costume would be ready.

Knotwork

22

I couldn't very well leave the client stranded in Liverpool, could I? Abandoned by Dreadful and Frightful. What I decided overnight: I would finish the unfinished sleeve. Yes! I thought this as I lay in the clammy bed beside Art, who I couldn't see and couldn't feel. I could hear him snoring like an engine, that's how I knew he was there—also because I *knew* he was there. And these twin circumstances, the real snoring and the virtual knowing, were comforting. Then I started thinking about comfort, which is such a cushiony notion, and even the word sounds fluffy. And I thought how comfort could be the point of everything, why we work, why we try to get on with people etc. Or maybe it isn't the point. Maybe doing without comfort is the point, because then you start on other things. I'm not sure what they are, but they'd be profound. I was thinking that you could spend your whole life going backwards and forwards on this issue, in a flower-petal kind of way. Comfort, profundity, comfort, profundity. And then just before you died, you'd come to the last one: comfort. Or maybe it would be profundity. But at that point whether your life had been comfortable or profound wouldn't matter, because it would all be over. I was gulping in the blackness of the bedroom, which was so very black. It was as if you had no eyes. I pictured the black cuff of the costume, and how I would fill it in with colour.

•

In the morning I packed the costume into a bag and went out to buy silks.

I would finish the unfinished sleeve because I could. And because, like the dog in Sam Hunt's 'Bow-Wow' poems, I had *nothing else to do*. This was a bit of a worry.

I walked up to the crest of Symonds Street and headed down the gentle slope towards town. On the off-chance, I'd phoned a sewing shop at the bottom of Queen Street, Oh Sew Good. The pun had me in stitches. I was surprised that they were open, and the woman who answered had sounded surprised too. It was a fine day, with some of those flat Auckland clouds lying about the horizon as if they were tired. In upper Symonds Street there were fewer shops open than there'd been a week earlier. One or two had candlelight. A boutique full of fifties tin monkeys and Bakelite radios. No customers, but then I'd never seen anyone in that shop even when the lights were on. There was a second-hand bookshop in the same state. I tooled on down the hill, past the Jewish cemetery. I don't suppose the dead minded the Blackout. It was hot in the sun, even in my bright checked World top which I hadn't known what to wear *with*, but oh well.

I crossed over to the Grafton Bridge side, where there was a bit more shade, and to the Everything Else cemetery, which fell away like a miniature Machu Picchu underneath the bridge. The street was quiet, a smattering of people, mostly street kids, the ones who usually hung out in the cemetery, but they seemed to have Moved Upstairs proper. They'd arranged their stuff—blankets, plastic bags, ghetto blasters—along the railing, neatly, as if they were keeping house; their new sitting room. I couldn't see much point in the relocation—the cemetery seemed more comfortable, with its snippets of lawn and handy graves—except that now, with the Blackout, they *could*. No one was moving them on. I was pretty sure my street kid wasn't there. One of the girls (it may have been a boy, nothing poked out from the baggy clothes) was squatting beside an ice-cream container with a couple of coins in it. They weren't doing a roaring trade. I didn't contribute and she stared at me: *fuck off, you.* I stared back. She could go jump in the lake. She half rose menacingly. *Fuck off, you.* Fine, I'd fuck off.

I fucked off down Wellesley Street, past the library, which had a throbbing generator and was lit up ghostily, if there's such a word. It beeped from within. Oh, so you could still get books out. When I got to Queen Street I saw that everything had basically ground to a standstill. There were a few police walking the beat, to prevent looting I supposed. Banks and department stores had temporary lighting rigged up, miles of wires and bulbs like spiders' webs with their pockets of food—a fly, a mosquito—bound and glowing. A few cafés and boutiques and bookshops were open for business with gas bottles and candles, but more had shut up shop. There was hardly anyone around. A few cars, the odd empty bus blew past as lightly as a shoebox. An eerie sense of going back in time made the streets sleepy. Sedated like fifties housewives, that's what I thought. It hadn't been long, fifteen years perhaps, since people had said, Oh, Auckland's a one-horse town, Auckland's no more than a wild colonial town. You could fire a gun down Queen Street on a Sunday afternoon and hit no one. Since the brief eighties boom and all those mirrored glass buildings, it had become bigger, taller, more bustling, more *cosmopolitan* (people said), so that the gun fired down the street would have caused several pedestrians to fall down dead. This seemed to be a good thing. But now, suddenly, Auckland wasn't a city anymore, it wasn't cosmopolitan, it was once again the old, quiet, dark, one-horse town. The outpost of the colony had been lurking all this time just below the eighties mirrored surface.

•

In Post Office Square I hesitated at the mouth of a shopping arcade. No one was about, and there was that abandoned post-apocalyptic feel I was getting so used to. I kept checking over my shoulder for creeps as I tromped up the disabled escalator. Walking on the ribbed metal steps was an aberration of nature; my feet felt like lead. By the time I got to the second floor, the daylight was gone and I was in hand-in-front-of-your-face territory. I almost ran past a ghost train of dark entranceways and locked grilles, but sure enough, there was Oh Sew Good nestled at the back and lit up like a Christmas tree. Slight exaggeration, but they did have a few lamps dotted about. As I entered, the shopkeeper who I'd talked to earlier on the phone half recognised me. I didn't usually buy this kind of stuff—it was a hobby shop, and for my business I needed the basics, which I got from a bulk supplier out west. But I'd been here once or twice before, and the shopkeeper nodded from where she sat behind the counter, popping a needle in and out of linen stretched like a drum over a round frame. She had a long bob like a college girl's only grey—a Remuera look, and the truth is, you had to be a bit of a Remuera matron to be able to afford to shop at a place like this; to do patchwork and knitting. The shopkeeper changed her glasses and looked up. Her tight V of a smile appeared to be embroidered on like the inscrutable mouth of a teddy bear. The thing about these shops is there's a great camaraderie which comes from a shared interest in making things, and from the beautiful materials.

The shop was stuffed to the gunnels with every sewing notion under the sun. Yes, that's the word they use (Professor Bleakley):

notion. Why they couldn't just say 'idea', I don't know. Shelves full of richly dyed felt, of delicate Pilgrimish patchwork chintz, banks of shiny buttons, zips in all their toothiness, swivelling racks of knitting patterns on which sultry women looked out from their mohair collars, bundles of rug-hooking wool chopped off like some kind of harvest, and against one wall, a pixel of balls of wool. It was exciting. I love this stuff. I don't know whether I can convey to you, if you don't sew, just how gorgeous the raw materials of sewing—the notions—are. There's this sense of possibility that you almost don't want to disturb by making something. But you do. So, notions on this scale, a whole shop full, well, they enlarged me, and made me feel small at the same time. Not joking. I made my way down an aisle of glinting beads and came to the embroidery silks, which hung in shiny six-inch skeins like the worms they'd come from. I hauled out the costume, held it close to the skeins and picked out the silver and gold. A colour is seldom an absolute match. You err on the darker side; a lighter colour would screech at you. Having matched the silver and gold, I moved on to the green. Mm, this was going to be a little more difficult, especially in this light. Greens are ambiguous.

The shopkeeper appeared at my elbow, tweaking the stock. 'We have some wonderful new lamb's wool in,' she said, and produced a ball seemingly from her sleeve like a magician. Under my hand I felt softness and looked down at a ball of pale pink fluff.

'Lovely,' I heard myself cooing. It was true. The wool was so gentle you wanted to take it home and feed it with a bottle. But a garment in this would cost several hundred dollars. The shopkeeper must have sensed my lack of disposable income. She moved on.

'That's an alluring shade, isn't it? Dollar Bill, it's called.'

We were back at the green skeins.

The shopkeeper peered at the costume, slightly overbearing, but on the other hand I was pleased to have help. As I said, these sewing shops are like clubs. People communicate. There's talk. On a good day—with the power on—there's chatter. Okay, you need a bit of money. And leisure. But the brilliant thing about these shops is that it's okay not to know anything. In fact, it's a cause for celebration. A convert! I know a thing or two, but it's not uncommon to see a woman who's never held a needle in her hand being gleefully shown what to do by a shopkeeper, or even by another customer. Compare this with a man going into a hardware store. He has to pretend to know everything, or he's an idiot, and so he comes away knowing nothing. Men and shopping: a permanent learning disability. But I digress. In the sewing shop, I didn't need much encouragement to hold up the costume like Exhibit A.

'Knotwork,' nodded the shopkeeper. 'That's quite some garment.'

I explained how I was going to embroider the lower part of the sleeve and the cuff.

The shopkeeper peered closer. The V returned to her lips. 'You'll have your work cut out.'

She spoke in tropes, which were comforting. You knew where you were. I went back to the greens. I tried shades that were wildly wrong. That's what you do. You consider everything, and the wrong ones help you choose the right one. That's what I've always found.

'Getting closer,' said the shopkeeper.

I'd narrowed it down to two greens, and went back and forth on those.

'Tricky, isn't it?' said the shopkeeper. She was very close. There was the whiff of perfume. 'Let me look.'

I handed her the costume and stood back.

She was a picture of concentration as she went back and forth on the two colours. 'I think your first instinct was very close. It's either the Dollar Bill or the Minaret.'

'I'm leaning towards the Minaret,' I said.

'Tricky,' said the shopkeeper again. 'Very tricky. See, I think the Dollar Bill might be your answer. Let's put some more light on the situation.'

She handed me back the costume and brought one of the lamps right up to the bank of silks. Together we peered at the colours and swapped them rapidly against the costume. I said that I thought the Minaret was closer.

'No.' The shopkeeper shook her grey bob. 'The Dollar Bill.'

'You think so?'

'I'm absolutely certain,' said the shopkeeper. Her beaky nose was right up close to the silks. 'It's brighter. The Minaret is dull.'

I was sure that the Minaret was the best way to go. I held it against the costume again.

'No, you see?' said the shopkeeper. 'It's going to look muddy compared to the rest.'

'To me the Minaret is the one,' I said, but less certain.

'I think you'd be making a grave mistake,' said the shopkeeper.

'You don't think the Dollar Bill is too bright?' I asked.

'Not for a second. Not for an instant have I thought the Dollar Bill too bright.'

I stood surveying the costume and the two skeins of silk. I wasn't sure anymore. Maybe it was the Dollar Bill.

There was a footstep in the doorway of the shop. Another customer had arrived. Two customers in an empty shopping arcade in the middle of a Blackout. Oh Sew Good wasn't doing too badly. The new arrival was a barrel-like middle-aged woman with a grey mitt of hair. She was wearing a belted coat, even though it was summer. The shopkeeper seemed to know her vaguely. She smiled her V smile and gestured her over.

'Would you mind helping us out here?'

The customer sailed over, a little shy, but pleased to be asked. The shopkeeper held the two greens one after the other against the costume. 'Our friend here is doing some knotwork. Which do you think is a better match, the Dollar Bill or the Minaret? Dollar Bill. Minaret.'

After considering the two colours for a moment, the customer smiled and spoke as if answering a question on a game show, with devil-may-care aplomb. 'The Minaret.'

The shopkeeper paused for a minute. 'Ah, interesting. You're sure? Dollar Bill. Minaret.' She held the greens up to the costume again for good measure. 'Because I'm sure it's the Dollar Bill. Look, look closely.'

The other customer peered closely again. 'No, still the Minaret.'

'Two against one,' I said, and laughed.

'Difficult,' said the shopkeeper. 'I happen to think you're both quite wrong. The Dollar Bill.' She left it dangling.

'No, that one,' said the customer, pointing a chubby finger at the Minaret.

You know how your nose gets tired choosing perfume? That's how my eyes felt. I couldn't have told one green from another if my life depended on it, Dollar Bill, Minaret or Mustard. But I would buy the Minaret, because it was two against one.

'I know how to settle this,' said the shopkeeper. A mad gleam appeared in her eye. 'We need daylight.'

The other customer pointed vaguely at some rug-hooking supplies. 'Ah . . .' But the shopkeeper was on a mission.

'We'll get this right. Lock up the shop, just for a minute, and take the silk out onto the street. Then we will see that the Dollar Bill is the best choice.'

'No, really,' I said. 'No need. I'll take the Minaret.' Although I wasn't at all sure. 'But please, serve this woman first.' I gestured towards the other customer.

The shopkeeper paused. It seemed she might go ahead and serve the other customer, but at that moment a girl of about sixteen appeared in the shop. She bobbed near the door. I had time to notice that she was 'dressed up' in a summer shift and cheap unlined blazer, cream. She lolloped in, in her teenage-girl walk, and went straight up to the shopkeeper. 'I'm here.' Her head wasn't even grown. Her features, her eyes and nose, were big on her face, emerging as if through plaster.

The shopkeeper took off her glasses and sighed. 'Brittany, I've told you, I don't need you today.' She smiled at the other customer and myself. 'Excuse me.'

The girl (Brittany) said, with the smile and a slight whine, 'I just thought I'd come in on the off-chance.'

'No.' The shopkeeper's V-mouth was firm. 'I don't need you today.'

The girl hung her head with theatrical disappointment.

'Or any other day,' added the shopkeeper.

Brittany looked up and gasped. 'But.'

'I've told you,' said the shopkeeper.

'I've come all the way in on the bus,' said Brittany. 'It cost me five dollars twenty.' Here she acknowledged the other customer and myself with a hard-luck smile. 'Crazy.'

'I didn't ask you to do that,' said the shopkeeper coolly. 'Now . . .' She resumed the silk debate. 'Let's go to the daylight.'

'Please,' whined Brittany. She was twisting the strap of her squishy vinyl shoulder bag. I thought it might snap.

I wanted to leave, but I needed that silk. 'I'll take the Minaret,' I said.

'No!' cried the shopkeeper. 'If we go outside, you'll see that the Minaret is all wrong.'

'But now that I'm here,' said Brittany.

'Did you hear me?' said the shopkeeper sharply. Then she sighed. 'Now you're here, you may as well help us choose the silk.'

'Okay!' said the girl. She brightened up and untwisted her bag.

'And when we have finished, you will get on the bus and go home.'

The customer in the belted coat now spoke up. 'I'm wanting a rug-hooking set. It's for my daughter-in-law. She's—'

'This won't take long,' said the shopkeeper, jiggling her keys. 'We'll be back in a jiffy.'

•

A moment later we were all trooping down through the dark complex on the still escalator. Out on Aotea Square, the shop-keeper produced the two silks with a flourish. The rest of us gathered around. The other customer looked around the square, disconcerted. She seemed on the brink of going off, but then she turned her attention to the skeins. Brittany was in boots and all, looking pleased. I held up the costume.

'Now,' said the shopkeeper. 'The Minaret,'—she sounded very sombre—'or the Dollar Bill.'

'I still think the Minaret,' said the other customer.

'I do too,' I said. And I did.

The shopkeeper looked beadily and expectantly at Brittany.

'Oh,' said Brittany, who had been in a daydream. 'I think . . . I think . . .'

We all waited. The shopkeeper did a quick exchange of the silks against the costume, eyeing Brittany like a hen.

Brittany ummed and ahhed.

'Brittany,' said the shopkeeper sharply.

'The Dollar Bill,' said Brittany and smiled.

'There,' said the shopkeeper. 'Two trained people think that the Dollar Bill is the better match. Thank you, Brittany, now you can go.'

'Let's go back inside,' I said. I wasn't even sure which one I'd buy.

'Trained?' wailed Brittany. 'You see, I'm trained.'

'My rug-hooking,' said the other customer.

But Brittany had started to cry. She'd planted herself in the square and tears were running down her cheeks. Her blazer had crumpled and looked, somehow, desolate.

'I just helped you, and you said I was in training!' she said, between sobs, to the shopkeeper.

'I said nothing of the sort.'

'I just helped you.' She looked from the shopkeeper to me. Me!

'Brittany. Go home,' said the shopkeeper.

'I won't.'

We all stood in the square while Brittany cried. At one point I patted her back and she wrenched away.

'Brittany, this is ridiculous,' said the shopkeeper.

'You said I had a job, and I said no to another job, and now I have nothing. And I just spent five dollars twenty on the bus, and I helped you. I helped you!' She gestured at the silks, which to me were beginning to feel like crimes.

'Brittany! I'm sorry, ladies.'

'It's okay,' said the other customer, then to Brittany, 'It's okay, dear.'

Brittany rounded on her. 'It isn't!'

There was another silence while we stood around looking at our feet and Brittany cried. Then she spoke again. 'What does it matter, anyway? The Dollar Bill or the Minaret! Ew, darlings, the Dollar Bill or the Minaret!' I must admit, she did a good impression of a Remuera lady. I wanted to leave. But Brittany was now beside herself. 'What does it matter! The Dollar Bill or the Minaret. You have no clue!' The few people in the square were looking at us as they went by. 'You think this shit matters? Do you? You have no fucking clue!'

Brittany reached out and batted the silks from the shopkeeper's hands. The two skeins flew in an arc and landed a few metres away. Brittany pranced after them and, with her high heels, ground them into the asphalt. When she'd finished she turned and glared at us all triumphantly. 'I don't have any money. I have to walk home.' She clopped off in her high, tottery sandals. The other customer and I bleated after her, offering bus money. She called over her shoulder for us to fuck off. After a few steps she bent to tear off her sandals and continued barefoot across the square.

The rest of us sidled over and looked down at the silks lying on the ground. They were pathetic, mashed and blackened and unravelled. The Dollar Bill and the bloody Minaret.

'Well,' said the shopkeeper. 'I'm sorry about that, ladies. Let's repair to the shop.'

The other customer and I traipsed meekly after her into the complex and up the dead escalators. In the shop it turned out that now there wouldn't be enough of either green for my needs (yes, my needs), so I took all the skeins of the Minaret, and all the skeins of Dollar Bill. I'd have to make do. Plus some gold and silver. The shopkeeper tootled a sigh as she wrapped it all up. I didn't want to buy them. I didn't want to buy anything in this shop, but I had to. If I wanted to go on mending the costume, if I wanted to go on with my business—really, if I wanted to go on with my life, I had to not mind about Brittany.

•

On the way up Queen Street, I felt bad, and the costume and the skeins of silk felt heavy in my hand. But soon I had my mind on other things. In fact, it proved to be an eventful trip downtown, all in all. I remembered I was going to the library and veered off up Vulcan Lane. As I was walking past the Magistrate's Court, I looked right into the foyer and saw that it was strung with lights like exotic fruits, and heard the low insect hum, the white noise of a generator, and it seemed if you were to step inside you would be engulfed in the heavy air of a tropical forest. And as I was standing there, I caught sight of Grant, the lawyer with the dry wit, approaching along the footpath with a woman by his side. She had a bruised face and a yellow dress, and he was in a camel-coloured suit. They were like double-yellow lines. Our eyes met, there was a slight raising of hands, Hi, a pause while Grant decided whether to go any further.

When he spoke, he leaned forward and his speech sounded slurred. 'I suppose you know about Glenda and Art.' He had a bitter, questioning sneer on his face.

A tapeworm of jealousy writhed in my insides. I could hear myself saying, as if it were another person, 'What? *What?*'

The woman with the bruised face seemed to be falling, stumbling. Grant took hold of her arm and propped her up. I was staring at her in a bit of a daze. Her face, up close, was grotesque, yellow, mauve and green, like she'd stepped out of a fairground. I realised I was panting. I repeated, What? Grant was shaking his head, ridiculously. I thought he might have been drunk. I wasn't sure if I'd heard him right. The atmosphere outside the courthouse, the rigged-up lights, the hollow-looking buildings, had a makeshift feel, like a dream. *What?* I said. But Grant walked on, almost dragging the woman, and I watched them make their way into the court. The whole street, the Edwardian buildings, seemed fake, like a film set or another time. I passed the court building—an Edwardian birthday cake—which slipped back into shutteredness, hiding its secret yellow life from the street.

As I continued along Lorne Street towards the library, I gave myself a good talking-to. One, I had probably imagined this whole thing. Two, it couldn't be true because Glenda is crazy. Three, I liked the client. That was what I said to myself. *I liked him. Shane.* Shane. Four, which didn't mean I wanted to be dumped. I'd never liked the idea of being the dumpee. Five, a little more secrecy was in order.

•

I'm a great one for researching, I really am. There was a long row of books on costume. I crouched down to take the biggest from the shelf. (Later I read a book about a giant library assistant.) *The Evolution of World Fashion: From early Egypt to the present with 700 individual figures in full colour.* Ireland wasn't even in it. I felt sorry for the Irish being excluded, then found there was also no China, no South-East Asia, no India and no Pacific. No Africa, no South America. Small world! I picked up *Folk Costumes of the World*, which had eighty magnificent colour plates. Figures smiled out from the pages. Some danced. The introduction went on about how national costumes were often associated with song and dance. England was represented by a Morris dancer in his white trousers and shirt, his red braces and bells strapped to his ankles. English women didn't have a national costume. They would get into difficulties at parties where people were wearing their national costumes, just like me. And there, sharing a page with England, a little sea of white between them, was Ireland: a woman in a close-fitting dress embroidered with knotwork which was, sure enough, like a hose tied up in knots, but nicely. In the twelfth century, apparently, the well-to-do Irish got into bright colours, apart from red which was associated with England. Bright colours were a mark of high social status, and commoners should wear only one colour. So my Irish dancing girls had ideas above their station with their bluey greeny confections. Not to mention the client.

There was a bit about the shoes. How there weren't any for the women, but their bare feet made them graceful. When the English banned dancing in Ireland, the men would teach the steps by sitting down and tapping their fisherman's clogs on the flagstone floor.

All very bloody interesting but it didn't help me with the pattern. The illustration was too pointillist, too blurry, as the figure whirled about dancing, to be any use. I'd expected patterns, diagrams of loops, knots, pathways that led you in and out until you'd forgotten where you started. But there were none. I checked the book out all the same, because I liked it. There was something about New Zealand too, by the way: How the costume of the Maori, the people of New Zealand, for instance, is constructed from grass that were swished vigorously back and forth during hypnotic dance movements.'

I walked back up the hill. At the top of Queen Street, I looked back downtown. Grey. The skin of the city was showing through the tear in the electricity.

By the time I got home, I'd almost forgotten about Oh Sew Good, and the customer-in-a-coat and Brittany, but not so much that I'd forget to tell it in the future. I hope this doesn't constitute self-centredness. I told the story about buying the silks precisely *because* of Brittany. I mean, what a class struggle. I hope she got home alright. I hope she's found a job by now. I'm sure she has. I'm sure she'll be fine. I also put the Grant thing out of my head. I wasn't even sure if I'd seen it. The whole of downtown seemed unreal, dreamlike. You couldn't trust anything anymore. And Glenda. I mean, she was a nutcase.

Anyway I had my silks. I'd have to alternate Dollar Bill and Minaret, to blend them together.

23

I needn't have bothered. What I realised was, he *wanted* to tell me. First of all there was the ridiculous stuff about his jacket. It was quite a song and dance. From one hooked finger he swung a Foodtown bag stuffed like a punching kit. 'Can you mend this?' Grinning like a clown. A tow-coloured suit jacket spilled onto the table, and he dived after it, fingering a spot. 'This.' Under my nose. I held it away to see it—torn buttonhole, minor, almost nothing.

We were back to tension and blushing and carrying on.

'Why?' I knew it was a ruse—the yellow jacket a red herring, and ugly as sin to boot.

'After *that*, of course.' He head-butted towards the costume, which hung over a chair. 'You wouldn't want to put one job ahead of another.'

It was Wednesday. Eleven days into the Blackout. Twelve. And late, almost eight o'clock. We were standing by the table.

He was busy, he said, a busy day. Almost breathless with it.

The jacket, as I said, was awful—the dark yellow had a sheen like a petrolly puddle.

'You don't *wear* this, do you?'

His eyes widened in mild offence. Greenish.

'This is what capitalism does to people.'

He laughed like a drain. 'You're funny.'

I don't know about funny. Unprofessional, yes. I'd never expressed an opinion about a garment before (or an economic system). In fact, I'd never given a toss. They could wear what they bloody liked. But this jacket, it was like sewage, and you put it on to make money.

'You know your problem?' he said. 'You're too privileged.'

What a joke. Art and I lived on the smell of an oily rag. There was his Grandma fund, but that was usually reserved for buying paintings. And—crucial point—it wasn't mine. I should have told the client about my original family. Privileged! We had a Skoda. My sister was a drug addict. I should have told him about how my father ran off with an exchange student, which epitomised our lack of privilege—in fact, was the jewel in the crown of evidence. I'd dined out on this story, literally, for years. I'd told it at dinner parties where, late at night after chucking back enough wine to stock a small bottle store, people spill the beans about how their uncle was a remittance man, or their father had a secret family down south. My story held its own at these parties. It sounded like a Peter Greenaway film (that's what someone said once and I thought it was clever): *The Girl, the Mother, the Father and His Lover*. I would've told the client this story, but he'd already told me about Mr O'Connell, and I felt it wouldn't have stacked up. But privileged. This client with the costume, *Shane*, thinks I'm privileged—that was going too far.

I don't mean to go on about myself. Wasn't someone going to tell me to stop?

Now he was making a great fuss, all rangy fingers, of finding a rumpled bit of paper in his wallet (his nice wallet), and handing it to me. It was the docket I'd written for Trisha on the first day of the Blackout, two weeks before. It seemed a long time ago. I'd spent much of it bumbling around in the dark.

We. We'd spent much of it.

I screwed the docket up and scribbled a new one for the dog-turd jacket, reciting as I went: 'Jacket, men's, yellow, tragic.'

'Oh, come on!'

I tore it from the book and fluttered it at him.

He made a grab at the docket but I whisked it away. We went through this charade a couple more times, laughing, and finally, when I was falling against the red curtain, I let him pluck the docket from my fingers. He folded it and filed it away in his wallet, looking at me the whole time.

I dusted myself off. 'You better rough it up a bit.'

'Oh yeah.' He took it out again and with great seriousness gave it a Chinese burn.

I watched this pantomime.

'Have you ever taken anything to be mended before?'

He shook his head.

'I rest my case.'

I propped the costume up on the table. It just about stood alone, with its embroidered armour. 'Almost finished.'

He squinted at it from afar. 'That was yesterday.' Oh, I was cruel!

I flattened it on the table. It was rough-and-smooth like a feverish dream.

'I would've written you a docket for nothing, by the way. Didn't need to bring your jacket in.'

'Would you?' He flushed slightly. 'Milly's coming home tomorrow night—just for the weekend,' he added. 'So if I could take the thing now.'

I clunked my chair in at the table, and gestured for him to follow suit (yes, suit), but he wouldn't. He folded his arms and positioned himself by the curtain. I had my bag of new silks. I threaded up some of the Minaret green. Licked the silk. We were taught by an elderly nun at school not to do that. It was considered disgusting. I remember deciding then and there, age six, that this was bad advice. I don't think I ever discounted anything so readily. I've licked thread all my life. I glanced up at the client, then poked my needle into blackness. I pushed forward into the blank bit. It was flat and expansive. I was a pioneer. I was finishing the sleeve, for God's sake.

I offered him wine. Well, it was after eight o'clock. The sun was just gone, that exciting loss.

He held up his hand like a stop sign. I poured him tea from the thermos instead. It was stone cold and he didn't touch it, didn't come near the table.

He looked at the naked cuff. 'Is it my imagination, or do you have a way to go?'

'It's your imagination. Either that or you don't know what you're talking about.' I smiled at him.

'I'm sure it's the latter. But why do I feel like I've handed my car over to a mechanic?'

'Don't you trust me?'

He hesitated.

'I'm helping you lie, aren't I?'

'Alright, just keep going.'

'I am. Stop interrupting me.'

'Alright.' He settled in at the table, cleared his throat. He wanted to tell.

•

Two months in a sticky boarding house in Liverpool. His ma bought them a set of cheap clothes at a chain store. They were watching their pennies. The six grand wouldn't last forever.

213

I could just see her, his doughty old mother (that was what I thought, *doughty*), looking at the labels in the shop and saying, *This, this, this* will do nicely. Her certainty, her plucking ability. And in the evening, while their alternative clothes soaked in a bucket, Ma worried about Dad's limp as she heated beans on a single electric coil.

And the Blackout would continue. We'd live on in the damp villa, carrying the light around with us at night, cooking dinner on the roaring 747.

I was starting in on a seaweedy green whorl.

I asked him why New Zealand—I mean, of all places. He shrugged and said maybe there were posters advertising New Zealand in the train station, although he may have been misre-membering it.

Misremembering. That's what he said. I told him I loved that, misremembering.

He paused and said, Do you? I thought, GoGo, you fool. You're a complete fool.

But it can't have been posters in the train station because they didn't go on the train. They didn't go anywhere. They didn't see The Cavern. They went to Liverpool and didn't visit the birthplace of Western culture. All he knew was that the ma was worried about the way the dad walked around on his new knees. They knew what new knees meant in Liverpool. And so Liverpool—which had been the promised land for so long—was now too close to the Wanted card and the Mass card and to the death of Mr O'Connell. Around this time, the dad must have got new papers done. There were ways and means. He'd never asked his dad, but that's what he must've done.

I seem to be telling this. I seem to have taken over.

What it was was: there were postcards from Dreadful and Frightful, who'd washed up in New Zealand, for some reason.

At the bottom of the world! Postcards of lambs and mountains. You could pick hops in the summer, which was really the winter, wrote Dreadful and Frightful in their convent handwriting, rent a whole house and have enough left over to go out on the town on Saturday night, such as the town was. But it was gorgeous. Ma should come over. One of the girls would say, There's a postcard from Dreadful and Frightful. Ma would say, Don't you call your aunties that! The dad scowled. If the family went to New Zealand, Dreadful and Frightful would meet them at Christchurch and help them find a house—a whole house—plus a job for Kevin and a group of girls for Ma to have a gas time with. They said it was paradise. The dad sat on a chair and practised the use of his reconstructed knees as if learning the steps of a dance.

The colour was draining from the room, the white floor going dove-grey.

The client didn't remember their exact route to New Zealand, but it involved a throbbing week in the air. He recalled steam in Dubai, acres of lino in LA, a warm wind in Hawaii. For our purposes: zap to New Zealand. Like a film. A film made by LambChop Productions.

When they wobbled off the plane in Christchurch, Dreadful and Frightful weren't there. They'd left word that they were on a farm on the outskirts of Nelson, picking hops. So the family went on a bus to Nelson, grinding over a mountainous pass, sleeping, and shading their eyes from the blue snow on the alps (I imagine). In Nelson they were told that Dreadful and Frightful had gone to Wellington weeks ago, because that's where the action was. Dreadful and Frightful were good about leaving messages with bearded men standing in the doorways of rickety wooden houses. So the bus to Picton, which turned out to be a tiny seaside village at the top of the South Island, from where they caught the ferry across to Wellington. In a shady street of Wellington, in the fold of a hill, a bearded man told them Dreadful and Frightful had gone on the Limited to Auckland a week ago, because that was where the action was. Piled onto the Limited and slept swaying clickity-clack through the night. In Auckland—you've got it, Dreadful and Frightful had skipped to Aussie. Sydney was where the action was. On the doorstep of a wooden house in a weedy windy suburb of Auckland, their bags around them, Ma broke down. That Dreadful and Frightful! she said. She wasn't going a step further.

'Paradise,' said the client.

He came close to the table. I took his hand and put it on the soft wool. He couldn't feel anything, you could see that a mile off; his unfocused gaze. It was off his map. He took his hand away.

I asked him if all this meant he could never go back and he said, Oh no, of course he could. His father couldn't though. His father still jumped a mile at the sight of a policeman.

The truth was, I was feeling a bit embarrassed that I'd told him my funny little bourgeois story about the national costume at the one-year-old's birthday party. Not when he had this big story to tell. I actually said this to him.

'Your sweatshop is hardly bourgeois,' he said.

I sat back with the costume in my lap. 'Sweatshop!'

'Well, cottage industry.' He looked around at the sewing machine, the cottons. 'It wouldn't be out of place in pre-industrial England. You don't need to worry about being bourgeois.'

'It's the Blackout,' I said.

'Even without the Blackout.'

'I thought you thought I was privileged. You can't have it both ways.'

'You can actually.'

'Oh really.'

His face was leaning in. It was bluish. Our eyes met, stuck a moment, then away. I was bemused, and perhaps a little annoyed. Before I had time to reply, he asked where my husband was.

'Out.'

'I know out. I mean what does he do?'

'He's working on a film at the moment,' I said.

I heard myself say *feelm*. I didn't really mean his transcribing job to come out that way.

'I notice you don't have any clients,' he said.

'Have you noticed it's half past eight in the evening?' I asked.

'But even in the late afternoon, no one.' He sang, *Where have all the clients gone?* I hate that tune.

'It's the Blackout. People aren't coming into town.'

'I thought you said they were coming to you.'

'Well, they're not.' I hurried on. 'People are moving out of the city,' I said. I'd heard this on the news. I felt on safer territory. I didn't like being accused of I-don't-know-what. I was a hard worker. 'They've set up offices in South Auckland, in West Auckland,' I said. 'Did you know that?'

'I did know that.'

'They're going to Wellington, Hamilton, Sydney even. Or they're staying home. There's nothing doing.'

'That's good,' he said. 'I mean, if it's just the Blackout. You wouldn't want to be living on what you can earn from one . . . dress.'

'I don't have many expenses.'

Which was true, not with 'the farm' bankrolling our villa conversion.

I'm not a materialist, you see. I'm really not. In fact, I quite despise materialism.

'What will you do if it goes on?' he asked.

'They're fixing the cables.'

'What say people forget to come back?' He was being ridiculous. 'What say they find other menders and keep going to them?'

'I almost have an MA in English.'

Now he laughed. 'Businesses are going bust all over town,' he said. 'No clients for a couple of weeks and already you're going down the tube.'

'I'm not going down the tube,' I said.

'You're already down it. Why didn't you rent another space, so you could keep working?'

'Because I don't have to,' I said. I was getting tetchy. I had choices. I could do all sorts of things.

'You're down the tube,' said the client. 'But you know what? I think you like it down there.'

This was really annoying. I came from an educated family, but we weren't capitalists. My father drove a Skoda. And this business, it was really just for fun. I told the client there were plenty of other things I could do.

'What?' he asked. To give him his due, he was genuinely curious.

'Lots of things.'

He suddenly said, 'Do you want kids?'

I felt myself blush. 'That's a bit personal, isn't it?'

'This is personal.' He indicated the costume.

This was true. I'd seen it all undone. I'd taken liberties with it. I shrugged—about the kids thing. (And by the way, I'd been popping little pink pills for years.)

'What say they want to go to university, like you, these kids?'

I was kind of outraged.

'They'll be hustling for the highest-paying job they can get,' he was saying. 'They'll be importing titanium.'

They wouldn't.

Something occurred to me. 'This is all hypothetical. Like your imaginary daughter. The one Milly talked about.'

He blushed. *He* blushed! He was shaking his head.

I started telling him how Pinnacle Power had quadrupled their profits and halved their employees in four years.

He said they had to do that otherwise they would've gone broke.

I told him how they increased managers' salaries by thirty percent.

Of course, he said, otherwise they couldn't get anyone to work at that level.

He shifted in his suit. Yes, his *suit*. 'It's not ready, is it?'

I peered down at the costume, which was an ink blot in the grey room. 'No,' I said proudly. 'Come back tomorrow.'

'I'll come by after work, latish, I have a busy day.'

'It'll be ready.'

'Will it? And I'll tell you about paradise. Sometimes I wished Dreadful and Frightful had taken it into their heads to go to hell.'

'But remember I know that bit already,' I said.

He stood up. 'Yeah, you probably do. Thanks for the tea.' Which he hadn't touched. Suddenly so formal. I couldn't stand it.

'You're welcome, as they say in America.' He was going. 'Wait,' I said. I wanted him there. I wanted to keep him there. 'About the Woolthamlys' company, the fruit drying, remember?'

'Yes, of course,' he said. 'Taranaki Dried Fruit.'

'They're going to ride it out, that's what they said.'

'Oh. That might not be very wise, but still.'

I groped my way across the room to get a torch. I shone it on the floorboards all the way to the front door, like an usher. A lovely yellow dot.

On the doorstep he said, 'Will this affect you?'

'What?'

He laughed. 'If they lose the company, of course.'

'No!' I was shocked. 'I'm not a materialist.'

'But you could lose your little life here.'

'My little life?' My cheeks flushed. I felt his face close in the dark, briefly, almost to touch.

'What?' he said.

And I said, What, nothing.

He shambled across the veranda and down the planky steps. I was formulating a theory: if we don't have any big stories to tell, we start feasting on ourselves. We eat our hands. It's called literary theory. Actually, I just thought of that.

There was a shred of lilac light over the Waitakeres. I heard him on his mobile phone as he walked to his car, an urgent tone, authoritative. I could tell it wasn't Milly, and I was relieved. So relieved some kind of chemical flooded through me. It felt like a colour. And as I stood on the doorstep I saw that the tenants from the villa one up from us, who I'd only seen once or twice in passing, were moving out, about four of them loading their stuff into a van and yelling at each other to hurry because the light was going. A woman with a beehive hairdo like Amy Winehouse noticed me in the gloom and called out as if we'd been having a conversation—they were over the Blackout, she said. As they slammed the van doors they all called out, Bye, bye, as if they knew me, and drove off. For a moment I didn't know whether they'd ever been real. I had the creepy feeling that electricity merely gave us the impression of lives being lived, but that once the power was gone there was nothing.

24

In the morning I made a few calls looking for *other premises*. To no avail. Every room, garret, nook and cranny within cooee of the city was spoken for. As I had predicted. I collapsed on the couch and read some of *Jane Eyre*, which was quite long, thankfully.

I looked out the window. I remembered that once when I was about ten, Mary-France and Dad (arguing all the time), with Lisa and me in the back seat, drove as far as you could up the steepest street in the Southern Hemisphere, which is in Dunedin (because Dunedin was laid out in Edinburgh by a Scottish town planner who knew nothing about the Otago hills). Near the top of the street there was a sign saying you couldn't take your car any further, with a cartoony picture of tyres skidding. You might fall off the street, like falling off the world. We all got out of the car and walked, or rather crawled, loped, low down like our ancestors, the few metres to the crest of the hill. You felt that if you stood upright or stood still you would slide, or worse, topple, all the way down to the bottom.

(And then there was Pinnacle Power. Ah, aren't coincidences wonderful! You couldn't make this stuff up. That's what I thought, actually, those afternoons as I worked on the costume: this was all just put in front of me. But what to make of it? I mean, isn't it the thing?)

It did seem that when I began working with my hands, I might have begun a long glide downwards—me and my sister too. Nobody really knew what Lisa did except shoot up when she could. There was a sense that the civilisation of a family had reached its peak, its golden age, and this was the westward slope. It was alright, though. You could do a lot worse.

•

The client started straight in on the chair from the side of the road. Didn't mention the costume, just stabilised his briefcase against the couch, sat at the table and said his dad found a chair by the side of the road. I poured tea. And was relieved, under the circumstances, that he didn't ask after the costume. I was plugging away at the cuff, alternating the Dollar Bill and the Minaret. It was a crisp evening, cooler, and the sunlight falling into the room was milky. Perfect for close work, for knotwork. I wanted to hear about New Zealand. How it was, and so on? I mean, hello (as they say in America), I live here.

I might as well just tell you myself. I might be leaving out a few ums and ahs.

It was bright. The cicadas fizzed all the time and the lawn out the back was springy like a mattress. It was awful, a wasteland. He thought, Where is everyone? They were in their cars. The immigrants were the only ones walking. They got lost every time they went out. They walked in circles like zombies, as if they were dead.

That's what he said. They had died and gone to paradise.

•

In paradise the houses were wooden and the gaudy sunlight chopped everything up. *Like bunting*, he said. When they got to New Zealand it was summer. In *January*, he said, all topsy-turvy, everything shaken up like a snow bubble. I know, a *snow bubble*. The metaphors. I loved them. And I loved *misremember*. I thought I'd like to do that. I'd like to misremember and toss it off, as if it were nothing, nothing to get it all wrong. Even if it were serious.

The New Zealand house was flimsy like a carton. His ma put on the apron she'd worn on the ferry under her coat, an apron similar to one of Mabel's—*That*, he said, pointing (although his mother's apron wouldn't have been made of organza because it would have needed to actually function as an apron). And cleaned briskly, like blessing herself even in the new godforsaken place. It was a dive—holes in the walls, mould on the ceiling, no working door handles. Later he realised his parents were ripped off for years, the rent they paid to the slum landlord. It was a kind of paradise. They'd never had carpet before and he regarded it as an entity, the way skin is an organ. There was a bath. He watched his mother scrubbing pink mould off the bath like you watch TV. No emotion. The wind got up in the late morning and exploded all through the rest of the day. It was a pattern he came to recognise.

End of story. He leaned back in his chair.

My hands in the costume. I looked up at the Carrara ceiling. A wedding cake. My chair creaked.

'Your husband?' said the client.

I put on a puzzled expression. My husband? Anyway, Art would be late. He was going to hear Billy Bragg over in Devonport with Glenda and Grant and some other old uni friends. I didn't think of myself as privileged. Privilege was a dirty word. I offered him wine. It seemed decently late enough. I poured it at the sideboard.

'Do you love him?' he asked.

I think my mouth fell open. 'Of course. What a question!'

'I know. Sorry. There's just something.' He stopped. 'It's almost finished, isn't it?'

'I know, Milly.'

'Actually, Milly.'

Yes?

Wasn't coming home tonight after all. He was going to her for the weekend instead.

Oh he was? To Wellington?

To Wellington. For that he would not require a costume.

'Oh, so there's no urgency,' I said.

He paused, then cackled. 'I'm sorry, but this is funny.'

'Is it?'

'Yes.' He wiped his eyes. 'Now there's no urgency! How long has this been going on?'

I didn't think it was that funny.

'I'm sewing the bloody thing. Look.' I held the costume up as if saying cheers, salut!

He settled down. 'Cheers.' With his glass.

'Cheers.' With the costume.

It wasn't that funny.

'Dad found a wicker chair by the side of the road.'

Oh, the chair.

He's telling it now. I give up.

'Dad appeared in the doorway, all chair. He said it was like bringing a hot-air balloon home, in that wind. It just about took him out to sea, like Phileas Fogg. Ma and the girls thought this was great. I didn't. I didn't like this development.'

He didn't like this development.

'Why? Why not?'

'You'll see. The chair was sort of round and chunky, like the basket of a hot-air balloon. It had paisley cushions.'

'Paisley!'

224

'I know. You wouldn't read about it. We needed a chair. I wasn't complaining about the chair. It wasn't that. It was that Dad had noticed it. A chair by the side of the road! He'd thought about sitting down. It was anathema. My dad. He'd always been a consumed man, burning. It was there on his face all the time, his eyes smouldering. He'd never had a job, but he didn't sit around all day. He talked to the men in the street. He paced around the house and thought with his intense expression and then he'd mutter to Ma he was going out, and grab his jacket and be out the door, and even the way he walked along the street showed he was a man with a mission. When he came home, he'd done something, I don't know what, but you could see it coming off him. No furniture on his back, no bloody chair from the side of the road.'

'Right,' I said. I had to say something.

Wine. Costume in my lap. Sun coming in the bloody window.

'So anyway, Ma and the girls thought it was great and they were all laughing about it being paisley. They were going to sit on paisley, put their arses on paisley.

'Ma was fixing the unravelled wicker and saying the chair had been waiting for us to come along. It was sent. Dad said, It was not sent! It was lying by the side of the road because someone else decided they were too good for it. That was more of the old Dad. Dana and Sharon had turns sitting in the chair and bouncing on it until Ma said they'd break it, and to give me a turn. But I was not going to sit in that chair. So the girls had more turns, and started fighting about it, until Dad said, Let your mammy sit in it, for God's sake. But Ma said, I'm too busy to sit in a chair, I have the tea to get—*you* sit in it. This was somehow a threat. Dad just walked into the bedroom. I watched the muscles of his back, which were as expressive as anyone's face, frowning. I knew how he felt, because I felt the same. Ma and my sisters

225

were stupid and blind because they couldn't see. I could see it. Dad had been a hero. He was a hero, and now he was looking for furniture by the side of the road. Maybe not looking, but seeing. *Seeing* it. And what I realised, but much later, was: he continued to fight for the cause, while slopping around the house in slippers, fiddling with the knob on the radio (when we got a radio). The day he left Ireland he began starving himself like Bobby Sands in Long Kesh.'

I was kind of blown away by this. 'Wow,' I said (again). 'You mean metaphorically?'

'Yes, metaphorically.'

'Is this true? You're not embroidering it, are you?' I was just about having a meltdown over Kevin McGrath starving himself, and I had to make a smart, ironic comment about it. This is what's wrong with our society, myself included.

'It's not a story,' said the client. He did his blowing mannerism. 'It's true. And for a long time, no one sat in the chair. It was like the bounty of the new land, and we didn't use it. But later I thought, What's the point of being here if you don't take advantage?'

He was looking at me.

'Oh, that's a question?'

What *was* the point? But I didn't have to answer that because I was born here. Hah!

He didn't wait for an answer anyway. 'We shouldn't have been here, of course. After three months we were overstayers. There was stuff in the paper about how there were too many Poms here.' He laughed. 'We were Poms! To all intents and purposes.'

He patted his pocket as if he'd forgotten something. His fags.

Then he was going on again. I wasn't stitching. 'But nothing ever happened. We enrolled at the school, nothing happened. Dad walked about with his wonky knees, craning around because he was worried about being caught. They could still have got him for whatever he did the night of the parade. He would've been extradited. Nothing happened. Later I found out they were too busy doing dawn raids on Pacific Islanders to be bothered with us. In fact, there were more English overstayers than Pacific Islanders.'

•

Now there was a little intermission. He asked, by the by, how much it was all going to cost. All these hours. I told him it would be the same as I quoted, a hundred and sixty dollars. He was aghast and I panicked. I was a money-grubber, and money was so obscene.

'Well,' I said, backtracking, 'it might be a bit less.'

'No,' he said. 'I mean, is that all? How much do you pay yourself an hour?'

An hour? It varies. It must. Obviously.

He shook his head. 'How do you make a living?'

'I make a good enough living,' I told him. 'What more could I want?'

He took this as a serious question, and a comic expression of pondering appeared on his face. Finally he said, 'I wouldn't know where to start.'

Fine. I motored on with the knotwork. The gold silk was glinting in the sunlight.

'The thing is, things aren't very good at the moment. You have heard of the Asian crisis?'

'Ye-ah,' I lied as if it was blinking obvious.

The truth is, I was in my years-long phase of not reading the papers. It started at university. The news seemed too non-theoretical.

I laughed gaily. Yes, gaily. 'Change of subject. New Zealand,' I said.

Because I knew New Zealand.

'Well.' He sipped his wine. 'Dana and Sharon came home and said, We've met some Girls. As if they weren't girls themselves because they'd come from away. These Girls, who lived across the road, had things—toys, a game called Trouble. The only problem was you couldn't understand them. They quacked. We got to know them all, of course, over the years. One of them was gorgeous, lovely, when she was older. But I remember Ma asking if they were Catholic, and Dana saying she didn't know, and Dad saying, As if it matters, it doesn't matter here. Ma said she knew it didn't matter, she was just asking out of curiosity, and what were their names? They were Penny and Olivia and Linda. Ma said, Oh they're Orangies. With a look of satisfaction on her face.

'Dana and Sharon ran about screaming with The Girls, and then they disappeared again into the mysterious New Zealand house, which was so bright on the outside that the inside looked dark by comparison.'

'Like this one?'

'Well.' He glanced about the bright front room.

'I mean the back. My workroom.'

'Your workroom. Yes, like that.'

A little something crossing his face. That day. The doorway. Where I hid him. GoGo, you're a nutcase.

He went on: 'When they came home—Dana and Sharon—they said they'd played another game, Monopoly, which was set in London where the Prods lived but they were buying it up and renting it out at exorbitant prices. I'd never seen them so excited. I hated it, because how could you abandon Clonard, just like that? They told me there were boys along the street, several. They were called The Boys. I went out to the gate and looked up the street. Sure enough.'

'Sure enough!'

'I saw The Boys crossing the road. They were like a pack of urchins, all scruffy. They were white kids, but they were the colour of saveloys. I was too pale, and too well dressed, in my new Liverpool clothes, so I went inside. Eventually I met them all, of course. They were my friends for the next five years. But that day, I thought I looked a right idiot with my pale skin and my new clothes. I'd been part of a gang of Clonard boys and now I was only one boy. Now I was shy, although I hadn't been before. You know how I felt?'

'How?'

'As if I'd left my skin lying on the road in Clonard. I'd shed a skin.'

The dress in my lap. It was all weird. Boy's skin, woman's dress.

'After I'd seen The Boys, I went inside and said to all and sundry, I hate New Zealand. Ma said, Would you rather be back in Clonard wondering if your Dad's going to come home in a box? I said, Yes, low so neither Ma nor Dad, who was tacking up curtain rails, could hear. Yes, the freedom fighter was tacking up curtain rails. *Much* rather, I said.'

•

The sun was slanting into the room. A beeline for—yes, the costume. I had to turn sideways from it. There's a hole in the ozone layer, you know, and New Zealand cops it more than anywhere. It's a bit of a worry. My hands were, at this point, embedded in the costume as if they loved it, but not moving, just lying there with it, but he didn't notice and I couldn't be bothered doing any more. I was sick of this costume, if you want to know the truth. Sick of it.

And he was rabbiting on anyway. He was away. About how his dad got the first job of his life. But I'll tell it. It's quicker. Remember, a few ums and ahs, a few sighs, a few gawuffs. Patting for fags, pacing about the room.

Anyway.

His dad went to the Labour Department and came home with a job more or less tucked under his arm. Had the interview, got the papers, everything, start next Monday. Grinning all over, fit to bust and saying to the ma, Concepta, there're all these jobs and no one wants them, all over this board! And you just go up and take one and go up to the counter and they send you for an interview. It's like the jobs grow on trees. So he'd found this job, apparently, and it was like a leaf, it was like a fucking leaf growing on a tree. And he said (apparently) that if you took that board with the jobs on it to the Brew and said anyone could apply for them, even Catholics, there'd be the biggest mob they'd ever seen in Belfast, including on the twelfth.

It was for the railways. A trainee shunter, he said. He'd be doing shiftwork, all hours of the day and night. The ma said, Okay, good (apparently). That night they had lamb for dinner. They knew where the *next* meal was coming from. Courtesy of the railways. And the parents had beer, and the dad went to sleep in the chair from the side of the road. If they'd been in Clonard they would've kept going all night, talking and getting hilarious and maybe having a dance if the wives came in, and then getting serious, as the night wore on, and sending the kids to bed because it was not for little ears. But now it was just them, the father, the mother, the kids, in paradise, and so the dad went to sleep.

They should've died. They should have all been dead.

On the first day of his job the dad was on Mornings, and was up at the crack of dawn, and the client—Shane—watched him drinking his tea at the kitchen bench, because there was still no furniture, apart from the chair. It was light early because it was summer. The ma was cutting the dad's lunch, and when she'd finished she brushed off her hands and put the packet next to him and went off to get dressed, humming. As soon as she'd gone there was an odd, animal noise. The dad had his tea on an angle about to spill, and tears were pouring down his cheeks. Shane hesitated, and wondered if he should run for the ma, but somehow he knew that the dad had been saving these tears for when the ma was out of the room. He stood there. It was like the world was coming to an end, because, well, this was a man crying, and he was crying like a baby, and the only other time he'd cried was when Bobby Sands died. Shane edged in close, which he hoped would make the dad stop, anything for him to stop. The boy didn't know what to do, because wasn't it meant to be the other way around, a kid crying and the parent comforting? Maybe it was topsy-turvy in the Southern Hemisphere, where grown men cried and kids, well—Shane suddenly hurled himself at the dad and hugged the dad's waist. The dad was saying through his sobs that he was sorry, he couldn't explain it, son. He knocked back his tea, tipping the cup back to drain every last drop as he always did. He seemed to recover and he said, My father was unemployed from the age of thirty and I've never had a job and now I have a job and *you'll* have a job. And here it became apparent that the dad hadn't recovered because he let out such a loud sob that Shane thought the ma would come running and be upset and then the girls would wake up and everyone would be upset, but she didn't. The sob must have been almost silent, something between them, just felt. The dad said again, *You'll* have a job, when you're grown up you'll have a job. Shane said he would, he'd get a job, don't worry. The dad was saying, That's my lad, you'll get a job that's a damn sight better than your old dad's. Shane was saying no he wouldn't—the dad was a freedom fighter, he'd risked his life for the armed struggle—of course Shane wouldn't have a better job than that. There was no better job. But the dad said fiercely, You'll get a better job than me, lad, much better. And Shane kept saying, No I won't, Dad, I won't. The dad suddenly exploded. For

God's sake, are you stupid? Why the hell d'you think we came to this godforsaken country at the end of the earth? Shane was alarmed. Godforsaken? He'd thought they were meant to be happy about coming here. Ma had shushed him when he said how much he hated it. So the dad was allowed to hate it. The dad was in a trigger-happy mood. Shane hesitated. Whatever he said would be the wrong answer. But Dad wanted an answer. Why d'you think we came here then? Shane licked his lips. Why? *Why?* thundered Dad. Because of the Mass card, said Shane. Dad stared at him. Because of the *Mass* card? Is that what you think? Shane said he didn't know. The dad stared out the window. The fucking Mass card, he said, we could've moved down the road to get away from that. We could've gone anywhere. We came here for you! We came to the end of the earth for you and your sisters, so you can have a better life, a better life entirely than me or your Ma or your Grandpa and Granny ever dreamed of. He sank down a bit, exhausted. That's why.

The ma could be heard moving around in the bedroom and the dad seemed to come out of some sort of dream or nightmare. He hugged Shane quickly. Don't worry, son, I'm going off to my first job and I can't believe it. Be happy for your old Dad.

The ma came into the kitchen and said, Kevin, the bus, it's twenty past. And the dad nodded and took his pathetic packet of sandwiches that the ma had packed for him and his jacket, and kissed them both—kissed them, the man who'd probably picked off an Orangie on the twelfth—and he went down the steps and the ma and Shane waved him off from the doorstep.

In the evening the dad was so tired he didn't eat his tea or wash off the dirt from the railway yards. He fell into bed. The ma hauled off his boots and shut the bedroom door. It was broad daylight. He was thirty-eight years old and doing the job of a sixteen-year-old.

When the dad got his first pay, they all met him in town and bought clothes at Farmers. More clothes, only better. The family looked spick and span. On the way home on the bus, the dad said, Now we'll look like everybody else. But they didn't, they looked like immigrants. The father added, Like everybody else in this godforsaken fucking place. People on the bus stared. Shane hissed, Dad, we need to not draw attention to ourselves! He wanted to fit in.

They didn't fit in. Shane wanted to look ragged like The Boys, but instead he wore the clothes he would've worn in Ireland if they'd had two pennies to rub together, which they hadn't. He remembered the ma asking why the rich children (everyone was rich apart from them) looked like peasants. He didn't know. All he knew was he wanted to look like a peasant too. But they couldn't afford it.

That's it.

He put the wineglass to his lips. He'd finished. He patted his pocket. 'I'll just pop out for a fag.'

While he was gone I tossed the costume over the back of a chair and got up and stretched my legs. I caught sight of him on the veranda, chugging away. I ran my finger over the spines of books. *The Post-Colonial Studies Reader, Outside in the Teaching Machine, We Shall Not Cease*. The room now seemed like a crucible of sunlight, which any moment would be tipped out. The light would slip through my fingers. There would be nothing I could do.

He sat on the couch, which was intensely red.

'There was another incident.'

'Oh, what?'

'Well, a couple.' He smiled. 'The school, and a piano. Seeing you're still going.' Flapped at the costume.

You know what? I should've been giving titles to these stories. *The Rats. The List, The Piano Lesson.*

'Wine?'

I went to the kitchen and fetched crackers, salami (I know, grease near the garment), and a jar of artichoke hearts, the ubiquitous dried apples. Yes, *fetched.* As I came back along the passage I could see sunlight like liquid running under the door.

I poured red.

'Thanks.'

'Blackout food,' I said.

He ignored this detail. He was neutral about the Blackout. I loved the Blackout. I'd never lived so well. He scoffed the food though.

I could have provided a few titles for myself: *The Pole House, The Dropout, Rip Burn Snag.* But I didn't.

Okay, so, *The School.*

I'll tell it.

(This was great. The costume over the back of the chair. He didn't even notice. Instead, we raised our glasses into the last of the sun. Cheers.)

The ma (he said) went to enrol the kids at the local Catholic school, and she was gone a long time. The dad was at home. (He was on Evenings.) All the time the ma was out, the dad was like a cat on hot bricks, pacing back and forth. The empty New Zealand house was perfect for pacing. In Clonard you'd encounter a wall within a step or two, but here the dad could pace to his heart's content. The girls were next door with The Girls. Shane said to the dad, Dad, don't worry (all of twelve years old), there aren't any snipers here. The dad stopped in his tracks and looked at Shane, and he said, Don't you go thinking Belfast is dangerous and the rest of the planet is safe. Otherwise you may as well go and get yourself a job on Fleet Street. Shane said, I'd never do that, not in a million years. And the dad nodded, Good lad, I know you wouldn't. Human nature was the same everywhere, he said, it just depended on circumstances how people behave. Shane said, I know, Dad.

But the ma still wasn't coming back. Shane said she was probably having a cup of tea with the nuns and the dad laughed and said, You're probably right there. Because Ma was always inviting the sisters and the priests in for a cup of tea and they seemed to be her friends, whereas a lot of people didn't think nuns and priests were friend material. They were too holy or weird, or dressed in too much black. But the ma got on with them like a house on fire and they always had a great old yak. The dad would hang about the edges, a bit nervous because he wasn't sure if they weren't too holy to be friends with, but he'd end up having a bit of a laugh too.

Except in the end they didn't come to the Clonard house, nobody did, because the dad had had the Mass card.

The client was thundering through the dried apples.

When the ma finally came home the dad seemed to stifle his happiness at seeing her alive. He stopped halfway towards hugging her and narrowed his eyes. What is it, Concepta? (he said). The ma had an odd expression on her face. She sat down in the chair from the side of the road. She said, They're to go to the state school. I had to get the bus to Mount Albert to enrol Shane at the intermediate school. And the girls will go to Mount Albert Primary.

There was a silence like the moment after an explosion, shattered by the dad going, *What?*

The ma said that was the way it was, St Mary's was full. It had a waiting list. The principal had put Sharon and Dana on it. It wasn't worth it for Shane because he only had one year left at primary school. Shane could hear the dad saying, way in the distance, *A waiting list!* But he'd flown into his own panic. He couldn't go to the state school. He'd be murdered. The ma was saying, You won't be murdered at all, this is New Zealand. But he would be murdered.

And then it occurred to him that all was not lost. This would be the deciding factor. Now, because of the state school, they would all go back to Clonard, to the squat, and the woman and her five—no, four—children would give it back because that was only decent. Shane would run outside and find his friends again, the gang of boys tossing rocks over the barricade, and they'd call out to him, Shane! Shane! And they'd admire his new clothes. And he'd start mucking around with them as if nothing had happened, as if New Zealand had never happened, as if it didn't exist on the face of the fucking earth. And when he went inside for tea, he'd even find his Superman lying on the floor, kicked into a corner. The new kid wouldn't have taken it after all. So it was good it had turned out like this. Thank fucking Christ for the state school.

They didn't go back. Obviously.

Meanwhile the dad was pacing about (again). He had the look of when he was planning something back home. He was saying to the ma, But they *have* to take Catholic children, surely they do, and the ma was saying, No they don't, they don't have to. Surely we have a right, said the dad. No we don't, said the ma, who looked like she was getting to that point where she'd say, *I'm too tired to talk anymore*, like she did sometimes. But she said, There's a waiting list and what's more, not only Catholic children are on it. Dad stopped in his tracks. You mean Orangies are on the waiting list? The dad laughed. Yes laughed, even though Shane might die at the state school. (Shane hated him.) Prods wanting to go to a Catholic school? This couldn't be true. Well, said the ma, not necessarily Prods—they could be anything, Jewish or Hindu, they could be atheists. They'll be Prods, said the dad. Who else would want to infiltrate a Catholic school? And they take them! They fucking take them! Five percent, said the ma. Five percent non-Catholic. Jesus fucking Christ, said the dad.

Shane said it didn't matter anyway, because they were going home, but no one heard him.

The dad was saying, God Almighty, we come all the way from the other side of the world because we're Catholic, when it comes down to it, no other fucking reason. We've been drummed out of our own country because we're Catholic, and we come to *this* country because they tell us you can practise your own religion and nobody gives a damn, nobody gives a toss whether you pray to the sun.

The ma interrupted. No one gave a toss about that in Ireland either, when it came down to brass tacks.

The dad said he knew that. Of course he fucking knew that. But anyway. Now, *now*, their kids were being turned away from the Catholic school in favour of fucking Prods. And after all they've been through (the kids, he meant). They were more Catholic (the kids, he meant) than that nun's little finger.

Actually, said the ma, she wasn't a nun. And the ma put her head back in the rickety chair and closed her eyes. The dad said (darkly), I might have known. She was an ordinary person, Mrs Somethingorother, was she? The ma, still with her eyes closed, said, Yes, she was an ordinary person. Jesus, said the dad, the *princi*pal is an ordinary person. The ma said the principal had told her she was of the Anglican faith herself. The dad was asking, Is this England, for fuck's sake? What's someone doing being an *Anglican* here? This is New Zealand! The dad went over to the window and stared out into the windy garden as if to verify that this was New Zealand. And at a Catholic school! He shook his head.

Shane looked at his back. The tense, muscled back that was like a face. Shane would die at the state school. He was being sacrificed for the dad, while the dad lived on in New Zealand. He felt hatred filtering through his body like dye. Like the barium meal the ma had to eat once when they thought she had a tumour, and she told them all about it, how the barium showed up brightly on the X-ray. That was how he felt. A meal of hatred glowing in his intestines. He let out a wail. The dad looked at him as if he was mad, fucking crackers. *What?* Without opening her eyes the ma reached out from the tottering chair and patted Shane. It's not like that here, son, don't you worry. The dad closed his eyes for a moment too. With both the ma and the dad with their eyes closed, it seemed that Shane was the only one left on the planet. Dad's face ironed out into something floppy and plain, like a sheet off the line. Then he opened his eyes and said to Shane, Don't you worry, you're going to the Catholic school. I'm going down to St Mary's straight away to have a word with the ordinary person. You and your sisters have a right to be at that school. I'm going down there. I'll just have a cup of tea first. Shane nodded. Of course the dad wouldn't let him be murdered at the state school. The dad was a hero. In the row, the dad was the most famous hero.

After he'd had his tea, the dad said he didn't feel like going down to the school that afternoon. He said he was too emotional and he'd probably give the ordinary person an earful he'd regret and then they'd be put on some fucking blacklist and the kids would never be allowed to set foot in the school. He'd go the next day. The ma kept her eyes closed through all this, even refusing the cup of tea which sat cooling on the floor beside her.

By the next day the dad was asking what the fucking use was anyway. He didn't go down to St Mary's to have a word with the ordinary person. And so for three weeks Shane lived in terror of being murdered at the state school. He'd never feared death back in Clonard. Even if he had, Clonard was worth death. It was worth joblessness, poverty and death. He hated paradise.

He was beaten up on the first day at school for being a whingeing Pom. They thought he was a Brit. And he hadn't bloody complained about anything. That night, he put his broken nose an inch from the dad's. He could feel the dad's breath. *What?* The dad was the reason they'd come to New Zealand. Shane said, I told you I'd be murdered at the state school. He growled the last word, like an animal, a dog. The dad looked away.

•

I remember the odd thing. I remember the cold, mushroomy clay under the pole house. The ironed smell of Sister Jude's embroidery being unwrapped. I remember the wind.

25

There was a period of restlessness. The client staring out the window. Me folding my arms and thinking. Yes, thinking. The client on the veranda having another fag. Me going to the kitchen for food, wine. Suddenly he appeared there with plates and things. (Never say 'suddenly', because it isn't ever really sudden.) His face went like a prune.

'What's that smell?'

'Oh,' I said, 'it's the waste disposal.' I felt kind of nervous.

Then he was under the sink looking at the pipes, asking for a wrench, which I found miraculously in the kitchen drawer.

'And a bucket.'

I got one.

Soon there was the sound of something tumbling wetly down, and the smell—well. Then he was charging through the kitchen with the bucket, saying out the side of his mouth, Out of my way, and I heard him pounding around in the undergrowth of the garden. He came back, and ran water through the waste disposal while we alternately gagged and had hysterics. I guess because, like a high wind, a smell is horrible and funny. And we kept laughing and gagging, and something had gone, something had given way, and he said, Why didn't you tell me, and I said, I don't know.

•

In the front room, after all that, the sun was almost gone. I shrugged on my Nom*d cardigan and safety-pinned it up. The client sat on the couch and ate another bag of dried apples.

'These are good,' he said.

'What about The Piano?' I said. 'We were up to.'

He was chewing again. 'Ma wanted to buy one. Dad's job.' He smiled, pointing at his mouth.

I'll be telling this one. I cuddled the costume.

'And there was nothing else to do.'

Like Sam Hunt's dog.

Paradise was boring.

He didn't mind going back to the piano.

Going back?

Exactly. But he pleaded with the ma not to buy the new-old piano from the old woman along the street. She'd seen it advertised in the Musical Instruments column of the *Dominion*, which she scanned down like an abseiler.

An abseiler. I loved that.

But the Ma ploughed ahead. This was providence, like the chair. They come all the way from Belfast and want a piano, and someone in their street has one for sale. And a good price. This was the universe telling them something. Telling us what? asked the dad. That there's a piano for sale, said Shane. The ma said, Keep quiet, you. They went to the house where the piano was for sale. The smell of cats greeted them at the door like a butler.

A butler.

Then came the woman herself. Gradually you saw cats as your eye grew accustomed to the darkness. They were everywhere, on every chair, on piles of newspapers, on the piano stool, and even an orange one curled on top of the piano like gum oozed out of the wood. In Clonard the ma would've rolled her eyes at Shane and said to this woman, Thank you very much and goodbye. Not here. What's more, the piano was a write-off. The case had a funny shape, as if someone had gripped it by the shoulders and shaken it. Even from a distance you could see a galaxy of borer holes. Ma nudged Shane to try the thing. The piano stool had a cat on it. Shane looked back at the woman. She gestured him to push it off. He sat down on a thatch of cat hair. The old woman went about her business, fondling a cat and watching Shane out of the corner of her eye. In the moment with his hands poised above the keys, he wanted to go back to Belfast more than anything in the world. He didn't care about the Wanted card or the Mass card. He'd rather that than be sitting at this horrible piano in a room full of cats, and the room dark compared to the glare outside. But there was nothing to be done. He played something.

'What?'

'I don't know. "The Happy Farmer".'

He pushed the costume out of my hands. I looked up, surprised.

'What?'

'Can I tell you this? Will you listen?'

'Of course,' I said. I sat back.

'"The Happy Farmer". It was all I could think of to play. As soon as I started, a mangy cat leapt off the top of the piano. The piano was terrible, of course—notes missing, the dampers gone. "The Happy Farmer" could've been almost anything, but it wasn't. I realised I hated it. I couldn't stand it. I got up from the piano. I thought we'd be going home soon—or at least back to the house we lived in. (That's the way to feel at home, by the way, find somewhere where you feel even less at home.) We'd go back home and leave this old nutcase to her cats and her piano.

But Ma was getting the bright money out of her purse (the money was so bright, purple and orange, I thought you could eat it and save the trouble of going shopping). Ma was counting out fifty dollars, and I was saying, Ma, don't. Don't buy this piano! She ignored me and went on smoothing out the notes. I said again, *Ma, don't buy this piano.* I thought the cat woman would see how much I didn't want it, and say, *Don't buy the piano if the boy doesn't like it.* But she didn't.'

In the front room, the sun going, greyness coming on, Milly in Wiggytown, the costume over the back of a chair, we laughed. *Don't buy the piano if the boy doesn't like it.*

'And now. Now you're—'

'I know what you're going to say,' he said. 'A capitalist.'

'I wasn't going to say that.' Well, I might've been.

'But the cat woman was stroking her cat and looking at me as if she was deaf.'

'Of course.'

'Of course. I said it again: *Don't buy the piano.* I wondered if the cat woman couldn't understand me because of my accent. Perhaps it sounded like I'd said, *I really want that piano, Ma, please buy it for me.* But Ma was gesturing for me to keep quiet, and she was looking at the cat woman apologetically. I'm sorry about my son, she seemed to be saying. I'm sorry about me, I'm sorry about our funny accent. She was handing over the brilliant fifty dollars. It seemed like we had to buy that piano because of the way we spoke.

'That evening, while we were all trying hopelessly to shift the piano down the old woman's steps, a group of men from the street came to help. They all had short names—Ken, Ted, Earl and Earl. (That's where all the earls went.) That was how Ma and Dad met the neighbours, so I suppose some good came of it.

'I was to go for lessons. Guess what the teacher's name was?'

'No idea,' I said. I fingered the costume and he pushed it out of my hands again.

'I thought you wanted—'

'No. Can you just listen?'

'I am.'

'Mrs Deethridge. I saw it written down by the phone. It said, Deathrage.

'I hated that. We had everything wrong—our clothes, our accent, the piano, the piano teacher. Mrs Deathrage. I never touched that piano, I never played it. I never played "The Happy Farmer" again.'

•

We were sitting in the gathering dark. That's what people say, gathering, and it was gathering around us like a blanket. We were on to our third glass of wine. 'Half,' he'd said, he was driving. I was feeling a bit light-headed myself. I'm not good on more than one, really. A ruby fell on the table as I poured, and I put my finger in it and licked it. I was tiddly enough to break the golden rule, no food or drink near the garments (the ruby rule). Although Rose didn't give a rat's arse, I told him—Rose who had taught me to mend and who drank coffee and smoked cigarettes all day long. Rose had been known to burn a hole in a garment by accident and mend it invisibly before the client was any the wiser.

He said, Oh, and looked a little worried.

Soon all the light would be gone from the room.

And I would see everything. Slight exaggeration.

'If you like music, what do you like?'

'Why do you think I like music?'

'The piano teacher, your ear, etcetera.'

'I hate music.'

I clicked my tongue. 'Go on, what do you like?'

'Europop,' he said, as if he didn't.

'I love Europop!' I said. 'And post-punk.'

'I like post-punk.'

'God, I wish I could put something on.'

'Why can't you?'

'The Blackout!'

'Oh yes.' He could never keep the Blackout in his head.

'Sometimes I forget,' I said. 'Sometimes I put my hand on the light switch expecting it to go on and it doesn't.' I blushed for some reason. I held up my glass in a semi-toast. 'Alright, instead of music.'

'Instead of punk, plonk.'

'Oh that's good,' I said. We drank. 'We could hum,' I said.

We hummed 'London's Burning'. The Clash of course, not the bloody nursery rhyme. Daa-de-da-da, da-de-da-da-da-da. The light was going. It was catastrophic. It was all over. I loved it. I loved the way everything became dangerous.

'How can you see in this light?' He'd been looking at my hands.

'I just can,' I said. There was no sunlight and no electric light, only wine and the song I was humming, then singing, 'London's Burning'. I broke off to say, 'I love that song.'

'I'm not surprised,' he said.

'Why?'

'Because you're a colonial.'

The funny ideas he had. 'That was yonks ago. Generations.'

Then, reaching for a needle, scissors, I don't know what in the half-light, I knocked over my glass and it was like a tree being felled. It didn't break, but red wine spilled onto the table and was absorbed by the stack of organza aprons. We were both up, dancing about with tissues and bits of material and he had grabbed the costume and was intending to mop up the wine with that, but I snatched it from him.

'Not that! Are you crazy?'

'I suppose I am crazy,' he said, 'to sit here day after day, when all I needed was this to be mended.'

I was saying, 'I'll wash these. It'll wash out.' I was slightly woozy on my feet.

He was saying, 'First the beads, then this.'

I stopped with the stained aprons in my hand.

'The beads, remember? Gone. And now these, these things, gone.'

'They're not exactly gone,' I said.

'And probably the dress too.'

'This is silly,' I said.

The costume was still in his hand, and he looked at it. He held it very close to his face, almost to smell it.

I took it gently from his hands and hung it over a chair.

'I'll be back in a minute.'

He nodded. He looked sad.

I went to soak the aprons—only four of them had been splashed with the wine. I bumbled around in the gloom. He followed me, appeared in the bathroom doorway. 'Can I help?'

'No,' I said, 'I'll only be a minute. Look, it's just rinsing out, it's getting on to it quickly, that's the trick.' I tried to string the aprons up over the shower rail but I couldn't reach and he reached up above me and hung them up like Miss Havisham's veils, and they dripped down our arms and we were laughing and saying, I hope to hell it comes out. Me too, I hope it comes out. It should. While his arms were still stretched up at the rail I remembered that Mabel was coming tomorrow to pick up *said* aprons. He asked who Mabel was, and I told him—the designer, only the designer of the aprons! We had another storm of laughter. Mabel is coming tomorrow. *Mabel* is coming tomorrow! He stepped out of the bathroom, suddenly awkward, leaving the aprons dripping noisily, and hovered in the passage and I brushed past him on the way back to the front room, and felt all of him, flesh and bones and his warmth, and I felt as if I knew his atomic structure.

When we were back at the table, I picked up the costume and held it in my lap like a cat and said, 'Sit down, it's alright, tell me about Trisha.'

'But you've stopped now.'

'Well, it *is* the light now. The lack of it.' Because the light had all but gone from the room, and from the garden, although the white daisies on the unruly bush through the window were glowing. As if embroidered onto the costume, I said to myself, and was pleased. A costume that consumed light, took all the light for itself as if it owned the light. I shook my head, saying a small *no* to something, I wasn't quite sure what. 'There isn't enough light now.'

'I suppose that means it won't be finished today.'

'Does it matter?'

'Can it matter?'

'Well, no!' I said. 'What choice do we have? It's out of our hands. Bloody Pinnacle Power!'

He was shifting in his chair, perhaps to get up, I didn't know.

'I can't come tomorrow.' He seemed flat.

'Why?'

'I'm busy. Work,' he said. 'Also, I'm going to Wellington the next day and I have things to finish.'

He got up and looked down at his arms as if he had woken after sleepwalking and was surprised to find his arms still there. 'You must have things to do.'

I stood up. Art would be home soon.

I said it was alright. I felt his mouth come out of the darkness against mine, tentative, then urgent. I tasted cigarettes, and him. This strange wet tenderness and hunger. He broke off and stepped back.

'I'm sorry.'

'No, I'm sorry.'

He fumbled for his jacket on the back of the chair. I heard him bumping against the chair and could just see his outline as he moved across the room. I was about to say something—I felt I should say something—and he hesitated, waiting, but I didn't say anything. There were no transactions about tomorrow or the next day or the day after that. He felt his way into the passage and let himself out the front door. I stayed sitting with the costume in my lap and for some reason tears fell onto it. Not rips, *tears*.

26

Change of subject but not entirely: once, in the Taranaki Museum, I saw a pair of nineteenth-century men's woollen long johns that were literally all patches, completely remade, with nothing of the original left, only different-coloured cross-hatching. And bad cross-hatching at that, all uneven and knotty. They'd belonged to a gum-digger who had mended them himself. Not many sheilas out there on the gum fields. You had to admire him. These long johns, with their pink and grey and cream darns, reeked of poverty but also of pride. This obstinate colonial still had a pair of long johns, even if they were a different pair. Here's an interesting parallel: our skin replaces itself every seven years. For instance, in the five years I'd been with Art, three-quarters of my cells had been replaced. And his. I was thinking this as we wolfed down our battered mercury on Friday night (not on the superfoods list), and went back and forth about the Blackout, about LambChop, about bloody Settler Literary Ephemera.

•

The outlook was terrible, Art said, terrible. Not the weather, of course, the Blackout. Work on the cables was slow. Three weeks, they were saying. I was reading on the back doorstep with a torch, not getting very far. Art was at the bench unwrapping a cake he'd got on the way home from that little place in Mount Eden. He sneezed every so often, out into the room to avoid the cake. He then brought the cake, a mini orange disc, outside with the lamp, and his hair cast painty shadows like Grahame Sydney cabbage trees onto the house. I'd held that hair in my hands—it was brittle, like seagrass. I'd clung to it as if it was the only thing that would save me from falling. But the outlook—I found it strangely exciting. In Wellington people used to say *The outlook is terrible* quite a lot, and sure enough the wind would arrive and assert its authority, cancel everything, lambast everything. And people would be delighted. It was a relief to hand over to the wind.

We hoed into the cake, nodding and agreeing.

'No cream though,' said Art. 'No icing on the cake.'

He waited for my rejoinder, but I couldn't think of anything.

'No worries about gilding the lily though,' he said.

I felt charged, like on a windy day in Wellington.

Later, I stood in the doorway of the front room and said goodnight. Art was rummaging through papers with a torch and humming Billy Bragg. What I thought was, he'd love the Wanted card, the Mass card. Ephemera. I almost told him about them, standing there. Ephemera when seen from the centre.

'Looking for an article,' he said.

The bedroom smelled like a billygoat—the damp waiting just underneath. Who goes there! I could hear Art sneezing his head off in the bathroom. Then he called out, 'Do you want these, GoGo?'

'What?' I bellowed.

'Just come!'

I'd once needed a light in the passage, even in the daytime. For a few days I'd used my fingertips to brush along the fuzzy topography of the flocked wallpaper, but after ten days of Blackout I could walk confidently in a straight line along the passage in the dark. When I got to the candlelit bathroom Art was naked, poised to get into the shower (which would be cold but hey, it was summer). The aprons were dangling from the shower rail.

'What shall I do with these?'

I harvested them, plucking them down, one, two, three, four, pink, blue, green, yellow. They were dry of course—the organza like drying air. They were ever-so-slightly wrinkly, but soft, smooth, like a penis to the touch. I'd iron them. His body so beautiful as he stepped under the cold water, shuddering. I laughed. Ah, but no iron! In the kitchen I smoothed the aprons out on the table—checked the marbly Formica first for wet spots, for stickiness; I wanted no more stains.

We slept on the aprons, Art and I. I was aware of them all night under the mattress. What I thought was, there's been a change, in me, in him. He had armour on, or something. But that was silly.

The next morning, Saturday, we went to 'the farm'.

•

Spur of the moment decision: me trying to light the flipping Primus stove in the early grey light, Art getting a whiff of some off milk. *Blow this for a fucking joke.* Next thing I'm shaking out dried food for Bell, and Art's stuffing the boot, and we're driving the length of the scalloping power cables—bloop bloop. Prue and Bert spent most weekends at 'the farm' and it was open invitation for Art and his sister and hangers-on (i.e. me) to meet them there. (I'm going to keep using inverted commas for 'the farm' because the word farm sounds down-home, but of course it was a business.) I must say, after the Queen Street thing—the hundred dollars and the boy—I felt the teensiest bit uncomfortable about seeing Prue and Bert again. This was overridden by the thought of a warm bath.

After we got shot of Auckland and the hour of transitty little towns, we plunged into the bush and tootled along singing Bic Runga songs and Don McGlashan songs as the ferns went blurring by. It was beautiful. At one point I thought, GoGo, you fool, and I wished we could drive forever and there'd be no Blackout, no dissertation, no longing. No I didn't. I wanted to go on. I wanted to push on, and I put my hand to my mouth to check, just as we pulled up at 'the farm' gates. These are quite a grand affair, iron spears set between concrete pillars topped with stone lions. The first time I saw these gates they seemed incongruous in the landscape of rolling hills and bush, but they'd grown on me. Now I felt a rush at the promise of the good food, deep couches and nice bathroom fittings that awaited us in the house. (Actually, they called it a homestead.) From the winding driveway we saw Art's older sister Issy doing dressage, leaping sideways like a spider on Blackie in the west field. Yes, west. The whole farm was west, for that matter. Issy released her hand briefly to wave. Issy had a girlfriend, May, but she never came to 'the farm', I suppose because she was a girl.

If there'd been any bad feeling about the Queen Street incident it was all on my part. Prue greeted Art, then me, warmly, with Bert tagging behind in his pebble glasses. That's the thing about Art's family: they rise above things. I kind of wish the pole house had been like that. I thanked Prue for the peaches and the socks. And the dried fruit. She said don't mention it—you poor souls in the Blackout. It was all a bit tense, but in a good cause. In the dining room, which was made important by its monstrous bits of carved furniture, we sat down to a lunch of salmon, salad and warm bread. The family discussed their various projects. Issy, still fluffing up her blonde helmet-hair and giving off whiffs of horse, fleshed out the details of her latest *Construction Site*. She was in her final year at Elam and she had an exhibition to prepare for. I must say I was quite looking forward to the day when Issy graduated. So far Prue and Bert were her only customers. *Construction Site No. 14*, which hung in our front room, had been a gift.

Issy was telling us how she'd been finding inspiration in this new subdivision in Sylvia Park.

'Have you, dear?' said Prue, touching Issy's hand. She called her children 'dear'. It was endearing. I thought I might do that when I had children, if ever.

Issy ignored her mother. She stretched back in the big uphol-stered dining chair. She was beaky like her father, but had the Woolthamly spiky gold hair like Art. 'So ugly it's beautiful,' she said. 'The angles on the hillside. I almost envy the poor sods who have to live there.'

'They're probably grateful for it,' said Prue.

'They're not poor,' said Art. 'Sylvia Park. It's middle-management types. Junior executives.'

'I know they're not poor,' said Issy. 'They're poor *sods*.' The long face—so like her horse. Sorry to make stereotypes.

Prue said it was probably a lot of Chinese immigrants with their Hong Kong dollars.

Issy was saying, Not dollars, Mummy, it's not *dollars*. But Bert said it was dollars. After the British lease ran out in ninety-seven, they kept the currency.

'HKD,' said Prue. 'Don't I know it.'

At this *rueful tone*, Issy roused herself enough to say, 'Why do you know it, Mummy?'

'Because we export there, of course, and to the mainland.' Prue had gone all clipped.

'Do you?' said Issy. I saw her wink at Art. 'I didn't know the Chinese liked dried fruit.'

'You don't need many Chinese to like dried fruit for them to like dried fruit,' said Bert. 'If you get my drift.'

Issy thought this was hilarious, for some reason. 'Get my drift! Daddy, you sound like an old hippy!'

I saw Prue purse her lips and share a look with Bert. 'Well, they used to like it.'

Everyone went silent briefly to hoof down some salmon, but it seemed there was a little *thing* going on with the Woolthamlys. This was about as ruffled as they ever got.

Prue put down her knife and fork like a cat crosses its paws, and she turned to Art. 'What have you been doing, darling?' I suppressed a yelp of laughter. For some reason. Both parents listened with rapt attention to the story of the serial killer, making mock gestures of shock—*for goodness' sake!* Bert asked about Art's dissertation, and remembered that he'd come across a book on First World War recruitment or something in the book bus that he'd show him later in the drawing room. Art pretended this was great. I liked that about Art. I loved that about him.

His sister butted in about how she was adding a sound layer to her *Construction Sites*. I suppose, when I think about it, there was always a frisson of competition between Issy and Art. Sibling rivalry, nothing unusual—although, I hasten to add, not in my family. Lisa had her drugs and I had, well, I don't know. All this.

Prue clapped her hands—about the sound layer—and said wonderful a few times. Issy could afford to ignore the praise. There was so much you needed a wheelbarrow for it to have any meaning. Just her, on bass, she was saying. Incredibly minimalist. Issy played in a band. For money she waitressed part time, which may not have paid much but was an endless source of anecdotes. In fact, now Issy launched into a story about a customer who wanted to read his poetry aloud in the café, and the other patrons couldn't bloody stand it. They got angrier than if he'd tried to hold up the place with a gun, said Issy.

Prue laughed. 'And it was just poetry! Aren't people funny?'

They are.

Bert was leaning back in his chair with his hands repeatedly cupping each other like a ball and socket. 'You could be psychoanalysing your customers, my dear, and earning a fortune.'

Issy had a master's in psychology. She often said she was qualified to work in the café.

'Oh, Bert,' said Prue, exasperated but in a comic way. 'You know Issy's too creative for that.'

This was what I loved about the Woolthamlys, they kept it all seemly. You could trust that nobody was going to go off like a skyrocket. Well, up until this day you could. Watch this space.

Issy was looking at her father with her head on one side. 'Couldn't I just, Daddy. I could analyse them to hell and back. But, Daddy, I'm happy to just serve them their meal. That way I'm much more inspired to sculpt and play music.'

Bert nodded in his fond, anxious way. Now that I think about it, he was kind of kind.

Prue turned to me. 'And how's your . . . business going, Megan?'

I gulped down my last mouthful of warm bread and said that things were slow because of the Blackout, but that I was hoping—

But Prue's mind was on other matters. 'Just a minute, will you,' she said. She called out to Mrs Muru. Prue didn't give a fuck, to coin a phrase. I didn't mind. I'd worked out a long time ago that if you weren't a Woolthamly, you could never belong, so there was no point trying. It didn't matter.

Mrs Muru came and leaned in the doorway. She was a middle-aged Maori woman with a gammy leg, and she'd been with them for a few years. Art and Issy—and even I—said, 'Hello, Mrs Muru,' all together like choir practice.

'Pudding in ten minutes, if you wouldn't mind please, Mrs Muru,' said Prue.

Art and Issy entertained their parents with their recent travels—art, cafés, films. I didn't blame them. You couldn't talk about politics, religion, gender, ethnicity or justice. But I suppose it was worth it for the warmth of the house, the roast dinners, the raised glasses, the funny stories about 'the farm'.

Sure enough, during summer pudding, which was so tart it took the lining off your mouth, Bert proposed a walk. A weekend at 'the farm' wasn't complete without a stomp over the hills with Bert while he breathlessly pointed out historic sites. *A Maori battle took place on this very spot!* There are worse things.

'Oh, Bert, don't this time,' Prue said. She called for Mrs Muru to clear the table and bring coffee.

Art looked puzzled. He asked why not—about the walk. We always went for a walk.

'You haven't heard?' asked Issy. She was bursting with news. 'Tell them, Mummy.'

Now Art was all ears, but Prue said it was nothing.

'What?' Art was going pink. 'What?'

'Oh, it's nothing, dear. A man took a potshot at your father a couple of weekends ago.'

Art stood up from the table, rattling the cutlery. 'What!'

Prue told Art not to make a fuss. She called for Mrs Muru in quite a sharp way, and Mrs Muru came hurrying in.

'Your mother's right,' said Bert. 'It was just a BB gun. It's these blasted tenants. They have no love for the land.'

I put my hand on Art's back. There was still this tenderness, a sort of instinct.

The Woolthamlys had leased out some paddocks, apparently. I wasn't quite sure why, all of a sudden, except that I knew 'the farm' had been carved up after the grandfather died. Several Woolthamly siblings had several blocks of land. Prue had bought out the others to get the house—homestead—on a much-reduced block.

Prue said it was true about the tenants. 'They don't love the land like we do. They're Chinese. They don't understand the meaning of it. Do they, dear?'

I rolled my eyes at Art but he was sipping his demitasse with great concentration.

Bert was waving his hand in a gesture of *non comprende*. Mrs Muru waited for his hand to go back on his lap before she took his plate. He kept on. He didn't know why they wanted to come all the way down here. From China.

'Because it's paradise, Daddy,' said Issy. She smiled the Woolthamly strong-toothed smile.

'Because it's cheap land,' Art said. He suddenly looked doubtful. 'Isn't it?'

But Prue was telling Bert to keep well away from the fence line. God knows there was plenty to go on with.

Bert shook his head. 'All I want,' he said, 'is occasional access to that site. There was an important battle up there. Occasional access, and it was in the terms of the lease.' Blah blah blah.

'Daddy!' said Issy.

It was true he didn't often get upset. I must say I wondered why he was so agitated. He'd only acquired the land by marriage. He was like me, or how I would be in the future once Art inherited.

Bert sucked on a cigarillo. 'Blasted tenants.'

•

When I came back downstairs with my jacket and walking shoes, I could tell there'd been a confab in the drawing room. Art, Issy,

Prue and Bert were emerging, all looking flushed. I heard Prue say as they dispersed, 'And we *certainly* won't tell Grandma Woolthamly tomorrow. It might kill her.'

Outside, I asked Art what all this was about—did Issy come out?

Art banged out his boots on the doorstep. 'We might have to sell the business,' he said. '*Might*. There's been an offer—the assets and the debt or something. Things aren't good.'

A slightly cold feeling went over me, I wasn't sure why. I took a breath to ask a question, but Art shook his head. Not the place. Bert was crunching around from the back of the house with his walking poles.

Bert, Art, Issy and I set off down the wide gravel path from the house and turned along the road. We were skirting the orchards, close enough to see gnarly apple trees with their fruit still small and sour-looking. As we came up over the north-west hill, I looked back and saw that some of the trees were shrouded in blue like an elderly woman leaving the hairdresser's. I thought of Grandma Woolthamly, and the secret that was being kept from her. Over a dale, you could just glimpse the blaring silver roof of the drying plant.

Bert was yelling into the wind, 'See that hill? The Maoris came swarming down it but the colonials drove them back.' I knew all this. There was a plaque commemorating a siege at the pa. But Bert had just read a new history on the area and he was telling us, breathlessly like David Attenborough as he climbed up the sheep tracks, how the siege story wasn't true. All that about women and children surviving on no food and little water for three days—rubbish. There was new evidence they were down at the village the whole time, gorging on paua. 'Fabulous stuff,' he said. The wind blew, the grass rippled, the cows eyed us. It was gorgeous.

We were walking north along the bumpy side of the hill when I saw something twitching on the ground up ahead. As I hurried closer, I saw it was a little flop of a rabbit caught in a trap. It was half-alive, its leg glistening with blood under the vice, its pulse fluttering like a kite. I called to the others urgently, but they were in no hurry. Art came up and stooped to wrench open the trap, and the rabbit tumbled out. I think I was saying, Oh God. I knelt down and slid my hand underneath the soft warm tiny-boned body. It convulsed and one brown eye below its furry eyelid wavered in and out of consciousness. I thought it looked up at me imploringly. Later, Art said that was fanciful, but I'm sure it did, it looked at me and it asked for help. What I thought was, this was what I wanted to do with the street kid. I wanted to cradle him.

Issy was saying something about how rabbits are more intelligent than we thought, she read an article. I was baying, Oh God, oh God. The rabbit's brown fur rippled as a shudder came from deep inside it.

'Okay, Sylvia Plath,' said Art. He took a rock, held it high up against the sky, and brought it down on the rabbit, which went into a rictus. Had another go. The rabbit slumped dead.

I felt dazed. Tears sprang into my eyes, but I tried to mop them up because it was only a rabbit. Issy thought they might eat it, but Art said it was too skinny. My vision was clearing, and I saw him turn it over and inspect it.

'See that hillside over there?' said Bert. 'Rabbit warrens all through it now that the blasted tenants have control of it.'

Art asked if this was the leased land, but Bert was striking out ahead. 'The Maoris came storming down that ridge, but we were too much for them.'

'Daddy!' said Issy. She was thumping off after Bert. 'Is this the leased bit?'

'The least bit!' said Art.

'Oh shut up!' said Issy.

Art seemed a bit stung and I felt sorry for him. This wasn't the Woolthamly way. He wobbled after Bert and Issy, over the uneven turf towards the fence. There was a stile.

'But shouldn't we not be on it?' said Art.

'They're only leasing it,' said Issy. 'Surely.'

I followed, feeling sick. Their voices sounded muffled. On the other side of the stile, we assembled again and continued in silence south, back down past the orchards. When we could see the house again, there was a sense of relief. Art took my hand and we smiled at each other, walking along bumpily together. Bert had cheered up enough to point at a stand of trees further down the gully. 'See those natives. There was an uprising happened there.' I looked at the trees intently and imagined the scene. I wanted to get the image of the rabbit's agony out of my head.

•

Before dinner we sat on the huge white couches sipping sherry and eating pigs-in-blankets in front of a roaring fire in the drawing room. It was March, and getting cool in the evenings. Not so bad, you might think, and you'd be right. Dinner was half a roast sheep in the formal dining room. Mrs Muru served. After dinner, back in front of the fire, I did the costume—meandering to a finish, of course, and there was the added bonus of the chandelier and the lamps. I worked right under a spotlight. It was good to have something to do with my hands. Practical things went down well at 'the farm'. Prue leaned forward in her armchair and had a look. Absolutely lovely, she said, and was inspired to get out her rug-hooking. I calculated she'd paid five hundred bucks for the materials, and could have bought it made up for less. We talked about art and films. Art had the book on First World War recruitment, which he was gazing at dolefully. Steered clear of the ballet.

Every so often I thought about the client, even though he was a philanderer and a capitalist. I remembered his mouth. A peculiar shot of electricity ran through my body and came out at my fingers, where they met the fine silk. I remembered the cigarette taste, and something voracious, and I looked up to see if anyone had noticed my body turn into something irresistibly sexy. They hadn't.

We went up to bed and passed, as always, under the razor gaze of the Woolthamly ancestor in his gilt frame. Fell asleep to the hooting of owls and the silence. The rabbit.

27

Grandma Woolthamly arrived late Sunday morning for lunch, in a cream summer coat and her feet stuffed into beige pumps. She lived in a care facility in Stratford because she was going a bit batty in her old age and had once set fire to the kitchen, despite Mrs Muru. Everyone greeted Grandma Woolthamly enthusiastically, including me. But it seemed that today something was up with Grandma Woolthamly. She stood in the vestibule tipping forward and trembling, and said she wanted to go back home.

'You mean to the care facility, Mummy?' shouted Prue, who was trying to wrangle off Grandma Woolthamly's coat. 'But you've only just arrived.' The linen didn't have much give in it. In the end, Issy and I held Grandma still while Prue tugged the sleeves backwards.

'Home,' said Grandma Woolthamly.

'You are home, Grandma,' said Issy. She said this again, louder, and asked Grandma Woolthamly if she wanted to stay the night.

Prue took up the theme. 'Do you want to stay here tonight, Mummy!'

Once Grandma Woolthamly was freed from the coat, she said again, 'I mean home.' Then her pumps and her stick clacked over the marble tiles to the drawing room.

We parked ourselves on the couches and ate canapés and drank more sherry while everyone shouted comments at Grandma Woolthamly, about ballet, art, sculpting. Grandma Woolthamly didn't seem to be listening. She munched on her mushroom square thingies as if she were starving. Prue tried 'the farm' as a topic of conversation, then meat. Bert mentioned the cloud formations, interesting at this time of year. It was the humidity. It got so desperate that Prue shouted, 'Megan's embroidering a wonderful dress, Mummy!' I smiled a gory smile, but Grandma Woolthamly swivelled her gaze to land on Art and demanded, 'What about the business?'

Everyone looked uncomfortable, and there was throat-clearing. Art laughed. I felt a bit sorry for him. It's not as if Art had *gone into the family business* kind of thing.

Prue announced lunch. During the soup, which Grandma Woolthamly had difficulty with and in the end abandoned with a clatter of her spoon, they had a conversation, shouted for Grandma Woolthamly's benefit, about the wedding of a second cousin, Danielle from Inglewood, who was marrying a minor member of the English royal family in Oxford in June. Issy said wasn't he, like, a hundred and ninety-seventh in line to the throne, the fiancé? Art said you'd need a lot of haemophilia to be about, and they both snorted into their soup. I might have let out a giggle myself. Well, these weren't really my jokes to laugh at.

Just as Mrs Muru had delivered the fish pie, Grandma Woolthamly announced that she was going to the wedding.

'Oh, Mummy,' shouted Prue, 'I told you, I don't know if you'd be up to the flight these days. It's twenty-four hours on the plane, not counting stopovers.'

Grandma Woolthamly said she had already arranged the present. When Prue said she could post it—and added, *if you must*, quite firmly, so everyone looked—Grandma Woolthamly said, more firmly, 'I'm taking it in person.'

Issy said, 'Don't say we didn't warn you,' sort of sotto voce.

'I'm forearmed and forewarned,' said Grandma Woolthamly.

I watched Art go all wide-eyed as he asked, 'What is the present, Grandma? A shepherdess?' He and Issy dissolved into giggles.

'A crystal bowl?' squeaked Issy.

'Twenty thousand pounds,' said Grandma Woolthamly.

I saw Art stop with his fork poised halfway to his mouth. Issy had gone silent too. I was already silent, but I went more so. Bert harrumphed, although he wasn't a harrumpher.

Issy turned to Prue. 'Mummy, this isn't true, is it?'

Prue had her eyebrows up by way of yes. 'You can't talk her out of it. I've tried.' She was getting up from the table, asking Mrs Muru where the lemon was, even though Mrs Muru wasn't there. Honestly! She disappeared into the hall.

Art was frowning and murmuring. 'In New Zealand dollars, isn't that fifty-something . . .' He shouted, 'Quite a lot of money, Grandma!'

'It won't be true,' murmured Issy. 'She's, you know.' Issy shook her head to indicate battiness.

Grandma Woolthamly was hoofing down her fish pie, making a right mess of the potato on the front of her cream dress. At least it matched.

'Grandma,' shouted Art, 'that's fifty-something thousand dollars.' He turned to me. 'Pretty good present,' said Art. 'What did she give us for our wedding?'

'It was hardly a wedding,' said Issy. 'And you're not exactly royalty, are you, Megan?'

Everyone laughed, including me. Except Bert, who was sitting at the end of the table looking, I noticed, slightly absent.

In the *spirit of mirth* I turned to Art and suggested, 'Didn't we get a villa?'

Issy sat back. 'That villa's not yours.' She turned to Prue, who was back with a dish of cut lemons. 'Isn't it in the family trust?'

'No, it isn't,' said Art.

Prue had a fixed smile on her face, and she was saying, What isn't, darling? What isn't?

'Oh well,' said Issy. 'I don't mind. I really don't. But back to the subject. Danielle's only a second cousin, maybe third. And as thick as two short planks.'

The fork fell out of Grandma Woolthamly's purple arthritic little fist. She fixed Issy, then Art, each with a *rheumy stare*. 'It's fifty-two thousand. Danielle is doing her bit. Marrying royalty, and inviting everyone to the wedding. She understands about family. That's how we built this.'

I could sense Art chortling away in his chest. He was asking, Was I invited? I don't think so. I noticed he didn't use the royal We. Issy said she *definitely* wasn't invited, she'd remember an embossed invitation. But hey, Grandma should be left to do what she wanted, it was only money.

Everyone stuffed their face, and it seemed the fifty-two-thousand-dollar question had been kissed goodbye. But after a while, Grandma Woolthamly turned to Art and started up again: 'What about the dried fruit? Are the Asians still buying our dried fruit?'

Art half laughed and told Grandma Woolthamly she was talking to the wrong person.

'Didn't he go to university?' Grandma Woolthamly asked the table.

'Mummy,' said Prue, 'he has a PhD. But he didn't study things like that.'

Art reminded everyone modestly that he *almost* had a PhD.

Grandma Woolthamly sat up straight. 'For pity's sake, why didn't he study something useful when he has a company to run?'

Prue said, 'We've been through this, Mummy, many times.'

I felt sorry for Art, really I did. I mean business, it just wasn't his thing.

But Grandma Woolthamly had focused her watery eyes on Art again. 'A PhD,' she said in a very doubtful tone.

Art said, 'In English literature, Grandma,' in a *slightly* condescending way.

'Mummy, once again, you don't understand. You can have a very good career in literature.'

'Doing what?' barked Grandma Woolthamly and scanned everyone, even me. That's how I knew she had such a pale, jelly-like stare.

'Well,' began Bert.

Grandma Woolthamly eyeballed him, but when he started to go on she talked over him. 'I can read a book. I used to read a lot of books before my eyesight went. Now I get talking books from the mobile library. They're very good.' She swivelled back to Art. 'Why don't you get some talking books?'

'Grandma . . .'

'Listen to them at night. Run the business during the day and keep the family afloat.'

Issy asked why Grandma didn't ask *her* that, but no one answered. Prue was busy telling Grandma Woolthamly that they were creative, these two, always had been, and Grandma knew that. At this, Issy put her head on one side a little coquettishly.

'I said they're creative,' Prue repeated loudly.

Grandma Woolthamly let out a high-pitched cackle. 'Who will tell me about the business? Is Japan still buying our dried fruit?'

All through this I was minding my own business. This was nothing to do with me. I have to say, it was a teensy bit uncomfortable. Prue passed the salad bowl, first picking something out of it with a frown. As she did this, I noticed she and Bert exchanging glances.

'Who will tell me!' Grandma Woolthamly rapped her stick on the floor. 'Is Japan buying our dried fruit!'

'No,' said Prue.

'*What?*'

'No!' shouted Prue. Her hair was slightly mussed and her silk scarf had come undone. She lowered her voice. 'It's the Asian crisis, but it'll recover. We just have to be careful.'

Grandma Woolthamly folded her monkey-puzzle hands in satisfaction. 'Finally someone tells me. I listen to the news. I'm not an imbecile. Since when have they not been buying?'

'Well,' said Bert, sitting up importantly in his wing chair at the end of the table, 'it's not immediate. There are contractual obligations, of course, and—'

'Tell me!' rapped Grandma Woolthamly.

'When there's no money, there's no money,' said Bert miserably.

Mrs Muru waddled in with a pavlova with strawberries and kiwifruit, and everything went quiet. The pavlova was eaten with relish by Grandma Woolthamly. Prue tried to make light conversation. Art's job, Issy's soundtrack. How Megan didn't like the rabbit. I tried not to catch Art's eye in case I got the giggles. It's hard to explain, but only a certain kind of giggles was okay.

•

In the drawing room over coffee, Grandma Woolthamly repeated that she wanted to go home. I was probably infected with the air of giving that presided over the Woolthamlys. Remember, Art never came home from 'the farm' without food, linen, a retro fan. I leaned towards Grandma Woolthamly, who was dissolving into the white couch cushions in her cream-and-potato dress, and I shouted, 'I'll drive you.' The truth is, I was dying to get out of the house. Those Woolthamlys, no wonder they didn't argue, because when they did, it was chilling.

Grandma Woolthamly looked at me as if for the first time, and I saw the puzzled expression in her oystery eyes. 'Drive me?'

I repeated my offer, and looked at Art for backup. He nodded. He seemed a bit freaked.

'What's the girl talking about?' said Grandma Woolthamly. 'Who is this?'

'It's Megan, Mummy,' shouted Prue. 'She's offering to drive you back to the care facility. Very kind of her, don't you think?'

Oh, I was kind. I was halfway to being a Woolthamly.

'Or Art will,' I said. We'd both go. I certainly wasn't staying here on my own.

The truth was, I was longing for the blacked-out house. I wanted damp, dark, the wallpaper at the end of my fingertips. I wanted to be in the front room, listening to the end of the client's story. I wanted that so much.

But Grandma Woolthamly hadn't heard. She was asking Mrs Muru, who had brought in more coffee, how her daughter was. Mrs Muru hovered a moment with the coffee pot, and corrected Grandma Woolthamly. Son, her son, and he was fine, thank you for asking.

'Has he left school now?' asked Grandma Woolthamly.

Mrs Muru said he had, three years ago.

'You knew this, Mummy,' said Prue.

'He's at the drying plant?' asked Grandma Woolthamly.

'Just in the holidays,' said Mrs Muru. She checked around the room. Everyone was looking at her and she seemed unused to the limelight. She bowed a little and smiled. 'To put himself through university.'

'Goodness. University these days.' She was wide-eyed, then something occurred to her. 'What's he studying?' she demanded.

'Oh,' said Mrs Muru. She was smiling, kind of bashful. 'Engineering.'

Grandma Woolthamly jerked back in surprise.

'You knew all this, Mummy,' said Prue tiredly.

A beady expression had come over Grandma Woolthamly's face. She fixed her stare on Mrs Muru. 'Not books?'

Mrs Muru swayed in the doorway on her gammy leg. 'Books?'

'He's not studying *books*?' said Grandma Woolthamly very distinctly.

'No.' Mrs Muru shook her head. 'Chemical engineering.'

'Well,' said Grandma Woolthamly, almost leering at Mrs Muru, 'let's hope the Asians keep buying dried fruit.'

A worried look crossed Mrs Muru's face. She waited for a bit, and then, because the conversation seemed to have ended, hurried away.

'Why, Grandma?' demanded Issy. She looked at Prue. 'Why?' Prue shook her head.

'See,' said Grandma Woolthamly triumphantly. 'Even they study something useful.'

'Oh, Mummy,' said Prue. 'Let's get you down for your rest.'

It seemed that the plan to drive Grandma Woolthamly back to the care facility wasn't a happening thing anymore. I was trying to catch Art's eye—get me out of here—but he'd busied himself in the pages of the library book Bert had got for him. Prue and Bert seemed to be brushing themselves off for the afternoon's activities. The thing I'd always liked about 'the farm' was that there was so little to do you were forced to find amusing activities. But this day felt different. I wished I'd brought *Heart of Darkness* with me, which I was ploughing through.

Issy performed a magnificent stretch on the couch. 'You should have done engineering, Art, instead of *books*. Then you could have made something of yourself.'

'Ha ha,' said Art, from his book.

Grandma Woolthamly was sitting bolt upright on the couch. 'I want to go home.'

Good development. I repeated my offer to drive her, but she seemed out of sorts. Cantankerous old bat might be closer to the truth.

'Home, girl. Home.'

'Yes,' I said. 'We'll drive you, won't we, Art?'

Art absent-mindedly assented.

'It's not far,' Prue said aside to me, then yelled, 'But, Mummy, shouldn't you have your rest first? That's what you always do. You have your rest and then Mrs Muru brings us afternoon tea.'

'Home!' shouted Gramdma Woolthamly. 'England. I'm going to the wedding. I want to go home!'

'We know that, Mummy,' said Prue. She helped Grandma Woolthamly into the spare room.

Bert thought we might all go for another ramble. He was polishing his binoculars at a side table.

'But what is it about Jayden?' asked Issy.

'Who?' asked Bert.

'Daddy, Mrs Muru's son.'

Art turned a page. 'And you should have been a chartered accountant, Issy.'

'Oh shut up,' said Issy. 'Daddy?'

Bert harrumphed. It seemed to be a new habit. He stood up and wrangled the leather binocular case onto himself. He looked strained. 'Well, he'll lose his summer job. And we'll have to lay off his father. And the uncles.'

'What, you mean Eddy?' asked Issy. 'All of them, all five? Why?'

'It's not pleasant,' said Bert, 'for anyone, but we've had to pull in our horns.'

'But, Daddy,' shrilled Issy, 'they've been working for you for fifteen years.'

'Fourteen,' said Bert. 'Fourteen.'

'God!' said Issy. 'This is terrible. Can't you just, I don't know, ride it out?'

'Apparently not,' said Bert. He took out the binoculars again and cocked them out the window.

'Why not?' Issy sprang off the couch. There was something threatening about her.

'It's complicated,' said Bert. 'Ask your mother.'

'Yeah, pretty fucking complicated for them,' said Issy.

'Issy!' said Bert. The Woolthamlys didn't swear.

'Did you hear this, Art?' said Issy. 'If you can get your head out of that book for a second. They're getting rid of the Murus, Eddy and Junior et al.'

'That's terrible,' said Art. His eyebrows were knit.

I must say I was sitting there, sunk into the opposite couch with my head swivelling like I was watching a ping-pong match. But what could I do? I was only here because I'd happened to sit next to Art at a Derrida talk at the Michael Fowler Centre back in 1993. Life is strange, and unfair.

'I think this is absolutely the wrong thing to do, Daddy,' said Issy.

'Do you, darling?'

'Yes I do. Don't you, Art?' asked Issy. 'Don't you think this is the wrong thing to do?'

I looked from one to the other.

'Of course I do,' said Art.

'Well? Well?' said Issy. She eyeballed Bert. 'Daddy?'

'The Muru boys got fourteen good years out of us.'

'Fourteen good—' Issy was pacing. 'Are you listening to this, Art?'

He was. He was in agony, his radiant face clouded. I could see it.

'Also, Daddy,' said Issy, 'don't forget *out of the Woolthamlys*. The Murus got fourteen good years out of the Woolthamlys. You're a Frome.'

Art sat upright on the couch and his book clattered to the floor. 'Issy!'

'It's true,' said Issy, almost smiling at Art. She turned to face the mantelpiece.

Art winced at his father. Bert was limping over to the French doors. 'Don't argue, children, not on my account. It's true, this is nothing to do with me.'

What I thought right then was: this was me. I was the Bert figure. Always would be. The client was right. I had no say in my own life. I felt my hackles rise.

Prue was in the doorway. 'What's all this ridiculous yelling? Mrs Muru is in the house.' Yelling was the worst thing. I have to say, part of me liked that decorum. Prue plumped the little dent in the cushion where Grandma Woolthamly had been embedded. There was a sense of power being restored.

'Mummy,' demanded Issy, 'tell us exactly what's going on.'

Prue straightened from her cushion-boofing. There was a brief glance at me, and then, it seemed, the decision to go on regardless. 'Darling, it's them or us. The business could go. We need to pull in our horns.'

Issy went quiet. From the open French doors, Bert asked who was up for another walk. The garden, 'the farm' beckoned, birds twittered. No one replied. I looked at Art. He was sitting still and frowning, as if this were a chess problem. I sat like a stone. Nothing to do with me. But it was. It was.

'For God's sake!' Issy had turned back to the room, and was framed by the candlesticks on the mantelpiece. 'Do they know? Have you warned them?'

'Who?' asked Prue. She picked up Art's book and added it to the pile on the massive coffee table.

'The Murus, of course.'

'Not yet.'

'Does *Mrs* Muru know?'

'Of course not,' said Prue. 'Come on, sweetie, nothing is finalised.'

I remembered what the client had said—to keep the staff on as long as possible, so the business would be saleable. Fair enough, I suppose.

Issy stepped forward and planted herself in the middle of one of Prue's fluffy hand-hooked rugs. 'Mrs Muru must be told.'

Prue told Issy firmly that it wasn't her business.

'It is my business,' said Issy. 'This is our business. Isn't it, Art?'

Art sat looking lost, saying nothing. I also continued my stone impersonation.

Issy groaned and turned to Prue. 'What are you going to do—wait till the day before you fire them?' When there was no answer, she said, 'You know what? I'm going to tell her myself.'

'Issy, don't!' said Prue urgently. Her voice had gone all deep and scratchy.

'What, Mummy? Are you worried Mrs Muru won't finish the washing-up? She'll probably walk off the job, and I wouldn't blame her.'

'Of course she won't,' sighed Prue. 'She needs the job more than ever.'

Issy put her head in her hands and wailed. Suddenly she looked at Art, her eyes on full-beam. 'What does the armchair socialist think? Should we tell Mrs Muru what we all know?'

Art gaped for a second like a fish. Then he said—and it sort of sounded important—'I think we very probably should.' I must say I felt sorry for him. It wasn't his thing. And he didn't like arguments.

'Oh, you think we very probably should, do you?' parroted Issy. 'You don't give a fuck about the Murus!'

Art turned the colour of pomegranates. 'I do, as a matter of fact.'

'And you.' Issy turned on me.

I was rattled by this. I mean, I was the Bert figure. 'This is nothing to do with me,' I said.

'Oh really?' said Issy. 'Why don't you go and give them a hundred dollars?'

I think my mouth fell open. The story of the street kid had obviously done the rounds of the family. It felt like something creeping on me to know they'd been talking about me.

'Cut it out, Issy,' said Art. He stood up from the couch. He had assumed a sort of parental authority that didn't sit well on him. He was struggling—his smooth face.

'Yes, that's enough,' echoed Prue. I thought she cast a brief, guilty glance in my direction, but this may have been far-fetched of me.

'It's okay,' I said. Even with my stinging ego, I knew this wasn't my business. Brother and sister were still glaring at each other.

Prue put her hand on Issy's arm. 'It isn't the right time, dear. We'll tell them in due course.'

Issy shrugged her mother off. 'Due course! I'm going to tell Mrs Muru.'

'Issy!' shouted Prue.

'Try and stop me,' said Issy. She looked ferocious.

Prue drew in her breath. 'Alright, I will. If you tell her, you will not get a cent from here.' She slumped a bit. 'What's left of it.'

Issy reared back as if Prue had hit her. 'That old trick. You never tire of it, do you?'

Bert came in through the French doors. 'Dear!'

'That's a bit unnecessary, isn't it, Mother?' said Art.

Prue waved away the objections. 'I'm not having the staff looking for other jobs at this . . . terrible, terrible point. When there's still a possibility.'

There was a long, poisonous lull. This was it, this was the unspoken thing that had always been there, I suppose, but I'd never seen it in action. I looked at Art. He'd hung his head. Shame, that's what he would be feeling. He respected his parents. Issy argued and trashed them, but Art—well, he loved them. He really did. There was no way out.

Issy sank down onto the couch beside me, put her arm over her face and cried. It was a strange, lonely sound. The others stared dumbly. I didn't know if I was meant to comfort Issy, seeing I was sitting right next to her. I'm not very good at that sort of thing, and also I anticipated being flung off if I tried. I sat still while Issy sobbed. 'It's not the money,' she wailed, 'it's the abuse of power.' Actually, I thought it was about the money.

'For goodness' sake,' said Prue.

Art seemed to expand like a bird fluffs its feathers. Everyone looked at him. Issy's crying petered out. Art cleared his throat and announced in a formal way, 'Mum, Dad, I'm going to tell Mrs Muru what's happening.'

The silence and the light seemed timeless—could've been right then, could've been 1900. Art walked stiffly to the door, his upright stride, and turned back to the room. I'd never seem him cross his parents before, and part of me loved what was unfolding. I wasn't sure he should be doing this. Maybe the client was right—having the Murus walk off the job could kill the business, and then there really would be no work. I didn't know. But even as I admired Art's stand, there was something else, the way Issy and Art could make these grand statements. Somehow it got up my nose.

Prue stood quivering, and spoke in her raspy voice. 'I mean what I say. If you tell her, you will not get a brass razoo.'

Art took one final glance at us all assembled—his eyes grazed mine—and then he could be heard haring down the passage. As the kitchen door opened and closed there was a snippet of dishes being twanged into a dishwasher, and the sound of Art's sonorous voice.

'I suppose our walk's off,' said Bert.

Issy blew her nose and turned on him. 'You callous, callous old man.'

'That's enough!' shouted Prue. She sailed out the French doors. Bert followed.

Issy got up quickly. She turned and said to me, 'You should be worried. Your comfortable little life could be gone.' She almost ran out the door to the passage and I listened to her thumping up the stairs. Then it was just me in the drawing room. I walked around looking at toothy photos of Art and Issy when they were kids, vases, the grand piano. What Issy had said was so untrue, of course. My life wasn't even that comfortable. I peered through the French doors at Prue and Bert having an agitated conversation beside the round garden. I felt all jangly, which surprised me. It wasn't my family. But it seemed like the light in the hall might be going out.

•

Half an hour later I saw Mrs Muru flapping down the drive in her raincoat, although it wasn't raining. I sidled along the passage and peered in at the kitchen, out of curiosity. I'd never been in there before. There were long wooden benches, a tiled table, an enormous china cabinet. It was all gleaming and tidy, every copper pot on its hook, every plate on its shelf.

Coming back into the hall, I jumped when I saw the figure of Grandma Woolthamly. She said she wanted to go home. I looked around. No one else was coming in from the garden, or out from behind doors.

'Do you mean the care facility?' I asked. I mean, I wanted to be sure, under the circumstances.

'Of course!' snapped Grandma Woolthamly. 'What else would I mean?'

I was still gaping when Art appeared from somewhere. I thought he'd be feeling on top of the world after standing up to Prue, but he was aloof, distant. For some reason it looked like cling wrap covered his face. All the same, we angled Grandma Woolthamly back into her linen coat, with Art bleating, Grandma, no Grandma, and delivered her to the care facility while the sun was still high in the sky. Then we continued on, threading back through the green blur. I drove. There was silence. No Bic Runga, no Don McGlashan.

Around Raglan I said, because otherwise I would burst, 'You won't really be cut out of the will, will you?' Art didn't answer immediately, and I thought he went a bit purple. I couldn't exactly look at him—driving is like sewing that way.

'Why do you ask?' he said.

'Well,' I said, 'if you're not being cut out, it's just a gesture. Maybe you've actually done the Murus out of a job, I don't know. But you don't know either.'

'It wasn't just a gesture. I meant it.'

The coast was rugged, it is around there. I normally love the way the waves crash in.

'Anyway, that's a bit rich, coming from you,' he said.

'Me?' I squeaked, and he said just concentrate on the driving. Fair enough. Didn't want to go off the cliff.

'Yes, you,' he said, after a while.

I took the opportunity to remind him that the family had been talking about me—the street kid business—which wasn't very nice.

In my peripheral vision I saw the blur of him shaking his head. 'That's nothing to do with this.'

'I rest my case,' I said.

After a few miles it did occur to me that the reason I had a hundred-dollar note dilly-dallying in my purse to give to the street kid in the first place was my low living expenses, thanks to the Woolthamlys. But there were strings attached. I more than paid my way in fixed smiles.

•

As we pulled up outside the villa conversion, tenants from another of the villas were leaving, their rented trailer piled high like the Beverley Hillbillies. In the half-dark, they rolled away and waved as if they knew us. The street was very quiet. We cracked open the villa conversion. Its thick smell of mould and dust rushed to greet us. I called Bell but she didn't come. She didn't come and she didn't come. I went like a zombie down the passage, my arms out in front of me, calling, Bell!

She never came home, by the way. We never saw her again.

It was still tense—I know, it was silly—and I plumped down at the kitchen table like Lady Muck and watched Art ferry things in from the boot. I couldn't be stuffed helping. On one of his trips he stood and looked at me with a box in his arms. 'What?'

'Nothing,' I said. But I thought about it and added, 'Except you Woolthamlys are all horrible.' Well, I was sick of it.

'I suppose you're worried about the inheritance.'

I think I gasped, but there was something freeing about hearing it said. Even Art looked shocked. It was complicated. It wasn't my inheritance, but it was. I was spluttering. 'No one can belong to the Woolthamlys who isn't a blood relation. I'll never be one of the family as long as I live. Same for your poor fucking father.' Yes, fucking.

Art shook his head, he said that wasn't true.

'Everyone feels sorry for him,' I said. I was cruel. But I had more. 'Soon there'll be no Woolthamlys anymore. They'll be extinct. Good job.'

Art's face, looking down at me, was something from the fruit-drying plant. He lowered his voice. 'You make out like you despise materialism, yet you want an easy life. You want to do a nice little job at home, while the Woolthamly estate keeps you. You want this inheritance more than I do.'

'I don't!' I yelled. 'I don't want a cent of your poxy squattocracy money!'

I hadn't thought of this before. But I didn't. I really didn't.

It seemed that my little business, my low income, had got under his skin all this time, yet he'd never said anything. That was what got me most, that he'd thought thoughts and hadn't said them. Later it occurred to me that I'd thought thoughts and hadn't said them, and I'd done things and hadn't said them.

Art moved things around in the kitchen and said he didn't want to listen to any more of my crap, he couldn't be bothered talking. I said, Don't then, and he said, I won't. I told him he talked shit anyway. Absolute shite.

But I had one more thing to say, something important.

'I thought you'd seen something wonderful. But you hadn't.'

'What the fuck are you talking about?' He turned from the bench.

'The day the power went out, you walked home and you said all these people were walking together and talking to each other and supporting each other.'

'This is ridiculous,' he said. 'Did you take notes?'

'I remember it,' I said. 'Why talk about things like that if you don't mean it? It's just ideas, and it's meaningless.'

'I don't know,' he said, 'you tell me. Because that's exactly what you do.' He folded his arms and said, sort of pompously, as if he were lecturing English 100, 'It's the Blackout. Everyone's acting strangely. The Blackout is making everyone behave differently.'

'That's garbage,' I said.

'And you know what?' he said. 'I don't give a fuck about this inheritance.'

I believed him. But it didn't change anything. 'Your grand gesture about the Murus was for nothing after all,' I said.

'No.' He stopped pacing and turned to me. 'It wasn't for nothing. I discovered that you're different. There's something about you, different.'

A bolt went through me. 'Maybe I am,' I said, sounding like I smoked.

It had all got out of hand. I know it was ridiculous. Art had just made a stand, perhaps kissed his inheritance goodbye, and we were having an argument.

At this point I felt like I did when I thought I was looking at Auckland for the first time. Like it had popped up out of the mist, and might disappear again. Or I might. Now I wandered into the passage. He called after me, Where are you going? I didn't answer, but went out to the back doorstep. I sat there fuming and looking out into the blackness. And you know what? I'm sure I saw something. I thought I did, something I hadn't seen before. Something was revealed. In the core of the darkness was a treasure. Yes, a taonga. Wellington was up, Auckland was down. South was up, north was down. The carefully planted villa garden was a wilderness. Shakespeare was no longer Shakespeare. The neighbours through the wall were seen for the first time just as they left. Fine motor skills resulted in things coming apart. You could hold darkness in your hands. You could smell it, eat it, you could cover your face with it. It seemed there had never been real darkness before, no one had had the full force of darkness upon them. But now, there it was, darkness staring you right in the eye.

I knew what I was going to do, and I had no earthly reason.

●

In the morning, a bit fragile, I put on a blouse, teal, flimsy, bloody Trelise Cooper. There'd never been an occasion important enough to wear it. (I hadn't known quite what to wear it *with* though. Jeans.) It was Monday, the seventeenth day of the Blackout.

28

He came in. He had flowers, a mixed bunch from the dairy, but nice. 'About Thursday . . .'

'It's okay.'

I went to put them in water. When I came back I asked, 'Are you finished?'

'Am *I* finished?' He gawuffed. 'I thought, Are *you* finished? was the question.'

'No. Yes.'

He said, 'Now you know why I didn't marry a girl from Clonard.'

'Why?'

'Hah!'

I did know, of course. Because he was in the New World.

It would be done today, couldn't help it. The costume.

He cooled his heels in the middle of the front room while I stitched over and over into the same spot, running on the spot; an Exercycle. Then sat down at the table. I was aware of him, his hefty torso, good for rugby, for felling the opposition. He'd chosen a wife that way, I knew that, like an All-Black scores a try, falling into the mud clutching her while spectators roared. For this, I suppose, he'd required a New Zealand woman. I smiled at the thought.

'What?'

I shrugged. 'What you're going to *do*.'

'What am I going to do?'

'Still hide this thing?' I held up the costume. 'At the bottom of the wardrobe? Trample it underfoot?'

He shook his head. 'I don't know.'

But he would. And it would be picked up and hung on a hanger. His messy life, his great life. He had everything—streetwise roots and a tertiary education; sob stories about poverty and a high-paying job; a Kiwi accent and an Irish turn of phrase; the beliefs of his parents and the freedom to trash them; a wife and a mistress. Everything. An Irish costume, and the wreck of it.

How far he'd come; he'd come so freaking far.

But I knew, I knew. His lovely little immigrant package—every bloody thing—contained the seeds of its own destruction. He'd find this out soon enough. At least, his grandchildren would.

I'm the grandchild. I am.

'It may be too late for trampling,' he said.

Something leaped in me. A sort of hope. The wind.

I might have kissed him again, right then. 'How was your weekend?' I asked.

'Good. How was yours?'

'Good.'

'How's the fruit farm?' Sarcastic as hell.

'Fine,' I tootled. 'Well, actually . . .'

'What?' He was intent.

I told him how the Japanese had pulled out. I was sewing the blinking air. The whole deal? he asked, and I said, Yes, the whole blinking deal. The poor Woolthamlys, I said, and he said, The poor Woolthamlys. I told him how the Woolthamlys were firing their workers. They're firing them? Yes, every last one. The poor stinking rich Woolthamlys, he said. We laughed. They would likely sell the business, I said. Really? said the client. Yes, really, I said. They'd had an offer. He said, Is that so, and I said, So.

'And what about Milly?' I asked.

'Milly? Yeah. They've dug in in Wellington, her firm. Till the end of the Blackout.'

'So there's no desperate hurry,' I said.

He waited a moment, then laughed.

Even I laughed this time.

What I realised: I had no choice now, it was out of my hands.

'But it's finished anyway.'

'It is. It's finished. I'll wrap it.'

''Kay.'

No earthly reason.

•

At that point that Mabel arrived, thumping over the springy veranda, bashing on the open front door. 'It's me!'

Me. It was endearing. I wish I were 'me'. She was halfway into her monologue before she reached the front room—more aprons, she had more aprons even though there was no *desperate* hurry but she thought she may as well drop them off on her way home. She stopped when she saw the pile of already-worked aprons, smiled. Then glanced at the client.

I introduced him. After the don't mind me, Mabel took up where she'd left off.

'How'd you get through these so *quickly*? Not that I'm complaining. My God no, the girls can get on with them. But I didn't *expect* (isn't she efficient?),'—directed at the client, who was still arranged at the table—'expect them for another few *days*.'

Then the look on his face. Puzzlement, and the residue of surprise at being included in Mabel's conversation. His eyes slid over to me, narrowly, and retreated again. He was mulling, I supposed. *Quickly?* The aprons are early? But the costume. The costume is late.

Well, what did he expect? Honesty? Straightforwardness? This was all about deceit. Deceit was why we were there.

Mabel was starting up again, addressing the room, the client, me, the slant of the sun. 'This *theme*,' she was saying, 'has taken off in directions I'd never dreamed of. That's the way it works, I suppose, creativity. It happens in your sleep, don't you find? This is *so* coming together I almost can't bear it.' An aside to the client, by way of explanation, 'The fifties. We're having a show. Hence the aprons. They were hard times, but boom times, well, the beginning of boom times. Not exactly booming for everyone, but everyone expected a job—except the women, of course. Everyone expected a section. Milk in schools. Apples. But it all came with work, bloody hard work. Hence the aprons. My mother used to get up at half past five in the morning . . .' Mabel stopped and brought an apron up to her black-rimmed glasses—a slight hesitation, the furrowing of the brow.

I looked at the client. He was frosty, but couldn't resist a smile. This was one of the wined-and-dined aprons. Wined-and-washed. A little dancing. I was trying not to laugh.

Mabel was packing the aprons away into a box. 'These are great by the way, wonderful, I can't *tell* you how much I appreciate it. I've had a wonderful idea for an eighties line, I'm quite excited about it. I think we're far enough out from them to *look* at them, don't you? Generally it was an ugly decade—I mean shoulders, my *Gahd.*' Mabel mimed vomiting. 'But also, beauty *isn't* everything. A little ugliness, like the zest of a lemon. Mm.' Mabel flung her bunched fingers out from her mouth. 'So I'm thinking eighties for Spring 1999. No, I'm serious!'

It was our laughter.

'I'll do the burst bubble. I'll do tatters. In fact, people *did* wear tatters. I wore the odd tatter myself. Ripped tights and T-shirts. The op-shop greatcoats. It's going to be the stripping down, the flaying, of everything. Hence . . .' She spread her hands as if to indicate the air around us. 'Has anyone heard what's going on, by the way, with the cables? I'm just hanging out for power again. Give me power!'

We shrugged. Well, I did.

'But the eighties, when they sold off everything, my *Gahd*. But it did bring us kicking and screaming into the twentieth century.' Here Mabel turned to the client. 'It's so easy to wipe things off as a bad deal, but there's always new growth, it's the way the world goes around. I remember when they sold the buses, the post office, the hospitals, the *elec-tric ser-vice*!' wailed Mabel. 'Ay-ay-ay! But we can *celebrate* this. You might not even remember this, GoGo. And I don't know how old *you* are . . .' A flirtatious rolling of the eyes in the client's direction. 'I'm not holding you up, am I?'

The client folded his hands and looked at Mabel. 'I remember when they sold the railways.'

'Oh, you do?' said Mabel. 'Shocking business.'

'My dad was the first to go.'

'The poor darling,' said Mabel.

The client frowned at me. If he'd known I was leading him on—well, Doris in Kingsland. He would've fired me. I was fired!

'Unqualified,' he went on, to Mabel, 'middle-aged, last on board.'

'What did he do?'

'Sponged off my mother.' He was performing for her, a monkey.

'The poor sausage.' Mabel clicked her tongue.

The client was calm. 'It fit like a glove.'

I shook my head. 'The little bourgeois troubles we have.'

'Oh, I know!' said Mabel. 'Don't talk to me about bourgeois. Don't think I don't struggle against it every day of my life. In this business, you have to be vigilant about that sort of thing, believe me.'

'I have bourgeois troubles,' said the client, and enjoyed the slight flush that came onto Mabel's face. 'What d'you call this?' Indicating the costume. And he looked at me, confronting, but funny. I almost laughed.

Mabel followed his gaze and snatched up the costume from the table. 'What *is* this?'

'It's his,' I said. I was tidying up the scraps. I'd finished. The costume was finished. 'It was his mother's. All the way from Ireland.'

'What a gorgeous thing!' said Mabel. She fingered the shoulder. 'What've you been doing to it, GoGo?'

I caught my breath. Doing to it? Was the ripping of the shoulder the night of the dinner party, the subsequent mending like a slow train—was it written all over it?

'Did you mend it?'

'Oh, yes. Here.' I showed Mabel. 'I reattached the shoulder, I repaired the knotwork.'

Mabel ran her fingers over the glittery mass of silk. 'What happened to it?'

'Long story,' I said.

Out of the corner of my eye I thought I saw the client purse his lips.

'Utterly gorgeous.' Mabel smiled at the client. He smiled back, and blushed in a bamboozled way—such fuss over a dress. Mabel ran her hand over one embroidered sleeve, then the other. She noticed that one was different at the cuff, I could tell by the way she looked from one to the other. I hoped she wouldn't say anything. At this point, especially after the client knew that I'd put the aprons ahead of this job, I'd look foolish if it was discovered that I'd gone beyond the call of duty as well.

'It's not authentic, of course,' said Mabel, 'but still nice. Still *very* nicely done.'

'Thank you,' I murmured, on autopilot.

Thank you! Mabel was going to spill the beans. Oh well, I'd been expecting to be sprung every day for the last two weeks. I began to rehearse, in my head, what I would say: how I couldn't bear to leave the sleeve unfinished (which was partly true), how, once I knew something of the costume's past, I regarded it as an heirloom, just like Milly did. I understood that now. Even after my pretty speech—the client would go away annoyed that I'd spent so long doing work that didn't need to be done, and that I'd actually made things worse. Because now, Milly would definitely notice. But I wouldn't give a rat's arse, because I'd probably never see this person again in my life, or only by accident because Auckland wasn't a very big place—

But Mabel was going on.

'Not the authenticity of your repairs—that's an oxymoron, isn't it? I'm talking about the authenticity of the garment. It's not historically authentic. It's a reiteration of something that never was, and therefore how can it be a reiteration?'

Oh, not my overenthusiastic patch-up job, but the costume per se.

'Not authentic?' I said, bristling, ready to defend the client. His mother and the dancing club, the box they took on the ferry—his rich culture going way back. Not authentic! The client didn't flinch, of course. I needn't have bothered.

Mabel shook her head. 'It's not as if Irish women ran around in embroidered dresses with capes attached to them. No, they dressed very plainly. In fact, there were sumptuary laws. Only the wealthy were allowed to look wealthy. That's why the poor needed to go all sumptuous later, when they got the chance. Who wouldn't? Come to think of it, history has been one big rollercoaster of sumptuary and sumptuary laws. But this,' said Mabel, pushing her glasses back to inspect the knotwork again, and again humming over the discrepancy between the sleeves, 'this is a product of the industrial revolution. Not this exact dress, of course, but the design. It was the textile mills. Suddenly a poor woman could have something fancy. Yeah, so, post-industrial, and not authentic. But still nice, still wonderful. Aren't you lucky?' Mabel turned to the client. 'It'll be an heirloom, this, won't it, even though it's not authentic?'

The client shrugged, but looked bemused, pleased.

'Of course it is!' said Mabel. 'And what else do we have to hand down? If we have children, that is. Myself, I seem to be waiting until I need artificial insemination. The choices we have! My fifties line, on the other hand, I mean talk about *no choice*—do you want to come to the opening, by the way? Bring a friend.' Mabel dug two flyers out of her bag and handed them to the client. He nodded thanks, and Mabel continued, 'We're celebrating the fifties women who went to live in the suburbs after the war. The sponge cake, the tomatoes on the windowsill, the antidepressants, the apron! Thank *Gahd* the venue is outside the Blackout zone otherwise we'd simply die. No *person* waits for fashion. I'd better get going, hadn't I? Will you come?'

'Hopefully,' said the client. 'I'll talk to my wife. Thank you.'

Meaning not a snowball's chance.

Mabel left in a cloud of cartons, words, silk skirt, black-rimmed glasses.

When she'd gone, I was as honest as I'd ever been.

29

The atmosphere was unbearable, somehow dehydrated, gasping. To break the silence, for no other reason because it was blinking obvious, he said, 'I didn't need to be coming all this time, did I?'

He was close, his skin. The table for support. I could smell him, cigarettes, ironed shirt. His face was hyper-real, blurry, like a Roy Lichtenstein. I wanted to touch it. I didn't. He seemed to come out of a trance, and did his puffing thing. Twice. His fingertips on the table. He shook his head. It was all over.

'Don't you want me to tell you about the girl from Clonard?'

'Do you want to?'

'I don't mind.' Come on. He was screaming to tell it.

'May as well then,' I said.

I was pulsing. The costume fell from the back of a chair onto the floor. I left it there and led him over to the couch. We sat at either end of it, perched like Victorians. Mr Rochester, Jane Eyre.

I give up. He's telling it.

He looked at me. 'They hoped I'd marry the girl from Clonard. This is about 1990. Ma always fought off the non-Catholic girlfriends with a stick.'

I opened my mouth.

He smiled. 'With pursed lips. You have to hand it to her, she was a good fighter. If I didn't find a Catholic girl in Auckland, they'd get me one from back home where there was an endless supply. There was a tap in Clonard running with Catholic girls and all you needed to do was line up with a bucket.'

Oh, a bucket.

'But why this girl?'

I got up to pour wine that was open on the sideboard and handed it to him.

'Already?'

'It's eight o'clock.'

'Is it?'

'Eight o'clock.'

'Thank you.'

'Don't mention it, Uncle Vanya. But why Trisha?'

He shrugged. 'I misremember.'

He misremembered!

'They knew her parents? They were Catholic? That was enough.' He stopped, then added, 'It ran deep. It ran very deep.

'There'd been letters. From her ma, and she was coming to New Zealand. Trisha. I remembered her. Buck-toothed Trisha. Now she was grown up and had a job and everything. There were jobs. She had a sunny nature, her ma said in a letter. My ma read it out. I remember that, a sunny nature.'

He laughed. I laughed. I'd met Trisha, after all.

'She did Irish dancing, and she'd turned into a beauty. Strange thing, the day I heard about this girl, I also came to blows with my father. I was visiting the house, having a cup of tea, hanging around like a spare limb. I always felt like a hulking teenager, compared to my dad (who starved as a child). Ma sat at the kitchen table and read me the letter from Trisha's mother. I was living in this wonderful country, teeming with New Zealand girls. I was doing my degree, and had just bought a car.'

I wondered how a student could afford a car and he said he made it his business.

'A Mazda 626. Blue.'

Blue. I smiled.

'What?'

'Go on.'

'So I thought I'd drive the new car out to see Ma and Dad. Who were on the bones of their arse. Ma with her letter, and Dad in his chair all day with his fags and his ashtray and his cup of tea, set up like a hospital trolley. Leaping sky-high every time there was a sirèn.'

'Wait. The paisley chair?'

'The paisley chair, poor bastard. Lungs rotting to hell. All day smoking and listening to the radio news, every hour on the hour. In case there was a tidal wave or parliament was dissolved or something. Five o'clock he'd start on the TV news. Anyway, Ma was telling me about Trisha's sunny nature, Dad was watching the news, when suddenly he stood up, knocking his trolley-load—the necessities of life—onto the carpet, and he was yelling blue murder. Ma and I came running in. We thought something terrible had happened. Dad was jumping up and down, pointing at the screen yelling, Conlon's on the TV! It's Gerry Conlon.

'I'm thinking, fine, who? Dad says fucking Gerry Conlon is what I'm telling you. So I ask who's Gerry Conlon when he's at home, even though I sort of knew. But I was sick of it, I was sick of the whole thing. Dad was foaming at the mouth—the Guildford Four, you don't know about the Guildford Four? They were wrongly convicted, in like 1975 or something. They'd just had their convictions quashed. When the ads came on Dad turned to Ma and he's going, How can he not know about the

Guildford Four? And Ma was saying, How would he? He was a boy. Dad put his head in his hands and he was mumbling about the Guildford Four and the Maguire Seven, who were related. Gerry Conlon's father Giuseppe, an aunt and two teenage sons, all put away, all innocent. Dad looked up and he said, Do you want to know what they did to them, down in London, to get them to sign the confession? I said I didn't want to know. Dad said, I'm fucking sure you don't. They were accused of running a bomb factory. The mother of these lads, running a bomb factory in her kitchen in London. She served fourteen years. Giuseppe Conlon never saw the light of day again. Dad turned back to Ma. Does he really not know? Ma said, Leave the lad alone. Lad! Dad was spitting. He's twenty! Actually, I was nineteen. Ma went back to the kitchen. Dad was still shaking his head and wittering on, For pity's sake, he doesn't know anything.

'I went right up to his face and I said, You're not there anymore, Dad. You're here. We came here so you wouldn't be shot in the street like Mr O'Connell. That's why we came here in the first *fucking* place. He said, That's rubbish for a start. It was for you we came here, for you and the girls. I would've died willingly. Every day I was ready to die for Ireland. But no. We had to come here, *here*—he meant the room, the room with the chair from the side of the road, the TV and the carpet. We came here for you.

'I told him we came here because he was a murderer.

'Ma bleated from the doorway—Shane! Well, he was, I said, he murdered someone, didn't he? In the July twelfth parade. He was a wanted man. That's why we were here, wasn't it?

'It all went slow-motion in the room—silent, but the TV still going. He looked me full in the face and said he had. He spat it out. He'd taken out an Orangie and he was proud of it.

'At that point I swung my fist at him. He ducked. I was pathetic. Well, he was the hero from the lane, and I was the university student. I hated him to hell. The news was back on. He turned away to watch the news, which had background stuff on the Maguires. I was sick of it. I couldn't stand it. I said, That's right, go back to the telly. You're like a little working-class fucking Englishman, with your chair and your telly and your ashtray. (This is what I said, all in my New Zealand accent. At home I could always hear my own accent.) I felt like dusting my hands. I'd been crucified at school for being a Pom, and I'd called him an Englishman. He was purple with rage, literally purple, and he was pushing his face right up to me. I thought he was going to hit me, so I swung at him again and this time I hit him in the mouth. It was as hard as a doorpost. He sort of staggered backwards onto the chair and looked up at me with this incredulous expression on his face. I couldn't believe it either. Me, his son! I'd won.

'Ma came running in, all upset. She told me I should go, and I said I'd go alright, and I'd never come back. She said she didn't mean that. But I meant it. I said I was never setting foot in there again. Ma was all, you know, crying, and went out of the room.

'I put some money on the kitchen table, which I often did. Ma cleaned houses. That's how they survived. They didn't go on the benefit because Dad kept a low profile. He was still terrified of being extradited. I'd give Ma a hundred dollars, and make sure Dad saw it, the red note. Even when I was a student I earned more in a year than he'd earned in a lifetime. Dad called out—he was still holding his chin—You can keep your fucking money! And your fancy car. But he looked sort of broken. I felt sorry for him. I remember he looked down at the chair as if he'd just noticed it. Then back at me. He said he should've been there, with Bobby Sands, and with the Conlons and the Maguires. And I would've been, he said, if I hadn't brought you and your sisters to this godforsaken fucking place! God, I hated him. Then he was watching the news again, not Gerry Conlon, but some other catastrophe. And I repeated, I'm never coming back.'

•

The client was pacing around the room. Wound up *like a spring*. He looked back at me, and I felt an odd tremor because there was this anger coming off him. He came up and jabbed a finger at the costume. I didn't like it.

'What?' I said. I glared at him.

'Nothing.' He turned away.

'So you never went back?'

'Of course I went back.' As if this was a ludicrous suggestion, but he'd said it. There was more. 'Ma came back into the room and she had something—guess what?'

I shrugged. I was screaming to know.

'She said if I was going I should take this.'

'What, the costume?' I said.

He nodded. 'She said when I got married, it'd be for my wife. It was this Trisha thing, she hadn't given up on it. In the other room, I could see Dad watching us. He turned off the TV, you know like shooting it to death, *load of fucking rubbish*.'

'I bet you couldn't even see it,' I said. I felt all jangly.

'What?'

'The costume, of course, what are we talking about?'

'It was a dress,' he said, his hands outlining one in the air.

'That's a terrible dress,' I said. 'I'd never wear that.'

'Wouldn't you?' He looked at me.

'No,' I said. It sort of all went quiet. I blushed.

Then he was off again. 'I told Ma one of the girls should have it, of course. But then I remembered Ma had tried to get them to do Irish dancing when they were young, but they wouldn't have a bar of it and she'd given up. Never, she said, sort of darkly. The dress was for my wife.'

'Trisha,' I said.

'Not that it was for my *wife*.'

'What? Pardon?'

'It was for a grandchild, the first girl grandchild, of course, Catholic. Who would carry everything into the next generation.'

The costume really was an heirloom. It did have some meaning beyond itself. The wool, the silk, the knotwork, they weren't just materials. I'd held it in my hands, in my lap. Okay, GoGo, don't get carried away. But it was *something*. I'd torn it, for God's sake. For I-don't-know-what.

He got up from the couch and stood in the middle of the room and the room was purple.

'Of course, they *wouldn't* carry everything into the next generation,' he said. He had his arms folded tightly across his chest. 'Not in New Zealand. Ma and Dad never understood that. No one warned them—the way you're warned about malaria if you go to Africa—that New Zealand would take away everything. Everything.

'But Trisha,' he said, 'she still had it, with bells on.'

'What? *What*?' I wanted to know.

'I don't know. Eight hundred years of oppression plastered all over her.' He guffawed. He gawuffed. 'As I stomped out of the house, Ma pushed the dress into my hands. I didn't want it. I took it back to the flat and tossed it somewhere. I thought I gave it to Dana or Sharon at some point. I meant to. It certainly wasn't going to the skinny, buck-toothed girl from Clonard, because I was never marrying her. I asked Rena to marry me.'

'Who the hell is Rena?'

'Previous girlfriend. Long story. She turned me down.'

'Sensible girl,' I said.

'I know.'

'Under the circumstances.'

'I know. It was okay. Well, it wasn't. But my next girlfriend I married. Milly.'

I knew *Milly*. I knew this part of the story.

'But you didn't marry Milly just for . . .'

I mean, he seemed to love her. God knew why. She was Bertha Mason.

'Oh, Milly was great.' He was pacing again.

Was.

'Is,' he said. 'When I met her she was doing middle-class finishing school.'

I didn't like the sound of this.

'She lived at home and went wild under her parents' roof. It drove me nuts. A lot of New Zealand girls were allowed to do this, I noticed. I'd meet a girl and her old man'd be offering me a drink and clapping me on the back in the living room. We'd chat about the weather. Half an hour later I'd be fucking their daughter in her bedroom while they watched TV. There'd be stuffed toys flying off the bed. My parents cared who I married. Milly's father broke out the champagne when he heard this stranger was going to marry his daughter. I might've been a psychopath.'

He came near the table and looked at me. You had to be close to see, in the dark. I knew where this was going. 'I suppose your family was like that.'

I looked up at him. 'Why do you think that?'

'Just a guess. Were you allowed to go wild?'

I opened my mouth. Perhaps I could've gone wild. Lisa did. I think my parents were the wild ones. Never mind. 'So the betrothed wasn't coming, then?'

'Not *betrothed*!' He was off again.

'Family fwiend.'

'She didn't come. It was all off. This was seven, eight years ago. Then, a few months ago, she turned up here.'

'Who paid?'

'She did, I suppose. She had a job. It's different now. Both England and Ireland joined the EU and it's been good for them. It was all to do with wealth, or lack of it. It always is. Now they have cafés on the Falls Road. So I hear. And there've been peace talks going on.'

'Did you see her?'

'Trisha?' He turned and looked puzzled. 'You know I did.'

'Tell me anyway.'

That blowing-out-air mannerism. Which I'd grown to like. It was endearing. 'I picked her up at the airport because I had a car. Slightly weird—the picking-up—because of the history of matchmaking. Milly even came too. She felt sorry for Trisha. Poor Trisha with the buck teeth.

'As soon as I saw her coming out of Arrivals I knew what was going to happen. She was beautiful. Dark hair, dark eyes. Her teeth. It's funny how something ugly in childhood can become beautiful in an adult. But it wasn't just that. She'd been around the block a few times, you could tell. She had poise, the most amazing poise. But it wasn't even that. It was that my parents had picked her out for me, and I *wasn't* marrying her. It was the way she smiled at me as if she knew something about me. Which she did. I watched her push her trolley through the airport in her black dress, caught sight of her in the rear-view mirror (she insisted on sitting in the back), and listened to her talk to Milly about the flight, Belfast, about the talks, all the way back into Auckland. She stared back at me in the rear-view mirror.

'I had no choice.'

The old *out of my hands* routine. Spare me.

'We drove Trisha to my parents' house. They were a bit shocked by her.'

'But there was Dreadful and Frightful.'

'Dreadful and Frightful were always on the outer. You couldn't remember a time. But Trisha. She'd been a nice Catholic girl. I couldn't keep my eyes off her. I remember looking around for Milly. I was worried she might notice something. I couldn't find her. Then I saw her sitting in the old paisley chair. For a moment I couldn't distinguish her from it. She was wearing a paisley dress. I remember thinking, she's invisible now.'

He shouldn't be telling me this. I loved it. 'Is she still?' I asked. 'Invisible.'

He waited a bit. 'Almost.'

He came close to the couch. I could've touched his thigh.

'While Milly was kissing my parents goodbye—which they hated, they've never got used to all the kissing here—I gave Trisha my card. She took it and crushed it like a leaf. A few days later she called at the office. We had lunch at Rakinos and went to a hotel.'

I couldn't bear it. I realised.

(*Yes, I am a bit like that little dog.*

Ha ha. Ha-ha-ha-ha-ha.)

But I wanted to know, I had to know.

'Milly often works late, till ten sometimes, and on those nights I took Trisha to a hotel after work. I know. I'm a terrible person.' He must have sensed I was on the point of defending him. He put up his hand in denial. 'No, I'm a shocking person.'

I didn't believe his self-abnegation for an instant. He was proud of it.

'There's more. My father was painting my house. Still is. It's been going on for months. On the first morning, as I'm going to work—'

'In your yellow jacket.'

'My nice yellow jacket. He's in his overalls. He says to me, You've made something of yourself, son. I thought, Here we go. Sure enough he says, But don't go thinking the men back home didn't make something of themselves. And I said, Of course, Dad. He didn't expect me to understand, he said, but they weren't *nothing* just because they didn't have jobs. And I'm saying, No, of course not. I worked with some great minds, he says. Not myself of course. (Always the modesty, which was real, and why people had liked him.) Not myself, he says. And I say, No, you Dad. And we go back and forth like this, just like we did in the kitchen on his first day of work at the railways. He tells me he knew men with great minds. I tell him I know that, I say they were all great men, given to the cause. I was quoting the words I grew up hearing. And now I have to go to work, Dad. But he says to me, he swings around and says to me, What the hell would you know about it?

'And you know what? Nothing. I know nothing about it. And I'm glad I don't. I went to work. After work, I brought Trisha back to the house. To the spare room. The woman they picked out for me was my—I don't know what.'

'Mistress,' I said. I was certain about this. I'd thought about this, through all the ripping and burning and snagging. 'Mistress.'

He smiled. 'Okay, mistress.' It sounded odd in his mouth. Prim.

He'd fucked her in the spare room, was what he was trying to say. How far he'd come, the immigrant kid with the funny accent and the new clothes. Now he had the career, the house, the wife, the mistress. How far he'd come.

'Was it good?' I asked.

He shook his head as if to shake off the question.

'I thought she was pretty,' I said. 'Her teeth.'

He ignored me. So politic.

'But you thought you'd be together?' I asked. I was a dog at a bone.

'Of course. For an evening.' A shrug.

'The evening of the national costume?'

He asked me what I meant.

'You know what I mean,' I said. 'The day it was ripped.'

'Yes, then,' he said.

'Tell me how it happened.'

'You know how it happened.'

'Tell me.'

'At the house one night,' he said, 'she was cold and she was looking for a dressing-gown—'

'She was naked?'

'Well, yeah.' Shrugged.

'Just checking.'

'She saw the costume hanging in the wardrobe. I told her it was for her. I told her the whole story of how it'd been given to me to give to her. She was amazed. Me? she was saying. Me! She was gobsmacked. She put it on. Actually, it didn't look too different from what she usually wore. She's sort of . . .'

'Punk,' I said.

'Oh, that's right. You know.' He was surprised. She'd brought me the dress, all that time ago, the first day of the Blackout. He'd misremembered. 'Punk. She was getting ready to leave in the costume. She wanted to wear it, you know, out. I didn't want her to, in case Milly. She said I worried too much, the chances of bumping into Milly on the street. She said it was hers anyway, it'd been given to her. The whole thing was weird. I'd never seen anyone in this dress before, I'd never looked at it before, and now it had come to life—in New Zealand. But it was strange. I tried to stop her.'

'And?'

'And the rest is history,' he said. He was a silhouette, a blush of light from the western hills.

Oh for goodness' sake. I'm telling the rest of it from here on in.

•

He was lying on the bed. Naked. He was naked. He got up and went towards her, his cock bouncing, his shoulder lifted and he grabbed the sleeve. She wrenched away. It was a joke, she was joking with him. He had another go but she kept jerking away. They were laughing. It was a game. She could've run out the door but she didn't. He could've held her but he didn't. She kept dodging away from him, just within his reach. This way, that way. Her dressed, him naked. (*Le déjeuner sur l'herbe* in reverse, I thought.) It was hilarious. But suddenly it went serious. Suddenly they were in a bubble where there were no rules, no limits. No New Zealand, no Ireland. He grasped her shoulder. She turned to glare at him. Almost hateful, but not. Not. There was a scratchy sound. Like a fart, he said. A fart! All he knew was, he had a flap of the dress in his hand, and her white shoulder was showing through. There was a bunch of threads in his hand. This shocked him. It was like veins, he said. Guts. She said, Oh shit. Then they were laughing again, and back on the bed, and he could feel the embroidery—the knotwork, yes the knotwork—rubbing against him. They probably did it more damage then. Hammer and tongs. Afterwards she said, I'll go now. He opened the front door for her and she stepped outside wearing the dress, her skin showing through the gaping rip. She put on a cardigan as she went down the path.

I swallowed, brushed threads off myself, if I could see any threads. 'Milly saw her in the supermarket,' I said. 'She told me that day you were—'

'Yeah, that was the first I knew. You wouldn't read about it.' He laughed.

I felt jealousy leap like a weak, unused muscle. I'd always been so *unjealous*. People said that to me, friends over the years. GoGo, unjealous to a fault, over Art's string of women friends.

I remembered the last time—in the Michael Fowler Centre, 1993. *Yes, I suppose I am a bit like that little dog*, and the exaggerated, swollen laughter of the woman.

'Now I know everything about you,' I said. I expected him to say, no, of course you don't.

'Yes,' he said. He looked sort of surprised, wide-eyed.

'Good that this is finished then, isn't it?' I stood up and pushed the costume into his hands in the dark. 'I'll light the lamp.'

He held it close to his face, turned his head on one side, curious like a bird, and seemed to consider something about it.

'It's done?' he said.

I nodded.

He let it drop, as if releasing a theatre curtain.

'I don't know anything about you, though. Do I?'

'No, you do,' I said. 'A few things.'

'The strange thing is, there's no urgency now.'

'Because Wellington?'

'Because of the Blackout.'

'That's the first time you've mentioned the Blackout.'

'Is it?'

'It is.'

He smiled. I followed suit.

'Because it may be too late,' he said. 'Maybe always was.'

I was trembling. I was. I said, 'Tell me again, is part of all this that you might end up together? There might be no going back?'

A beat, as they say, in a screenplay. I was close and could feel his warmth. He looked dazed. I prompted him: 'No choice. Out of my hands.'

The client seemed to come to. 'Yes. Of course. Otherwise.'

'Otherwise why do it?'

'Yes.'

A strange energy rushed through me. 'I need to wrap this,' I said.

'I remember you said that, that day.'

'Did I?'

'And you went to wrap it.'

'Did I? I'll wrap it now.'

''Kay,' he said. Just the 'kay, not even that, the click. I remember that.

In the passage it was a bit lighter because the front door was open. A mauvish colour came in. He followed me down to the workroom. I could feel his footsteps on the floorboards. The Wah Lee lightshade passed overhead like a moon. I turned in the doorway. We fell together suddenly just inside the door, in the metre space between the table and the door. Half a thought, that it wasn't right, because of the others, *the other parties*, but finding I was lost in his mouth for a long period of time and that it was impossible to let go, even if you might decide to let go, several times, because of the other parties. You could never break off. There was no human power strong enough. Our clothes gone somehow, out of the way, pants yanked, skirt pushed up all bundily, shirt open, belt fumbled undone. Then disappearing into it, all your body parts, your thumping heart, your limbs, neck, arse, tits, all gone from the known world. His name coming out of your mouth. Shane. Later wondering at which exact point there was no choice about what would happen next. Out of my blinking hands. And in the mirror later, getting undressed, twisting to find small bruises like rare moths on your back from the bones mashing against the workroom table but being unable to remember any pain.

Skin

30

I was looking down a road and there must've been rain recently because it was shiny, a silk road. The seal was bumpy, textured, and as I squinted into the distance I saw that the road looped in a paisley or perhaps a koru shape like a road on the side of a hill. By the side of the road were bundles of something bristly laid out at regular intervals as if ready to feed animals or to thatch a roof. Inside the loop were other roads just the same, concentric, getting smaller and smaller like Russian dolls. And like Russian dolls, each one was perfect in detail; although perhaps as it all got very tiny, they weren't quite so perfect. I know, I'm mixing patterns and metaphors like nobody's business—Indian, Maori, Russian, where will it end? But this was our familiar old red brocade couch, and I'd never seen it up so close.

The client came back. Even though I'd pushed the costume, all finished, into his hands on the way out the door, he came back the next day. He said hi and I said hi and we stopped for a minute, fell against each other in the passage and toppled onto the floor, then moved into the front room where I kicked the door shut and swished the curtains across. It was like cinema during the day. He swallowed me.

After that, he came back again and again. At first I numbered every time—workroom, passage wall, red couch, floor—then I lost count. I could give you details, but I don't want to be self-centred. Suffice to say I had a very exciting idyll, when secrecy was my jacket and lies my skirt, not to get too flowery about it. There were other things going on, which I'll get on to, but this glory was the main thing, even though I told myself every morning *not to*. I said—as I carefully picked out my clothes—GoGo, you fool, you're riding for a fall. I proceeded as if it were temporary, for several reasons. One, I knew how the client operated. Two, the Blackout would come to an end and his wife would come flapping back from Wiggytown like a homing pigeon. The client told me he'd hung the costume in the wardrobe, all prepared for that very day. As if I cared a hoot. He hadn't mentioned putting it on the wardrobe floor and trampling it underfoot—the original plan, but perhaps redundant if his wife happened to notice the finished sleeve. He hadn't noticed it, of course.

And number three was blinking obvious: I had a husband. Who I didn't want to deceive, but I had no choice. It was out of my hands. And so now I started on my period of deceit. I liked the secrecy. In the beginning I liked it.

I liked that he was wiry and heavy, light and dark, smooth and rough, gentle and unpredictable. He was a whole bundle of dichotomies. I know, book me in for a lobotomy.

I went with the client into paradise.

•

In the mornings I couldn't wait for Art to leave the house. I'm sorry, but it's true. Things were a bit high-strung. For a start I had adopted sex-avoidance techniques like suddenly getting busy late at night, or falling into bed yawning at nine o'clock. I tried so hard to be normal, it must have looked like a neurosis. Over breakfast we would go back and forth about the news a little bit, and then I would wave him off like a fifties housewife, smiling my gory smile. I'd never done this. I was a nineties housewife. As he got smaller and smaller, disappearing down the path and onto the street, I would stand in the mandolin, its grey light. A layer of brightness had been stripped away as if with a flat knife. I was twitchy, ecstatic. I was *on* something. When Art was completely gone—no chance of him returning for a forgotten thing, Frantz flipping Fanon f'rinstance—I would go into the bedroom and whirl clothes about. I was a character in a sitcom. A flockcom, seeing we were as far from a nuclear family as a split atom. Nothing went with anything, of course. The agony. That had always been the case, but now I really cared. What I'd discovered about my clothes was, they were nice, but they were intellectual. A Russian constructivist would like them, if you get my drift. What I wanted was sexy. There were a few things. A vintage fifties dress, a wafty op-shop blouse. Anyway.

Then I would have all day. Did I mention Megan Sligo Mending and Alterations was on the verge of collapse? Perhaps I would ratchet it up again, perhaps I wouldn't. I hadn't had a client for weeks. The upshot was, I read the odd novel. *Wide Sargasso Sea*, by Jean Rhys, for instance, about the madwoman in the attic from *Jane Eyre*, why she was mad—when I could tear my thoughts away from my own little roman à clef, that is. I must say I thought about the client *quite a bit*.

•

Around seven o'clock he would arrive. As per usual, you might think, and you'd be right. The Wah Lee moon would shift on the breeze from the front door. We'd kiss on the doorstep. The audacity—it was like petrol. The sun in our hair first, then plummeting in the bay window. Then *curtains* again. It was after hours. I knew the feeling of his mouth on my neck. His body crushing me and then rolling over, me sitting astride him and spilling myself onto him on the rug. Up close he had a lovely upper lip, its tender shape. I moved onto his body like an immigrant, carved out a new life on terra incognita; his torso, my sweat, his arms and legs, my arse (yes, *my arse*). He tasted like me now, his mouth, skin, wetness. My hand on his bristly hairline was connected to him filling me. I won't go on.

I said his name. Shane. Shane. Shane.

Of course we listened for Art in between, like commercials. On the second visit, we seriously thought we heard him, a thump on the veranda, but it was the wind. Fell back screeching. We were a young country with weak infrastructure, wiring that might fizz out at any moment, not to put too fine a point on it. I could lose everything in the next instant—chuck everything away. It was glorious. We lay squashed up on the couch and talked. He smoked there once or twice, the tendrils curling upwards like a Renaissance hymn. My hand on his damp chest, knee across him. We talked about stray things, what kind of weather we liked, the worst teacher we ever had, talked to the ceiling. Sometimes I turned uncomfortably to look at him close-up. And he turned. Like pecking birds.

He asked me to tell some stories, like he did. I told him he already knew about the pole house, and he said yes. And the books, and the Skoda.

Yes.

And my sister Lisa.

Yes.

And my invisible national costume, and he laughed, and said, That's just bits and pieces.

I suppose it's true, things had broken down a bit—but that's alright, I said.

He said it was. After a fashion.

After a fashion! I said.

I didn't know any long versions anyway.

I knew all about him of course.

'This is just till the power comes back on, isn't it?'

'Yeah.'

'I hope the Blackout lasts forever.'

'Me too.'

I can't remember who said what. I said a lot, a lot of garbage, like thinking aloud. No stories, stories were over. It was snippets now, ephemera. They seemed important.

He said, 'I love you though.'

And I said—amazed—'Yeah, me too. I love you.'

We laughed because it was so funny, because you know, I was the mender and he was the client, and it was true. And everything was suddenly beautiful and exciting. Honestly, it was as if I'd turned my head and seen the whole world from a different angle, one I'd never looked from before, and it made the air, objects, even ideas glittering and larger. It made things wonderful.

Our lingering goodbye was dreadful, in the half-light.

'I have to go.'

'Don't go.'

'I need to.'

'Go then.'

'In a minute.'

'I don't want you to.'

Some shrieking and groaning, pulling away like chewing gum. It was a pantomime. Agony. It was the best time in my life.

When he'd gone I washed at the basin by candlelight (a whiff of mould in the long bathroom) with a cloth, as if I was in a

French film with a soundtrack, the foily tinkle of water. I was Juliette Binoche. I thought Art might think it odd that Juliette had had a shower mid-evening, so I sponged myself, the slick of sweat from my stomach, between my legs, a spit of semen plopping onto the floor, water everywhere. Also to be quick, but it took longer. Shortcuts are always more trouble. I would have cleaned my teeth but thought Art might wonder why Juliette smelled of toothpaste at dusk.

I could smell the client, for hours afterwards. As I walked about the house, his smell clung to me like perfume. I wondered why Art didn't twitch his nose as soon as he came in the door, dropping his dissertation in the passage. I almost wanted him to. It would all be over. But he didn't, he couldn't. He sneezed. But even without hayfever, Art would probably never have noticed. The smell of the client lay on the air like a fresh mend.

In bed I turned away, my nostrils in the crook of my arm. It rushed at me again, how I was in love, a fresh wave of ecstasy or deceit, I don't know which, surging through me. Now I was like the client, like all the clients whose tracks I had covered. Cases 1, 2 and 3. I was Case 397, or thereabouts. I loved the risk. I felt like I had the day I'd dropped out of university, walked down Church Steps, and come home to an empty house, where a pencil rolled across the floor.

•

These other things going on? Well, they were working on the cables for a start. I heard that on the news. Plus, I had no clients. Plus, the Murus had walked off the job. There was a new Warehouse opening in the town, and they'd thought it would be a safer option. The Taranaki Dried Fruit Company had come to a standstill. Art told me this, in the kitchen. It was like a dream. I might have dreamed him. He talked and I thought about the client. Who I must stop calling the client because he was Shane. But then I did hear, slowly, like a reverberation. The vultures, I suppose, were descending.

In my half-dream, it occurred to me: 'But you're cut out of the will anyway.'

'Might be.' He sort of blushed.

Of course. Might be. I knew how it was—just the threat of it. He hated that.

'I could be, but I'm not. At present.'

We almost laughed. I didn't care. About any of it. I had everything. I revised my thoughts on *the highest point*, the peak, which I had originally put at the time Mary-France and Dad and Lisa and I drove, then loped, up the steepest street in the Southern Hemisphere, Dunedin, c. 1980. No. It was *this* moment, standing in the middle of the yellow kitchen in the Blackout. I had absolutely blinking everything.

I felt like singing.

I thought about how on the doorstep I might notice his teeth and the inside of his mouth more than anything. Or his hips. My hands. It was like lying down in the snow. I gave up everything.

In the passage, the wall as a prop. His throat.

Once, a conversation about cars, all arms and legs wrapped up on the rug. He had a new one, don't ask me what. My knowledge of cars stopped at my father's Skoda. He laughed. The university professor with the Skoda. Then went a bit thoughtful and said his dad could've bought a Skoda but he couldn't have afforded the money for a taxi. I laughed.

At night I undressed in the bathroom and wrapped myself in a dressing-gown so Art wouldn't see the marks on my neck. The bruise from a week ago still just visible on my spine, a yellow smudge. I kept my bruise to myself. Time would mend it. I need do nothing but wait. He was a good man, he was lovely, but I didn't even care. All the same I was jittery in the night, on a permanent full moon. I would wake with a start, having dreamed I'd pricked my finger on a rumbling sewing machine. For a few moments I wouldn't know who I was, or where I was, what the meaning of the blackness in the room was. I would realise, then, that the rumbling was Art's snoring and that there was no pain in my finger, I had just thought it was pain. The taste of the client was in my mouth, and the smell of him in my nostrils.

•

Then my lovely routine again. Waving Art off, getting dressed, my choosing-clothes routine, my whirligig (I needed to look as though I'd just tossed them on without any thought, which was where all the thinking came in). One morning I came upon a whole bunch of my Mabel garments. They were certainly beautiful—wool and fur, chiffon and linen—but it struck me for the first time what was wrong with them: they weren't sexy. They might have been funky, powerful, interesting, but they had zero sex appeal. I packed them up and put them away in the Winter suitcase on top of the wardrobe. Ditto my shoes. I had one good pair, bought to go to a wedding once, from the stylish shop on Ponsonby Road. I looked like a ward matron in them.

I dressed in an op-shop thing, a dress. Then I read a novel, or tried to. It was hard to concentrate. I read a page upside down like Blanche Ingram.

Then the client was in the warm sun of the passage.

'Hello.'

'Hello.'

In the front room I walked my fingers on the bones of his neck. And looked at him. Somehow different today. I don't know why.

'We're not falling in love, are we?'

He swivelled his head with difficulty. My finger slipped away. 'Maybe we are. What do you think?'

'I think maybe,' I said.

'When the power comes back on.' He looked back at the ceiling.

'When the power comes back on what?'

Then he said, because I'd got up and opened the curtains and the garden was broadcast by the sun into the room and my Singer sewing machine was glinting (I think it was this): 'You should employ people.'

I told him I liked working by myself, he knew that, and he said what did liking have to do with it?

'What you should do,' he said, and he propped his head on his elbow, getting all enthusiastic, 'is take on four or five immigrant women and make some decent money.'

'Immigrant women!' I sat up. 'You're a fascist!'

It was all a joke, you understand.

The client got dressed. It was time anyway. (Art.) 'My mother was an immigrant,' he said. 'She worked for a pittance. You don't want your kids to be like that, do you?'

'You're a capitalist.'

'Of course. You are too. You're having a break. That's what capitalism gave you. It's a bit like this.'

I stopped with only my sleeves on. 'What? Us?'

'Yes.' Fastening everything, buttons. 'Just because your parents had degrees and a nice house.'

We laughed and rolled over and over on the rug again and I said stop, I was getting fluff all over me. And Art would notice, I meant.

He was ridiculous. He was gorgeous. We laughed and pressed together in the doorway. While the power was out. Pressed tight. There'd be an imprint of him on me. One day I'd be a fossil and the memory of the man would be a carbon picture. When he'd gone I brushed crumbs from the couch into the palm of my hand. I was dreading when the power would come back on. I was.

I did wonder if Milly would notice the newly embroidered sleeve. Perhaps she would bring the knotwork right up close to her eyes and decipher the two colours worked together, the Dollar Bill and the Minaret.

31

Once or twice he popped in at lunchtime (yes, popped). On one of those lunchtimes we were in the front room with the curtains drawn, though obviously it was broad daylight, not to put too fine a point on it, when there was a *major development*.

He said, 'I see the house is on the market.'

There was no wall anymore. You could fall through into the other side of the villa conversion, through one of the blocked-up doorways in the sunlight.

'I see *all* of the houses are on the market.'

I told him about the fruit empire shares taking a tumble.

He said, 'Oh, they took a tumble.' As if he knew nothing. He knew I knew.

A key clattered like a maniac in the front door lock. The inevitable, I thought—and the client thought, and sprang up like a cheetah. Perhaps this was for the best. I realised I wanted the Truth, and the client did not, he wanted Lies and Beauty. Even at this point I knew this. However. Yes, however. Even in the first nanosecond the rattling didn't have the particular timbre of Art opening the door. Next, multiple footsteps in the passage, a herd, then Prue's Taranaki voice, Bert's pleasant bleating, and another voice, a shrill rejoinder. We scrabbled, the client and I. Our eyes met briefly like a ding. A moment later the door was flung open as if by a poltergeist. The tail-end of *wonder why this room is*, and Prue's blue stare followed (like Art's, but it occurred to me in that moment she'd had her eyelids pegged back).

'Oh, Megan! I didn't expect to find you home. I'd forgotten about your . . . little business.' Prue took in the scene and frowned as much as she could. Me sitting at the table pawing over an apron, the sun beating down on the mad garden. '*Lovely* to see you. We have rather unfortunate news.'

Bert waved from the passage and disappeared as if pulled by the clopping heels of the shrill woman. *Master bedroom*, if you wouldn't mind.

It was a visitation.

As you've no doubt guessed, the house was on the market. Come to think of it, Prue looked dreadful. Blue, her skin. They tromped up and down the passage and in and out of the rooms again and again as if the spaces might have changed since the last time. I sat at the table pretending to be busy. At one point the real estate agent—bottle blonde, business-suited (the kind I'd like to wear, but never could), wound up like a spring—made a circumnavigation of the front room. She stood in the bay window and took in the garden. As I watched I saw the curtain beside her breathe in and out. Her polished brass head turned to look at it. It happened again, in out, like a lung. The real estate agent pushed the curtain aside and saw the client, standing like a sentry, if sentries were naked from the waist down. Prue and Bert were craning up at the Carrara ceiling. Ah, the ceiling, the ceiling has always been an asset. Prue wiped a tear from her eye. Bert told her not to be a silly sausage, they'd be alright. And Prue sniffled, Yes, it was just money, they had their health and their happiness.

She might have just said health, on second thoughts. I might be embroidering a bit here.

The real estate agent let the curtain drop and turned back to the room. 'The garden has potential,' she said. 'A little neglected, but nothing a bit of landscaping can't fix.' She caught my eye on the way out and I tried to smile my thanks, but she stayed in character, in her suit.

That was the day I ripped my teal blouse.

When they'd gone, the client and I had an episode of hilarity during which I thought I might have a heart attack. Then he went back to work, and I stood outside in the frying sun looking at the For Sale sign that had been stapled to the fence. It flapped in the tough little wind. The gully was quiet apart from the mechanic down the road and the building site. I looked up the street. There was a For Sale sign on each of the four villas. The whole blinking row was on the market.

I got to know all about the baht of course. Things were toppling like dominos through Asia.

Over the next few days, when prospective buyers came to inspect the house, I lurked in the garden. The house wasn't at its best—ponged like a trench, carpets matted, though the real estate agent sent someone around with a carpet sweeper. Prue-short-for-Prudence and Bert were desperate. The thing is, the villa conversion was fading away anyway. It was light and flimsy.

The next time he came I reached out behind me for his fingers and we walked along the passage joined tenuously like paper dolls. On the workroom table he entered from behind. I reached back blindly to clutch his thigh, his hair, in my clenched hand. He was solid and silky.

It was urgent, no stories. I knew all about him.

Everything was gone.

Everything?

Everything except the couch, the floor, the table. I'd brought these with me. I'd moved, you see; I'd emigrated.

•

In the evening I washed clothes by hand in the bath while Art stalked up and down the passage, and outside, talking on the phone about the villa being sold, having to move and so on, with a succession of people. Villa-z, I heard him say. Not just villa, villa-z. He was stunned, I thought, the proverbial mullet, but was putting a good face on it, in true Woolthamly fashion. I lugged the clothes out to the yard and hung them on the line. They were dripping, but the heat would dry them. Art followed me in and out, still on the phone. I think one of the conversations was with Prue. I almost wanted to tell him about the funny incident with the real estate agent, because that was what we used to do. I didn't, of course. Are you crazy?

We'd sort of stopped talking, we'd stopped our banter. I didn't miss it. It felt like there were more urgent things. Banter had seemed like an excess, like a burn-off of oil.

Plus—to tell the truth—I couldn't sit still. I was a bundle of nerves. When there was a bump, Art's foot knocking the rubbish bin, I jumped like a firecracker. I imagined the client turning up out of the blue. Not exactly *blue*. He'd gone mad, and was knocking on the door, coming in and walking through the rooms until he found Art. I'm fucking your wife. Or even, I'm in love with your wife. There had been this fear or hope sitting there in my head all these weeks.

I loved the risk. I had a Wanted card. I had a Mass card.

When he'd hung up the phone, I turned from the line and said I was sorry about the house. I wanted to say something. Art said there was no need to be sorry on his account, he didn't care. He was knocking back a glass of wine. And anyway, the house was mine too, he said. I said I thought it *wasn't* mine, I thought we'd established that and he got all het up and said no, no, of course it was mine, that was just a silly argument.

'What's mine is yours. The house is yours,' he said. 'Or would be if we owned it,' he sniggered.

There was a little banter, but I wasn't taking part. I hung the dripping clothes.

•

On the day I gave him his yellow jacket, which I'd mended, things racked up a bit. He took the jacket and screwed it up unconsciously as we were falling backwards. Careful, I said. He said, Oh yeah, and laid it out like a body on the table before returning to the rolled arm of the couch.

This was during a period of rain—the house particularly zoo-like—two, three days' worth. What am I talking about? It was two days and it cleared up on the third day. The rain applauded quietly at the window. I sat down in the front room to mend my teal blouse, all threaded up with teal thread. I stared out at the nutty garden. The old lady's lavender looked like it was off its face at Woodstock. The blouse lay in my hands. Actually, I couldn't be stuffed mending it. I sat there thinking. That's the thing about thinking, it goes on all day and all night like a factory with a night staff. I wish it would stop sometimes. I thought about my clients whose best clothes were ripped and burned and snagged. I knew what they were on about. They wanted conflicting things, and it was exciting to want them: stability/fresh sex, responsibility/carelessness, family/freedom. Ooh, I hadn't used a slash for a while! Tradition/modernity, not to put too fine a point on it. The thing is that these days—yes *these days*—it was possible, at least in the West (although the very term, the West, is melting in front of me, like the Wicked Witch). For a wild moment, with the rain spattering the bay window and me plumped there with my teal blouse, I felt like I'd picked up the essay I'd left unfinished on my desk the day I withdrew from university. What I thought: *Having an affair was the most democratic, even-handed, racy, classy, gendery thing in the world.*

The garden coming in the windows onto the table and onto the books, the shelves lined with books and the stacks of books teetering on the floor. I tossed aside my teal blouse unmended. I waited for him among the books. There were so many, always had been. They were like crutches, like built-up shoes. I looked at the books so I could stop thinking.

When the client arrived I said it was raining the first day he came to the house, and he said he knew that, he remembered.

It rains a lot in Auckland.

I found his hand on the cushion and pressed each fingertip with my own. I told him how he had felt that day, a gravitational pull and all of me, all my mass, pushing down on your fingers.

We fell asleep on the couch and he woke in a panic, sweating. He'd dreamed something. What? I said, smoothing his brow. Something. What? A colour that filled the room, he said, but then, like a glob of colour captured in glass, he would turn his head and it would've snapped into a fine line.

The things you say to people.

The power stayed off. That was good. The longer it went on, the more I wished it would stay off forever.

'When the power comes back on, maybe we'll keep going?'

'Maybe we will.'

'Do you want to?'

'Yes.'

We kissed. Now it was not just sex and fun and elation, it was tenderness.

I remembered what he'd said. That an affair wasn't exciting unless there was the risk of falling in love. Yes, risk.

I remembered my client with the indigo shirt.

I fingered his upper lip. 'Would you leave her?'

He looked at me. 'Yes. Would you? Him?'

My lungs pumped up like a tyre. 'Yes. Yes. Yes.'

'That's settled then.'

I regretted doing the sleeve because it was deceitful. But if I hadn't done it, I wouldn't have got to know the client, and I went around and around like this a bit.

•

Change of subject but not entirely: once I saw a group of people going to the church at the top of Newton Gully, young women dressed in the clothes of their mothers, their grandmothers even—floral polyester dresses, flesh-coloured pantihose and slingback shoes, cardigans. And the men in chain-store suits, white shirts, ties. They looked sexy! No wonder they had piles of children. They couldn't keep their hands off each other. The women dressed to look like women and the men to look like men. The women were like baboons with great red arses hanging out for the men, and the men were like big dark blocks of manhood with penises hanging down their front. These were their church clothes. There was no confusion. It would make the species go on.

Yes, but we don't need to go on—well, not at this rate. Maybe that's why fashion makes women look like men, and like interesting drug addicts. How I'd love to look like the women going to church in their polyester dresses. But it's too late, far, far too late. If I put on a floral dress, a cardigan, Pakeha pantihose, I'd feel like a drag queen. There's been too much splitting off, dropping out, ripping up, blowing up, boiling down, paring down. There's been too much bloody theory.

But sex somehow struggles through. Chemistry can dissolve things like acid.

•

That day he came home while I was on all fours throbbing like a baboon, the rug scrubbing my knees. I heard the thud of his satchel on the doorstep. I looked up and saw that the door to the front room was open a crack, and felt the client's breath still hard on my neck and saw Art walk past the gap in the front room door, not fast, taking his time. In fact, pausing there outside the room for a moment of almost meditative stillness, but not looking right, not turning his head the forty-five degrees it would take to end our marriage. Walking on. I pulled myself away with a pop and loped, as if I'd regressed several stages of evolution, over to the door. And taking the door knob in my hand and feeling it, weighing it, judging the effect turning it will have on the internal apparatus which will close the door, and only when I feel I have an understanding of the door handle's relationship with the snib, rotating it and closing the door in absolute silence. Looking back into the room and smiling with the client in conspiracy but he isn't smiling, he's wearing nothing but an expression of lavish anxiety. Coming back to the rug and resuming position but he's hopping around putting clothes on, stuffing everything into them, and shooting me looks to indicate I'm a monster. Me! He's the monster. I try to smile at him, and wipe my brow in an exaggerated gesture of relief, urgently, as if it's wartime, as if there isn't much time left, and there isn't. These are extraordinary circumstances, the Blackout. People are behaving like they've never behaved before. It's wonderful. Why not me? I hiss at him that I feel like

I'm coming home. That he's home. He shakes his head madly as if to say, don't do this. But all in mime, he won't breathe a word aloud, and he's still doing a three-legged race with his trousers. And I go quiet too, because actually I don't do this sort of thing, I don't fall in love, I don't come home. But now, at this moment, I misremember. I do, I misremember, and I think I will never leave home again. I'll know where home is, what's possible. That will be enough, for a lifetime.

When he had gone, I sat on the red couch, alone, and I thought clearly. I hadn't been thinking before, not at university, not as a mender—only blabbing and listening, blabbing and listening, like a glutton, a gourmand. And I thought now, I am not a liar, I want the truth, yes the Truth like Keats. That the client was a wonder, a glory, and I was in love with him, and that was the only Truth. The events of the past—the pole house, *If On a Winter's Night a Traveller*, my hands, my hands, getting married, Rip Burn Snag, the costume—all had been leading to the moment when I would ruin my life. And I must ruin it. At the same time I am even thinking about an English teacher at school trying to teach us grammar who said, *I will drown and no one shall save me*, and *I shall drown and no one will save me*—which is the suicide? And I'm thinking and feeling I will ruin it. I will ruin it and it shall never be fixed. I shall ruin it and it will never be fixed.

I padded into the kitchen. Art was forking lamb steaks around in the pan. He'd thought I was out. I must've dozed off, I said. Lamb was on the list of superfoods on the fridge. It was the healthiest animal, until it was butchered, then it wasn't in the best of health. But before that it had gambolled in the fields and eaten grass, a superior life to your average chicken, pig or cow.

There was nothing to say. We wrestled with the lamb chops on our white plates. Trails of blood glistened in the lamplight. Even laughed. I needed to end things. And he did, the client. Why didn't we just call it quits with our respective *spice*? I don't know. Yes, I do know. Because he'd told me everything. Because we were in paradise, down in the Pacific, and it was borrowed time, and it was the Blackout, and in the light everything would be revealed.

Later, I was in my workroom. A ridiculous hour. Art creaked by in the passage, his torch making the gap under the door into a thermometer—a bout of flu coming on and receding. He looked in at the door.

'Couldn't sleep?' I asked.

I was sweating slightly. I'd just turned from the end of the rack.

'What are you doing?'

'It's a full moon,' I said.

'Is it?'

'No.'

'Lunatic,' he said. That was better. Back to normal. But it never would be.

In the kitchen he poured brandies and we sat down to keep each other company. Stewart had a new theory about Shakespeare.

The villas going, being sold from under our feet, but there was Stewart and Shakespeare. I sort of admired it.

'Do people still do their PhDs on Shakespeare?' I asked, kind of tiredly.

'Of course,' said Art. He was all animated, like an old *Archie* comic. Honestly, he was. I don't know why I'd never thought of that before.

'Anyway, what?' I asked. I'd never actually met Stewart. That's Auckland for you.

'That Shakespeare was the son of Elizabeth the First, the Virgin Queen,' said Art. 'Which just about makes him Jesus.'

'How did he dream that one up?'

'Oh, he read it somewhere.'

So that's what a theory was.

'That's not a theory,' I said.

'A turn of phrase—Jesus!' said Art. Quite tetchy, for him. 'He is a sort of Jesus, culturally, for the West, for the second millennium.'

'Shakespeare?'

'Yes.'

'What is the West anyway?' I said. 'I don't even know anymore.'

'Us, you idiot,' said Art. 'It's us.'

I looked at him across the kitchen table. He seemed to have gone small, like a landscape I was receding from—plains, cabbage trees, rocky outcrops, out the back window of a train. God, I was cruel. I even looked at that from a distance too, my cruelty.

This was almost the last gasp of the millennium, and we were spending it in the light of the hurricane lamp.

32

And then, on the last day—of course—the last day. It was lunchtime. He'd come at lunchtime. I was in the bathroom mopping up when I heard a commotion coming from down the street, yelling, cars honking, a *general hubbub*. I padded back to the front room. The client, naked, had his hand on the light switch. 'Ta-da!' Dangling from the Carrara ceiling, a dazzle on a string. Deadpan for a second, then going nuts. Aah! I turned on a lamp, and the dehumidifier, which purred. We danced, a waltzy thing, sawing back and forth under the light.

Then hauled on clothes and went out onto the veranda because the whoops were ricocheting up the gully. A man in overalls ran past the house hollering. Someone replied, into the air, About fucking time! There was laughter, more shouting. Yee-hah, as they say in America. A woman from up the street who I'd never met before waved to us from a veranda. A stereo started up, some funk. This pantomime went on for a while. The client and I stood on the veranda watching it, like Christmas in the Park. Then we looked at each other. Time to go forward, into some other thing. I walked along the passage, stabbed at the Wah Lee light switch.

The beautiful paper lantern glowed. The client followed. In the kitchen I woke up the fridge and it began humming. The fan coughed out a whole lot of dust. I plugged in the kettle. It creaked and hissed. I turned to the client, who was hanging about in the middle of the room.

'What?' I said.

'Your husband.' His hands dangled like the first day.

'He's out,' I said.

He smiled, okay. Turned on the light, although it was broad daylight, turned it off again. We cackled. He looked about, plugged in the CD player. There was a mix in it. The Clash started up, 'Should I stay or should I go?' I turned it up to blare on the way past. Coffee? Yes, coffee! The client got a whiff of the waste disposal and feigned vomiting. That! I said. Would need some careful thinking about. I said *will need some thinking about*. The client said he heard me. I turned on the pantry light. There were eggs. Omelettes. *Omelettes!* I heard you, he said. I cracked *oeufs* in a bowl and the client found the plug-in hand-held beater and blasted them. A fork will do. I said a fork will do! I know. I tossed some flour into the breadmaker while I was at it. There was still mayhem out in the gully. I suddenly ran into the passage and boinged the hot-water switch, came belting back again. Hot water! He had the toaster going. 'Poi E' was belting out of the stereo. God, I love that song.

We sat at the kitchen table shovelling in omelette, toast, coffee. Looking at each other. Everything on, blaring, bubbling, throbbing. The End. Finis.

He had work. He had to go back to work. Regardless. He got his jacket from the front room and went out onto the veranda. I followed. There was still the odd shout and horn flaring down in the gully. He turned at the top of the steps and stood wavering. It was one o'clockish, the sun pelting down.

'This is it, isn't it?'

'It is,' I said. 'The end of this bit.'

'Yes, just this bit. The end of deceit.'

'Now we'll be truthful.'

'Yes,' he said. He was nodding.

And I was. We were nodding like anything.

'Are you pleased this is happening?' I asked.

'Of course! Yes!'

Of course. A rhetorical question.

'When will I see you?'

'As soon as possible.'

'How to arrange this?'

'How to?'

We were saying how to, how to, and kissed and for a long time, the length of the Blackout, five weeks. Then tore away like suction cups, literally, pop. He had tears in his eyes. And *I* did. Just because, well, it was going to change. We were coming out of paradise into some other place. He bounced down the weedy steps, waved at the bottom, blew a kiss. A circular saw grated on down the street.

I went into my workroom, stood there for a minute, excitement drumming through me, then tried the light switch. Darkness dried up like a puddle.

Now it would begin.

•

When I woke in the morning, I was on my own. Art was gone. I had a sudden mad panic, I don't know why. As if I'd leaped ahead to some future time. I went out into the passage and walked along it, and I felt like I wasn't anyone and I wasn't anywhere in particular, I'd just been plunked down somewhere. I thought I could walk forever along the passage and it wouldn't lead to anywhere, and I wouldn't ever be anyone. I creaked open the front door onto the day, the silence, the strawberry roofs, the Waitakeres looming out west, and it was just me. I didn't know what to do. Later, the sun scorched through the banana palms and I read a novel on the back doorstep, can't remember what. But I do remember thinking how useful novels are.

I needed to tell Art and when he came in. I paced about and then it was nineish, almost dark, and I was standing in the mandolin looking out on the garden and the lights across the gully, which now seemed festive, like a floor show. I remembered that at the beginning of the Blackout, on the first evening, Art had gasped to see me standing there, but this evening he didn't flinch. He looked like he'd been in a fight. Yes, a bar-room brawl. His satchel strap dragged like a clenched fist on his lapel. I could smell the medicinal smell of *one too many* on his breath. He walked past me into the front room and fell onto the couch. I asked him where he'd been but I didn't care.

'It's bad news,' he said.

'The business?' Well, it did have one foot on a banana skin anyway.

'I don't care about the business.' His face purplish. He was a derro. 'It's not the money. Don't you know that?'

'What—not "the farm"? Are you sure?'

He'd never liked my inverted commas. 'Yair, "the farm",' he said in inverted commas, which were heavy. He'd been there for the day. There'd been a divvying up of things. Art's beautiful shiny privileged face crumpled like a can. He twisted his painty head. 'It's gone.'

The royal We. I sat down beside him. I hesitated, put my hand on his cheek, but it felt unreal, fake, my touch, and it must've to him too because after a moment he wrenched away.

'Gone.'

I tried to say it wasn't like that, his parents had their house in Wellington, he had his own life, his career, but even as I talked I knew it was rubbish, balderdash, and I petered out. They'd been the Woolthamlys, and now Art was just a Frome.

And me? Well, as you know I'm not a materialist, I despise materialism. I suppose I'd got used to there being a light on in the passage, and it had been extinguished, but I didn't care, I didn't give a rat's arse. And anyway, I liked the Blackout. I liked what the Blackout had brought me. I wanted my mouth mashed against the stretched sinews under his chin.

Now Art embarked on a meandering version (because you know, off his face), about the Asian crisis, how when it got to Japan it was curtains for the Woolthamly prune empire. Which I knew anyway. And then the Blackout, to compound it, and the villa tenants moving out like *nobody's business*. Which might have seemed small fry compared to the 'the farm' and the business, and it was, but it all added up. Or didn't. Apparently there was a moment, said Art, and he leaned forward into my face and everything in him was loosened, when it could have been salvaged, and I said, Oh, and he said, Yes, there was a moment.

He told me how at the house, Prue, Issy and himself had divided up the furniture. Even then, I noticed how it was just the blood relatives. It wasn't pretty, he said. He told me vaguely what was happening to the sideboards, the big dining room table and chairs, and how some things would be sold to the new owners, who were white South Africans. How it was kind of heartbreaking, but it had to be done because his parents obviously couldn't squash everything into their Wellington house. I nodded a bit, I watched him. He was sort of twitchy. He sat forward, reached into his pocket and dipped out a handful of earth and told me he'd literally knelt down and scooped it up before he drove off the land. He held it out to me and I looked at the earth but I couldn't tell if it was good earth or bad. I thought how his jacket pocket would be all dirty. He'd shed tears, he said. Yes, *shed tears*.

'It was heartbreaking,' he said again, 'but even so, even so,'—he groped for words—'GoGo, it was wonderful.'

I screwed up my face. 'Was it?' I asked.

He said it was, it was wonderful. He kept telling me about the stuff in the house and what was happening to it, the portrait of the old guy, Woolthamly, being gifted to the National Gallery, the big chiffoniers auctioned. And how they'd stopped Grandma giving the twenty thousand quid to Danielle who was marrying royalty, in the nick of time. We sort of laughed at that, but as he was talking I was thinking about the walks over the hills with Bert, the battles and the skirmishes, the camping in the summer, free as a fucking bird, the girl who was murdered, and how the farm was carved up and carved up among the siblings, and the lions at the gate. When he'd told me it was gone.

He said again, there was a moment when it all could have been saved.

I asked, 'What was that moment?' Well, I had to.

'When the Murus left,' he said, 'and production at the plant stopped. Completely,' he said. 'Did you know that? Completely?'

I said I did know.

'And you know why it stopped?'

And I said I did, but it was okay.

'It was,' he said. And he laughed, but it wasn't his usual laugh, it was a cackle. 'And then,' he said, 'and *then*, an investor made an aggressive offer, yes, a very *aggressive* one, and it was sold for a song, *a song*.'

He was falling asleep, wilting on the couch.

'It's all over,' he said.

'Yes,' I said.

He blinked at me, trying to focus. 'But in the end, you know, GoGo, you have to do what makes you happy.' He was flickering asleep, his bright eyes shutting down. 'Do what makes you happy.'

'I will,' I said. I put a blanket over him and went out of the room.

·

In the morning I turned on the vacuum cleaner. Art sneezed. This won't be pretty, I yelled. He went to LambChop. I did the whole house, which took ages, was like hoeing up the dust. Then paced about. It was back to normal. It felt foreign. There might be clients. I'd almost forgotten. Probably not, the first few days.

In the passage I touched the phone. It was still. I didn't have his number—I'd never had it, hadn't thought of it. He had mine, of course. My docket.

What I realised was: those clients, they didn't love their wives, their husbands. They loved the lover.

Somehow there was dinner (the oven), and chilled things from the fridge. I was distracted. He even said that, Art—GoGo, you're distracted. It's the electricity. Back on, he said, and I said, Yes, back on.

(Oh, and by the way, there was a false start with the power—it went out again for a few days, but that's another story.)

The next day I thought, I thought of taking a novel to bits. I thought, I am the granddaughter of the storytellers. Stories are over. Now we can just undo them.

I felt like absolute shite, in my own words. Whatever shite feels like when it's at home.

·

The *next* day I went downtown. I set the answerphone.

I expected the city to be bustling. It wasn't. Trolley buses were whining up the steep bit of Queen Street. The big shops were open, banks, and a few neon signs were blinking. The water sculpture by the Art Gallery burst on and a bunch of kids jumped in, screeching like monkeys. But overall the city was still on reuptake inhibitors. A lot of small shops—lunch bars, tobacconists—were dark. They were like strips of land from which the serfs have been turfed off for not paying their rent. I walked and walked. I didn't know what to do with myself. I remembered the day I dropped out of university. I remembered a pencil rolling over the wooden floor.

33

It had been a week, and I couldn't stand it any longer. Art was at home, packing his papers morosely. I said I was going out to buy a dress. He looked up—a dress? I suppose it sounded odd. I flung out the door, took the car. Soon I was nosing along Ponsonby Road like a fish. I found a miraculous park, and I actually did go to buy a dress. In a posh shop, first the lovely sensation of my hands in racks, then a Marilyn Sainty dress. Navy blue, very fine cotton, almost like tissue, it clung like tissue. I ended up not wearing it to the *thing*. Long story. But I knew where I was going. I got back in the car, and drove to the client's house.

Yes, the client's.

It was down one of those dinky little Ponsonby streets lined with everyone's late-model BMW. I cruised along rubbernecking at the house numbers, all in brass. Soon I found number 96. I wasn't going in or anything. I just wanted to see. I purred with the brake on over the driveway. It was a cottage, cute as a button, as they say in America. Periwinkle weatherboards, white lacy veranda. I got out of the car, and instinctively looked around for Milly. I felt a sick thrill at the possibility she might be home. I know, book me in for therapy. The front garden was neat, jasmine trailing delicately over the picket fence, a path of crushed white shells and little box hedges lining it. And shrubs, hebes. The front door had new-looking stained glass, red. Which I knocked on. They had a security system, a little piss-off sign. No answer.

I was at the Lilliputian picket gate on my way out when I caught a drift of smashed-up jazz, all tinny, coming from around the back. I hesitated. I crunched down the side path, ducked under banana palms and arrived on a little patio with a wooden table and chairs, red like a redhead, and a grapevine all tendrilly above it. I looked out into the garden. Big band was coming from a boom box on a chair under the clothesline. This seemed strange. I couldn't picture the client listening to any radio program, let alone early-evening jazz. It just went to show I didn't really know him. So what the hell was I doing? Which made this all the more exciting, and at the same time made me feel lonelier than I'd ever been in my life. I turned my head.

An oldish man, grey-haired, was sitting on a stool by the far corner of the house, carefully painting a windowsill oxblood. When he saw me he stood up and winced from his back. He wasn't that old, sixties, but wizened, prematurely.

He called out over the radio, 'You're after Milly, are you?'

I knew it was the client's father from the accent, and from the likeness. The same long arms, the blue-green gaze.

I hesitated for a second, then: Yeah, I was after Milly.

The father walked over to the clothesline and turned the jazz down to a squeak. 'She's in Wellington. She stayed behind to, ah, wrap things up after the Blackout, apparently.'

Well, thank Christ for small mercies.

'And he's out of course, working late.'

I said never mind.

The father stood holding his paintbrush, waiting for me to leave.

'I'm painting my son's house.' He walked back over to the house, easing his back, and spread one hand as if to introduce me to the painting.

'It looks nice.'

'It does. Not bad, though I say it myself.'

When I just stood there under the grapevine like an idiot, he went on.

'For six months we've been going back and forth about it, while the wood deteriorates. I thought if I don't let him toss some money my way, the whole house is going to go, so I'd better do it. I'd do anything for my son. I even let him pay me so I won't have to stand by and see his walls rot.'

He laughed and I laughed.

'He can afford it,' I said.

The father looked at me sharply.

'I mean, Donovan Brothers,' I said.

'They're big, aren't they? They're players.'

I said yeah.

The father creaked down onto the little stool and started painting again. 'Between you, me and the gatepost, I always thought he was doing alright. But didn't like to pry, you know?'

'I understand,' I said, quite sombrely, but I felt excited—this strange circumstance, being drip-fed information about the client.

'He's had some big thing happen, just the other week,' said Kevin.

'Oh yes?' I was blazing.

'A sale. He brokered a sale, for some big company—ah, if I could remember the name. Made a mint.' He glistened. 'They're out celebrating. As we speak.'

I sidled around the garden furniture and stepped off the patio onto the grass. It was the wall-to-wall-carpet kind. Springy. I loved this. I loved that I was having a conversation with the father about the son! No preamble, straight into it. God, it was great. Because I had been fucking the son, not to put too fine a point on it. Talking to the father made me feel horny as hell. Rabid. I can't quite explain it, but I was at some inner temple. I pictured the son, and wished I could tackle him to the ground and fuck him stupid.

I pointed to a white sill. 'Shall I?'

He considered the possibility for a moment. 'Ah, it's fine.'

His sill was becoming more and more bloody, the window underlined as if for emphasis.

'And how do you know Milly then?' he asked. 'Out of curiosity.'

And out of bloody nothing-else-to-pass-the-time.

I hesitated, then lied through my state-funded Child Dental Service teeth. 'From a long time ago.'

'She's a lovely girl, Milly.'

Suddenly the father hobbled across to the boom box, more agile than before but you noticed the cacky knees. He twiddled with the volume and listened with his ear cocked. As he returned to the house, he gave a light guffaw, just like his son. Gawuff.

'Missed it. The Black Caps playing South Africa at Eden Park. Never mind.' When I looked blank he added, 'Cricket. I listen to that bloody thing a lot.' He lightly kicked the air in the direction of the boom box. 'It's quite good, you know, I shouldn't complain. The National program's quite good. I quite like that Wayne Mowat in the afternoons. Have you listened to him?'

I hadn't.

'I like that Kim Hill in the mornings, but she's a bit aggressive, mind.'

He'd killed someone.

He moved to another windowsill. Without its red trim, with its empty stare, it had a picked-clean, skull-like quality. The sun was still pelting down on the house. I'd go in a minute.

He pushed the tin of paint, which was as dark as a scab, towards me.

'Maybe you could after all, if you wanted to.'

I looked about. 'A paintbrush?'

'Good point.' He tromped down the garden and ducked into a rustic little shed that had a climbing rose weeping apricot petals on one side. Reappeared. 'No weapons of mass destruction in there.' Laughed. Handed me a narrow paintbrush. 'Did you see that in the news? Resolution Seventy-One or whatever it is.'

I hadn't. Knew all about it later, of course.

But mass.

Mass destruction.

'We watch the news at ten o'clock every night. Me and herself.'

He watched it day and night. I knew that. The client had told me.

He stood up. That crick in the back again. This time he groaned. 'Were you affected by the Blackout, then?'

Right in it, I told him, for five weeks.

'Give over,' he marvelled.

I'd loved it. I dipped my brush in the oxblood.

'Bloody Pinnacle Power,' he said. 'Ah well, at least the weather was warm.'

He knew what winter without electricity was like. He wasn't letting on though. He wasn't a blabbermouth like the client. I don't mean that pejoratively. We painted in *companionable silence* for a few minutes. I was buzzing, excited. I was painting with the client's father.

'Will he pay you too, d'you think?'

He laughed. I laughed too much.

'Nice house,' I said, for something to say.

'He's doing well for himself then.' A question, but he knew the answer.

'He is.'

'Donovan Brothers, eh?'

'Yeah.'

'If I could remember the name . . . And Milly, of course. She's doing well.'

I didn't have a clue about Milly, nor did I give a rat's arse, but I nodded vigorously. We kept painting. The oxblood was going on like nobody's business.

He said he was proud of his son. He looked at me with that green-blue stare. 'Between you, me and the gatepost, I'm so proud I could burst.' I was reminded of a Go-Betweens line, Da de-de-de-dee de-de-dee. Didn't say it of course. He looked away quickly. I didn't know why his pride had to be a secret. Yes, I did know. I just did.

'For me,' he said, 'it was all over a long time ago.' He smiled at the wall, or it was a grimace. 'But for himself, well.'

He listened out for the radio again, the cricket, then gave up. 'Ah.'

I'd go soon. I should.

'We hoped he'd marry a girl from home,' he said. 'At one time. Between you, me and the gatepost. Lovely girl, but no. No. But it turned out alright.'

I nodded. He couldn't see me. He was painting.

'Lovely girl, Milly. In Wellington for another week, after the Blackout. They relocated.'

'Yes.'

'Hope to get there myself some time. I've only been to the South Island once. Been here fourteen years and never got the ferry across the straits. Like to though. With this'—he held up the paintbrush—'me and herself'll get the ferry.'

He was a wanted man. He'd had the Wanted card.

'What's your name?' It suddenly occurred to him. I told him and he said, 'Catholic name. There's a town called Sligo. In the west.'

Never say the West unless you want to spend a long time defining it. He could just say it.

I asked him his name and he said it was Kevin, which I knew anyway because of the stories. Not stories, the truth. *You've got his blood on your hands, Kevin.* Etcetera.

He balanced his dark red brush (I know, the colour, but this is true!) on the rim of the paint tin and straightened up. Groaned a bit, then bent to unscrew the lid from a thermos. He poured a cup and offered it to me first. Tea? I shook my head. I smiled to myself, remembering the cups of tea I'd offered his son, which the son had declined, often. The father swilled down his tea, his eyes on me, and an expression of curiosity crossed his face as he noticed my silly grin.

As we painted, again there was a silence apart from the low squawk of the radio. The pips sounded. It was seven o'clock. He studied his watch as if to confirm it.

'Missing *Coronation Street*. Ah well. I want to finish up that side wall.'

He'd had the Mass card.

'I'll head off then,' I said. I was on top of the world.

'I'll tell Milly you came around.'

'No, it's okay,' I said, too panicky. She wouldn't have a clue anyway, who I was. Yes, she might. The mender. She might remember.

I misremember.

'No need. I'll email her,' I said.

'Okay, so.' He started cleaning his bloody brush at the tap and the water ran red and twisted like veins. 'You seem like a nice girl. You come to see your friend and you end up doing painting and listening to me raving on.'

'It's been great.'

'It has. It's been grand talking to you.'

342

We shook our oxblood hands. It was fantastic.

And I would've gone then, full of the client, but Dreadful and Frightful arrived.

Kevin saw them first out of the corner of his eye and I heard him say, Here we go, under his breath, and our hands fell apart. They were twenty years older than the client had described them, but unmistakable. *Hey-ho* as they picked their way over the lawn, one dark, one a redhead. They were like spinning tops, top-heavy in their frilly blouses, reducing downwards in their spindly white slacks, down, down to their strappy spiky heels. They stopped when they saw Kevin and me.

'Hey-ho,' said one of them again, who may have been Dreadful or Frightful, and who was wearing a red blouse. 'Where's the missus, Kev? We thought the missus was helping you today.' She craned her neck as if the missus might be inside.

'Ah no,' said Kevin, wiping his hands. 'She's been cleaning today. She's had her rounds today.'

'And who's this then, your lovely assistant?' asked the other one, the one in a green blouse. They both cackled, and the green one tottered forward and fell onto my cheek in her attempt to kiss it. I got a whiff of Winebox No. 5. She razzed her brow. 'Has he got you helping him then, the old sod?'

'Give over,' said Kevin. 'She's a friend of Milly's.'

Names were exchanged. The green blouse was Deirdre, the red Finoula. I looked at Kevin. There was something wrong. He kept on painting. He didn't like them. And now Deirdre was shaking my hand. 'Look!' Oxblood stained my palm. 'Honestly, this family. Where's himself, anyway?' More craning.

'Ah, out,' said Kevin.

'We thought the whole fam-damily would be here this evening— except for herself, of course. When's she back, Kev?'

'Next week, I believe.'

343

'Which is why we came around, didn't we, Finoula?'

'We did,' said Finoula, 'which is why we brought—ta-da!' She looked down fondly at the sloshing box of chateau cardboard she held tucked under her arm. 'Join us,' she said to me, and they set off weaving across the grass to the lacy white wrought-iron furniture that nestled under the trees at the edge of the garden.

'That's kind, but.' I'd go. But this was interesting. I was meeting the entire clan.

Kevin had retreated to his paint tin. He looked across at me, a shared something, not exactly a wink. Dreadful and Frightful! He was stooping to do the honours with the oxblood again, but craned back up, knees creaking. 'Taranaki Dried Fruit!' he announced. 'That's the company. Knew I'd remember in the end. That was the sale. Made a mint, he did.'

I'm stuck, glued, my feet. And my heart's going. I'm not sure what to think. I'm partly ra-ra-ing for the client. The audacity! And partly angry, yes—very, very angry. Everything goes small. I look down into the shade under the trees, and with the contrasting gashes of setting sun, Dreadful and Frightful are almost invisible. Their silhouettes perform an elaborate ritual, moving the chairs, dusting them, I'll sit here, no you sit there, moving them again, almost falling, a chair falling over, laughing. Finally they've plonked themselves on the chairs and they're tilting their heads across the lawn. A couple of glasses, please, if you wouldn't mind! What's her name? GoGo. GoGo, a couple of glasses from the kitchen. Talk about cheeky, Deirdre. Well, she's right there, Finoula. The wine, Deirdre. I can't see them for the sun, the blinding yellow Auckland sunlight. I'm looking for Dreadful and Frightful at the bottom of the garden but I can't see them, I can see them in my mind's eye, their top-heavy bodies. Did I mention the rings? A bunch of diamonds like white grapes on their ring fingers, both of them. They must've married sugar daddies. And

I'm thinking about the client. You fucker! I can't see the aunts for the life of me, under the shade of the banana palms, under the nutty creepers, the jasmine, the wisteria. But I can hear them, one of them. A couple of glasses, please, GoGo, make it three. Deirdre! Well, why not? She's joining us for a drink.

I skirt around the overly red outdoor table. The French doors are open. I stop. From the doorstep I watch stands of banana palms shaking their silly heads at the bottom of the garden. Through them I glimpse other cottages, their lacy backyards and timber fences, flashes of white sheets on a clothesline. I step into the kitchen and listen to the hush of the house, to the radio squawking outside. It's all modern, renovated, with one of those island benches in the middle, copper pots hanging above. The dining area is off to one side, the living area beyond it. All really nice—nice couches, rugs, bit of art on the walls, and venetian blinds everywhere giving it a cool underwater air like a Sylvia Plath poem. The house is smallish, of course—it's a Ponsonby cottage. I step from a squishy rug, that sinking feeling, onto the polished boards of the passage. I gawk. GoGo, you're an idiot. I don't care. I continue down the passage. It isn't long, there isn't much of it. I peer into a bedroom. Theirs. An enormous bed with a white embroidered quilt on it. It's unmade, the quilt half on the floor. I'm tempted to go in, to look closely at the bed, look for hairs, smell it even, finger the knick-knacks on the bedside table. I restrain myself. I turn and there's another bedroom opposite, the spare room—yes, spare. I move towards it. I can see another bed, a chair. I'm in the doorway. I see, just inside the door, a pair of tartan Docs. They're pigeon-toed as if someone has just stepped out of them, there is the ghost of someone in them. I stoop and push my hand a little way inside one of them, and it is still warm.

Everything in the book happens to me: mouth dry, palms sweating, a shudder up my spine, the hair stands up on the back of my neck. I am in the room, the spare room. The double bed is jammed up under the window, neatly made with a taro-patterned quilt. I stand stock-still, and I cast around. There's a bit of junk, boxes, a desk, a stuffed bookcase. I jump when I see a figure in the wardrobe mirror. It's me! I look for a while longer. I want to cry, but I don't. I rasp tears away quickly. It's silent in the house. I'm getting out of here. Never again. Never again. I want to cry but I don't. I hate the reflection of myself in the mirror. I don't want to look. I swing it to one side, the wardrobe door, and get a start—there's the costume, hanging, swaying a bit with the sucking motion of the door being opened. I have a sense of déjà vu. I've stood here before, with the costume in my hand. If so, maybe this isn't real either. I touch the site of the mend, the shoulder, where my hands had been busy for so long. It all comes galloping back. I know the fabric well, the coolness. I touch the sleeve. The client hasn't put it on the floor. He's forgotten to put it on the floor as he said he would, and to trample it underfoot. I would never have forgotten that detail, to put the costume on the floor and mess it up, with things on top, so it looked as if it had fallen of its own accord. So it looked authentic. But of course, I have changed it. I have finished the sleeve, so it doesn't matter.

I hear movement on the path, the shells being crushed. I'm breathless, my heart pneumatic-drilling in my chest. I have the costume. I bundle it up like a baby in my arms. I remember its weight. I go back through the house and out the French doors. I can hear the boom box, an announcer, a burst of cabaret. The father is on the other side of the house. Kevin. He's whistling. The garden is sunk in shade. I can't see Dreadful and Frightful. They must be there, at the bottom of the garden, but I can't see them. They're in the dark. He's whistling. Don't whistle after dark. I've heard that. It's a Maori proverb. Don't whistle after dark because the birds don't. I crunch along the shell path, hurl banana fronds away from my face. The sun is dropping. It's late summer, it's autumn. That fine light, delicate light. I get into the car, put the costume on the seat beside me, and I must've driven home. I don't remember doing it. I remember the road, through tears. *Tears.* They should have picked me up for drunken driving, for grief-in-charge.

•

I sat in the kitchen, shaking, yes, like a leaf. Everything was on—lights, radio, breadmaker going nom nom. I hated it. Everything was over. Everything. The back door was open. I was looking out over the city lights. There was nothing to see. Dots. A few wild palms.

I went into my workroom. Didn't turn on the light. Hah, sometimes I forgot that you could. A snippet of moonlight came in. I was trembling. The costume hanging there looked bigger than it should. It might push down a flipping wall.

34

I went back and forth about going to the fashion show because I didn't want to go anywhere, anywhere on earth, but I sort of needed to go because *the aprons*. I felt like crap, I mean absolute shite. The worst I'd ever felt. Like you may as well give up. In the end I went because if I stayed home I'd go crazy.

He was on the doorstep. My heart went up high, then plummeted like an elevator. For a split second I thought he'd come to get back together. Then I realised. That moment, that realisation, was the nadir. It was the well.

'You've got the dress,' he said. 'Give us it back.'

I didn't reply. I don't know what I did.

He frowned. 'Can I come in?'

'Are you joking?' I said. My voice sounded croaky.

He gawuffed. Then he said no, he wasn't. Joking. He needed that dress. He said he heard I met his father. I said, He's nice, your father. I was cold as ice. We went on with this nonsense, like we weren't separate people, like we were talking to ourselves. That's what s e x does to people. He was wearing a black blazer over a check shirt. The effect would've been preppy-looking if it weren't so messy. I told him I was on my way out and when he asked where, as if it was any of his business, I said off-hand, To a fashion show.

'Oh, thingie's?'

I didn't bother answering.

He'd been there that day, of course, the day Mabel came around to get the aprons. *I didn't expect them for another week!* she'd said. He'd blinked at me, and understood that there'd been no need to wait for the costume, no need to talk, no need to sit and drink wine, no need to wince into the afternoon sun, to look out at the wild garden, or to watch the room change suddenly from yellow to grey. There'd been no need for all that, but it had happened.

I was half in the mandolin, half out, swaying back and forth on the doorstep. I felt jittery. He was boinging on the veranda. He said, Just get the dress, and I said, Fine.

I slopped inside. He'd have a fag on the veranda anyway. But he followed me inside.

I turned. '*What?*'

We leaned against opposite walls of the passage (our shoulders like the men in Clonard). I asked him why he didn't tell me and he said tell you what and I said you know. But maybe he didn't know, because there were two things. He shook his head back and forth. I asked him if he was even sorry and he said he was, about the whole thing, from start to finish. He looked upset—*he* looked upset—and said it was just the way it was, that was the nature of it. You mean the sale, I said, and he said, no not that, that was just business, it had nothing to do with anything.

I told him it did have something to do with something.

He shook his head and screwed up his face. 'Why do you care about those people? Why should the Woolthamlys have the money? Any more than anyone else?'

I don't know. I didn't know.

'They've had their turn. That's the nature of it.'

'Of late capitalism,' I said with a kind of sneer.

'Yeah,' he said. 'And I thought you were finished with him anyway.'

'Did you? I thought you were finished with Milly. *And* Trisha.'

He didn't say anything.

I said I couldn't trust him an inch, and he said of course not, and I can't trust you.

I knew this, of course. The thing was, I knew I'd never do this again. I'd lived out something, I don't know what, some sort of brokenness. I turned on the Wah Lee light, turned it off again. Didn't need it. I leaned against the passage wall and felt the flocked wallpaper through my fingertips.

He stepped forward and searched my face. 'I did fall in love with you. I did think we'd be together, otherwise.'

'Otherwise,' I said. I was pinning myself to the wall, like a butterfly. 'Otherwise.'

Suddenly he flushed like a lantern. 'I loved you, and I told you everything. I told you things I've never told anyone. And you didn't tell me anything in return. I don't even know you!' He grabbed my shoulders and I jerked them and said get off, but we wrestled a bit and I sort of biffed him, because I could, it was pathetic. We fell back against the wall, against the fuzzy flowers. Right into his face I said I felt the same, I don't know you. Even as I said it I knew this wasn't true. I'd known him as well as you can know anyone. I told him that without the Blackout things would have gone on as they were, and no one would have known anyone.

'That's just shit,' he said.

He told me the Trisha thing was nothing, it was fleeting.

I put my hand on his face and he hurled it away as if I'd burned him. Then I went into the workroom to get the costume.

In my workroom I wriggled out of my Marilyn Sainty number, dropped it in a puddle on the floor. Shadows leaped up the walls.

There seemed to be at least two of me. I liked the company, because I was so nervy, almost feverish. I bumbled the costume off its hanger. It was heavy. I'd never got used to its weight. The client called out from the passage, what was I doing. I heard him stomp outside, no doubt for a fag. I spread the costume on the table and tugged the zip undone. It was like roadworks, that zip. I held the costume in front of me and stepped into it as if climbing big-gauged stairs. One, two. Shaking like a leaf. Doing up the zip was like being strong-armed by a mobster, but I managed to secure it, right up to my neck. It fit perfectly. No, it didn't. It was a little big, but not much. It felt heavy, protective, velvety, like a special cello case made for my body. If I were a cello. I watched a ghostly image of myself in the mirror twirling a single revolution, the bell of the skirt swishing around my thighs. I'd never tried on any garment belonging to a client before. I ran my hand over the roughness of the knotwork, where I had torn it, and mended it, and a thrill of transgression (ah, a trans word, the like of which I hadn't used in a long while) rushed through my body. I peered along my shoulder and under my arm as far as I could see, at the scar where the seam had been torn. The mend was almost invisible. Except to the eye of the mender. I could see it because I knew where to look, and what the mend was made up of. I knew its history. I wasn't a rider on a galloping horse. I knew though, even then, that it was better to be the rider, and not look so closely.

In the bedroom I hauled on black pantihose and rooted around in the wardrobe for a pair of black lowish pumps I'd got from the op shop one time. They were a bit mouldy. I tumbled the things from my common-or-garden bag into a squishy black handbag. At the last minute, because I didn't want to look too eccentric, I pulled out a black lacy wrap of Mabel's and draped it around my shoulders. Also, the nights were beginning to close in. It was autumn. All this happened in autumn.

'It's a wrap,' I said to myself in the mirror.

I might have laughed once. But I was trembling.

(*Those Were the Days.*)

When I came back out the client was sitting on the front steps, reaching up and drumming his fingers on the handrail. I had liked those fingers. I was so strung out it was hard to walk a straight line. I stood in front of him, looking down. He didn't notice what I was wearing. Men; I tell you.

'The dress?'

I opened my wrap like a stripper.

'What!' He jumped up quickly.

'What?' I said, smiling.

'Take it off.'

'Here?' I walked down the path.

I heard him gawuff. I told him I didn't have time now, which was true. He said, How long can it take to change? and I said, You'd be surprised.

'Just go and get out of it!' A neighbour watering his garden across the road craned up at the raised voice. The client said through his teeth, 'Do it.'

'I can't,' I said.

He sighed musically. He asked where the show was and I told him. This ballroom thing, in the old Blind Institute. I made to set off up the street.

He called after me. 'You're not driving?'

The neighbour was having a good old gawk, I noticed.

'Art has the car,' I said over my shoulder. 'And anyway, there won't be parking within cooee.'

He said come on, I'll drop you off and I said ta and scurried back and got in the car. Probably shouldn't have. Don't get into a car with a stranger. Or someone you fell in love with.

He bumped his head getting in, and while he was putting on his seatbelt, talked to the steering wheel with exaggerated patience (the poor steering wheel). 'I'll drive you there. I'll pick you up afterwards. We'll come back here and you give me the dress.' Now he looked at me. 'Agreed?'

•

I must've agreed. He drove rather erratically through the Domain and over to Parnell. All the way through the kinky streets I was thinking, *This is the last thing I'll ever do*. I didn't even care. He pulled up screechily outside the venue. The ballroom.

'Ta,' I said.

'You look ridiculous.'

'How can you tell?'

He laughed bitterly. I laughed bitterly. You know what? We kissed, involuntarily. A thirst. A hunger. Then I got out. It was a beautiful autumn evening, by the way, hazy and apricotish.

I was speeding. As I was skedaddling towards the ballroom—because it was almost time for the show to start—a double-breasted-suited person put his head in the car window and started yakking to the client. I saw this out of the corner of my eye. They seemed to know each other. The client got out of the car and was, I have to say, schmoozing with this person. I could tell by the obsequious body language on the part of the client, a notch short of bowing and scraping. As I disappeared inside I saw the client being towed—as if he was being led by his tie, if he'd had a tie, in any case he looked like a goose—towards a tall pashmina-engulfed woman who was undoubtedly the wife of the double-breasted person. They all did European kisses. I left them to it. The client would be gone in a sec anyway.

Inside the foyer, everyone seemed drunk, a roiling sea. The Irish Sea. There was an air of hysteria, shrieks of laughter like

Bedlam or an orchestra tuning up. Perhaps they were all tripping from the chemical smell of new clothes. Perhaps it was just me. I was jostled through the double doors into the ballroom, which was gold and curly and plush, wouldn't have been out of place at Versailles. Mabel's friends and followers filled the place. There were distinct groups—I'd noticed this before. Tribes. The forty-something wives of businessmen, whose skirts were of a type as if they all came from the same village. I'd hand-finished loads of them. Then there were the young heroin-chic types dressed in Mabel's black range. I didn't know a soul. I also shrugged off my Mabel wrap, and felt pleased with myself in my bell skirt and embroidered sleeves. I noticed the odd person casting a glance at me.

And there was Mabel, glowing with life and shiny black glasses, surrounded in a cloud of well-wishers, and reaching out to crush me in an embrace, blasting in my ear, twice, 'I said, *you'll love the aprons when you see them*. That tinge of oppression, only joking.' Then groping for the man next to her, pulling him into view. 'My second husband, Bruce. The most supportive husband I've ever had, the most loyal.' Bruce blushed. She'd once told me she and Bruce didn't have sex for five years before they got divorced, and hadn't wanted to so it was simple, you could be friends, she'd said. Which might tell you something about bitterness, where bitterness comes from. Then Mabel was pointing and saying, 'Isn't that your lovely client?' I heard myself call, Mabel, like a wail, but it was lost.

The client was nodding ridiculously, like a horse with a feedbag, to a little knot of silver-haired people, the double-breasted person and his wife among them. You know what I thought then, seeing him kowtowing? *He's still the working-class boy from Belfast.* He was nodding and smiling and carrying on across the sea of heads. It was like hell, it was like the inferno. Only happy, on second thoughts. Paradiso. And now the client was stabbing at his watch theatrically, and making big movements with his mouth, words, like this was a Christmas pantomime, and he was backing away from the suited group, and then bumping into Mabel, and turning and giving her a possumish look, and studiously ignoring me. Mabel was pecking his cheek and bellowing something at him, then Mabel was swept away and I was swirled further into the Va (yes, the Va).

•

I found a seat one from the end of a row nearish to the back, and plonked down into it. I glimpsed the client in the distance, looking distraught and making a beeline for the double doors. As he passed my row, he paused and stared down at me for an instant. A glare fizzed between us. He looked up as the doors began to creak closed, and made a jerky goosestep towards them, but he was stilled by something. I followed his gaze along the row to where the wife of the double-breasted person was waving coolly. The client smiled sickeningly, showing his longish teeth, and waved back. He had one more glance at the doors, which were now shut, and plopped down beside me as if this were musical chairs.

I turned to him. 'Is that the CEO or something?'

Like a ventriloquist, the client answered in the affirmative out the side of his mouth. He stared straight ahead. He didn't know me. I got it. I turned back to the stage. You could tell by the hush that the show was about to begin.

This was bloodsport. Being out in public with your illicit lover—even though it was *all over*—was man against Nature, i.e. woman against Nature, me. It was a lot of things. It was childhood fairground excitement. The odds of bumping into someone who knew us were about as low as the likelihood of a car flying off a fairground octopus, but the consequences were as dire. I pretended not to know the person sitting beside me. Whose guts I now hated. I had taken him in my mouth. I was in a rage.

But on with the show.

35

It began with no preamble, straight into it like the bit of a film before the opening credits. A model strode out onto the catwalk looking, I'm sorry to say, very uninterested in life. No wonder. She was wearing a ridiculous green blouse with a cape collar so big it would get caught in machinery, a gathered skirt cinched in tight (you thought whalebones), and high high heels, stilts really. I wouldn't be seen dead dressed like this. Is that the point? More dead-looking models followed, women like horses, lanky and loping. They walked the way models did in Europe, angular and wildly swaggering, but still with the stamp of New Zealand on them, I don't quite know how. The way they turned in a slightly galumphing way, and glanced up sometimes, forthright, almost aggressive. After this desolate prologue, bebopping music began, and the models started dusting furniture while a host of fine feathers fell onto the stage.

In the semi-darkness, I felt the client looking straight ahead at the models. He glanced at his watch.

There were women dressed in red coats and tent-like jackets swinging down the catwalk, but once again an unmistakably Kiwi kind of swing, like meat on hooks at the freezing works. Clunk clunk clunk. I couldn't take it seriously. I suppressed a giggle or two, and felt the client stiffen beside me. You know what it was (I decided)—it's the smallness of our dinky little country, the intimacy. These women weren't models, they were just girls from Glenn Innes, from Howick, dressed up. Therefore (I reasoned), you could never quite believe in the clothes they wore.

I caught the eye of a machinist who was sitting diagonally in front of me. I waved, and commented to the client, 'She works in the sweatshop. I mean workshop.'

I felt his arm laugh and I inched away. But not before fibres from my wrap caught in his jacket as they rubbed up against each other. The tangle.

It went as dark as a power cut, and some men in black could just be seen spinning out with a Thing on wheels, which was revealed to be a washing machine. Hypnotic music, and the models wobbled onto the catwalk wearing creepy hoods over dangling clothes, monk-like. They circled the washing machine as if they were worshipping it. I have to admit, this made the hackles rise. It was still absolute shite.

I snuck a look at the client. It didn't look as if his hackles had risen. His hand gripped mine, then dropped it again quickly. I snatched it away anyway. I glanced at my hand: burning. I thought at that moment that there was love involved, and falling, and actually used those words in my head, I had fallen in love, and it was a shame that I had. There had been no control over it, which was why they called it falling. You could plan all you liked, you could study and save and read self-improvement books and there would still be these words and this rush of ecstasy. The words came out of my mouth. I'd actually said these things. *I fell in love*. He twitched at the words, but looked straight ahead. Tears came into my eyes and I thought, I am going to cry and there is nothing I can do. And what does it matter? In the scheme of things. Are we meant to hide all this? Are the clothes more important? I wanted to stand up and announce to the room that I had loved this man, and now I knew about love. I wanted to laugh and cry and have everyone applaud.

Why can't we do this? Why can't we?

Then someone got up to talk about wells in Africa. The show was doing a fundraising thing and a very articulate woman who looked like Mabel's sister but probably wasn't, just had the same black glasses, spoke about how women and girls in Africa spent their lives carrying water. The girls couldn't go to school because they were needed to carry water. How a single well in a village would change the lives of several hundred girls and women. People might have some inkling now, with the Blackout, of how hard life could be without basic facilities. People nodded.

At intermission the rest of the audience rose in a body and spilled out the double doors and I could hear the clink of glasses outside. The client and I sat in our seats like statues. At one point I giggled and he gawuffed and I said, Oh, for goodness' sake, and we went back to our statue routine. It was excruciating. I looked at his lovely hand, his sleeve.

'I thought you were going.'

'Well I may as well stay now seeing I'm driving you home.'

•

When the show resumed, there were people in trench coats and dark glasses sidling around corners. A KGB number, apparently, but seriously, the show could've been anything by this stage for all I cared—bullfighting, a man gored to bits, a Shakespearean play or a play by the artist formerly known as Shakespeare. I'd gone into a sort of reverie. For some reason I remembered Derrida in the Michael Fowler Centre, and the little dog from Kansas. How Derrida was that dog.

I vaguely remember the aprons. I felt warmth coming from the client. I felt warmth passing into the client. I hated him. At that moment I remembered a sickening series of posters from my very early childhood—Love is . . . followed by a cutesy array of epithets. I thought: Love is Wanting the Other Person to be Happy. At that moment marriage, contentment, stability, stood back and took their hats off and watched Love walk by, recognising that they were humble and that this was greatness.

As you can see, I was a goner.

•

We might have left the ballroom like zombies, but when we got out into the dusk and the client discovered his car had been towed, his zombie state vanished. He was instead a whirling dervish, all arms and legs and swear words. 'Two hundred bloody dollars, the bastards.' I stood and watched—I didn't know him from Adam, you see. Other people watched too, in passing, including the double-breasted person and his draped wife. The client didn't notice them. I did. I might have waved like the Queen. After a while the client's tantrum subsided. By this time the crowd had thinned considerably. I caught sight of Mabel gathering her dinner troops around her, a lot of people in black-rimmed glasses. From a distance they looked like they were about to spray-paint a car. Then, there was nothing for it, the client had to talk to me even though we were In Public. I responded civilly even though I hated him. The client's primary interest was in the costume. We discussed who would walk where, trips involving towing yards, his place, my place, and the fading light. Eventually I graciously agreed that we would both leg it to my place, I would change out of the costume, he would take delivery of said costume and get a taxi to the towing yard.

On the way through the Parnell streets, past the ivy-covered Edwardian houses more English than the English, I power-walked ahead because I hated him, and he traipsed a few metres behind so as not to be associated with me. I must have looked like a sway-bummed Olympic walker.

At the entrance to the Domain I stopped and felt him arrive beside me. He'd got over his Wouldn't-Be-Seen-Dead thing, it seemed. There was no one else about. We stood looking into the shadowy arcade of trees, in which the birds were doing their crazy bedtime routine. You wouldn't want to be stuck in the Domain after dark, but I decided riskily, deliciously (I felt it in my lungs), that there was just enough light to get through to the gates on the other side. I set off helter-skelter into the Domain with the client following. Past the beds of summer cannas which now, in March, were like oily rags. Past the Teletubby-like rise that led up to the museum. The odd car illuminated the trees madly. On I went, with the client slightly breathless behind me. I was fitter than him. I led him a Merry Dance. He caught up sometimes, sometimes he was behind.

By the pond he said breathlessly, 'That was crap, wasn't it? I mean, the pretentious thing with the women ironing.'

I bolted ahead and called back over my shoulder that I quite liked the women ironing.

'And the pretentious thing with the Queen's visit.'

I'd quite liked that.

'The pretentious thing with the Russians invading Czechoslovakia. I was thinking what if there were Russians in the audience.'

I turned to face him and walked backwards for a minute. Looking back, yes, *looking back*. 'What if there were any Czechs in the audience?'

He was following, out of breath, loping like an ape. He'd devolved.

'*I* was thinking,' he wheezed, 'what's it to you? This is clothes, isn't it? And this is New Zealand.' He caught up. 'Your aprons were good though.'

'You wouldn't notice an apron if it bit you on the bum.'

'No, I did. They were good.'

I turned back to face the path ahead. The pond caught the last reflection of the purple western sky, and went under the arthritic monkey-puzzles, and then the pohutukawa trees.

'I don't know why you're doing this, though, this piecework.'

Oh puh-lease, as they say in America. This again. The corporate capitalist. I remembered seeing him talking to the CEO, smiling, nodding, bowing, scraping, like a Pinnacle Power meter reader about to be given the push.

We weren't meant to be talking.

I was off again, along the gnarly path. I caught sight of the fake Classical statuary down on the slope, a tooled Greek body twisting and glowing white in the dusk. That was the last landmark I could make out clearly—we were about two-thirds of the way through the Domain. The big trees, the big fat flax stands, the little lawns were beginning to blur into one deep greyness, but there was still enough light to see in front of us. The thing about these long twilights, though, is that you think they're never going to end, but they do end. We seemed to decide simultaneously to quicken our pace along the path, and once or twice knocked against each other and jerked away. When we saw the trees break apart and the western sky outside the park show itself—it was really still quite light out there after all—we ran towards it.

In case you thought we were going to get stuck in the Domain in the dark: we didn't.

I power-walked past the hospital, which had spread like a disease—building after building. He blundered after me. On the

other side of the road the verandaed flower shops were all closed.
I got to Grafton Bridge first. It was elegant in that light, or lack
of it.

•

In the months following the Blackout, if I was out late at night on
my own, I was aware that I now thought of the city differently,
saw it differently, as if seeing right through it. I would look up
dark alleys and think, I know you, I know darkness. It was
dangerous, a crazy thing to do, to peer into empty buildings, but
I wasn't intimidated. They were like tents pitched in a frontier
town. There was nothing to them. Nothing to it, this city. I'd seen
it all undressed and there was nothing to it.

I suppose this was the last of me going a bit wild. The client
asked me, as I mended the costume, if I'd done that. I didn't answer
him. But it was true, I had enrolled in the middle-class finishing
school. It was hard to plot exactly when it had begun. Perhaps it
was when I became blasé about novels because I discovered you
could take stories to bits. Continued on through getting married,
dropping out (in that order), going to New York, falling in love.
Perhaps it came to an end a few months after the Blackout, when
things had settled down, I don't know.

When it was over I went very sensible.

•

The client wasn't going to let me out of his sight until I handed
over the costume. Let him come and get the bloody thing. When
we got home I would skedaddle into the bedroom and unzip it.
I would stand at the front door in my stockinged feet and shove
it out at him. Take it!

(You might think the costume is a McGuffin. It isn't. I'm the
McGuffin. We're McGuffins. The costume is the deal.)

As we traipsed across the bridge in single file, I starting thinking about the walk Art had had through the streets that first evening of the Blackout. His sense of wonder. I hoped that we—I—would be able to salvage something from all this that would be important, real, wonderful. The air above the bridge and all around was a beautiful mauve with the dusk. Everything was quiet apart from birds, sparrows chattering and the odd native, a bellbird, well, belling clearly above everything.

'There is a certain wonder about this, don't you think?' I said over my shoulder.

'No,' said the client.

I turned and saw he had that broody Mr Rochester look. I wasn't Jane Eyre, I wasn't Charlotte Brontë. I was blinking Jean Rhys. I was the nutty colonial.

I finally led him down into the cemetery.

36

When we were about halfway across Grafton Bridge I spotted three or four street kids ahead of us. At least I thought they were street kids, from their *Lord of the Rings*-ish hoodie shapes, and their milling. I remembered that they'd occupied the street above the cemetery during the Blackout. Maybe they'd got accustomed to the extra space. Street kids on a deserted city street on a dark night: spiffing, fan-bloody-tastic. I crossed over to avoid them. The client followed and we trotted along like person and shadow. I was the person. Just as we came off the bridge, with Karangahape Road stretching ahead and getting dimmer in the dusk, I stopped. I could hear a strange sound that resembled a cat—Ouww! But it wasn't a cat. I looked sideways and realised we were standing above another entrance to the cemetery, and that the cemetery stretched under the bridge. I'd never noticed this before. The sound came again—Ouuuuww! After a while I knew it was a boy. I squinted down the path that led into the cemetery.

The client's voice was hot and tight in my ear. 'Keep. Going.'

'Listen,' I breathed.

The mewling again.

'Let's go!' said the client.

We really needed to, and I turned. At that moment the owner of the voice, a tangle-haired boy, stepped out from behind bushes. He hesitated, looked back down the path that plunged into cemetery. 'I fought it was you.' It was the boy. Even in the half-light I could see he had a tender troubled face, and a jagged mark on the side of his temple. I think I gasped. He was alive.

'GoGo!' The client's voice was ragged in my ear.

I mumbled a query after the street kid's health. I mean, my last proper sighting of him had been when his so-called friends were kicking him in the head on Queen Street. 'Is . . . that alright?' Indicating his noggin. Then we'd be off like a robber's dog, my shadow and me.

'F-fine,' the boy said. He had a stutter and an urban accent. *F-fahn*. I got it. He was a sandwich short of a picnic, you could tell from his uncomprehending expression, the odd way he held his head. His eyes looked hard and grey like concrete, but with something underneath. I thought of the cemetery, the long-decayed bones. No, I didn't, I think that now. Ah, the benefit of hindsight.

The client was close to me. 'You know him? What is this? Let's *go*.' His breath brushed my neck like a petal. Oh, he was a blinking rosebud. 'GoGo, we're going.' I wasn't scared. I'd been here all my life. He thought I came from some cushiony bloody background. I didn't. The street kid tugged my sleeve. I looked down. His dirty hands. He just wanted more money. Couldn't blame him.

'He's bullshitting you.'

'Ain't no b-bullshit,' said the boy. He kept glancing back down the path. I could just make it out, a Jacobean pattern between the jutting graves and the little grey pockets of lawn. Stone angels arched their wings in the gloom. Everything was bathed in a pigeon-coloured light, and fine specks of pollen and insects filled the air. It was ethereal and somehow soothing. I felt torn, standing there, the client on one side, boy on the other. The client backed away onto the pavement. I could see the tense angle of his body. He was like a bloody heron. We were going. The boy stepped forward and took my hand. I snatched it away. It was rough and sticky, his hand.

'S'alraht,' he said. 'Don't want n-nuffeeng.'

There was a giggle from the darkness below. I froze. The client called out urgently. GoGo! I made a lunge for the street, but a figure leaped out from behind the bushes and I felt a vice grip my arm. There was pain in my shoulders and sweat and yelling, and I was half carried, half frogmarched down through the scratching poking bushes into the cemetery. I thought my heart would stop. Behind me the client was following, going demented. It got darker and darker on the way down.

I was deposited on a piece of grass. The client was beside me. I felt him grope for my arm. 'Run!' A burst of reggae, overblown and distorted, came from somewhere in the dark, a boom box followed by a shout. The client and I stumbled a couple of metres back in the direction we'd come from. Something whacked my shins, an agonising pain, and I heard the client groan, and we both tumbled. I lay, cupping my legs until the pain subsided. When I looked up, a new figure was barring our way. He was bigger than the slender boy, stocky and deeper-voiced.

'Youse aren't going anywhere.'

The hair on the back of my neck bristled like a pig's. The client went all authoritative. 'Oh yes we are.' But as we simultaneously made a frantic scrabble to get past the stocky guy, two other figures appeared above us on the path. One was short with a halo of hair, the other very thin and tall. In the dark, their shapes were all that defined them.

A new pulsing sound emanated from further down the darkness, a guitar body being slapped. I felt the client go slack beside me. There was a high-pitched giggle. I noticed that the skinny one dangled a shining machete casually like a towel. In that moment I was transformed into a gibbering wreck, shaking and pleading and crying. My knees were literally knocking together. Bang bang bang. They all ignored me.

'Let's go,' said the haloed kid. He produced a torch. We trooped down the hill a few more metres, Halo in the lead with the dancing torch, then the stocky deep-voiced one who had barred our way, then the Boy, who had a bumpity gait, then me, then the client, and Skinny Arse bringing up the rear with his machete, I think, I didn't really want to find out. I was certain this was the last thing I'd ever do. I thought of Art, how sad he'd be.

At the bottom of the path, a group of ten or so hooded figures were sitting in a circle, wedged between graves, around a fire. Dotted about were candles in jars, like fireflies (sorry to be Eurocentric). We milled around, the client and me and the tour party. I was sweating, even though I seemed to have come over all cold. I didn't want to look at the client. To look at him would somehow make it more real.

'It's the rich chick,' said Halo. I could see he was Maori and that Skinny Arse was Pakeha.

I caught a glimpse of the client's uncomprehending face, and looked away again.

The Boy wobbled forward. He had a donkeyish gait. 'Hey, I f-found her! She gave me a h-h-hundred dollars.'

It was me they were talking about? I was the rich chick? A tsunami of panic surged through me. I felt my bowels lose the plot, and I hung on, hoping I wouldn't shit myself.

'Fuck off, Ben,' said Halo. To the client and me he said, 'He's mental.' Well, I could work that out for myself. This Ben character seemed anxious, wringing his hands. He subsided into the shadows as if he had wounds to lick.

I could now make out a big guy sitting on a grave, higher than the street kids, stroking his beard. He was clearly in charge, not remotely a kid, about thirty, Maori. 'Welcome,' he said, and left off stroking his beard to gesture extravagantly at the graves. 'Please, take a pew.' There were giggles from the rest of the party.

The client and I sat lightly on the edge of a grave. I could feel him quivering beside me. On my other side were two hooded girls who said hello and cackled as if this was a great bloody joke. The stocky guy who'd accosted us on the path came forward with a rope and made a he-man grab for the client's hands to tie them up. The big guy waved him away. Ah. Unnecessary. Skinny Arse said what the fuck to Stocky Guy. We could hear cars going by overhead on the bridge, and the dull roar of the distant motorway. The machete flashed in the torchlight. I was aware of the boys who'd led us down the path standing behind us, restlessly jostling and joshing each other. I wanted to weep but I didn't. It's amazing how quickly you can come to terms with the fact you're going to die. You don't know this unless you happen to be in that situation. But I can tell you, we're fast learners, human beings, when it comes to dying.

The big bearded man twiddled his thumbs and contemplated us. 'We probably won't hurt you,' he said, and smiled, 'but of course we do want your money. That's only fair.'

The client had his wallet out, pulling out wads of jittery notes. Halo counted it on a gravestone. It looked like a couple of hundred dollars. Halo stepped across the firelight to hand the money to the big man. He returned to rub his fingertips together under the client's nose. The client, who I noticed at this point wasn't a blithering wreck like me, handed over his nice Italian wallet. I remembered it from when he'd paid for the costume.

The funny things you think. Halo dug two credit cards out of the client's wallet, then turned to me with the same finger-rubbing exercise, like crushing herbs. I was shaking like the proverbial jelly. I managed to croak out that I'd dropped my bag up the path. This was true. Halo jerked his head at the sentries. Skinny Arse and the Torch Bearer headed up the path we'd come down.

We all sat in a silence punctuated by the odd giggle. A glowing joint danced like a bug as it was passed around the circle. I was trembling uncontrollably. Nearby a stone angel benignly watched over some poor sod's grave.

Ben wobbled forward again, creased head to foot with anxiety. 'She's a r-rich bitch.'

The others immediately told him to shut the fuck up. The two hooded girls next to me laughed.

I shook my head. 'I'm not rich. Believe me.'

'She is,' said Ben to the big man, who nodded but didn't look at him. Ben turned to me. 'I s-saw you, all dressed up.' He mimed a shrugging approximation of fancy clothes. The others went into hysterics, and Ben's face solidified into a kind of rictus. He shook his hands in front of him like a cheerleader's pompoms.

I was gulping colossally again and again.

•

After what seemed like enough time to die and be reincarnated, Skinny Arse came back holding my black squishy handbag triumphantly aloft like a thing he'd killed. It gave me a lurch to see it in his hands, as if he had a pet of mine. When Halo snatched it, Skinny Arse muttered, What the fuck. Halo rummaged through it and found my money card. He shook his head over the few dollars and said, Is that fucking all, that's fucking typical.

When Halo asked the client for his PIN number, he said, I misremember. I felt his voice vibrate into me. The machete was produced and the client recited his number like a choir boy. I gave mine. Halo wrote them with a biro on the back of his hand. He turned to us again. If you go to the cops, he said, and did the slit-throat gesture understood throughout the world as curtains. He may as well have been speaking Esperanto. I continued my quaking. Halo and Torch Bearer disappeared back up the path. We could hear their whoops disappearing into the bush. Skinny Arse stayed behind this time, dangling the machete and saying, What the fuck.

The big man turned to us majestically. 'I'm Walrus, by the way. Now, how can we entertain you while they're doing the banking?'

The others all cracked up at this great witticism, but it seemed it was a serious question. A guitar was produced and someone did a few prongy chords to tune up. The client and I sat hunched like birds. It was probably about half past nine. The singing began. 'How Bizarre,' dirgy and hypnotic.

A way into it, the girl next to me buzzed close to my ear. 'It's not too late to run. I'd get the hell out of it if I were you.'

I looked quickly at the client but he hadn't heard. Then up the path. It was now pitch-black. A car screamed past on the motorway up above.

'No, don't,' said the other girl. And an aside: 'She'll regret it.'

Walrus leaned back and looked cock-eyed at the client. 'So what do you do for a crust? Shane.'

He knew his name. Well, there were the cards.

'Banking,' said the client, his voice like a bloody fantail.

There was an explosion of laughter. We could hear the word *banking* being repeated around the circle, to more laughter. I expected Walrus to ask me what I did for a living but he didn't.

There was more singing. The trees were shaking in the firelight. Figures leaped about in the shadows like Matisse's flipping dancers. I mean flippin' dancers. There was crackling from the fire and cackling of the street kids. Except for Ben, who sat apart wringing his hands. I could hear low conversations, and was straining to hear in case it was about our demise. Someone said, What do you call Maoris on Prozac? Once were worriers. I tried to ignore the client, and I'm sure he was ignoring me. If we looked at each other, the worst would happen, I was certain of it.

A few minutes later, Halo and Torch Bearer came blatting back down the path, looking cocky and important. They swooped past the client and me, and Halo showed Walrus the stack of cash he had in his mitts, which must've come from the client's account. I had about forty dollars in mine. Halo had a high-level conference with the Walrus, who nodded and looked over at us from time to time. During this conversation, Halo eyeballed the client and once again did the international sign for it's all over, cunt.

Halo came and stood over me menacingly. 'What other cards you got?'

I shook my head.

He bellowed, 'Where's your other money?'

I was going to die.

Ben shambled forward from the shadows. 'She's l-lying,' he said. 'She's a r-rich bitch.'

Someone scragged his hair. 'Go back to sleep, Ben.'

Ben. 'Wasn't asleep.' He flapped his hands.

'She's not rich,' said the client. Everyone looked at him, and he jumped a bit, all nervy. He told them I didn't have two pennies to rub together, a quaint expression.

Halo turned his attention to the client. 'Who the fuck asked you, cunt?' (They called him cunt all the time, but not me, I suppose because I had one.)

Everyone laughed like hyenas. I felt the client move beside me. I wished he wouldn't tremble.

'She's r-rich,' said Ben. 'She gave me a h-hundred dollars.'

Halo turned on Ben. 'Shut the fuck up about your fucking hundred. You don't know what you're fucking talking about.'

Ben flapped his hands and groaned in anxiety.

Halo pointed to the client and announced to the group, 'He's the rich one. In't that right, Walrus?'

Walrus was stroking his beard and watching the proceedings. He wouldn't be drawn.

Then Halo loomed over the client. 'Gis your other cards then.'

The client reached into his jacket and pulled out a card folio.

'Now he tells us,' said the Walrus and this statement caused uproarious laughter. It was like the bloody comedy hour.

They discussed the limits on the cards, how much they'd be able to get out tonight. The fire crackled, the guitar pulsed. The odd burst of song. 'Tihei mauri ora.'

'We should kill the bastard,' said Halo.

I felt the client jump like a wire beside me.

'Don't be a cunt,' said Stocky Guy.

I put my hand on the client's back and he shrugged it off. I whispered, Are you okay? and he replied, Don't talk to me. Walrus was looking on and I suppose was pleased with the way we were divided. But we were already divided. I heard a bird fly up into the dark as if disturbed by something. Just the one.

Halo and Torch Bearer gathered the client's other cards and went up the path a second time.

Walrus leaned back on his grave and twiddled his thumbs. A few of the boys were tumbling in a play-fight routine like kittens. The girls were doing cat's cradle, leaning towards the firelight. A boy went by and groped one of them and she pushed him away with her cat's-cradle hands—Get fucking off me. Ben came and sat near the girls. He'd gone all soft and sleepy. At one point I saw him sitting with his back to a girl who put down her wool and started combing his hair. He relaxed. I heard someone say, How you get virgin wool? Ugly sheep.

A joint went around. The sentries didn't smoke. I wished they did. But it was still pitch-black out there, of course, so we were, in effect, prisoners of the darkness. The joint was passed to the client and me. They must've thought we were crazy. The girls looked at the stars and were saying, There's the Southern Cross, There's Orion's Belt. Someone was cutting open a can of corned beef with a knife, and soon wads of white bread with beef inside it were passed around and everyone was wolfing them down. My guts were tight as a fist. There were more jokes. Why did the chicken? What do you get when you cross? There's Mars. But it was clouding over.

Walrus ate his sandwich ruminatively. He stretched and pointed out a tall grave to the client and me. 'Governor Hobson,' he said. 'Captain William Lieutenant Governor Hobson.'

As if I gave a rat's arse.

Ben, chewing his sandwich, was looking at me. 'I f-found you.'

I think I nodded.

'I f-found them, didn't I, Walrus?' with his tripping way of talking.

Walrus patted him on the back.

One of the girls went behind a gravestone with the boy who had pawed her earlier and you could hear them at it, quite loud, shrieking and carrying on. The other girl didn't seem to have any admirers.

When Halo and Torch Bearer came back a second time they had a wad of money. They counted it out on a grave. 'Bit more like it,' said Halo.

What do you call?

Ben turned from where the girl was combing his hair. 'She's n-not his missus.'

Torch Bearer snarled out the side of his mouth, 'What you talking about, idiot? He's mental,' he added, for the client's benefit, and mine.

Ben flapped his hands and the girl patted them to soothe him. 'I s-saw her,' he said. 'On Queen Street. Told youse. That,'—he pointed to the client—''s not her hubby.'

Halo bundled up the money in a tight wad and delivered it to Walrus. Walrus received it like a sacrament, and stood up. Everyone stood up. It seemed they were all going somewhere. I felt the client's head twitching like a bird.

'We may as well have the clothes,' said Torch Bearer.

'Oh yeah,' said Halo, as if the detail had slipped his mind. 'Take them off.'

I turned to the client. In the firelight, he looked dazed, drunk.

'Take them fucking off,' said Halo. Skinny Arse rotated the machete.

The client had his outer clothes off in a jiffy. They were snatched away. I was still fumbling with the zip on the costume. My fingers like paper. Then it was in a puddle at my feet, I tripped, stood up. Someone whisked away the costume and my wrap. 'And the shoes.' The shoes went. No one said anything, but we were free to go. This caused general hilarity for some reason. Extinguished when Halo strode around the fire and told everyone to shut the fuck up. They all trooped off up the hill. Skinny Arse swished his machete as he went. It sang through the air and lopped off an azalea head and the flower landed a way away. We could hear the bristly thud.

Then they were gone.

•

'Are you there?' said the client, much later.

It was pitch-black. Now I felt the client's hand reach for mine. We wrapped together in the darkness, whimpering. Relief is too weak a word. We tried to go up the path, but it was so dark you couldn't tell up from down. We didn't have a chance. There was nothing for it but to wait for dawn. We lay down in the leaves. The stones were around us, and I felt like Tess of the D'Urbervilles. We didn't talk. Too scared, of course, in case they came back. After a while we shuffled together and lay like spoons. It was cold. I felt the shape of his body, and his breath, the place where his story had come from. I lay in that. I guess he lay in something coming from me. I couldn't tell because all the boundaries had dissolved and they would never be rebuilt, I knew that.

The night went on for eternity. I thought about things. There wasn't a lot else to do. I thought about the centre of the road, about the interstitial space, about sign, cosine, no sign, signifier. You can see how far gone I was. Looking out from the arms of the client, I could see as much blackness as I'd ever known. I was yawning it in and gulping it in, and there was no delineation between the client, the blackness, and me. I thought about the connections between everything. I remembered Saussure, Barthes, et al. I remembered how it seemed. They were great guys, S and B, even though they upset you so much. Someone had to say it, and they said it. I felt words being reinstated: *discourse*, *hegemony*, *prolepsis*, *dialectic*. They popped up; up they popped. I felt the cold wind of ideas rushing back into place. The notions raged like banshees. How to look at things—line them up on a wall, blow them apart, put them back together, run them down the middle of the road, turn them inside out, make them into polar opposites. How to read things, if you didn't already know. You might have thought this was paradise, but it was death. This is how you read paradise: death. You needed the colon. You read it like a garment. *Black dress, ripped gusset*. What it really meant. *Desperate hurry, sex*. Now there was no excuse for not knowing.

I loved the client, but it was hopeless.

At one point, just before dawn, I turned my head and we kissed, and it was like a marriage, going on forever, full of love and compromise and argument and delight.

Birds. That's what I heard. A bellbird. It was dawn.

The client and I stood up, creaking and brushing ourselves off. I looked down and saw that the grave we'd been curled up next to was none other than the final resting place of the Woolthamly ancestor, the one who bought the frigging farm for twelve blankets. You wouldn't read about it.

The path was just visible, blurry, like the arms of a school blazer. We scrabbled up it like monkeys. It was gravelly, and my hands and fingernails were planed by it. I knew those bitty stones very well, almost more than I've known anything.

There was a pinkish dawn going on, and the birds. We were almost naked. We had been in great danger and now we were okay, picking our way barefoot up Symonds Street. There was no one about. We didn't look at each other. It was wonderful.

The sun broke over the horizon as we reached the villa conversion, and spiked the back garden. The front was in shadow, cool and somehow trembling. I went around the back to get the spare key from under a pot plant, came back and jittered it in the lock. I stilled it. I tiptoed in, pulled on tracky clothes, got the car keys, drove the client home. It was all wordless, not a backward glance from the path of the Ponsonby cottage, and I drove away without checking the rear-view mirror.

37

Art was in bed, just waking and realising it was morning. He said, Where've you been? in a custardy voice. Long story, I said, and I sank onto the bed. Well? he said. I said nothing and we just looked at each other. I wrapped Art in my arms and I knew that this bit of love would save me from being destroyed. He wrapped me back. I felt lucky, because I knew I couldn't love *completely* the way I wanted to, only in secret.

After a while I said, Change of subject but not entirely. He didn't exactly laugh. I said, into his shoulder, that for some reason I was thinking about the time Mary-France and Dad and Lisa and I tried to drive to the top of the steepest street in the Southern Hemisphere, how we had to do the last bit on foot, and it was all downhill from there.

I said I was starving. Art went and got a huge bowl of Weetbix, about six of them, and I shovelled them in to keep body and soul together. He sat and watched me. Milk, I said, or tried to and he said, Yair, good to have milk again. Even then, I thought things would fall apart, I really did, that's why everything was so flat. And maybe he did too, I don't know. And they could've. What I knew then was that things would only ever be climbing or falling, like the free market. Never still.

Then he told me, sitting there, that he had something to say, and he had tears in his eyes—a canary down a mine, when a man cries—and I got a bit alarmed. But then he didn't say it, whatever it was. He said, instead, that he'd thought everything was going to end because the farm did, but it wasn't going to.

I finished the Weetbix and lay down. I was exhausted, in my bones, in my blood. I fell asleep and slept like death until one in the afternoon.

When I got up, Art was crashing about packing pots in the kitchen because we were moving, of course. I started to help, getting jars with dead flies in them out from the back of the pantry. Art turned to me and said, Do you think it will be okay? And I said, Yes, do *you* think it will be? and he said, Yair.

38

Some last things:
A few days later, I went downtown to Darby Street, a higgledy-piggledy lane off Queen Street, in which there is a shop called the Recycle Boutique. I went in and fossicked about. I had this crazy notion I might find the costume there. I mean, what would a street kid do with a dancing costume apart from sell it? If it *was* in the Recycle Boutique, by any chance, I would buy it (like they do in *The Red Overalls*—'We'll just have to buy them again'). The shop assistant would run her hands over the knotwork as she wrapped it and say it was beautiful. I'd agree, although I was sick to death of its beauty. I'd had a-blinking-nuff of it. I would go home and get the car, drive to the client's house and park by the brass 96. The place would be sparkling, all periwinkle and oxblood, white lace and jasmine. Milly would open the door. Yes, Milly. I'd push the parcel at her, and she would look rather astonished. Here, I'd say, your husband had the sleeve finished for you as a surprise. Pleasure would cross her well-groomed intelligent-looking accountant's face, and I would tromp back along the shell path and through the dinky picket gate.

But the costume wasn't at the Recycle Boutique. Which meant Milly never got it back, which meant there must've been some kind of comeuppance. I hoped it spelled curtains (to be honest), but I suspected it didn't. Like a plastic bag, a marriage is hard to kill off.

●

Megan Sligo Mending and Alterations went bust, as you may have gathered—the clients didn't return, and I had to sell my machine and overlocker. It shouldn't have. I should've been able to go to the cleaners over the Blackout, and come back again all sparkling *because my overheads were so small* (to quote you-know-who). But in any case, the house had been sold and the settlement date was approaching like a meteor.

We packed up fast. Sorting through my workroom felt like an archaeological dig. I bundled up offcuts of fabric like a baby. I turned on my good light. I opened my workbook, and there was the last job I had done.

Costume, black, torn sleeve, embroidery

Which meant:

No choice, out of my hands

I understood this.

It was all over. Which is not to say I didn't imagine the client standing in the doorway, finding me at my electric sewing machine with pins in my mouth. He would laugh, he'd say I couldn't survive because I was a sweatshop of one, no really, he was serious. And I would answer him, out loud, out into the room, pins falling out of my mouth.

●

Three months after Prue and Bert sold them, the villas were on
the market again. This was the shortest amount of time you
could turn over real estate. Someone was laughing all the way
to the bank. I went to have a nosy at the open home, although
I shouldn't have gone. It was *rather* depressing, especially seeing
we couldn't afford to live in the inner city anymore. They'd put
our conversion back into one house—and renovated it *to within
an inch of its life* in the process. It felt like a new world. What
I realised: the house hadn't been cut in two when we lived in it
at all, it only seemed that way, like a magician's sequinned wife
sawn in half in a chambered box. As I paced about at the open
home (a bit self-conscious, as if measuring), I saw that the yellow
kitchen had been stripped back and they'd started again. It was
white. In the passage I looked through the space where a wall
had once been into the side of the villa I'd never seen before. The
rooms were big and square and elegant, and the yellow Auckland
sunlight came flooding through them. There would be no need for
a Wah Lee's paper lantern to be glowing during the day. I stood
in the mandolin and looked back at the place where the beads
had run under the door like honey, and I thought *it is over*, and
I boinged down the weedy steps for the last time.

39

In the car park at St Luke's Shopping Centre are two stiff little green blazers that look as if they're still on the hangers, but they have children inside them. A girl and a boy, about five and seven respectively. The girl has a tiny tartan skirt and white pipe-cleaner legs. It's the uniform of an expensive Anglican prep school. The children have dropped down from the high door of an SUV, almost as if from a building, but gently, like Spiderman. I am sitting in the driver's seat of our little bomb under the low roof of the grey, oily parking building. I turn my head and see the client closing the shiny door of the SUV that the children have tumbled from. He's fatter around the middle, greyish, going grey young, and his hand is reaching to engulf that of the younger child. There's Milly, older, harassed in a happy kind of way, her hair breaking free of its bun, tottering in her high heels from the other side of the car and gathering the boy's hand, and her bag. I happen to be in her line of vision and she smiles vacantly as if she thinks she might know me, perhaps would wave even, if her hands weren't occupied. As they walk away across the wasteland of the car park, the client turns to fire at the car, which jumps with the force of all the locks shooting home at the same time. At this point, he looks at me. A bolt of shock goes through him like the car locks, I can see it. But no, it's me, it's going through me and I am welded, until he looks away and, in a few strides, catches up with his family as they trail across the heterotopia. Yes, heterotopia.

So that's the girl, the little five-year-old uniform on legs, who the costume was for. Who I toiled away for in the front room back in 1998. It was her blinking heritage. When she's older, if someone asks her at a party, Why didn't you wear your national costume? she'll have to say, like me, I don't have one. It's gone.

I remember it intimately. I remember every last stitch of it.

You know what? I could make a costume for my own daughter, if I put my mind to it. I could run her up a so-called Irish dancing costume in velvet or soft wool, in black or blue or green. I could embroider the hem, the cuffs, the sleeves, the edges of the cape. Oh yes, in knotwork. I know all about knotwork. My daughter could have a costume hanging in the wardrobe at home. I could do this for her. But I don't.

She is six. At the local state school.

I won't.

Art is buckling her into her car seat. Oh, Art? Doctor Frome? He has a part-time gig teaching academic writing in the evenings. The pay is stink. Hopefully a position in his field will come up soon. It's been a long time. I've taken up my studies again, now that Sadie is at school. I'm looking into current theories behind Deformance: The Subjective in New Zealand Women's Poetry. From there on it gets involved. But thanks for asking. I have a bit of cleaning work which almost covers the fees.

Sometimes I do wonder what would have happened if there'd been no Blackout. I might have mended that particular dress in a pool of electric light, which I, like everyone, took so much for granted, and nothing would have changed. I would have kept on working with my hands in my workroom. I never would have moved into the front room and looked out through the wobbly glass at the overgrown garden. Now my hands are mostly still. I have a narrow office like a strip of land. Just this afternoon I had a conversation by the lift with a fellow student who, for some reason, was under the impression that I was about to drop out. Drop out! Nothing could be further from the truth. I had in my bag right at that very moment Helene Cixous, Gayatri Chakravorty Spivak, Derrida—Derrida who I'd actually seen, heard, in the Michael Fowler Centre, 1993! And the fellow student in the foyer, a slightly eccentric woman (I mean, drop out!), said, Wow, Derrida! Did you touch the hem of his garment? I shook my head and was about to say that in fact I had been a mender, had done hems, and had taken small snippets from the insides of hems to mend a hole elsewhere on a garment. I could've made a hole somewhere on Derrida's jacket almost invisible. But I didn't say that. Better not to go down the meandering avenues of my mad-but-good fellow student. Anyway, there I was, book bag on my shoulder, wearing my Nom*D cardigan with the big safety pin, left over from the days when I could afford to buy the odd designer garment—yes, garment—and on my way into the staff room to heat up lunch in the microwave. I realised—I did—that it was a relief after all to be thinking again instead of doing.

40

I'm afraid I've got a bit self-centred about all this, but I really couldn't help it. I set out to write about culture, loss of culture, economic movements etc., but I've ended up telling you quite a bit about myself. It was hard to unravel the different parts. I suppose, along the way, you've got the message that another man, apart from my husband, loved me. He really did. I loved him, of course. But I didn't intend to go on like this. I'd like to thank you, though. If I hadn't told you, I don't think I would have been able to stay on an even keel, I don't think I would have been successful in keeping it secret. My life would've been destroyed. Thank you. You're worth your weight in gold.

Acknowledgments

Permission to reproduce the following is gratefully acknowledged:
Slavitt, David R. "Tityrus." *Eclogues and Georgics of Virgil.* p. 3. © 1971, 1972, 1990 by David R. Slavitt. Reprinted with permission of The Johns Hopkins University Press.

Espada, Martín. "My Native Costume". *Alabanza: New and Selected Poems 1982–2003.* New York: Norton, 2004. Reprinted with the permission of the author.

I am indebted to the following publications for accounts of life in Belfast: Parker, Tony. *May the Lord in His Mercy Be Kind to Belfast.* New York: Henry Holt, 1994.
Conroy, John. *Belfast Diary: War As a Way of Life.* New York: Beacon Press, 1987.

The book that GoGo finds in the library is: Harrold, Robert. *Folk Costumes of the World.* Illus. Phyllida Legg. New York: Stirling, 1990.

Many thanks to Creative New Zealand for a grant that helped with the writing of this novel.

My grateful thanks to Laura Mitchell, Ali Lavau and especially Jane Palfreyman; to dear writing friends, Kathy Phillips, Deborah Ross, and Erica Reynolds-Clayton, and to faculty and students (from whom I learned so much) at the University of Hawai'i at Mānoa. Thanks and love, as always, to Robert Sullivan, Temuera Sullivan, and Eileen Kennedy.